Readers love ELLE E. IRE

Dead Woman's Pond

"Psychics, ghosts, and supernatural events, sign me up!"

—Quiet Fury Books

Vicious Circle

"I'd recommend this story to readers who enjoy descriptive, action packed, sci-fi stories, regardless of character gender or sexual orientation."

—Love Bytes

Threadbare

"I relished every flare of anger or sullenness because I knew that when the time was right there would be joy and happiness given the same attention. I loved this book. I hope you will, too."

—Joyfully Jay

By ELLE E. IRE

Reel to Real Love
Vicious Circle

NEARLY DEPARTED
Dead Woman's Pond
Dead Woman's Revenge
Dead Woman's Secret

STORM FRONTS
Threadbare
Patchwork
Woven

Published by DSP PUBLICATIONS
www.dsppublications.com

DEAD WOMAN'S SECRET

ELLE E. IRE

DSP PUBLICATIONS

Published by
DSP PUBLICATIONS

5032 Capital Circle SW, Suite 2, PMB# 279,
Tallahassee, FL 32305-7886 USA
www.dsppublications.com

Mass Market Paperback ISBN: 978-1-64108-342-3
Trade Paperback ISBN: 978-1-64108-337-9
Digital ISBN: 978-1-64108-336-2
Mass Market Paperback published January 2023
v. 1.0

Printed in the United States of America
∞
This paper meets the requirements of
ANSI/NISO Z39.48-1992 (Permanence of Paper).

The Nearly Departed series is set in real places, some retaining their true names, others with the names changed to fictional ones. I live in "Festivity." Yes, there is a Starbucks here, just like in these novels. Yes, there are also sometimes homeless individuals who frequent the outside patio. And yes, there was one particular gentleman with a long beard and wild hair whom my spouse and I fondly dubbed "Ferguson, the Wizard." Our "Ferguson" had a kindly and quiet demeanor, kept to himself, sometimes muttered "spells" under his breath, and never bothered anyone. When he stopped coming to the coffee shop, I inquired after him and was informed that he was struck by a car crossing one of the major roads and was killed. This book is dedicated to him and all those like him who deserve a lot more magic in their lives than what they've been granted.

Acknowledgments

ANOTHER TRILOGY complete, and as with my previous series, there is a certain melancholy that settles over me when I finally must leave a set of characters behind for now. I've lived with Flynn, Genesis, and Chris (quite literally, since "Festivity" is my hometown), for a good ten years or more as they waited for their chance to get their adventures out into the world. But at least with this group, real-life connections to them are never more than a short drive away.

Thanks go out to all the usual suspects. My incredible and talented spouse comes first as always, there by my side with constant support, encouragement, and faith without which this series would never have been written, let alone published.

Much gratitude to my former writing group: Amy, Ann, Gary, Evergreen, and Joe who read all three books in this series and helped catch inconsistencies and trap plot bunnies.

Thank you to my patient and determined agent, Naomi Davis, who is always on the lookout for new ways to get my work out there, and the administrative team at DSP for taking a chance on a fairly new author to be one of their first if not THE first writer of adult lesbian and bisexual science fiction and paranormal romance in their house.

Thank you to Gin for the awesome back cover copy and other blurbs, Naomi for her promotional and marketing expertise, Anna Sikorska and the entire art department for creating the most amazing covers from my vague descriptions and somehow coming up with exactly what was in my head.

Thanks to my awesome editing team: Gus, Yv, Brian, and Katie. I can't imagine there could be any more misplaced/missing/extra commas or hyphens in this one, but if there are errors we missed, they are entirely my own.

Finally, thank you to my readers. Sometimes writing feels like shouting into a black hole of nothingness. Your messages of praise and encouragement on Facebook and Twitter keep me going. Especially thank you to MB, Riley, Meredith, Mari, Arielle, Bob, Kathy, Jenni, and Rob, and all the OWLS. Mimi, I hope you like the pixie telekinetic named after you. Thanks for entering my contest.

DEAD WOMAN'S SECRET

ELLE E. IRE

DSP PUBLICATIONS

Chapter 1
Making Mistakes

"Ooof." My impact with the conference room wall behind me knocks the wind from my lungs and rattles the lighting fixture hanging above my head. I slide down the smooth surface to thump ass-first on the parquet wood floor.

"Let's go, Dalton! It's not nap time. Heroes aren't born. They're made."

I favor Nathaniel with my best glare. My vision's a little blurry from the disorientation of the hit, but my expression is still formidable, judging from the way he clamps his jaw shut. He's not part of this fight. He's not even breaking a sweat. He's the coordinator, the spectator, the assessor, standing off to the side in his neat tan trousers and white Polo shirt, leaning against the wall with his loafer-clad feet crossed at the ankles like he's waiting for a golf match.

"Look, asshole," I wheeze, and that's as far as I get before another blast of psychic energy wraps around my torso and drags me upright until my steel-toed boots leave the floor. I'm reminded of a scene from *Poltergeist*, helpless and flailing, Harrah's Casino T-shirt riding up to reveal my white sports bra beneath, before I'm tossed aside to land on my left shoulder.

Two days ago, that would have hurt like a bitch. Okay, it *still* hurts like a bitch. But Cassandra, the National Psychic Registry's best healer and love potion maker, took care of the water moccasin bite damage there. So it *only* hurts like a bitch rather than like a sonofabitch.

I roll sideways with the landing, the first move I've done right this whole match, and come up on my feet, panting and sweating. Turning, I face my attacker, and even though I've been fighting her for the last half hour, I blink.

Mimi is, at most, five three, and that's counting the white tennis shoes she wears. Slight of build with delicate hands and feet and spindly limbs. Pixie-style blond hair, bright blue eyes, a narrow face with high cheekbones and a slightly pointed chin. Add in her brown corduroys and green sweater, and she'd blend in with storybook forest nymphs.

At five eight I tower over her. My strength, built from years working in construction and a youth of competitive bowling, gymnastics, and swimming, could snap her tiny body in two.

And she's got me completely, utterly whipped.

She gives me a sympathetic little smile, as if to say, *Sorry, it's not personal*, and extends her hands toward me again.

I bring my own up out of instinct, palms toward her, in a pointless attempt to ward her off. It does me no good whatsoever.

The megablast knocks me ass over teakettle so hard I do a perfect backward roll and again plant my soles firmly on the floor to stand. Muscles I haven't used since high school scream their protest, but memories of my gymnast days reawaken in the rattled corners of my brain.

I'm supposed to be fighting back. Using my succubus power, I took a *pull* from Mimi's telekinetic energy a half hour ago, and if I could concentrate for one goddamn minute, I could figure out how to manipulate that power to return fire. Except she hasn't given me the chance. She hasn't given me a single break.

Just like a real enemy, dumbass.

I tell my internal critic to shut the hell up and cartwheel right as another orange-yellow—at least to my sight—beam streaks my way. She misses my moving target. Her first miss since we started.

Might just be on to something here.

If I can't fight back, at least I can keep myself from being turned into one massive purple bruise. Though judging from the welts already visible on both my arms and the soreness in my back and legs, it might be too late for that.

And I'm supposed to take Genesis out for her birthday tonight.

I do a dive-roll that brings me up beside Nathaniel, who is studying the sparring session with his magic-sight; he sees power usage and can identify it, analyze its type. I can only see what I'm immediately using and interacting with.

"You're not fighting back. You're not using her energy at all. You're never going to survive a confrontation with that rogue succubus, Tempest Granfeld, if you don't start taking the offensive."

"Only thing I find offensive around here is you, you little toad," I mutter, scrambling sideways like a crab to avoid another jolt. The telekinetic power zings close enough to raise the hairs on my arm and lift the long brown ponytail off the back of my neck like extreme static.

Mimi pauses to gather her strength. I'm wearing down her reserves, but that's not a technique I can use in a real fight where someone's actually trying to kill me. I would have been long dead by now if I faced Tempest instead of Mimi.

In the brief interim, I grab a hold of the telekinetic power I absorbed, turning it over inside myself, trying to narrow its intensity to a beam like my opponent's.

And failing.

Her next blast hurls me into the double entry doors, slamming the push bar inward and tossing me across the outer hallway running the length of the convention center of the hotel. I hit the carpet hard enough to shove my T-shirt upward and give me rug burns down my spine. The startled elderly couple standing over me stares, mouths agape, no words coming out.

I use the gray-haired woman's walker to haul myself upright, then pat her wrinkled hand. "Thanks. And sorry. Stuntman convention."

Her husband, I presume, glances toward the still-swinging doors to the conference room, eyes wide as if he expects God knows what to come out after me. He's not too far off the mark.

Mimi steps into the doorway, holding the right-hand door open with her palm and shooting me a disapproving look. "You're breaking the boundary rules," she scolds. "You never know who might—" She spots the couple and freezes, face blossoming into a friendly smile. The slight gold spark, easily explained away by the gaudy overhead chandeliers, fades from her eyes. "Oh, hi! Martial arts class," she says.

"I thought you were attending a stuntman convention." The old woman narrows her gaze on me, like she's caught an unruly student cheating on a test. I'm betting she's a retired teacher.

"Yep, martial arts demonstrations are part of the convention activities. Gotta go!" I hobble away from them, sliding past Mimi into the conference room. The doors bang shut. Her power catches me between the shoulder blades and flattens me.

"Aw, come on. That was a time-out," I groan.

"Granfeld won't give you time-outs," Mimi says. Then, "Sorry, Flynn. I'm under orders to work you hard."

And I know just whose orders she means. Linda Argyle's. Madame President. The woman who blackmailed me into the Registry's service by threatening to punish Genesis for her second use of dark magic.

What Argyle doesn't realize is I would have agreed to help anyway. Granfeld's tampering with time has put all the Registry members at risk. Including Gen. Including me. Any one of us could vanish from existence, and we have no idea who her next target will be. Which means they needed a hero. And I'm just a sucker that way.

Being the only other succubus alive with the ability to walk through time doesn't hurt either.

I lever myself upright once more, frustration and failure warring for dominance. Can't get out of the way. Can't use Mimi's power.

But I can still use mine.

I turn and face Mimi just as she hurls another blast, and catch the beam mid-arc, *pulling* it into myself. It surges in my core, mixing with the rest of the energy I obtained from her. Her eyes widen, and a grin curls her lips.

Between my legs, arousal builds, a heated, aching need that always comes as a direct result of the usage of my "talents." I swallow a moan and picture innocuous images in my mind: Mother Theresa, Gandhi, the Pope. Not enough. Casino mogul Donald Trump. The lust vanishes, replaced by faint nausea.

Mimi tries again, and I do the same thing, storing more and more of her telekinetic power and draining her of her ability to use it herself. She's already tired, her levels low. It doesn't take long before she has nothing left.

Then, suffused with her energy, things click into place. I'm still too clumsy to create a nice narrow beam, but I can throw a wall of it in her direction, and I do it, with all the grace and finesse of a sumo wrestler in a ballet recital. She flies backward, slamming into Nathaniel, who happens to be right behind her, which he mistakenly assumed to be the safest place in the room.

"Take that, spy."

President Argyle had Nathaniel watching me and Genesis for months, spying on my abilities, testing and tormenting us both. It felt good to toss Mimi into him.

Then I notice neither of them is moving.

Aw hell.

"I REALLY am sorry," I say, placing two ice-cold beers on the table in front of Mimi and Nathaniel. I take the black-leather-covered bar seat opposite them, hauling myself onto its cushion. Much of the Irish-pub themed establishment is empty, the hotel guests preferring to get their drinks for free at the gambling tables and slots, and at six dollars for domestic, I don't blame them. But a few customers occupy tables scattered throughout the small lobby bar, so I keep my voice low.

Mimi gives me a wry smile, while Nathaniel presses the chilled bottle of Bud to the swelling lump on his temple. He got coldcocked when Mimi flew into him, the back of her skull connecting with the front of his.

"Are you sure you don't want a doctor?" she asks, studying him. I'd only stunned her, but he'd been out for a few seconds before we revived him.

"No, thank you." He glances at his cell phone. "I'll have Cassandra take a look during the session break in an hour."

"Well, at least I managed to *do* something," I say, folding my arms on the table's surface. I'll need to wear long sleeves tonight to hide the welts. Genesis doesn't know anything about my upcoming mission. She knows I'm being trained, but not the aggressive nature of that training or its purpose. And I'm not telling her. She'll worry. And she'll blame herself.

"Too little, too late," Mimi says, watching my face for the inevitable scowl.

I don't disappoint her.

"Sorry, Flynn, but you know it's true," she continues. "It took you too long to figure out how to defend yourself and how to defeat me. We need to get you to the point where you can channel any psychic's talent and make use of it immediately. Tempest Granfeld was a succubus, but many have multiple skills, like Cassie with her love and healing magic."

And Genesis who communicates with the dead. And uses dark power to kill people who threaten those she loves.

I shake that image away with a jerk of my head, then regret it when the bar rocks around me. Mimi grabs my arm, holding me on the chair. Damn, I hate these high bar seats.

"You need some rest," Mimi says, frowning. "You look flushed. Go upstairs. Take a nap. Get a meal."

"I always get a low-grade fever when I use my—" I can't quite bring myself to say *magic*. "—abilities. I'll just grab some aspirin. There's no time for anything else." I glance at my own phone and slide off the chair on purpose. "It's Gen's birthday. I've got an hour to shower and change before I take her out to dinner." The limo would pick us up in front of the casino to drive us to a romantic restaurant the concierge had recommended. I'd made reservations, but apparently the place was small, well-reviewed, and always booked solid, so we didn't want to be late. It was also about forty-five minutes away.

"Well, that's rest of a sort," Nathaniel puts in. "I'll let Linda know we made some progress today. I'm sure she'll have something else to throw at you tomorrow."

"Try to make it something soft. I'm getting married in two days. Don't need to break bones before the ceremony." That earns me a chuckle.

"And if I don't see you again," Mimi says, "good luck, with both the training and the wedding."

"Thanks." Damn. I could get to like the little pixie. But she's right. New day, new challenges. I never face off against the same person for more than an hour or two, tops.

I make my way from the bar, across the lobby, past the casino entrance to the tower elevators. My arms and legs ache while I wait for the car to arrive. How I'm gonna keep this hidden from Genesis, I have no idea. She's occupied by panels and meetings in the daytime while I'm training, but at night, she wants to show me affection, and normally I'd be all for that. Not so much when every inch of my body hurts. Maybe the hot shower will help.

A well-dressed middle-aged couple reeking of cigarette smoke shares the elevator with me to the twelfth floor. They've had a few drinks, and the woman wobbles a bit on her high heels. The man busies himself with his phone, scrolling through what looks like his appointment book on the screen, but the bleach blond examines me out of the corner of her eye. When the car stops and they step out, she turns back and holds the doors open. "Don't let him beat you up like that, honey. Get some help. There's a good shelter on Bayfront Drive."

I laugh and hold out my hand at about shoulder height. "Would you believe it was actually a girl, about this tall?"

She stares from my fingers to my face and back again, then cracks a wide smile. "Kinky," she says and steps into the hallway, letting the doors close.

I ride the rest of the way to the penthouse honeymoon suite alone.

Two bedrooms, two and a half baths, a living room with a ten-person jacuzzi and a wet bar, all done in blues, silvers, and golds, and all irrelevant compared to the bed. It takes a force of will not to drop onto the king-size mattress in the master bedroom. Maid service has made it and fluffed the pillows, and I can't think of anything more inviting.

Have to shower. Have to change.

God, I'm tired.

I indulge in a quick lean against the wall, closing my eyes, feeling the weights of the lids holding them down, blocking the sunset outside the huge windows. I drift, forgetting what I came upstairs for.

"Flynn?"

Male voice. Close by. Threat.

I throw out my hand toward the sound, a perfect narrow beam of telekinetic energy shooting from my palm across to the master bedroom door, wrapping itself like a lasso around the speaker and yanking him off his feet. He yelps, his head bumping the ceiling, looking down at me with wide, innocent eyes.

"Chris?" The shock of seeing Gen's brother in my room breaks my concentration, and the beam cuts off, dropping him eight feet to the carpeted floor. He lands with a dull thud and a muffled groan. "Shit."

I crouch by his side, legs aching in protest, and help him sit up.

"That was… impressive," he manages, his usual cocky grin returning. "You're definitely getting better at picking up guys."

I bark a quick laugh. "Funny. You're okay?" Should have known he'd be here. He flew in this afternoon to help us get ready for the wedding, and he's occupying the other bedroom in the massive suite, the one across the living room from ours.

"I'm fine," he says, rubbing at his backside. "You been tapping into telekinetics?"

I spread my hands. "Training," I say, avoiding details. Chris knows enough about the magical world from his sister and his parents, though he has no obvious talents himself, save an uncanny way with finances that keeps his business, the Village Pub, going strong back in Festivity, Florida.

"I'd say you're getting the hang of it."

Yeah, interesting that. Panic and adrenaline help me focus. Good. I'm sure I'll have plenty of both when I find myself in a real fight.

We give each other a hand up, and he studies my face while I grimace. I know what's coming next.

"Flynn, you look like hell."

Yep, that was it.

A hint of perfume wafts off him, a scent I can't quite place, though it's very familiar. Not Gen's, and while I like it on her, I don't wear flowery stuff, or any stuff, for that matter. Hmm.

Before I can sort through it or he can corner me on how worn I look, I catch sight of the bed-side table alarm clock's glowing red numbers. "Gotta hurry. I'm taking Gen out tonight, and I'm running late." Avoidance—always a great strategy. Except when I make my quick turn toward the master bath, my back locks up and sharp pain shoots across it. My breath hisses between my teeth.

Chris grabs my arm, right atop several bruises, and a humiliating whimper escapes my throat.

"What the—?" Without another word, he drags me over to the bed, pushes me facedown onto it, and shoves my shirt up. He's close enough to me now that the mysterious perfume on him smells much stronger.

My brain finally adds two and two and comes up with… *Cassie.*

Oh boy. Gen is gonna shit.

"Holy fuck," he breathes, stealing one of my favorite epithets and cutting off whatever I might have said about his secret relationship with Gen's biggest enemy.

"That bad, huh?" My voice is muffled by the comforter, but he gets the gist.

"You've got a band of bruising all the way across the center of your back, and it's swelling up too."

"Yeah, that would be from when I got thrown into a door's push bar."

Chris grunts and starts rolling up my sleeves, then my pant legs as far as he can. When he's done, he plops down beside me on the mattress, which sinks under his added weight. "Why do you look like you just went twenty rounds with Mike Tyson? And your skin feels like it's on fire. You wanna tell me what the hell is going on?"

"Not really. You wanna tell me when you started dating Cassandra Safoir?"

Dead silence in the master bedroom.

"I'm not the only one who needs a shower," I add. "You'd better wash off that perfume before you run into Genesis."

"You aren't going to tell her?" His voice is soft... and hopeful.

Dammit.

I let out a long sigh. "Not really my business to tell, is it? Cassie and I are cool, but Gen... she's not gonna let that breakup go."

"She's going to have to. Cass and I are pretty serious."

Yeah, I kinda figured. "Good luck with that." I use the interruption to try to squirm away, off the opposite side of the bed, but he catches my arm and tugs me back toward him.

"Flynn…."

I know that tone. It's the same one Gen uses when there's no way I'm getting out of something she wants me to do. Must run in the family.

I heave a defeated sigh. "If you can listen while I shower, I'll tell you what's going on."

"Deal."

Chapter 2
Overprotective

I GRAB a couple or three aspirin from my bag to down with a can of Coke Zero. While I wash off the training session's sweat and grime and let my bruised muscles soak under the steaming hot water, I first check on our dog, Katy, the husky/shepherd mix Gen and I sort of inherited after I killed Max Harris for murdering his wives and trying to kill Gen, Chris, and me.

"She's great," Chris says, keeping his back to the shower for modesty's sake. I hope he can't catch my reflection in the mirrors, but I'm too sore and tired to worry about it much, which testifies to exactly how exhausted I really am. "I checked her into the Posh Pet Hotel this morning before I flew out. The staff fell in love with her immediately, and there's another husky staying the week, a male I think she's got a crush on."

I snort in response, inhaling some of the shower spray and setting off a coughing fit that buys me another minute or two.

"Flynn, you're stalling."

Damn right.

But I can't keep stalling him forever. I swallow hard, lather up my hair, and give Chris the rundown on the Registry's plans for me. While I rinse out the shampoo, I swear him to secrecy. Not an easy thing, asking him to keep secrets from his own sister, and I'm surprised he agrees. But he knows she's battling the dark magic addiction, and giving her another reason to stress (and potentially a reason to angrily use dark power on some Registry members) doesn't seem like a good idea to either one of us. Besides, I'm keeping a secret for him. Fair is fair.

"I'll keep it to myself," he says, continuing to turn his back while I change into dark pants, suede boots, a wine-red long-sleeved shirt and black vest. "But you have to stay healthy. She'll never forgive me if something happens to you and I knew the possibility and didn't tell her."

"Glad to know your concern stems from self-preservation," I say, teasing really. I swipe the brush through my hair and prepare to pull it into my usual ponytail, but Chris spins around in the bathroom doorway and grabs my wrist to stop my brushing, his face angry next to mine in the mirror.

"It's not about me, and you know it," he growls.

He's got my attention. In the year and a half I've known him, I can count on one hand the number of times I've seen him angry. It's just not in his character.

And all those times have something to do with me.

"Okay," I say, keeping my voice soft and calm. I can get mad too. I'm rather quick to it. And us shouting at each other in the bathroom isn't how I want this evening to go, for Gen's sake if not mine. "I get it. We're both worried about Genesis."

He heaves an exasperated sigh. "No, Flynn. No. I mean, yes, I'm concerned about her, but no." Chris turns me to face him, resting his palms on my shoulders, lightly since he knows I probably have bruises there, too, and he'd be right. "You, Flynn. I'm afraid for you. You're family. The—" He pauses, a hint of his infectious grin tugging at the corners of his mouth. "—the brother I never had."

That earns him a laugh, but when he quickly sobers, so do I.

"You weren't even aware of the magical world until a few months ago. You've been sticking your toes in the kiddie pool, and now they want you to dive in the deep end headfirst. You're strong and smart and you roll with the punches, but no one's prepared for this much this fast. Quite honestly, Gen and I are surprised you've stayed sane."

At first I think he's teasing again, but the set of his jaw and the intensity in his eyes tell me he's not.

Chris and Gen thought I'd lose my mind.

I guess it shouldn't shock me. Seeing ghosts, getting possessed, finding out there's a whole population of magic users inhabiting the world and I happen to be one of the strongest among them—yeah, it's a lot to take in. And insanity runs in my family. Okay, Dad's nuts because the Registry has punished him with madness three days out of every week for the rest of the year. But Mom....

She stood over the kitchen sink, the knife gripped in her right hand, the blade and her left wrist dripping crimson into the pure white basin.

I froze in the doorway, schoolbooks in my arms, my letterman jacket too hot in the winter-heated house. She had something in the oven, a roast, judging by the smell, and it was burning, curls of smoke escaping around the oven door's edges. "Mom," I whispered, "what are you doing?"

"You're home early," she said as if she were simply chopping the vegetables forgotten in the bowl beside her.

"No swim practice. Pool heater's broken. You didn't answer my question. What the hell are you doing?"

She turned toward me slowly, trailing a line of dark red across the counter, then the dingy yellow linoleum floor. It clashed, the red and the yellow, and when she stepped forward, her shoe smeared a streak into orange-brown.

"Protecting him. Protecting them all."

Him? Him, who? "Do you mean Jonathon?" And what was she protecting him from? She'd been seeing a guy, an accountant for a law firm over in Princeton. They'd dated a few times. Things were just starting to get a little more serious. It hadn't thrilled me to come home after losing the state bowling tournament and find them making out on the couch, but I liked him well enough, and it was good for her. She hadn't gone out with anyone in all the years since my father left. It made her happy. It eased her chronic depression.

Or I thought it did.

"Jonathon, your father, all of them. They're all the same," she said.

"No, they're not." My dad left, yeah. And I was a lesbian. Knew it even in high school. But I didn't hate men. Quite the opposite, actually. I liked hanging out with them. We had more in common than I had with other girls.

"I'll end up hurting him. I always end up hurting them." And with a despairing cry, she brought up the knife and deepened the gash in her wrist.

"Shit!" Throwing my books aside, I leaped forward. I grabbed her arms, keeping the blade from her skin. Blood poured from her wound, ran over my hand, hot and sticky, and soaked into the sleeve of my jacket.

"Watch your language," she shrieked, as if that was all that mattered here, my dirty mouth.

Never mind the suicide attempt. Just don't curse where I can hear you.

"Fuck that," I said and wrenched the knife from her grasp. Even on a bad day I was stronger than my mother. Had been since I turned fourteen.

In some ways, I had been all my life.

I tossed the blade to clatter in the sink and dragged her to the closest kitchen chair. After dropping her on it, I went for the first aid kit she kept in the cabinet.

She slumped over the round table, face on her arms, uncaring of the blood widening in a pool across the wood surface. "I'll hurt him. I'll hurt him," she moaned over and over.

"It wasn't your fault," I whispered, tugging at her arm so I could get at the wound. Mom blamed herself for Dad's departure. She always had. I never understood that. I guessed she'd convinced herself that she'd drive Jonathon away too. Didn't make any sense to me, but I shouldn't have expected rationality from a crazy woman.

I set the kit on the table and popped it open, then removed gauze and tape—something to slow the bleeding while I called 911. When I had her taped up, I phoned for an ambulance, shut off the oven, and tossed the roast in the trash. The acrid smell of burned meat kept us company while sirens wailed in the distance.

"Earth to Flynn!" Chris waving his hand in front of my face brings me back to the present.

"S-sorry." I have to clear my throat before I can continue. I wonder how long I've been standing there, staring at him. Not the best way to continue convincing him I'm in my right mind. "Memories," I explain. "My mother."

Chris grimaces. "Sorry. She's in an institution up here, right? I didn't mean to—"

"No, it's okay." It's not, really. Since arriving in New Jersey for the conference, I've managed to avoid thinking about the fact that my mother lives in a mental hospital only a couple of hours from Atlantic City.

And that I haven't seen her in ten years.

"You going to visit her while you're here?" he asks, echoing my thoughts.

I shrug. "Probably not. Not much time in the schedule."

He looks like he's going to argue, then thinks better of it and closes his mouth. "Here," he says, taking the ponytail holder and brush from the counter. He gives my hair a few quick brushes and ties it back, surprising the hell out of me. If it were anyone else, I'd pull away, but this is Chris, and I love him like family, too, so I allow it. "Used to do it for Genesis when she was a kid," he explains with an embarrassed smile.

I return the smile. "Thanks. For everything," I add. "I appreciate the concern. I do. And I'll try to be careful." Though I don't know how much good trying will do me. So often, lately, I've found myself in situations beyond my control, with no choice of direction to take other than forward and through.

From his frown and the sadness in his eyes, I think Chris knows that as well as I do.

"And I'm really happy for you and Cassie." It's the truth. Chris has thrown his whole life into first raising Genesis and then making the Village Pub a major success. He almost never dates. He deserves some happiness for himself. And Cassie's been through a helluva lot with the breakup with Gen, married at nineteen and divorced with a baby at twenty—a baby who is now a four-year-old with leukemia. Cassie's told me about her during my breaks. I've seen pictures. Cute kid, even bald from the chemo. I think Cassie's been trying to make me understand why she did the things she did to me a couple of months back and forgive her, but I'm already past that. She fixed my arm and leg after the magical snake bite incident, helped me negotiate with the Registry about my upcoming assignment, heals me when I'm injured by my lessons, and I consider her a friend. "I hope it works out, and that Gen can deal with it."

"She's coming to the wedding," he admits.

"She's not invited. I wanted to, but Gen wouldn't have it."

Chris starts putting my toiletries back into my little kitbag on the counter. Well, God knows I wasn't planning to do it. I mean, I'm just going to have to take them all out again tomorrow. "She's invited if I'm bringing her as my plus-one," he says, wrapping my toothbrush in a tissue before storing it away.

"Um, I'm not sure that's the best way for you to—"

The phone (yes, there's a freaking phone in the honeymoon suite's master bathroom) rings, and Chris grabs it, seemingly grateful for the distraction. He listens for a second, then says, "Hang on," and passes it to me. The bellman on the other end tells me my limousine is waiting out front and Genesis is already downstairs. I thank him and hang up.

"Gotta run," I say. "Or at least hobble my way out of here. Gen's waiting."

"Go." He places a kiss on my forehead, and I rub it away with a grimace, making him laugh. "I was getting worried about you there, Flynn. Letting me fix your hair and all. That's more like it."

I finish reassuring him with a punch to his arm, grab my wallet and room key, and leave the suite.

On the elevator ride down, I use the mirrored walls to undo the ponytail he put in much too high, reminding me of a cheerleader out of the 1950s, and redo it to my satisfaction. The rest of me looks better, the hot shower having worked wonders. I'm not as stiff or sore, though the shadows linger beneath my eyes, and I wasn't going to deal with makeup. I took my turn in a dress and some simple cosmetics our first night here. Once a year is about enough of that for me. Actually, once in a lifetime would be plenty.

My conversation with Chris distracted me from the power usage arousal side effect, but it's returning with a vengeance now, and I'm a little worried about the upcoming lengthy ride in the limousine. Maybe Gen will provide another distraction.

I step through the casino hotel's glass front doors and stop, realizing exactly what kind of distraction she's likely to provide.

Gen leans against the shiny black limo's rear passenger door, striking a seductive pose, her legs crossed at the ankles, one arm draped across the car's roof. She's got to be freezing in that tiny spaghetti-strap red dress in a shade matching the shirt I'm wearing, though she has a full-length black velvet cape draped over one arm. The other hand clutches a mini red purse. Never understood those. It's not like you can fit anything important in them.

The dress hangs to about midthigh, and my eyes trace her toned, shapely legs down to the black stiletto heels she wears, then back up to the ample cleavage the plunging neckline reveals.

"Oh, holy mother of God," I whisper. The fire inside me burns fierce.

Genesis must read my lips because she laughs, her gaze roving over me as well. A little knot of tension unties itself in my chest when she nods and smiles with approval. She crosses to me, swaying her hips, and takes my arm so I can lead her back to the limousine.

"I'm liking that vest-and-shirt combo more and more, and that's a great color on you."

"You too," I say, meaning it. She's dyed her normally fire-engine-red hair to a more subtle shade, and the dress complements it nicely.

The chauffeur appears and helps her into the passenger area while I linger outside to give directions and confirm payment. He's all deference and professionalism, and we have things taken care of in seconds. "All set," I say, sliding in beside her.

It's a nice limo, spacious inside, with seats across the back and along both sides, a fully stocked bar, and a moon roof, now closed against the late-October chill. There's plenty of heat in here, too, and I don't just mean what's coming through the vents.

Gen's already got her shoes off, her feet pulled up on the seat, revealing even more of her thighs to my hungry gaze. She takes one look at my expression and giggles. "You look like you're ready to tear this dress off me."

"I'm not sure I'm not." I study the interior with more intent: carpeted flooring, seats wide enough to accommodate lying down, the partition between us and the driver firmly sealed. "You think that's soundproof?" I ask, nodding at the separator.

"I think we should test it out," Gen says, winking and shifting to face me. The engine starts up, and we're moving, the casino and conference rooms passing by outside the tinted windows. No one will see us, either, not with tinting that dark and night coming on.

Sex in the back of a limo. Not something I would have considered six months ago. But we have a forty-five-minute drive, I'm more than a little desperate, and my relationship with Gen has changed me in more ways than one.

Not all of them positive.

I shake that thought from my head as I kneel before her and gently part her thighs.

Chapter 3
Overdrive

"OH GOD, Flynn. Yes." She writhes on the leather seat, slick bare skin squeaking against the material and making us both chuckle. Her moans rise to crescendos, and I'm wondering if I'm really that good tonight or if she's being extra loud on purpose because we're in a limo. Because the chauffeur might hear her. I know the thrill of public display increases her enjoyment. Me, I'm wishing for something soft and sexy to gag her with. But I don't stop what I'm doing with my tongue. I'd never tease her, except in a good way, no matter how loud she gets.

Despite my nerves, Gen's pleasure heightens my own arousal, almost to the point of pain. Due to all the magic use and its side effects, she's been seeing to my needs first lately, but tonight being her birthday, I wanted to devote more time to her desires. I'm not sure how much longer I can hold out.

Gen's hips jerk once, twice, out of rhythm, and I know she's close, losing control of her body. I pick up the pace, focusing on the spot where she's most sensitive, and a moment later, her thighs clamp around my head, her hands tangled in my hair, pressing me in tight.

"Yes, there, now—" She bucks upward, almost dislodging me, but I've ridden this bronco before, and I hang in there until the last throes of her orgasm subside and her legs release me. Then I climb onto the seat next to her and cuddle her to my chest. Her heart races beneath the thin material of her dress. Her panting breath tickles my neck.

"Quite a concert for the driver," I say with a glance toward the closed partition.

She smiles up at me, unrepentant. "You ready for an encore?"

"More than you know." I spare a moment to check my cell—only twenty minutes left before we reach our destination. I took my time with her. She deserves everything I can give her. But....

"Don't worry," she says, reading my mind as she often does. "Just lean back and relax."

I follow her instructions, extending my sore legs out before me across the limo's open floor space. She retrieves her red lace underwear and slips it on, then wriggles her tight dress back into place. Quite the reverse striptease, and it stokes my fires higher. She undoes my belt, unfastens my black pants, and works them over my hips while I lift myself for her. "You don't think there are any hidden cameras in here, do you?" My eyes dart to the corners, searching for lenses.

Gen's voice goes low and sultry. "If there are, will that stop you?" She strokes her cool fingertips down the lengths of my heated thighs. My muscles twitch in response, and I hitch in a breath.

"N-no," I manage, earning a laugh from her.

"Good. Now shut up and let me concentrate."

I grin. God forbid I should break her concentration.

She begins by running her fingers across my center. Her eyes widen at the moisture she finds there, and she purrs in appreciation. I love that sound, and tremors ripple across my abdomen and lower. "Yes," Gen whispers, her breath warm and teasing as she leans in, "I'd say you're ready."

"Lots of… magic use today. Training."

"Guess they worked you hard. Just like I plan to." She presses two fingers into me, and my head drops against the backrest, my eyes sliding closed in response to the pleasure. So good. It's so fucking good.

In fact, it's better than I can remember it ever being. Gen knows my body, knows exactly where to touch me to set me off, but it isn't just that. It's my damn succubus side. Even now, not tapping the power at all, it curls within, heightening my sensations, and it's been growing steadily more intense with every use.

Gen slips her fingers from me, ceasing the soothing in-and-out motion. My eyes snap open to stare down at her in pained disbelief. "Why did you stop?"

She's got her cell phone out on the seat, the time displayed on its screen, her tiny purse open beside it. "Just timing things," she says. "We'll only get one shot at this. I want it to be impressive."

Fifteen minutes. She wants to tease me for fifteen minutes. Under normal circumstances, that wouldn't be a long time, and I'd enjoy the build-up. Right now I want to grab her by the shoulders and *force* her to continue—an impulse I've never experienced before. It scares me. "Not so sure that's a great idea," I grind out through clenched teeth.

She laughs. She has no idea how serious I am about the potential danger she's in. Never, ever, have I wanted to hurt her, and I'm not there yet, but I can feel the tension mounting, the anger at being denied prickling beneath my skin. And I don't have the strength to warn her further. All my energy goes toward controlling myself. "You'll be fine," she says and reaches into her purse.

Gen removes a small package of baby wipes and what looks like a ridiculously large lavender pill capsule or a too small lavender egg. She sets the wipes aside. I blink at the egg-thing. What I thought earlier about tiny purses containing nothing of importance?

I was wrong.

"Is that... what I think it is?" Big, bad Flynn. Psychic warrior. Former construction worker. Survivor of snake venom.

Can't say the word *vibrator.*

"Yep. There's a sex shop down the street from the casino."

Which, in Atlantic City, doesn't surprise me at all.

"Have you used one before?" Because I never have. Not to say I haven't been curious, but the idea of going into a public store to buy one, or receiving that unidentifiable brown-paper-wrapped package in the mail that I'll bet every mail carrier recognizes, sends me into embarrassed fits.

"Tried it out last night," she confesses. "While you were training so late."

A pang of guilt goes through me. She shouldn't have to resort to mechanical help. That does explain why she was just as keyed up as I was when I got back to the suite. We both had a good time, so maybe it's no big deal.

She twists the egg at its center. A low hum fills the passenger area. Crawling up on the seat beside me, she puts one arm around my shoulders, as if to hold me steady. "It's... intense," she explains at my confused look.

Oookay. At this point, intense would be welcome. A thin trickle of sweat drips down the back of my neck between my shoulder blades. I need relief and I need it fast, or not only is Gen's pretty dress getting shredded, but we're never climbing out of this limo.

Gen lowers her hand holding the… thing… between my legs and touches it to my center, just once, very lightly.

Intense doesn't begin to describe it.

My body jerks, hips leaving the seat cushions. I flop down. My spine arches in pleasure. Gen pulls it away with a soft laugh. "Good?" she whispers, stroking my face with her fingertips.

I'm panting from the brief contact, eyes squeezed shut. A growl threatens to erupt from deep in my throat. "Don't… stop." I flail for her wrist, wrapping my hand around it, drawing it back down. She gently but firmly peels my fingers from her skin. It's all I can do not to fight her, force her. I'm much, much stronger than Genesis. If I wanted to, I could break her arm. And, oh God, why is that thought even in my head?

She laughs louder, oblivious to my internal struggles. "Let me handle this." Fabric rustles against leather as she shifts position. Her arm brushes my thigh, and then the sensations return, faster this time, and she's pressing it harder against me, all my nerves responding like embers popping from a fireplace full of dry wood.

My hips rock. My head turns from side to side. My breathing comes hard and fast like it does during my sparring sessions. Muscles tense. I'm close, so close.

Laughing, Gen pulls her hand away.

"No!" In a flash, I'm on her, wrenching and twisting both our bodies so we fall from the seat and land with a thud on the carpet-covered limousine flooring. The vibrator goes skittering beyond my reach, but I'm not interested in that right now. When we stop rolling, I'm on top, kneeling above Gen, gripping her shoulders, panting like some wild animal ready to tear out her heart. The world tinges green, and on some subconscious level, I know how bad that is. Green equals dark. I shake my head in an attempt to clear my vision, but it doesn't fade.

"Flynn?" Genesis blinks up at me, only now regaining her bearings. I stunned her when I knocked her to the floor. She's surprised to find herself there. Her eyes meet mine, and fear flickers in hers. "Flynn, let me up." Her tone soothes, like ointment to an open wound, but I hear the tremor there too.

The tension in my fingers eases. I've dug them into her soft skin. She'll have bruises on her shoulders tomorrow.

Bruises caused by me.

"Oh… fuck." I fall sideways off her and wrap my arms around myself, trembling with need. My pants rest around my ankles, my bare skin in contact with the limousine floor and the engine's vibrations keeping me on the edge. "Gen—"

"Stop," she whispers. Crawling on all fours, she retrieves the sex toy, returns to me, and wraps her arm around me.

"Five minutes, ladies," comes the chauffeur's voice over the intercom. Outside the tinted windows, forest gives way to huge vineyards. New Jersey may not be known for fine wines, but this area is different.

Gen curses under her breath and hits the button on the armrest to respond. "Give us another fifteen, please. Drive around a bit before parking."

"Yes, ma'am," he replies with a chuckle. Yeah, he knows what we've been up to, or he thinks he does. I doubt anyone could quite imagine our current scenario.

Once the com clicks off, she holds me tight, turns the vibrator to its highest setting, and presses it firmly between my legs. At the same time, she grabs and massages my breast through my shirt and vest, adding to the pleasure. Her lips come in close, blowing warm air into my ear, then nuzzling the sensitive tendons in the side of my neck.

I jerk and twist, bucking and heaving, groaning as every muscle tightens, but she never loses contact, and a moment later, the world explodes in blissful relief.

Chapter 4
Aftermath

WHEN I return to my senses, I can't face her, instead crawling to the seat and snatching the wet wipes to clean up. Facing away, I pull up and refasten my pants, then jerk the shirt and vest into place.

"Look at me," Genesis demands, soft but undeniable.

"I'm sorry," I say, shifting toward her. "I couldn't help it. I tried—" My voice cracks. She looks ready to sob, angry red marks, finger indentations, marring her pale-skinned shoulders.

"Don't. Just don't." She stands, crouching, and crosses to me, pulls me onto the seat, and wraps her arms around my torso. "My fault. You were using your power all day. I should've known better. We can't treat sex as casually as we used to."

"I should've been able to control it." Tears slip down both my cheeks. I don't try to stop them.

"You did. Longer than you had any expectation to have to. I teased you, ignored your pleas. You tried to warn me. I thought you were playing."

No more playing. Not for us. The thought makes me very sad.

"Eventually, the training will end," Gen says, reading my thoughts or echoing them in her own.

"Maybe…." I hate this, hate what I'm about to say, but I have to. "Maybe we should wait on the—"

"No. Don't even think about postponing the wedding. I'm marrying you, Flynn, if I have to drag you down the aisle."

"But I *hurt* you." There. I said it. I made the nightmare real.

"All right if I park now, ladies?" the voice on the intercom asks.

Gen reaches the button before I do. "That will be fine, thanks." She clicks it off.

"Gen…."

She pokes a finger in my chest, and I shut up. "I'm fine. It's nothing. You could have done a lot more damage, but you held back. I'm proud of you, not upset, not scared, not angry. Proud."

I don't deserve her pride.

I don't deserve *her.*

"But—"

"No buts." The limousine pulls into a parking slot; the purring engine dies. "Now, get your sexy ass out of this limo. It's my birthday. We're cele-brating. And I intend to enjoy it."

I grab her cape from the side row of seats. "Wear this?" It'll cover the bruising, though that's already fading, so maybe it's not as bad as I feared.

She smiles, taking it from me. "Until the redness goes away. I don't even think it'll leave a mark. Stop worrying, Flynn. You didn't really hurt me. It could've been much, much worse."

That's exactly what I'm afraid of.

Chapter 5
Dinner Dilemma

I HELP Gen on with her cloak, the soft velvet rustling beneath my fingers, and paste on what I hope is a convincing smile. She exits the limo with the driver's assistance, though I wave off his hand. His calm, professional demeanor impresses me as we turn toward the restaurant. The chauffeur has to know what we've been up to, but he never cracks a smile or gives any indication except the brief humor I heard over the intercom.

Limos get premium parking in the gravel lot, so we're only steps away from a stone walk leading to large wooden double doors. Gen's having a little trouble with the uneven surface in her high heels, so I take her arm to steady her, closing my hand so very gently around her forearm.

"I'm not a china doll," she says, placing her hand over mine and pressing me to grip her more tightly. "I'm pretty tough. Don't you dare start treating me like I'll break if you breathe on me too hard." Genesis stops halfway up the walk and turns to face me. "I need you to believe in my strength, Flynn. Otherwise I can't believe it myself."

She doesn't have to tell me she's referring to her dark magic addiction. I know from the semi-hopeless look in her eyes. I take a deep breath of the honeysuckle growing to either side, watch fireflies darting in the bushes under the twinkling decorative lights the owners have strung along the path. It's dark and quiet except for our breathing, the crickets, and faint sounds of dinner conversation and rattling dishware from behind the closed doors.

"You are one of the strongest people I've ever met," I say with all seriousness. "Maybe not physically, but you have inner strength. You'll beat whatever you decide to."

Her smile lights up the darkness.

"Now, tell me where we are," she says, leading me onward.

I shrug. "It's a winery. The Renault Winery. The concierge said the food was amazing and the atmosphere was—"

"Very romantic," she finishes for me, placing a kiss on my cheek. "Very me and not you at all."

Another shrug. "It's your birthday." She's right. For my birthday, I'd prefer burgers and fries at a football game, or maybe concert tickets to see Pink. But that's two months away. I reach to grasp the wrought iron handle and pull open the right-hand door, revealing a short stone-walled tunnel.

We walk up a brief incline, passing several massive wooden wine casks, and arrive in a lovely stone-and-wood foyer with a check-in podium. A tuxedo-clad gentleman behind the podium smiles and welcomes us.

While Gen excuses herself to the ladies' room, I finagle with the host. We're late for our reservation, which would normally entail a wait of up to an hour, but a fifty quietly passed from my palm to his solves that problem. I also mention we're celebrating her birthday and remind him of the special arrangements I made when I called.

"Right this way, ladies," he says upon Gen's return and leads us through a large, oval room of elegantly dressed diners at regular tables to one of the odd wooden booths off to the side.

Gen slides in on the right while I study the thing. It's covered, rounded across the top and curved down the sides, the wood in long planks separated by strips of metal....

"It's one of those wine casks," Gen says, figuring it out. "They've been cut down the middle and made into booths."

"Indeed." The host beams. "These are over a hundred and five years old."

And yeah, I can see it now that I know what I'm looking for. The cask booths line both sides of the restaurant, many containing very lovey-dovey couples holding hands or kissing across the tables or choosing to sit side by side to snuggle.

My first impulse is to do the same, slide in next to Gen so I can keep my arm around her between courses. Then I flash back on the limo and frown, bending to place myself across from her.

"Oh, no you don't." She pats the cushioned wooden bench seat beside her, then reaches out for me and pulls me in.

"Your server will be with you in a moment," the host says, handing us each a menu. He plucks Gen's peaked napkin from the table and spreads it across her lap. I grab my own before he can and take care of that for myself. With a deferential nod, he leaves.

Genesis pores over the food offerings, quietly squeeing at some of the selections she'd like to try. On the phone, the manager told me it was a set price at thirty-five dollars a person. You pick an appetizer and an entree. The other two courses are chef's choice. Each comes with a wine pairing from their vineyards. I give the menu a quick glance, find something I can tolerate—filet mignon is always a safe bet, right?—and go back to surveying the room.

To find we're the ones being surveyed.

New Jersey is known for liberal attitudes, and they approved gay marriage years before Florida did. That doesn't mean the state's wealthy elite aren't homophobic.

Or maybe it's just me. I'm a little underdressed.

Not terribly so. I'm not in jeans and a T-shirt. My shirt has a collar, and the vest spiffs things up.

But compared to the elegant cocktail dresses and long skirts most of the women sport, I'm pretty casual. The men wear expensive suits and ties, their shoes polished and shining under the incandescent lighting. Genesis blends fine.

I never have.

Between my relative shabbiness and my obvious butch tendencies, even with my long hair in a ponytail, I'm attracting a lot of stares.

I pointedly return some of the more direct ones, making eye contact and glaring until they blink and turn away. Genesis says my glare could ignite fires when I'm really pissed. The diners are getting the full force of it now.

The waitress's arrival startles me, and I break off my glaring match with a gray-haired woman three tables to my left.

"Good evening," she says in a rich alto. She's young, attractive like all the other staff members I've seen, wearing a short black skirt, black stockings, black ballet flats, and a white blouse with a black vest similar to mine. My eyes travel appreciatively up her calves before Gen squeezes my arm.

"Remember who you're with," she scolds, playfully.

Well, if the waitress had any question about us being a couple, Gen's clarified it for her. The woman takes it the right way, smiling with genuine warmth. "What can I start you two with for an appetizer?"

Oh shit. I forgot to look at those—the only other choice we have with dinner.

Gen must read my momentary panic because she jumps in and orders me the asparagus, not one of my favorites, but I'm guessing it's the selection I'm most likely to eat. She goes with the grilled eggplant, which I wouldn't touch, along with the "pan-roasted paiche," whatever that is, for her main course, and I manage to stammer out my filet mignon, medium rare.

"Excellent. I'll return in a moment with your first wine pairing and your appetizers."

"What's wrong?" Gen whispers as soon as she leaves. "You're so nervous."

"Not used to this kind of place," I say, studying the three forks, two knives, and two spoons.

"Just follow my lead."

"Pretty much always do." That earns me a kiss on the lips, and though I blush fiercely, I enjoy it, the other diners be damned. "What was that you ordered, anyway?"

"It's a type of fish. Really delicious. You'll have to try some of mine."

We make small talk while we enjoy the meal, and it really is fantastic despite the frou-frou. My steak is so tender, I could almost cut it with a fork. The vegetables are soaked in some sort of cherry-flavored liquor and cinnamon, making them tolerable even to me. And all the wine samplings lighten my mood and untense my shoulders. When we get to the "palate-cleansing sorbet interlude" between the main course and dessert, the waitress pours sparkling blue liquid into long-stemmed glasses and sets them before us.

Gen raises her eyebrows. Good. I'm not the only one wondering what this is.

"Winery specialty," our server explains. "Blueberry champagne. New Jersey is famous for growing blueberries."

The confusion on Gen's face shifts to pleased surprise. She loves berries of all kinds, especially strawberries and blueberries. She takes a tentative sip. A slow grin curls her lips. Her eyes close. I know that expression. I saw it in the limo. "Oh, this is better than s—"

I jump in. "Don't say it."

The waitress laughs. "We sell it in the wine shop here. By the bottle or the case."

I try it. Okay, I'm not a wine gal. I prefer beer. But this stuff is amazing: fruity, scintillating, and pretty with its blue color. Champagne and limousines. Guess I'm finally making the shift to the wealthier lifestyle.

"Can you just add a case to our check? We've got a limo out front. We'll arrange for shipping it ourselves."

The waitress makes a note on her order pad, then gives Gen a big smile. "I'll see to it."

After she leaves, I say, "We don't even know what it costs." Maybe I'm not so used to this after all.

"Doesn't matter. I'm taking it home."

We sip champagne and cleanse our palates while I drink in the sight of my Genesis—beautiful, sexy as hell, and mine all mine.

"So," she says, focusing on her wine flute. "I'm thinking you should visit your mother while we're in New Jersey."

I fumble my tiny sorbet spoon, clattering it against the cut-crystal goblet I'm eating from. A pair of older gentlemen turn at the sound, one wearing a bow tie, the other in a bright pink button-down beneath his gray suit jacket. They're frowning, but when they recognize us as a couple, they both smile and return to their meals.

Huh. So we're not the only ones.

I focus on Gen's observation. "I'm buzzed, not drunk. You're not talking me into that."

"I shouldn't have to talk you into it. You should want to. Besides," she continues before I can list all the reasons it's a bad idea, "I'd like to meet your mother. After all, I'm going to be part of your family."

Such as it is.

"She doesn't want to meet you." That comes out harsher than I intend, and Gen's face falls. I grab her hand, holding it between mine. "Look, it's not personal. She's crazy, and she hates me."

And she'd hate Genesis, for no reason other than that she's bisexual and with me.

Again, I'm struck by the enormity of what Gen gives up to be mine. Being bi, she could have found a nice man, kept her sexuality a secret, fit into society with no prejudice or discrimination against her. Instead, she chooses me.

I take a bite of my sorbet, but it's gone sour to my taste, and not just because it's lemon-flavored.

"She doesn't hate you. She's your mother," Gen says, quiet and serious.

"I embarrass her. She's ashamed of me." And yes, she hates me, though I'll never convince Genesis of that. Her own parents love and accept everything about her, even if she can only talk to them through her psychic talents since their tragic deaths in a boating accident. We've met. They welcomed me with open arms, and I love them.

"Things change. People change. It's been what? Ten years? She's had psychiatric care, medications, counseling. Who says she hasn't changed her views?"

I do, but I don't say that out loud. Instead I try for humor. "You and Chris tag-teaming me now?" It falls flat.

"Yes, though we didn't plan it. We both think you'll regret it if you don't see her. She's not getting any younger."

Okay, that hits home. But not as much as Gen's next question.

"Do *you* hate *her*?"

Do I?

I take a long chug of my champagne, aware this isn't how such things should be consumed, but I don't care. I need the alcoholic armor.

I did hate her, once. When I was a kid, I despised her, resented her for being weak, for dropping all the responsibility in my lap as soon as I hit puberty, and with Dad gone, that was a lot to ask. Then she suggested having doctors "fix" my lesbian nature, sealing the deal.

If I'm completely honest with myself, yes, I hate her still. I love her too. She's my mother, and I cling to the few happy memories I retain of my early childhood.

Which makes me a hypocrite, because that probably means, somewhere deep down, she loves me too.

All the food sits heavily in my stomach, the wine sloshing around in there like rolling seas. "If Argyle gives me a training break, we'll go see her," I mumble around another forced mouthful.

A second later, Gen's arms are around my neck and she's hugging me for all she's worth. "Good. Great. I'm so glad. Don't you feel better?"

Not really.

"Yeah, sure. What do you want for dessert?" I hand her the laminated cardboard rectangle displaying the list of offerings.

"Oooh, crème brûlée. And bananas Foster." She turns hopeful eyes to me. "Can we get both and share?"

So much for the seven-layer chocolate cake I'd been kicking around. Then again, I probably won't eat more than a few bites of either, and it's her birthday. "Sure."

Dessert tastes as orgasmic (Gen's term) as the rest of the meal. The table-side igniting of the bananas Foster puts on a good show of blue flame burning alcohol, and I push the upcoming mother/daughter reunion from my mind long enough to enjoy it, along with a second glass of blueberry champagne.

Gen's fairly tipsy by the end of the meal, and I'm still pretty buzzed, but I planned for this, arranging in advance for us to take a tour of the winery to walk off all the drinking. We're not the only ones. A group of old ladies, all in matching purple hats, accompanies us through the dank, dark tunnel-like corridors to see the vats and casks and hear about the wine-making process from a rotund gentleman in homespun gray trousers, suspenders, and a dark shirt of rough fabric.

Our plan backfires when we discover the tour includes more wine tastings, and of course we must sample all of them, leaving us giddier than when we started.

I've got Gen by the elbow, guiding her out to the parking area, but I'm none too steady myself. We're laughing and sneaking kisses in the shadowed gardens surrounding the restaurant—testament to how drunk I am, kissing in public—when a throat clears behind us.

I spin on one heel—bad move since it puts me further off-balance—but manage to brace my feet apart in a defensive stance. Gen ducks behind me… then giggles.

I'm facing down one of the purple-hatted old ladies. Her friends are nowhere to be seen, but I hear them chattering shrilly nearby.

She points a disapproving finger at us both, waggling it in the air like a blunt sword. "God will save you if you give yourselves to him," she says.

Outrage wars with amusement, and given all the alcohol consumption, amusement wins. Besides, I'm in no mood to fight the elderly. "I'm agnostic," I say with a shrug, then pull Gen around her. Some powerful force created the universe. I'm sure of it. But I can't bring myself to attribute that to a thoughtful, rational, single entity who discriminates.

Before we can get past, the woman reaches out a shriveled hand and catches Gen's cloak. "And what about you? Will you let this heathen creature lead you down the dark path? Or will you let God guide your way?"

Okay, that's enough. I reach to remove the old woman's hand from my girlfriend's clothing, but Gen raises a palm to stop me.

"I'm Wiccan," Gen says. She nods in my direction. "I will follow her anywhere, including down *this* dark path, right to our limo, where I intend to make passionate love to her. Unless you'd like explicit details of where my tongue is headed, I suggest you let go."

Huh. Okay. Not sure I'm up to it, but I'm not arguing.

She pulls away, but the woman grabs her again, this time by the upper arm. And Gen's patience disintegrates.

In the darkness of an October New Jersey night, the green glow in her eyes flares bright and frightening, so much so, even I retreat a step or two before recovering and returning to her side. The old woman stares, dumbfounded, riveted to the stone walkway, mouth agape and sucking in air like a fish out of its bowl.

"Leave us alone," I say in low, measured tones that could be interpreted as calm or menacing, depending on one's perspective.

The lady jerks her hand away as if Gen had caught fire, crosses herself, and flees down the path, her sensible heels clattering on the stone. The light in Gen's eyes dies. She blinks at me.

"I think we should go," she says.

Understatement of the year.

Chapter 6
Addiction

NEITHER OF us needed the reminder of Gen's unhealthy attraction to the dark magic. Not tonight. Not after what happened earlier. Not on her birthday, dammit.

She's pale when we reach the limo, so much changed from when we arrived that the chauffeur shoots her a concerned frown while he holds the door open. "Is she all right?" he asks me quietly, once she's aboard.

"Just a little too much wine," I assure him, drumming up a smile.

He nods and returns it. "If she needs them, there are sick bags in the drawer on the right side of the wet bar. Oh, and speaking of wine, watch out for the case of champagne on the floor in there. I tried to set it off to the side, but I wouldn't want you two banging your shins on it."

Right. The blueberry champagne Gen wanted
to take home. "Thanks." I slide in after her. The
door thunks closed.

Instead of fetching the sick bags, I skirt
around the wine case, find some paper towels on
the bar, and soak one with a bottle of water from
the fridge. Then I dab Gen's face with it while she
closes her eyes, her breathing too fast.

The engine starts; the limo moves out of the
parking area. Too buzzed for balancing acts, I sit
before the motion dumps me on my ass.

"Hey," I say, touching her hand. "You okay?"

"I almost hurt her. She's probably someone's
mother, someone's grandmother." She bites her
lower lip, stopping its trembling. Shit, she's about
to cry.

"You didn't," I remind her. "You held on and
let me get you out of there. That took willpower,
strength." And the woman was a real bitch, but I
don't mention that. Regardless of her narrow re-
ligious beliefs, she didn't deserve to get hit with
some force of darkness.

"I came so close."

"Close doesn't count. Or are you telling me I
should feel guilty too?"

She opens her eyes. "What are you talking
about?"

That sparks a sarcastic laugh. My timing
sucks, but I can't help it. "Right here? Before dinner? Really, you've already forgotten my attack?
How about the way my vision went green? Don't

know if you could see that from your side, but it looked bad to me. If you've forgotten all that, that's some powerful wine you drank."

Gen's lips part as if she's going to argue. Then she clamps them shut. For a long moment, the only sounds are the limo's engine and the traffic outside as we hit the causeway heading for Atlantic City.

"You're right. I can't blame myself if I'm not blaming you," Gen finally says.

Of course, the other side of that coin is we should both be blamed, but I don't say that either.

"Your eyes didn't glow," she adds, squeezing my fingers. "You might have seen the darkness, but you weren't using it. You aren't evil, Flynn."

So they keep telling me.

"Neither are you," I assure her, pulling her in close.

"We'll see," she whispers, almost inaudible. "We'll see."

Chapter 7
Vanishing Act

CASSANDRA STRODE down the hospital corridor, purpose driving her steps. An hour. She had one hour to visit her daughter. Then she had to return to the airport to catch a flight back to Atlantic City and the National Psychic Registry's annual conference, leaving her only child in the care of her grandmother and the hospital staff.

She'd had to beg—*beg*—to convince President Argyle to release her for the day. They needed her healing skills. Flynn and those training her needed a gifted healer on standby. But Cassie couldn't be absent from the four-year-old's side for a full week. The child's condition depended upon Cassie's talent, as well as those of the doctors and nurses who attended her.

Besides, Nathaniel had promised an easy day for Flynn. After all, she was marrying Genesis tomorrow. Wouldn't do to put Flynn in a cast the day before her wedding.

Cassie caught the doors of a closing elevator and stood alone in its cell-like space. A smile crept across her face at the thought of the construction worker turned magical hero. Who would have thought they'd form an alliance, even, perhaps, a friendship of sorts? Cassie found herself rooting for the woman and happy she and Genesis had found one another.

After my foolish high school self so carelessly discarded Gen.

"I'm not gay," she muttered under her breath. But she fell a little left of center, and Gen was special. She would have been a loving companion, a steadfast partner in any relationship.

Flynn was a damn lucky woman.

She smiled to herself. Of course, Cassie had been lucky too. With Chris, Gen's brother.

They'd been seeing each other pretty steadily for about two months, ever since they'd met at Genesis and Flynn's house—the same night Cassie had discovered Flynn was a time walker. Both Cassie and Chris had agreed to keep the budding relationship a secret. She'd made her peace with Flynn, but Genesis....

The woman certainly knew how to hold a grudge.

Chris and Flynn both understood Cassie's freak-out and break-up with Gen at the age of eighteen. But Genesis just wouldn't let it go. Add to that Cassie's attack on Flynn at the bidding of the Psychic Registry, even if Cassie was doing it to keep her own daughter alive, and, well, there was no getting on Gen's good side.

In Genesis's book, two strikes made you out.

Sooner or later, Chris would have to tell his sister about the two of them. Probably sooner rather than later, since, despite not being invited to Flynn and Genesis's wedding (even though Flynn had privately apologized for that), Cassie *was* attending as Chris's date. His reasoning? Gen would be so happy that day that discovering her brother was dating her ex-girlfriend from high school would be no big deal.

Cassie doubted that very much.

The elevator dropped her off on the fourth level. Cassandra hurried over the polished tile floors, breathing through her mouth so as not to inhale the smells of bleach and sickness. She passed the nurses' station of the children's cancer ward and waved to the head nurse on duty—Isabelle—who seemed to be there every time they admitted little Tracy.

Odd. Isabelle's brows drew together in confusion. The gray-haired nurse peered at her through her bifocals, squinting as if she didn't recognize Cassie. But that made no sense. They'd chatted at length during Tracy's procedures, had coffee together, sobbed over the leukemia diagnosis and the child's setbacks.

Maybe her eyeglass prescription had expired.

The head nurse raised a tentative hand in return greeting, the gesture people made when someone knew them and they ought to know who it was but didn't. She didn't question Cassie as she passed the desk, but Cassie felt the woman's eyes on her all the way to room 408—Tracy's room.

Walls painted in bright yellow. Blue-sky ceiling with stuffed-pillow clouds hanging on wires overhead. Empty bed.

Cassandra didn't panic right away. She didn't know today's treatment schedule, hadn't called in advance since she had such limited time. Tracy might be undergoing more tests. An orderly might have wheeled her down to x-ray (floor two) or over to chemotherapy in the west wing.

Except Tracy wasn't the only element missing from the private room.

No stuffed animals decorated the bedside table's surface. No flowers stood in pots on the windowsill. When Cassie left three days earlier, she'd set pink chrysanthemums there herself. Tracy loved pink. And she'd arranged with the hospital florist to have another batch of blooms delivered daily, and Isabelle agreed to water them....

A knot of worry tied her intestines. She stepped to the storage cabinet which held Tracy's street clothes, her Disney Princess suitcase, her toiletries, and swung it open. All gone.

"May I help you, ma'am?" came a familiar voice from the doorway.

Cassie spun. "Isabelle! Thank God. Do you know where they've moved Tracy? I've only got a little time, and I'd like to see her." She didn't voice the other possibility—that something had happened to Tracy overnight. They'd spoken on the phone at her bedtime, just the day before. The hospital would have called her if the unthinkable had happened, if

Tracy had— "Please, just tell me where she is." Her throat closed on the last word. She swallowed hard.

"Ma'am," Isabelle said, stepping closer. She placed a gentle hand on Cassie's arm. "I can see you're upset. Clearly, there's been some sort of mis-understanding. This room has been unoccupied for several days. And we don't have a Tracy in the ward at this time. Are you certain you're on the right floor? That happens a lot. This is the cancer unit."

Cassandra jerked away from the comforting hand. "Of course I'm on the right floor. Tracy's my daughter. She has leukemia. She's been a patient here, right here in this room, for the past several weeks, and on and off for months. And why do you keep calling me ma'am? Isabelle, don't you recognize me?"

The head nurse leaned back, studying her from top to bottom, holding at Cassie's face. "Maybe? From a few years back? Why don't you come out to the nurses' station and have a seat so we can clear this up?"

With no other ready alternative, Cassandra followed the older woman to a plastic chair just inside the squared-off area of chest-high counters set up as the nurses' station. A couple of younger nurses and a candy striper gave her curious looks, but with Isabelle overseeing her, they didn't interfere.

Isabelle got on her computer, each passing minute without results sending Cassie's pulse racing higher. Then she remembered—her cell phone. Surely if she showed the nurse a picture of Tracy, she'd remember.

She pulled the phone from her purse, scrolled across the screen to the folder containing images, opened one after another: herself, friends, her business, Orlando Match, when she'd first opened the downtown office.

Not a single picture of Tracy.

"Impossible…," Cassie breathed.

It was like the child had been erased from—

"Oh no." Rising on shaky limbs, she touched Isabelle's shoulder. "Thank you for your time and effort," Cassie choked out. "I'll be going now."

"Ma'am," Isabelle said quietly, turning to face her, "I think I might have something." The head nurse ran a hand through her gray hair, her fingers trembling a bit. "There's a record of a Tracy Safoir having been a patient here three years ago when she was an infant. She had leukemia." The nurse took a deep breath. "She died." Isabelle rested her palm on Cassandra's arm. "Sometimes… sometimes our memories play tricks on us. Things we want to be, we imagine them to be. Let me call someone for you."

Cassie jerked away. "No. Thank you." Sedatives, psychiatrists, they'd stop her, keep her from getting back to Atlantic City and reporting what had happened to Tracy. Tracy, who, in the last year had begun showing some psychic ability, a talent for nurturing plants beyond basic gardening skills.

Tracy, who had become the mad succubus, Tempest Granfeld's, latest victim.

Chapter 8
Erased

"FLYNN!"

Cassie's voice. Panicked. The shout breaks my concentration. A blast of clairvoyant energy I'm drawing from a young female psychic named Toni (and why are my trainers always female, anyway?) slams into my brain, and I'm struck by a dozen or more simultaneous images of my closest friends and family in their current states: Genesis sitting in a late-evening panel, taking notes; Chris on the phone up in the suite, probably arranging for my "bachelor" party tonight; Rosaline and her daughters decorating the adjoining rooms we got them in pink-and-white crepe paper streamers for Genesis's bridal shower; and more, followed by a brief period of nothing but blackness.

It disorients me, and I lower myself to the floor before I hit it harder than I want to. I cover my face with my hands, waiting for the darkened vision to pass.

"Flynn, please, get up. I have to talk to you." Something wet drops on my forearm, mixing with the sweat I've worked up from today's training. Cassandra grabs me by the shoulders and gives me a small shake.

I've been at it all day. As promised, President Argyle and her toady, Nathaniel, went easier on me since I'm getting married tomorrow—mostly defensive rather than aggressive skills, but my arousal levels burn from all the power usage. I'm worn out, dirty, smelly, and horny as hell. I'm also nervous as shit about the wedding. I do not need another crisis.

"Give her a minute," Toni advises, her voice coming nearer as she crosses the conference-room-turned-training-center to where I sit. "She just took in a bunch of my energy, and I think she caught it hard."

"I don't have a minute. It's Tara." A pause. "No, that's not right. Oh God, I'm forgetting my own niece."

"I thought you were an only child," come Nathaniel's peeved tones. He doesn't like this interruption any better than I do, but for different reasons. Nothing should interfere with his precious schedule, and he's missing all the conference events to oversee my lessons.

Cassie's response comes back stilted and confused. "I… I am." Her clothing rustles as she seats herself beside me.

"Then how could you—?" Nate begins, but I cut him off, the pieces slowly coalescing in my weary head.

"Are you talking about Tracy?" Her four-year-old. A very sick four-year-old whose name she should have absolutely no trouble remembering. I force my eyes open.

"Yes, Tracy. She's my... she's my...."

"Daughter," I finish for her.

Cassie's shaking and sobbing, more wet tears falling on my arm as she throws herself against me. I'm no good at this sort of thing, but I awkwardly put my arms around her and pat her back.

"Daughter? You don't have a daughter." Nate crouches beside the two of us.

"Yes, she does. She showed you pictures yesterday, at the bar. Big blue eyes, pale skin. She's in the Orlando Children's Hospital undergoing cancer treatment," I tell him, heart sinking further.

He shakes his head. "I don't remember any pictures." And then it clicks, and all the blood drains from his face.

"Is she spelled or stoned?" Toni asks. "How do you forget your own daughter?"

I give Nathaniel a pointed look, and he nods. "That will be all for today, Toni. We'll finish this lesson at another time."

The clairvoyant opens her mouth to argue, scans between the three of us, and closes it again. "Right. See you later." She exits by the closest door.

Only a few members of Registry President Argyle's inner circle know what's going on—psychics being erased from time by a rogue and likely insane succubus named Tempest Granfeld. It's what they brought me in for, to stop her, and it's best not to cause a Registry-wide panic with general disclosure.

Toni left way too easily, so I'm betting she, and other members low on the totem pole, are accustomed to being out of the loop. I wonder if she even knows why she's training me. Some of the psychics who've taught me have, others haven't.

And again I'm struck by the realization that every one of them has been female. Something I need to ask Nate about when things quiet a little. Right. Like that's gonna happen.

"I need to let President Argyle know we have another victim," Nate says, beginning to rise.

I reach a hand past Cassie and yank him back down. "You need to listen to what she has to say." Holding her out from me, I make her eyes meet mine. "Tell me what you remember, Cass."

She blinks a few more times, processing. "I flew down to Orlando this morning to check on her. Her room was empty. All the toys and flowers gone. They told me... they told me...." The light of understanding leaves her eyes.

"Tracy," I prompt.

"They told me Tracy died. Three years ago. As a baby. And I remember that. In detail. But that's wrong, isn't it? You remember her being alive now, don't you, Flynn? I'm not crazy, right?"

"No, you're not crazy. I remember her. I remember the photos. I remember her being alive. Clearly."

So this is how it works. Those distant from the victim, like Nathaniel, forget immediately when they're gone. Those closer take longer for the memories to fade.

And me? Another psychic succubus? I get to keep it all.

Nathaniel gives me a look, and I dismiss him with a nod, hoping he can keep this in his head long enough to inform Madame President. He stands and leaves by the closest set of double doors. My attention returns to Cassie.

"Tell me everything else you can about the day Tracy died, but didn't." God, that's confusing, but she seems to understand what I mean, and though it chokes her up and more tears form in her eyes, she gives me all the details she can recall.

When she finishes, she's a total wreck.

"Go call Chris," I tell her, registering her blink of surprise that I know about the two of them. Guess Chris didn't mention it yet. "Get him out of the suite and let him keep you company, but don't tell him what's up."

"What *is* up?"

She knows she's upset, but she's forgotten why. Already. Jesus.

I shake my head. "Just do it. Spend some time together, but someplace else." I give her a nudge, and she stands and moves toward the doors, confused but willing.

I'd wondered what would happen if Genesis were a target. Now I know. I'd keep her in my memory for all time while everyone around me forgot she existed. I'd lose my mind.

And though Gen may never forgive me, wedding or no wedding, even though I never personally met her, I'm going to do whatever I can to get that little girl back.

Chapter 9
Confession

"GEN, WE need to talk." No positive conversation ever starts with those words, and from the look Genesis gives me, she knows it.

She stops brushing her hair and turns from the mirror hanging over the wet bar in the honeymoon suite's living room. "What's wrong?"

I came up to the penthouse floor an hour ago, searching for her, before I remembered my clairvoyant view of Gen at the conference. Then I grabbed a shower, changed clothes, sat on the couch and waited. She arrived and immediately began telling me all about the panel on "Blending Into Society as a Psychic," not letting me get a word in edgewise and primping herself for the bridal shower Rosaline is throwing for her in about two hours.

Fate's timing really sucks.

"Maybe you should come over here and sit down," I suggest, patting the pale blue couch cushion beside me.

She narrows her eyes. "Okay, spill it. What's going on?"

"Sit. Please."

Gen crosses to me warily and sits.

I'm not sure where to start, so I fuck around a bit, fiddling with the zipper on my leather jacket, talking about the training sessions in general. Genesis grabs my hands and stops my fidgeting. "You're scaring me," she says.

Well, that makes two of us.

"Okay, fine. So, here's the deal. The Registry didn't bring me up here just to teach me how to use my skills. Argyle has a job she wants done."

Gen presses her lips together and rolls her eyes. "No surprise. She always wants something. If she thinks you have a talent she can use, she'll find a way to use it. What does she want from you?"

Holding her hands in mine, I tell her.

The emotions shift across her face as I speak, going from stunned to afraid to outright angry in seconds. I think there's a little pride in there, too, but it's quickly obscured by the other three. I leave out the part about President Argyle pardoning Gen for her dark magic use if I comply with her wishes, instead stressing the threat that faces the entire psychic community if I don't complete my mission and stop Tempest Granfeld.

"That's insane," she blurts when I finish. "They can't use you like that. It's too dangerous. You're not doing it."

"I *am* doing it," I say softly. "In fact, I'm doing it tonight." And I tell her about Tracy.

"No." Pulling away from me, Gen stands and paces in front of the couch. With me sitting there, she doesn't have quite enough room to get by, so she gives the coffee table a violent shove with one foot. It skids across the carpet and bangs into the armchair. Then she continues pacing.

"She's a little girl. With cancer," I say.

"Right now she's nothing. She doesn't exist."

"Gen… seriously?"

Her callousness stuns me. It's not like her at all. And when she turns and faces me, I realize it's the frustration talking. She's just as upset about it as I am. Tears stream down her cheeks, ruining her makeup. Her face is red and her eyes flash with fury, but she's sad and scared and concerned. I read it all.

She throws herself on the couch and buries her face in my shoulder, letting me wrap my arms around her and rock her gently. "Why now? Why does it have to be now?" she sobs, her voice muffled by my jacket. She raises her head and gives me a hopeful look. "You work with time. If you wait a couple of days, it shouldn't matter, right? I mean, you're planning on going back to see where Granfeld messed with Tracy's existence. What difference does it make when you go? The past is the past. It's not going anywhere. It can wait until after the wedding."

Well, at least she's stopped trying to talk me out of it altogether. Gen knows as well as I do that I'm the only person for this job and that I won't be able to live with myself if I don't try to fix things.

I just hope I end up living at all.

"I don't know if it can wait," I tell her. "I don't know enough about this to make that judgment. What if the longer I hesitate, the harder it becomes to undo it? I can't take that chance."

"What if it can't be undone no matter when you try?" she asks, her voice a whisper.

"Then the sooner I find that out, the better. The question is, will you help me?"

She fixes me with a hard stare. "You know you're asking me to potentially help you commit suicide."

I try for a nonchalant shrug, but it doesn't come off well. "I'll have a better chance of surviving it if you're here by my side."

"If you don't survive, I'm not sure what I'll do."

Okay, that's ominous. And I suspect I know exactly what she'll do. She'll give in to the pull of the dark magic. But what choice do I have? I can't give up that little kid and all those other erased lives to stay and protect Genesis, who might very well end up becoming a target of the rogue succubus herself.

No. I have to stop this, and I have to come back. It's the only way to save us all.

My face twists in a grimace. "Have I mentioned how much I hate this hero shit?"

Gen shakes her head, and a sad smile curls her lips. "No. You love it."

I start to protest, but she presses her fingers to my mouth.

"You're suited to it. You thrive on it. It's who you are, who you've always been." She brushes a strand of hair away from my face. "And I love you. So tell me what you need me to do."

Chapter 10
Time Warp

ALTERING TIME took finesse and skill. Changing the wrong element could bring disastrous results. Adjusting something too far into the past might damage her own future. Tempest had to watch what she manipulated, foresee the long-term effects… and select targets to create the most havoc for the National Psychic Registry.

Since the late 1800s, the Registry had been her enemy—persecuting her without justification, interfering with her natural abilities to draw power from others, her gods-given *need* to feed off that energy. All other talents they let behave as they chose, provided they didn't delve into the dark magic. Her, they shunned from their meetings, hunted if she used her skills, punished if they caught her.

Punished with madness—perhaps their biggest mistake.

Because even though she knew she'd gone beyond what was fit revenge, she didn't care. She craved more and more chaos, and as a time walker, she could evoke it at will.

Tempest stood in the corner of the undertaker's office, staring down at her own body—an emaciated, pale, pitiful corpse, half-starved, disease-ridden with gonorrhea and syphilis. Unlike women she'd seen in the distant future, she couldn't easily find male partners with good hygiene to satisfy the sexual needs using her power produced. Instead, she'd resorted to prostitution, earning herself quite the reputation in her small New England town.

A reputation that resulted in a pauper's burial—a wooden coffin, soon to be placed in an unmarked grave.

It was fortunate that she'd been out-of-body when she died, her spirit continuing to live after the physical husk expired. Of course, the longer she remained incorporeal, the less sane she would become.

But she was strong, strong enough to continue interacting with the physical world even without a return to her body. She'd trained herself, practiced the use of her skills all her life, despite the warnings, and now? Now she had no need of her body at all.

If she could only eliminate this new threat, she'd be safe to do as she wished, picking random targets connected to the Registry, erasing its board members, and maybe someday, causing it to cease to exist. Revenge—plain, simple, satisfying.

She couldn't work with the past. Too risky to her own existence. But she could fight the future. The Registry's rules had changed, they allowed succubi to practice without punishment, but that didn't excuse their history, and it presented new problems. Not for the first time, another succubus was hunting her.

Maybe more than one.

She felt the energy, sensed interference she wasn't causing herself. And that meant others. They had to be after her. There was no other explanation.

Was there?

Chapter 11
Tag Team

I STRETCH out on the couch, long enough to accommodate my five eight height, and try to get comfortable, wriggling into the thick pale blue cushions. Gen kneels on the floor beside me and takes my hand in hers. "What do you need me to do?" she asks again.

I hate the choke in her voice, the pain I'm putting her through, but that little girl....

"Just keep the contact... I think. When I've gone out-of-body before, hearing your voice always brought me back. The way I figure it, if you're touching me, that might make returning easier."

"You haven't practiced this during your training?"

It's hard to shrug while lying down, but I pull it off. "We haven't gotten to that yet. It's only been a few days. Mostly, we've concentrated on drawing and using others' powers. I'm pretty good with telekinesis."

She smirks. "Yes, so Chris told me. He's still got bruises from you tossing him around. So, now what?"

I have no idea, but I don't voice that. "I concentrate on Tracy and I use the *push* skill. Cassie told me everything she could remember about Tracy's life, but the longer we talked, the more she got... overlayed I guess would be a good word... by the newer memories of Tracy's death at age one. Orlando Children's Hospital. Cancer ward. By the time she finished, she was sobbing and angry with me for reminding her about her child dying. Then she forgot we'd talked at all, just knew she was upset about something. No one else remembered Tracy living to age four except me. God...."

Gen reaches out her free hand, touching my face. I hold her palm to my cheek for a long moment, then let that hand go.

"I don't remember Tracy living either," she admits. "It's so hard to believe. I have vivid images in my head of attending that little girl's funeral. I went, even though Cassandra and I aren't friends. Everyone in the Orlando psychic community was there. I'd swear it was real, that there's nothing else, but I trust you." She gives my hand a squeeze.

And that's all I need. I close my eyes, take a few deep breaths, and form a picture in my head of Tracy from the photographs I've seen. I try to concentrate on the ones Cassie showed me a couple of days back, the ones of Tracy as a baby, not a four-year-old, because that's when I need to encounter her. I imagine the children's hospital I looked up online in the business center downstairs, the one I've driven past a couple of times but never set foot inside.

And I *push.*

I know the moment my spirit leaves my body because the aches and pains of today's training fade. They don't when I stay in my own time, but when I go back, I end up in whatever physical state I was in at *that* time, or whatever physical state I imagine myself to be in, if I can concentrate enough. Gen gives a slight squeak beside me, and I wonder if having contact while I'm doing this was such a great idea. Then there's no time for coherent thought as the now familiar disorientation sets in: whirling, nausea-inducing darkness, the sense of traveling down a never-ending tunnel, the desperate struggle of my mind to remain conscious and failing.

For once, my physical body doesn't fall. I'm already lying down, so there'll be no new bruises to add to my growing collection. Thank God for small favors.

I'm not sure how many minutes pass. It doesn't feel long, but I have a hard time judging without sensory input.

Then my knees meet concrete. Again. And I'm struck with more sensory input than I could ever want.

I've got my eyes squeezed shut, but bright sunlight pounds against the lids, and a fierce headache screams in my temples at the onslaught. Car engines roar, too close for comfort, and footsteps tromp on either side. I'm hit with wave after wave of nausea, and the gut-twisting sensation of other spirits intersecting with and passing through mine. I don't have a physical stomach to empty, but my confused incorporeal brain refuses to accept that, sending me into dry heaves for several painful moments. I crack open one eye, and blinding, sun-glaring white concrete draws tears, blurring my vision.

Well, at least I'm not in the street.

That could have been bad. I can interact with nonliving things, things without their own spirits, even when I'm out of body, and they can interact with me. I have no desire to get hit by a semi just to see how that feels.

I need to get out of the way of the foot traffic. Every living soul that passes through me makes things worse. So I crawl away from the car sounds until my fingers hit grass, and I crawl some more. I flop facedown and lie there, panting, breathing in the earthy scent, waiting for my equilibrium to return.

To my right, someone gags. Probably some wino or homeless person. Maybe even a dog hacking up some crabgrass. Or, with any luck, I'm on the hospital's small but decorative front lawn. Hospitals attract sick people. It makes sense.

A hand falls on my shoulder.

That doesn't make sense. No one should be able to see or touch me.

No one except occasional small children… and psychics with an affinity for the spirit world.

My stomach drops further.

"Flynn?" comes a very shaky voice to my right. "I think we've got a problem."

Chapter 12
Along for the Ride

I OPEN my eyes, blurred vision making out Gen's familiar form, and roll over onto my back. "Oh fuck."

Well, this is what I get for going in untrained. Did I really expect a handful of days, a scattering of random lessons, to stop me from making mistakes? I'm betting even with a degree in psychic power usage I could screw things up just fine.

"You pulled me with you," Gen breathes, as if she's trying to wrap her head around what's happened. "I'm out of my body."

"Yeah. Sorry."

"I don't like it." She rests her head on my chest, probably as dizzy as I am.

"I'm not a big fan of it either," I admit and hold her to me.

After a few more minutes, the world stops rocking. My stomach returns to its normal location, and my sight clears. Gen must feel better as well, because she levers herself up and stares down at me. "You… you don't look so great," she says.

"Nah, I'm fine. It's only bad when you first 'step out.'" And if you stay too long out-of-body, but I don't mention that, because I don't plan on letting that happen. Then again, with her here, there's no one to anchor me, no one to call me back.

That could be a problem.

"No," she says, shaking her head, then wincing and closing her eyes. Guess she isn't as recovered as I thought. "I mean, you—" Gen waves a hand over me. "—you look… rough."

Huh?

I sit up and take in the hospital's front doors a few feet away, people coming and going, the cars on the nearby street crawling with late-afternoon traffic. Then I glance down at myself… and do a double take.

Rough is an understatement. I look like hell.

Dirty jeans, torn at the knees probably before my impact with the sidewalk, fresh bloodstains there now (and how the fuck does a spirit bleed, anyway?), sneakers with holes in them instead of my usual work boots, grungy T-shirt like it's been worn a few days. I'm thin, too, the thinnest I can recall ever being. I piece it all together. Three years into the past, give or take a few months. That would place the timing right around when I broke up with—

"Kat," I say, swallowing hard.

"What? Where?" Gen looks around for the offending feline, which earns her a laugh from me.

"No," I say, continuing to chuckle. "Kat. As in Katherine. I'm guessing you're seeing me shortly after she walked out. It… wasn't a good time."

That's an understatement. I'd just lost my job too. Laid off indefinitely. Sporadic work had already moved me out of a nice two-bedroom condo to the rent-by-the-week hotel I still occupied when Gen and I first met. On top of her deciding she preferred men after all, I hadn't been able to give Kat the lifestyle she thought she deserved.

So she'd gone back to millionaire Max Harris.

And ended up with no lifestyle at all. And no life, though her one-way trip to the depths of Dead Woman's Pond, courtesy of Max and Leo's evil charm, wouldn't happen for a little while yet.

And I hit rock bottom.

It was the closest I ever came to attempting suicide myself, but I hated my mother so much for that, I never did it. It took a while, a long while, but I got myself back together.

One glance at my Genesis tells me things do get better, no matter how bad they seem at the time.

I'm not good at hiding my emotions, and Gen must read everything on my face, because she leans in and presses her lips softly to mine. "I'm here now. And I love you so much."

"Ditto." And then, because that seems to be a thing all spirits say, I laugh.

"What?"

"*Ghost.*"

She raises her eyebrows.

"You of all people never saw the movie *Ghost*?"

She shakes her head while I keep laughing. "Never mind. But yes, you're here, and while I'm always glad when you're around, maybe we should go back." *And get you out of the danger zone.* Assuming I can figure out how to do that.

But her head's still shaking. "Not until we do what you came here to do. I can help. I can see spirits too. I'm not a fighter, but if nothing else, I can be a second pair of eyes for you. This is dangerous enough without you having to try it twice."

I want to argue. I want her to be safe. But deep down, I'm really glad she's here, that I'm not alone in this again, and from the set of her jaw and the flash of her eyes daring me to get into it with her, I know there's no dissuading her from helping me.

Chris keeps reminding me Gen and I are a team, that I have to make adjustments to my attitudes if I'm going to be half of a real partnership. He wouldn't care for this, but I'm finally grasping what he means.

Standing, I reach a hand down to her and pull her up beside me. I nod toward the hospital's rotating front door. "Sooner we finish, sooner I can go to my bachelorette party. I think Chris has hired strippers."

Though she's still a little unsteady, she manages to punch me in the arm, hard. "Maybe I'll ditch the bridal shower and join you instead. Yours sounds like more fun." The scary thing is, she doesn't look surprised, and she's got me wondering if Chris really *has* planned strippers for my event. If he did, he'd check with her first, and she'd know. And nix that idea, I hope.

A fierce blush creeps from my neck to my forehead, making her giggle.

"Come on," she says, taking my arm, and tugs me toward the doors. "Let's go be heroes."

Chapter 13
Search and Rescue

WE PUSH our way through the rotating door, grinning at the confused looks the other people give a door that moves by itself. I'm not out to scare anyone, but we have to get inside the hospital, and a little poltergeisting lightens my mood. The entry dumps us in a grand lobby, and we pause to get our bearings.

Orlando Children's Hospital does as good a job as any medical facility can of keeping things bright and cheery: light colors—lots of yellows and vibrant greens—colorful cartoon murals painted on the walls, upbeat music playing. They all contribute to a festive atmosphere lost only to several sources of crying, a few terrified young screams, and the stressed-out faces of most of the adults we pass.

And the smell. Nothing can quite mask a hospital's specific smell: too strong cleaning agents, sweat and sickness and, well, fear.

Gen's heading for the reception desk before I can stop her, and she gets halfway through her request to locate Tracy Safoir when she stops, stares at the elder volunteer receptionist's blank expression as she scans the lobby, and turns to me with a sheepish smile. "Guess I'm not used to this out-of-body thing." A kid runs right through her, maybe five years old with wild red hair, freckles, and a cast on his left arm. Genesis freezes where she stands, then pales, and I grab her before her knees buckle. "Definitely not used to that," she says, leaning on me.

"No, that part sucks," I agree.

"Do I feel like that to you? I mean, when I touch you, flesh to spirit, not like this." Because right now, spirit to spirit, she feels perfectly normal to me, and I suppose I feel the same to her.

I shake my head and smile. "You feel like home. Warm and comfortable. And you don't pass through like other living people, I guess because you're a psychic who can see ghosts. It's the passing that's really unnerving."

"Huh." Gen stares into the distance for a moment, and I get the impression she's reevaluating some aspects of her profession.

Spotting a directory on the wall by a bank of elevators, I pull her in that direction. We study it for a minute before locating the cancer unit—fourth floor, wing B. I press the button to call the elevator, and we board when it arrives, along with a woman rolling herself in a wheelchair. "Excuse me," she says, brushing past my leg.

Gen moves aside for her. I just stare.

"You can see us?" I finally blurt out.

The elderly woman peers up at me through thick glasses. Her hospital-issue gown wafts around her thin wrinkled frame, hanging over bare legs. Pink fuzzy slippers cover the feet propped on the wheelchair's footrests. "Of course I can see you. Diabetes hasn't blinded me yet."

"But—"

Gen's hand lands on my arm. She mouths the word "ghost." I shut up.

Now that I'm aware of it, I notice a faint glow about the old woman, tracing her edges like a background spotlight. Right. This wasn't always a children's hospital. At one time, it served patients of all ages. I say nothing more while we ride to the fourth floor, then disembark. She offers a pleasant wave of her withered hand. When the doors close, I can't suppress a shiver.

Turning, I face the short hall leading to the children's cancer ward. And freeze.

Dozens of children, in wheelchairs, on crutches, lying on gurneys, fill the narrow space. And all of them, every single one, carries that telltale glow. Some moan in pain. Others laugh and play like nothing ails them. One little girl in pigtails pokes a freckle-faced boy in the arm. He pokes her back, and they erupt into a fit of giggles. Another older boy, maybe thirteen or so, vomits again and again into a receptacle by his gurney. What he expels is tinged with red. The sour stench hits me a moment later, and I shudder and turn away, leaning on the nearest wall. I press my forehead against the cool decorative mosaic tile depicting a scene from the movie *Shrek*. I think I've got my nose up Donkey's ass, but at the moment, I don't give a shit. I'm trying too hard not to puke.

"I hate hospitals," Gen says in a whisper beside me. "I avoid them as much as I can. Sometimes, like when we fought Max and got hurt, they're inevitable. Makes me work really hard toward recovery."

Most of my snake-bite hospital stay is a blur. I'd been in bad shape, in and out of consciousness for a while before stabilizing. I don't remember seeing any ghosts then, but I don't tend to see them when I'm in my physical body unless they're people I knew well, like my grandmother, and Kat.

And the last couple of times I'd gone for existential walkies, I'd been in a high school locker room and an airport. Maybe if I'd glanced out the window at the tarmac, things would have been different, but I hadn't seen any ghosts in either location, so this number of them comes as a bit of a shock.

"You gonna be okay?" Gen asks.

I think of Tracy and steel my resolve. "Yeah." But facing so many dead kids, it's heartbreaking. All those too short lives, all that lost potential. I hurt for their families, and for them, though most seem oblivious to their current state, just like the woman in the elevator. "Why don't they know? Why haven't they moved on?" When I met Kat's ghost, she knew, and so did the ghost of Max's second wife. They chose to stick around to help end Max once and for all and resolve things with Dead Man's Pond, but they knew they were dead.

"Kids and elderly," Gen says, "and many others who die unexpectedly, they tend to get confused about death. So they keep on going, usually doing whatever it was they did shortly before they died." She gives me a hopeful look. "If we had more time, I could help them cross over. That energy is about as good as energy gets. Maybe afterwards?"

I have no idea how long I can keep us here, how long it's safe for me to do so. We have Tracy to rescue and Tempest to defeat, but I can't deny Genesis or the pleading in her eyes. "We'll try to come back for them," I tell her.

A teenager tosses an ephemeral ball up and catches it, over and over until he misses and it flies in my direction. I snatch it out of the air, surprised when I close my grip around the little rubber sphere. "Sorry," he calls, giving me an embarrassed grin.

I force a smile. "No problem." And I toss it back for him to continue his eternal game. "How did I do that?" I whisper to Genesis.

She shrugs. "The stronger the will, the more solid the apparition, and anything that apparition brings with him. Or her." Her tone shifts to something more serious, and a little scared, and I realize she's speaking of Tempest Granfeld.

There's a woman with a strong will. She's sought her revenge for over a hundred years. What might she be able to manifest?

"Besides," she adds, "when you pulled me with you, you probably took a bit of my power as well. Whatever I can do, you can do, too, at least temporarily."

That might come in handy. I'll keep it in mind.

We slide past the ghostly kids, through a pair of double doors at the end of the hall. Hospital designers laid out the ward in a courtyard style, a square of rooms with a central nurses' station. More bright colors. A small playroom off to the left where several bald children seated on beanbag chairs watch cartoons popular three years ago.

Yes, I know my cartoons. Gen and I love the Saturday morning shows, and we get up early just to catch them and eat unhealthy, overly sugary cereal, though I admit I did that before I ever met Gen. Now my knowledge helps reassure me I'm in the right place at the right time.

A wall calendar behind the nurses' desk area confirms it, big arrows with smiley faces pointing at September fourteenth, three years past. A Disney wall clock, complete with Mickey arms for the hands, tells me it's 6:35 p.m.

Right on target.

Before I spoke with Gen in the penthouse
suite, I confirmed as many details of Tracy's death
as I could wring from Cassandra, including time
and date. I've hit it with about ten minutes to
spare. Quickly, I fill Genesis in on the specifics.

"We'd better hurry," she says. "Do you know
the room number?"

That, unfortunately, Cassie couldn't remember, and I shake my head.

"No problem." Genesis slips around the front
desk of the nurses' station, leans over the young
woman seated there in her tunic and loose-fitting
pants covered in rainbows, and grabs the mouse
of her Dell desktop computer. I shift position to
look over both their shoulders. A few clicks later,
the nurse is tapping the side of the monitor screen,
and Gen has the room assignments brought up for
us to read. "She's in 417," Gen announces with a
grin.

The nurse wrenches the mouse from Gen's invisible grip, picks it up, turns it over, and shrugs,
setting it aside. I notice she leaves what's on the
screen alone, though.

We duck back under the raiseable counter section, not wanting to really freak the nurse out, and
rush down the hallway toward 417.

When we arrive, I stop behind Gen in the
doorway where she's halted, rest my hands on her
shoulders, and give her a comforting squeeze.

So sad. So scary. The room has the same
bright colors—sky-blue ceiling, sunshine-yellow

walls, though the lights are dimmed for evening hours. Flowers and stuffed animals obscure every available surface, including some of the less sensitive equipment tops. And in the center, a single crib holding a single child, tubes protruding from a number of veins, wires attached with adhesive pads to her chest. They worm and wind their way from beneath an oxygen tent covering the entire crib, so Tracy must have been having difficulty breathing. Machines click and whir and hum, but the girl sleeps through it all.

Cassandra's overlayed memory recalled a bout of pneumonia, on top of the leukemia, when Tracy was one. In the correct timeline, feisty little Tracy fought off the additional ailment like a trooper. In the new order of events, the child never came home from this visit to the hospital.

Cassie had gone downstairs to grab a quick dinner from the cafeteria. She'd returned to her worst nightmare: ringing alarms, rushing medical personnel, and a daughter who'd suddenly and inexplicably stopped breathing in her mother's brief absence.

"The doctors said they weren't worried, that she was responding to the antibiotics. No one understood what happened. Maybe if I hadn't left…." Cassie had sobbed against my shoulder down in that casino conference room.

Tracy isn't the only new victim here.

I have to help them both.

I yank Genesis back into the corridor as the door to the room's private bath creaks open and a faintly glowing figure steps out—a woman, wearing a white long-sleeved shirt with lacy ruffles across the chest and an ankle-length flowing black skirt. Shiny black button shoes peek out from beneath the skirt she's holding up with her left hand so she doesn't catch it beneath her heels. A poofy mass of brown hair tops her head, curled over and styled with I don't know what to make it stay in place. Then again, do ghosts need hair gel?

Though her clothes don't scream "money" (in fact, upon closer inspection, they show some wear), she's perfectly put together, a haughty, self-confident air about her that makes my skin crawl. And me? I look like I just crawled out of some gutter after a three-day bender.

Force of will, I remind myself. She can will herself to look any way she wants. I've done it too, unintentionally, when my subconscious made me look eighteen to blend with Genesis's high school self.

Which means I should be able to make it happen now.

Tempest pauses to study the room, searching for something. She opens a drawer, then a cabinet, and digs around inside.

I close my eyes and concentrate. Gen's quick intake of breath tells me I succeed.

When I open my eyes, I'm wearing steel-toed black boots, black leather pants, a tight-fitting black T-shirt, and black leather fingerless gloves. Okay, I don't actually own a pair of gloves like that, or the pants, but hey, if I'm going to be this badass time-traveling psychic warrior, I should look intimidating. I feel behind my head, finding my hair's pulled back in a long, tight braid, out of the way. I've bulked up some, too, from my earlier too thin self. My regular construction-work muscle tone has returned, and I feel strong, powerful. And pissed off.

"Let's do this," I whisper. *Fuck with sick, helpless, innocent kids? You're going to have to come through me.* I nudge Gen farther behind me and check on Tempest's progress.

She's found what she was searching for—an extra pillow tucked in a rainbow-colored cabinet in the far corner. Though she closes the cabinet with care, she stomps her way to the crib's side, anger in every step. I wonder at the dichotomy, then figure it out. The nurses might hear the cabinet closing. No one but another spirit can hear her footsteps.

She pulls back the oxygen tent with one hand and lowers the pillow toward the girl's face.

I move into the room.

"Killing a baby. You must be the biggest coward I've ever seen," I growl.

Tempest's head snaps up. Her eyes go wide. She raises the hand holding the pillow and hurls it at me. While I bat it away, her other palm extends in my direction, green energy forming a sparking ball at its center.

Oh… fuck.

During training breaks, President Argyle, Nathaniel, and I have speculated about what powers Tempest Granfeld might possess. As a succubus walker, it's a given she can pull skills from other psychics, but she'd have to have those psychics available. We know she's crazy. We hadn't considered she might be a dark practitioner, because that takes dangerous to a whole other level.

Massive oversight. Potentially fatal mistake.

She hurls the ball of green fire at me, and I dodge right, ducking behind a rolling cart with a flat top for serving food in bed. The energy mass bursts against the door frame and disperses, glittering embers trailing like fireworks to the floor and disappearing. No visible damage to anything in the real world, but I have no doubt it would have hurt if it touched me.

The cart doesn't provide much cover, since the tray section is thin. I'm pretty much protecting a narrow strip across my chest and nothing else. Instead of seeking some other shield, I shove the whole cart at her. It rolls across the tile, one wheel squeaking a nails-on-chalkboard screech, and slams into Granfeld. She staggers back, cursing some ancient oath, and collides with one of the half dozen machines surrounding the crib. Two wires jerk from its casing, and the machine howls a low-pitched whine.

"Shit. Genesis!" I shout as I stalk after Granfeld.

Gen appears in the doorway, then fixates on the last scattering remnants of black magic power seeping into the tile.

Crap. "Gen, snap out of it!"

She blinks, head jerking toward the sound of my voice, and finally meets my gaze and nods.

Gen darts around me, keeping low, and uses the crib to block her from Tempest's view and power. While I distract the other succubus with a couple of hurled stuffed animals, Genesis crawls around the crib, reaches up, and reconnects the dangling wires. The mechanical whine stops.

The baby wakes.

Tracy screams like babies do, though her cries sound weak and breathy, and I wonder if even this could kill her without the need of a smothering pillow.

Pounding feet sound in the corridor, and a nurse bustles into the room. She sees no one but the child and hurries to calm her, making soothing noises and tucking the blanket around the tiny figure.

I launch an attack of my own, sending a beam of orange *pulling* power at Tempest. For a few seconds, I feel her energy entering me, sickly sweet like syrup, honey, and caramel combined, cloying at the back of my throat until I want to gag. But if I can weaken her, maybe I can—

The rest of my attack bounces off her like she's standing in a glass case.

Well, shit.

"Is that the extent of your skills?" she snarls.

"Nope." And instead of using magic, I tackle her ass.

I charge her headfirst, wrap my arms around that dainty little waist, and throw both of us to the tile. Rolling, we collide with the parental armchair, but it's heavy wood and plastic, and it only skids a few inches.

The nurse glances up from the crib, blinks a couple of times, and returns her attention to Tracy, cooing and singing some forgotten lullaby.

Granfeld reaches up and claws my cheek with her nails, deep enough to draw blood. It trickles down my cheek, a warm, wet stream.

So I'm not the only one who can fight dirty.

Grabbing both her wrists, I slam them against the floor at her sides and hold her while I close my eyes and concentrate. *Knife*, I think furiously, *or gun. A gun would be good.* I picture a holster at my side, a 9 mm tucked within it, loaded and ready to fire.

I open my eyes.

Nothing.

Figures. Either I'm not strong-willed enough, or I lack the proper training, or there are limits to what spirits can conjure up with their minds. She hasn't used a weapon on me either, so I'm betting on the last one. Which leaves me with my spiritual body or my power.

Granfeld gets her legs up under me. She's stronger than she looks, and though the move is untrained and awkward, she sends me rolling backward to hit the nurse's legs, pass into them, and rock the crib. Disorientation hits hard. The bright-colored room spins. My stomach churns. With everything shifting, I can't manage my feet, and I can't separate myself from the body of the nurse. The dizziness increases like I'm stuck on a never-ending carnival ride.

Tempest rises from the floor and moves to stand over me, practically nose to nose with the oblivious nurse. "So you're the new hunter. Not much, are you?"

"More than you," I say. Might as well talk tough, because I can't do anything else at the moment.

Granfeld holds out a hand, palm toward me, orange energy erupting from her skin.

She's going to drain me.

"Flynn!" Genesis rises from behind the crib, green eyes flashing with barely controlled dark magic.

"Don't!" I warn. If she uses the black power, she'll intensify her addiction. "I've got it." And suddenly, I do.

Amazing what adrenaline can do for a person's focus.

I use my *push* skill to create a barrier of my own, an orange/yellow shield between myself and Tempest Granfeld. Her beam of *pulling* energy drills into it like a laser, appears to penetrate about halfway through, then without warning, bounces back and strikes her in the shoulder.

She jumps and yelps, shaking out that arm as if she's taken an electric shock. When she stops, the limb hangs limply at her side.

"Stalemate," Tempest growls. Her gaze shifts. "So how about your partner? Never seen two of you come after me together before. Not a succubus, is she? She doesn't feel right. I wonder what she *is*. Let's have a taste." Granfeld raises her left hand, adjusts her aim, and lets loose.

Before Gen can move, the beam of orange *pulling* power hits her in the dead center of her chest.

"No!" My scream echoes in my ears. She's falling, sinking to her knees, her eyes wide and panicked as Tempest sucks Gen's power from her. The nurse steps sideways, putting her body in even more contact with my form, and I can no longer focus on anything beyond blues and yellows, undulating furniture and figures, whirling and spinning.

Chapter 14
Army of the Dead

"Mmm." Granfeld purrs with pleasure, as if Gen's energy tastes like the sweetest confection. "A psychic in the traditional sense. Spirit talker. Useful."

The nurse succeeds in quieting Tracy and decides to leave at last. She steps toward the door, and I flop onto my side, sucking in deep breaths and waiting for the room to still. I make out Tempest with her eyes closed, her brow furrowed. A golden opportunity, and dizziness prevents me from doing a damned thing. She's no longer drawing from Genesis, but she's clearly up to something.

"Gen," I whisper, shifting a little to bring her into my view. She's kneeling, panting, but she lifts her chin at my call. "Can you do anything?"

She shakes her head, then closes her eyes as if that caused her pain. Her figure dims around the edges, like she's fading out.

Shit.

I close my own eyes and crawl toward her, ignoring the roiling in my stomach, the imaginary
movement of the cold floor beneath my palms.
My spirit touches hers, and I panic when it starts
to pass through. Wrapping my arms around her, I
quite literally *hold* her in place.

When I look at her again, she's solid, or at least
as solid as she's been since we got here, and stronger.
Her breath evens out; her shoulders straighten.

"Thank you," she says.

"Not sure you should. You would have been
safer back in Atlantic City." Assuming that's where
she would have gone. I don't know what the hell
I'm doing. Would she have dissipated completely?
Ceased to exist like Granfeld's victims? Or would
she have returned to her own body and the relative
safety of our time? I acted on instinct. I want her
with me. But I may have done the wrong thing.

"I don't think I can go without you," Gen says,
touching my face. "I think you have to take me
back. That felt… wrong. Like a soul feels when I
help it cross to the other side." She stares into my
eyes. "I think I was dying, Flynn."

I give her a solemn nod. There's nothing to
say to that except "Stay close."

We both glance at Tempest, still in the same
spot on the far side of the small room by the window, back-lit by the glow of the setting sun. Still lost
in deep concentration. Gen's nearly drained. I have
power, but I'm not sure what to do with it. I can't
pull from Tempest so long as she uses those shields

of hers. And I'm in no condition to do anything physical just yet. If I try to stand, I'll likely fall.

A shuffling noise from the hallway suggests we might have additional concerns.

"What's that?" I ask, glancing toward the door.

Gen's eyes go wide. "Oh no."

And the first ghost child hobbles into the room on old-fashioned wooden crutches, followed by the teenager with the ball and the pigtailed girl wearing a pink cast on her arm. Behind them, I pick out at least another half dozen glowing children, pushing forward, working their way into the small space.

"What the—? Tempest's a succubus like me. I can't do this. Calling ghosts isn't one of our skills."

"No," Gen says, a slight tremor in her voice. "But it's one of mine."

I catch movement in my peripheral vision and turn toward Tempest, now waving her arms about, eyes open and glowing with green dark energy. I guess her earlier injury wasn't permanent. Pity.

"What's the point?" They're just a bunch of poor dead kids, and in their current states, all of them sick or injured.

Then the boy with the crutches swings one at my head and I'm ducking and dragging Genesis behind the crib and out of the way.

"If I used dark magic, I could also control them," Gen says. Her mouth forms a grim line.

Oh. Crap.

Chapter 15
Energy Source

"FLYNN?" GEN'S voice wavers.

"Get power from somewhere, anywhere safe," I clarify, grabbing the crutch and wrenching it from the boy's hands. "You've done it before." She told me about trying to save her brother, Chris, after a car accident all those years ago. She'd taken energy from plant life, but it hadn't been enough and she'd resorted to the dark stuff. I'm not letting her do that now.

"Right," she says, teeth gritted.

I hurl the crutch aside, where it impacts the truly solid wall of the room and dissipates into nothingness. The poor kid staggers on his single support, and a pang of guilt twists in my chest. These children aren't responsible for their actions. They're under some kind of mind control. And dammit, they've suffered enough.

A moment later, the missing crutch reappears in the boy's left hand. He tucks it under his arm. My guilt fades.

It's every spirit for themselves.

I'll do whatever I can to avoid causing them further pain, but the kids are dead. Gen and I aren't. There is nothing more that can be done for them, except....

I duck the girl's swinging pink cast aimed at my skull.

"Cross them over!" I shout, putting myself between Genesis and the girl and taking a hit to the shoulder. It doesn't hurt much. She isn't all that strong. But if all of them come at me at once... and that looks like the plan as the others close in. In the corner, well out of my reach, Tempest continues her orchestral conductor motions with both arms, her eyes glowing green and focused on nothing, her mouth curved slightly at the edges in a satisfied grin.

"I need more time, more power," Genesis shouts back.

The ball I caught earlier hits me square in the jaw, a distraction more than anything, but it does its job, preventing me from catching the next swing of the crutch. Solid wood strikes my temple and sets the world rocking once more.

By the time my vision clears, we're surrounded, and things are dying all around us.

In a vase by the window, the chrysanthemums droop, then wilt, the leaves and pink petals dropping off one by one to form a pile of brown brittle bits in the pot. Some daisies on the bedside table follow suit, and a pretty green fern withers and fades in the corner next to where Granfeld stands. Even a tree outside the hospital window starts losing all its leaves, like a sudden blight has afflicted it.

Gen glows with energy.

She rises to her feet. "I've got it," she says in a steadier voice.

And she does.

While I continue to block flailing limbs and random kicks from striking her, Gen reaches out to the closest adolescent spirit, the girl with the broken arm, and touches her fingertips to the teen's forehead. It causes an instant transformation in our attacker, the expression of hatred and pain shifting to beatific peace. The glow around her intensifies even as her form grows more and more transparent. Her feeble punches falter. I no longer feel their impacts, even though I'm taking them all on myself. She ceases her flailing, blinks, and smiles at Gen.

"Thank you," she says. Then, "I'm so sorry." The girl's gaze shifts to Tempest, and the briefest flash of green enters her eyes.

"No," Gen says. "Don't taint your spirit. Move past this."

The teenager nods, the brightness of her reaching the point where I must shield my eyes or be blinded. It means taking more hits from the others, some of which actually hurt even through my leather clothing, but it's so beautiful, I can't completely look away. At last, with a sudden flare of light, there's a pop, almost like a tiny breaking of the sound barrier. The energy fades away, most vanishing into the room's shadows but a small amount seeping into Gen's form, lighting her from within.

"Oh... yes," Genesis breathes beside me.

Damn, that energy must be good. I never hear that tone unless I'm making love to her... or she's drinking blueberry champagne.

I can't risk keeping my attention on her. One of the older boys has manifested a baseball bat, and judging from his high school team uniform, he knows how to use it. But I manage to ask, "Are you okay?"

"More than okay," she says while I duck the bat. "It's pure goodness. I'd forgotten how that feels. It's been a long time since I crossed over a child."

"Well," I tell her, planting a boot in the hitter's chest and shoving him backward as gently as I can, "snap out of it and keep doing it. Do it a lot."

"Right." The focus returns to her tone. She pushes past me and earns herself a few kicks in the process, but they don't seem to bother her. In the meantime, she's making contact with child after child. The more they close in, the more she can reach. Pretty soon she's cleared a wide circle around us as four, five, six of them vanish in bright lights and a firecracker's worth of pops.

I dare a quick look at Tempest. The fury on her face contorts her into something grotesque, the green flaring in her eyes and filling them entirely, whites, pupils, and all. "Stop it!" she demands. Aiming one pointed finger, she turns her orange energy loose in a blast that envelops Gen… and bounces off the white glow suffusing her. Gen smirks back at Tempest, reaching forward to send two more kids to their eternal rest.

Guess I'm not the only badass around here. And Tempest's face—she's dumbfounded, staring and blinking those glowing green eyes. I can't help it. I laugh. "Is that the best you can do?"

When will I learn?

There's a flash of light brighter than any we've seen yet. A boom like a bottle rocket going off shakes the entire room, knocking both me and Genesis to the floor. Vases topple and shatter; the rolling tray table falls on its side, narrowly missing Gen's head, and only because I shove her out of the way. It crashes between us. I don't hear it impact the floor. I don't hear anything. My ears are ringing too loudly.

By the time I clear the sparkles from my vision, Tempest is gone.

"I WONDER if I do that every time I leave," I ask aloud. Then I cough and clear my throat and try again with no greater success. I can't hear myself. I can't hear anything.

"What?" Gen asks, sitting up beside me and rubbing her temples.

I don't hear her, but I read her lips. Pointing to my ear, I shake my head. She nods her understanding.

The nurse rushes back into the room as my hearing returns. I can just make out her startled cry when she takes in the disaster before her: broken pottery, overturned furniture, stuffed animals and dead flower bits scattered everywhere... damaged life-saving equipment. Loose wires dangle from the insistently beeping machinery I'm only just beginning to hear.

She slams her palm against an emergency call button and a distant alarm sounds, probably summoning support personnel to our location.

Gen and I scramble out of the way, flattening ourselves against the walls as the small space is filled to near capacity by doctors, nurses, and orderlies. In her crib, Tracy cries weakly again.

The press of living bodies becomes so great that we're forced to retreat to the bathroom, where we stand, trembling and leaning against each other for support and comfort. "She'll live, right?" Gen whispers, peering through the space of the half-open door.

After everything we just went through, if there's any justice in the universe, she'd better. Out loud I say, "She'll live." And because I say it, Gen believes it. She settles at my side, her muscles untensing.

Sometimes I worry about the power I hold over her. I wonder if she worries the same thing about the way she affects me.

We wait and watch, listening to the demands the doctors give for an explanation and the poor nurse stammering that she has no idea what happened. Some kind of localized earthquake maybe? Except Florida pretty much never has earthquakes, and certainly not of this magnitude. An explosion on one of the floors beneath them? An orderly snaps a walkie-talkie off his belt and confirms that is not the case.

Eventually, things are put to rights. Machines are reconnected. Tracy stops wailing, her cries more of fear than physical distress.

A woman races into the room.

It's Cassie, and I recognize her, but only just—younger, but with reddened eyes and circles of exhaustion beneath them, her hair a more vibrant blond than it is three years from now, her normally perfect attire rumpled and disheveled. The nurse catches her before she reaches the crib, reassuring her that it's all right, that the child is stable.

But will she stay that way?

What if Tempest comes back for another try?

"I can take care of that," Gen says behind me, letting me know I voiced my concern out loud.

I turn to her, my expression stern. "Not with dark magic."

Genesis shakes her head, red hair flipping from side to side. "Don't need it. Look at me."

I look, really look. She's angelic in her beauty, all aglow as she is. She smiles at my stunned expression and smacks me in the arm, bringing me back to reality.

"Did you manage to take any of Tempest's power?" she asks.

I close my eyes, searching inside myself. Fatigue mixes with the now familiar arousal. I touch my own energy first, erratic and unstable but steadier than it's been, then the power I took from Gen when I accidentally *pushed* her here with me. That's warm and soothing, like flannel on a cold winter's night. And finally… there.

My instinct is to pull back, recoil from the static-electricity zap of Granfeld's tainted energy, but I force myself to focus on it, drawing it from my body into a crackling orange sphere in my palm.

I open my eyes. Not much to look at. It's about the size of a golf ball, nothing like the softball-sized spheres she kept hurling at me. I frown at Genesis. "Is this enough? And what do you want it for?"

"It'll have to do, because I'm going to use it to ward Tracy against any more attacks from that bitch."

We step from the bathroom as Cassie enters to splash some water on her face and wipe the relieved tears from her eyes. The medical personnel are just leaving the room. Tracy blinks up at us when we approach the crib.

"You think she can see us?" I whisper. The child's gaze follows my motion when I finger wave at her over the crib's edge.

"Makes sense. Her mother's a powerful psychic. Her daughter will likely be one too." To confirm,

Gen reaches one finger toward the baby, smiling when Tracy wraps her own tiny hand around it.

Only a talented psychic, one who has an affinity for spirits, can see, hear, and touch us in this state. So now we even know where part of Tracy's skills lie.

Gen tugs herself carefully free, then strokes the baby's forehead, tickles her tummy, plays with her toes. Despite her illness, Tracy responds with happy little chortling noises.

And I'm grinning like an idiot.

We did it. We saved her. And Gen's going to make sure it doesn't happen again.

I'm also watching my girlfriend's motherly instinct manifest full force. If I ever had any doubt about Genesis eventually wanting children of her own, this has wiped it out.

My grin fades.

I'm slapped once more with the reminder that Gen is bi. That she could fall for a man, have kids, raise a family. But with me....

"I can't give you this," I whisper. It's something we should have discussed long before getting engaged. But I have so little maternal instinct, it never occurred to me. If it never occurred to her, either, but she's realizing it now, will she still want to marry me?

Her free hand falls to cover mine, where I'm gripping the side of the crib so tight my knuckles have turned white, my other hand trying not to drop the bit of Tempest's power I'm holding.

"I want everything you *can* give me and nothing more," she says.

My grip on the crib loosens.

A toilet flushes, and I nudge Gen's shoulder. She reluctantly lets go of the teeny little toes. Closing her eyes, she takes a deep breath and releases it. At the same moment, the glow around her fades, and a misty cloud of white separates from Gen, floats toward the crib, and settles over the child.

Without looking, she reaches over and plucks the golf ball of orange power from my hand and drops it into the glow.

"Hey, what are you—" I start, but it's already diffusing, mixing with the white, then fading from view.

"Done," Gen says. "Tempest can't harm her again. At least I don't think she can. I've never done this before, but I've witnessed it. With Granfeld's own power mixed in, the wards should specifically protect her from that succubus's interference. I can't guard her from all magical influence. I'm not that strong. But Tempest is through with her."

The message comes across loud and clear. Tracy might be safe, but every single other psychic is still at risk until I stop Granfeld for good.

Wish I had some clue how to do that.

Before I can sink back into my ineffectual depression, there's a tug, a pull on my inner core. Judging from the way all Gen's muscles go taut, she feels it too. "What is that?" she asks, blinking up at me.

"A warning." We've been out of our bodies too long. "Time to go."

We head for the door as Cassie returns and takes up her vigil at her daughter's bedside. My first try to twist the handle and let us escape fails with my hand passing through the metal. So does my second. Eventually both Gen and I have to wrap our hands around it before we can get a firm enough grasp and reach the outer corridor.

The smell of antiseptic assaults my nostrils as I consider our options. Normally—hah, as if there's anything normal about any of this—but normally I'd have to touch my physical body in order to return to it, or stand wherever it lies in another time period, with Gen's voice guiding me to the right spot. Not possible here. My body is three years into the future, in Atlantic City, some thousand miles north of our current location. And Gen is here with me.

With more time, I suppose we could sneak onto a plane. It's only a few hours by flight, but after my previous experience, well, I'm already thinking we're renting a car to take us back to Florida after the wedding.

Presuming I figure this out and we return to New Jersey at all.

The internal tugging continues, but it's directionless, seeming to pull every way at once.

"Flynn…." Gen's voice fills with tremors. She stares down at her hands, and through them to the tile floor below.

"Shit." I grab her and pull her in close, my fingertips sinking several inches into her ethereal form before getting a firm enough grip.

"Don't let go," she begs, but she's fading, her voice weak and almost beyond my hearing. "I'm scared, Flynn."

Yeah, me too. Terrified, actually, if what she said earlier about dying is true. But I don't let her know it. Instead, I hold on tight, focusing on pouring more of my own energy, *pushing* my strength into her. I need to calm her down. Her panic is contagious, and if I don't concentrate, I can't get us out of this.

There is *no way out of this.*

I tell the voices in my head to shut up.

A cart full of meal trays, pushed by an orderly, squeaks its way down the aisle where we stand. We can't spare the strength to get out of its path, and when it passes through us, I almost lose Gen entirely. My power surges with my fear and the adrenaline rush that always follows. Her form solidifies in my arms, but I know it's temporary. Even less used to this than I am, and that's saying a lot, Gen gags, then vomits… right down the front of my T-shirt and leather pants. I stare at the mess in disbelief.

Yep, badass. That's me.

Not.

It's another distraction I don't need. The former contents of her stomach drip and run, some more congealed bits sticking to the material, as disgusting as anyone might imagine….

Imagine.

"Gen?" I catch her attention despite the way her mouth and throat are working up for round two. "You don't have a stomach."

She blinks at me, fear and panic warring with nausea and the tiniest hint of amusement in her expression. Then she swallows hard. "Right. And those aren't your real pants."

"Huh?" Oh. Yeah. I close my eyes, willing my appearance less disgusting. When I reopen them, the vomit is gone. "Hey," I say, hoping to lighten the mood a little more. I let her go just enough to wave one semisolid hand down my body. "How do you know I don't have these stashed in my closet somewhere?"

"Because if you've had those squirreled away and haven't worn them for me in bed, I'll be really annoyed."

I bark a laugh, make a mental note to hit the Harley Davidson store in the near future, assuming we have a future, then freeze as the faintest whisper carries to my senses. "Flynn? Gen? Come on, knock it off. You're scaring us."

"Do you hear that?" I ask, struggling to hold on to Genesis. I have no power to spare, but I'll *push* what I have into her, even if giving her more means losing myself to the ether to buy her time. However, if that's who I think it is, I may not have to.

"It's Chris!" Gen says.

We have a lifeline to follow home.

Chapter 16
Sleeping Beauty Meets Snow White

CONSCIOUSNESS RETURNS, slow and painful like an impacted wisdom tooth extraction. I take a deep breath, aware of the air filling my lungs, extending them fully for what is probably the first time in a while.

Somewhere nearby, someone gasps.

I open my eyes and immediately squeeze them shut. "Too bright," I manage through clenched teeth, bile rising in my throat. If they don't dim the room soon, Gen won't be the only one throwing up.

Gen.

Bright lights or not, I force my eyelids up, then my body, swinging my legs off the honeymoon suite's couch and kicking Gen in the process. She's lying on the carpet, completely still. Not a sound, not a motion. I want to reach for her, but between the pounding in my head and the swirling in my gut, I can't do more than grind out, "Help her."

"We've been trying," the voice comes again, high-pitched, strained, and desperate. Cassie.

My head lolls in her direction, across the living room by the light switches. The recessed lighting in the ceiling and the lamp on the side table all go dimmer. I let out a relieved sigh.

"We didn't know what to do." Chris appears from behind the wet bar carrying a water bottle and a soaked washcloth. He drops onto the couch beside me, sending a bounce through the seat cushions. Lunch threatens to make a reappearance.

"God, don't do that. I'm sick as hell."

"What happened, Flynn? Why is Gen out?" He's doing all he can to stay calm, but panic underlies his every word.

"Long story. Help me get her on the couch."

Through sheer will and stubbornness, I lower myself to the floor, moving slowly to minimize the motion of my head, and grab Gen's legs. Chris takes her shoulders, and we ease her up onto the cushions. He perches on the armrest. I kneel on the thick carpeting beside her and study her face.

Pale, impassive.

Lifeless.

I give myself a mental slap. She's breathing, although rather shallowly. But she's not dead.

Not yet.

I turn to Cassie. "She went out-of-body," I tell her.

Cassie blinks and moves to stand beside us, resting a comforting hand on Chris's shoulder. Chris brushes some loose strands of hair from his sister's closed eyes. "How? That's not possible," he says.

I study the carpet between my knees. "It is if I accidentally pull her with me."

For a moment, his only reaction is incredulity, which shifts far too quickly to an angry glare. "You *what*? Flynn, how could you? It's one thing if you want to take all those stupid risks. You're so hardheaded, no one can stop you, no matter how much we try. But to drag Genesis into that kind of danger...."

He's furious. With me. Again. And I deserve every raging word.

"Okay, stop," Cassie says, putting a hand on my shoulder as well. "This isn't helping. Flynn can explain later. We need to wake her up."

"You're the expert. How do we do that?" I ask, nodding my thanks when she takes the bottle from Chris's trembling hand and passes it to me. I uncap it and take a long swig, the cold liquid running down my throat and easing the churning in my gut. Then I press it to my forehead. I'm sweating and feverish, as usual.

"We make a connection. Genesis has always managed to bring you back from your 'walks,' right?" Cassie pulls a couple of aspirin from the pocket of her tight white skirt and passes them to me.

"Yeah." I swallow them together with a gulp of water.

"The same should work for her. The closest person to her should be able to bring her out of it."

I nod, and it doesn't hurt quite as much as it did a minute ago. Maybe I'm getting used to this shit. "We heard Chris calling us. We followed his voice to get back here."

Chris shakes his head so fast it blurs in my already unsteady sight. "I've been talking to her nonstop since your pulse picked up about five minutes ago. You woke up. She didn't."

My heart sinks. The water forms an icy pit in my stomach, sloshing around as I shift my position on the carpet so I can see all three of them at once. If Chris, her only surviving family member, the person she loves above anyone else, can't bring her out of it—

You've finally done it, Flynn. You've fucked up something you can't fix. No one can say this isn't your fault. You did this.

"That's because you're the wrong person," Cassie says softly to Chris while I berate myself in my head and a scream threatens to tear from my throat.

"I'm—" Chris stops and stares at Cassie, then me, understanding clearing the anger from his features. "Oh. Of course."

I look from one to the other and back again. "Somebody want to clue me in here?" *And now? Before I break something?*

Chris's smile is sad. "You, Flynn. It's you."

"What?"

He touches my arm gently. "I've been sup-
planted. Go on, call her."

"I don't—" Realization dawns.

Me?

"Chris was the closest to you both while you
were both gone," Cassie clarifies. "But once you
came back, Flynn, things… shifted."

*Yeah, you big dolt. Gen loves you. She's mar-
rying you. She intends to spend the rest of her life
with you.*

I clear my throat, heat creeping from my
T-shirt collar up my cheeks one flaming inch at a
time. "No one will take your place in her heart,"
I tell Chris. "Not me, not anyone." Then I turn
to Genesis and lean down to her ear. "Gen? Hey,
we're all waiting on you. You've got a bridal
shower to get to, and I'm late for the strippers, so
get your ass back here, 'kay?" I force the words
past the massive lump in my throat. Everything
comes out in a squeaky whisper.

Nothing. Not a breath, not a twitch.

I throw a frustrated punch into the couch, making Gen's body tremble with the reverberations
through the cushions—the only movement we've
seen from her since we laid her on it. "Dammit, I
don't know what else to—"

An idea forms. Swallowing hard, the blush
fiercely burning in my face, I stretch a little further
over the couch and press my lips firmly to Genesis's. It takes a few seconds, then she's kissing me
for all she's worth, her arms coming up to wrap

around my neck and pull me in closer, her tongue snaking into my mouth to tease mine. It's passionate and very, very public, and I'm breathless when I finally break away and rock back on my heels.

Cassie applauds. Chris whistles.

"Shut up, both of you," I mutter, but I can't keep the goofy grin off my face. "You all right?" I ask, wiping away the tears that have escaped and run down both my cheeks.

Gen brushes off one I missed, blinks while she apparently takes stock, and nods. With my help, she pulls herself to a sitting position on the couch and I stand, then drop down beside her. "I feel fine," she says, sounding surprised. "I guess I didn't catch enough of your energy to suffer the aftereffects." Then she studies me. "You don't look so hot, though."

Actually, it's quite the opposite. Despite the aspirin, my skin burns with more than embarrassment. I'm dizzy and glad for the seat beneath me. And her kiss has roused all the usual sexual heat that follows an expenditure of my power. It held off while I worried about her, but now…. Fuck it. I'll deal. Gen's okay. Hell, if the others weren't around, I'd do a freaking cartwheel, no matter how lousy I feel.

One additional plus, she's so concerned about me, she doesn't notice Chris quietly sliding his arm from around Cassie's shoulders or Cassie removing hers from his waist.

"I'll live," I tell Genesis.

Beside me, Gen sits bolt upright, all her attention suddenly on Cassie. For a second, I worry that she saw them showing affection for each other, but she doesn't look angry.

"Tracy. Is Tracy okay? Did it work?" she blurts out, grabbing for Cassie's hands and pulling her down in a crouch by the sofa.

Shit. In all my panic over Genesis, I hadn't asked. Gen seems to sense my chagrin. She releases Cassie and pats my knee.

Cassie blinks. "My daughter? The treatments are going fine. Why?"

"We just sav—" I begin, but Gen clamps her fingers tightly around my leg, cutting me off.

"Oh, good." She shoots me a look. "Flynn told me she was in the hospital. I was just concerned, that's all."

Right. Why freak Cassie out telling her that her child temporarily vanished from existence? We can fill Chris in on the details later. And maybe, once he has them, he'll stop being angry with me for dragging Genesis along for the ride.

"Um, sure. Thanks for asking," Cassie says, eyebrows raised. There's plenty of bad history between her and Gen, so I understand her surprise. She stands and pulls her phone out of her pocket. She scrolls through several screens, searching for something. "You're going to be late to your bridal shower if you don't get going," she tells Genesis, stopping on what must be her schedule for the both of us.

Leave it to her and Madame President Linda
Argyle to even have our personal lives' itineraries
on file.

"And the guys are probably waiting downstairs
in the vehicle I rented," Chris adds, checking his
own phone for the time. "You up to this?" He peers
at me. "We could cancel. Do a post-wedding party
or something when we get back to Florida."

I study my hands in my lap. "If you still want
to take me out, I'm up for it." I nearly got Gen
killed. Why would he want to throw me a party?

It takes him a minute to get what I'm saying.
When he does, he sighs. "I'm sorry, Flynn. It was
the panic talking. I'm sure there was a very good
reason why you pulled Gen with you, or it was an
accident, or she did something to get herself taken
along because she's tired of seeing you risk everything by yourself."

"Hey!" Genesis says, indignant. But she
doesn't correct him.

That grabs my attention. Has Genesis been
talking to Chris about the fixes I get myself into?

"I know you wouldn't intentionally put her in
danger," he finishes, pulling me up for a hug.

I'm not big on public displays, but I allow it,
mostly because I'm glad my knees aren't buckling.

"Come on," he says, hooking his arm in mine.
"Let's go tie one on before you tie the knot."

I don't know for sure what he's got planned,
but a few beers and some good friends should be
exactly what I need.

Chapter 17
Retreat and Regroup

SHE'D BEEN trounced. Utterly and thoroughly. For the first time in over a hundred years, if Tempest's memory served her correctly—which had become more and more questionable as time continued to pass, forward, backward, and sideways.

Oh yes, she knew she'd become quite mad. She simply didn't care. Which perhaps, in itself, was an indication of the extent of her madness.

But never mind all that. Targeting the child had been a tactical error. No force on earth fought as bravely or fiercely as a mother protecting her child, and while neither of those female psychics had been the baby's mother, they both possessed the instinct.

At least, the spirit talker did. The other one....

Rage flared at the thought of the rival succubus. Tempest paced the floor of the living room in the tiny three-room house she'd rented during her physical body's lifetime. That time had long passed. She'd died, the owner never bothered to re-rent, and it had fallen into disrepair and dilapidation. If she'd allowed herself to solidify fully, the floorboards would have creaked beneath her heels. Mold dotted the walls in dark splotches, and rainwater dripped through holes in the rotting roof. But the structure possessed one thing no other location in the history of time held for her—the familiarity of home.

Tempest manifested completely and sank onto one of the remaining pieces of abandoned furniture—a dining chair, already scarred with use when she'd bought it secondhand, now barely capable of supporting her minimal weight. Stuffing protruded through the torn cushion, and its legs groaned as she brought one leg up to rest upon the nearby table.

How long had all this been there? What year was she in? Nothing to judge by. No calendars or newspapers. But so long as she was alone, it didn't matter.

With a thought, she discarded her clothing, the long skirts and ruffled shirt of her time period vanishing along with the button shoes that pinched her toes. No stockings. No corsets. No undergarments of any kind.

Nothing to inhibit her needs.

Blissfully naked and reveling in it, she let the leaking raindrops drip onto her heated skin. They trickled between her breasts, ran over her taut belly and between her legs to soak into her already damp curls.

One hand sought out a taut nipple, pinching and pulling it to the point of near discomfort. Tempest liked a little pain. Pain was good. It reminded her that even without her body, she could *feel*. Part of her had always wondered if this were unique to her or common to all succubi.

If she managed to catch up to that other succubus, maybe she'd ask.

The thought made her laugh, a rough sound that shook the fingers she'd forced inside herself and heightened her lust for more.

She thrust them in and out, building her need, the heat of her imagined skin making the raindrops turn to steam where they hit. She added another finger and another, none of it filling her quite enough. The curse of the succubus. The payment for their power. The weakness they all shared—an insatiable need for sexual satisfaction.

Her muscles tightened, clenching around what was now her entire fist. When she came, she came screaming, bucking so hard against the table that she shoved it several feet across the pitted wood floor. Her foot dropped with a thud to the floorboards.

And still she was unsatisfied.

They had it wrong, the Psychic Registry. They thought the only thing psychic succubi shared with their ancient mythological counterparts was intense lust and an ability to draw someone's magical energy.

Maybe because in hundreds of years no other had accomplished what she had after death. Because without her physical shell, Tempest Granfeld could perform all the acts of which the myths told. Who knew? Perhaps others like her, from ancient times, were what had started the myth in the first place.

Licking her lips, she pondered upon who her male victim should be. Whom would she go to in spirit form and drain of all his life force while providing the most wonderful pleasure he'd ever experienced?

Her thoughts flicking back to her rival—the spirit talker had called her "Flynn"—Tempest smiled.

Whoever Tempest's chosen male prey was, she'd make sure it was someone close to the rival succubus. Someone whose loss would hurt Flynn beyond all hope of recovery.

Chapter 18
Partymobile

I WANT nothing more than to grab Genesis, throw her screaming and giggling over my shoulder, now that I can actually do that again, and carry her into the suite's bedroom to make love to her for the foreseeable future. Instead, I'm standing next to Chris in the elevator, shifting my weight around to try to relieve some of the arousal in my core and hoping like hell he doesn't notice. I love Chris, and I'd never hurt his feelings by backing out on the bachelorette party he and Tom have planned, but really, I don't need this torture.

I'll stick it out for a few beers, then lay claim to the very real migraine already beginning to overwhelm the painkillers Cassie gave me and bow out as gracefully as I can. Maybe the alcohol will mellow me.

I use the trip down to fill him in on the details of mine and Gen's out-of-body adventure. By the end of my tale, he's not meeting my eyes.

"Yeah, after I yelled at you, I figured it was something like that. An accident."

"I should have been more careful," I say. "Shouldn't have let her touch me."

He makes eye contact. "From what you've said, sounds like without her help, you might not have survived against Granfeld."

He's right. She would have drained me in the first few minutes of our fight. But I'd rather die than put Gen at risk.

He must read that in my expression because he lays a hand on my shoulder as we're crossing the lobby and stops me before we reach the front entrance. "Let her help you, Flynn. Protect each other. I trust you to keep her safe."

Great. Now if only I could trust myself.

I offer a tight-lipped smile and keep walking.

A cold New Jersey October wind howls through the opening sliding-glass doors, and I zip up the front of my leather jacket. The icy air pierces my black jeans as if I'm wearing cotton shorts. In fact, from the waist down, the only warm parts of me are my feet, snug in my black boots and double-thick socks, and between my legs, which is warm for a whole different set of reasons.

Out front, I stop, staring at the monstrosity before me.

It's a Hummerlimo, covered in tiger stripes *and* leopard spots, the words PARTY EXPRESS emblazoned on the side in neon orange. A steady glow of rainbow-colored undercarriage lighting illuminates the black pavement of the valet lane, and I'm wondering if that's just for me or if it comes standard. The back end has been cut away, where a hot tub bubbles with steaming water, empty of bathers, thank God. I love my construction crew guys, but I so don't want to see them in swim shorts, or—I shudder—naked. Heavily tinted windows block my view of the interior, but I can only imagine velvet seats, gold accents, maybe a disco ball in place of the dome light. It's got to be soundproofed, but pounding bass music still carries to where we stand. That's gonna be great for my headache.

In my peripheral vision, the bellman is laughing his ass off at my expression, but I ignore him.

I can't tear my eyes away from my ride. It's kinda like watching a circus train wreck.

"Chris," I begin, still staring, "I'm not getting in that."

He opens his mouth to respond, but at that moment, the side door swings open, cutting the word "Party" in half, the music swells to near-deafening, and out pop Tom and Joe. It's been weeks since I've seen them, and I'm so glad for the familiar faces of my friends that I take three steps forward before catching myself.

Tom laughs, raising a bottle of Heineken in my general direction, though it sways a little in his hand. I've seen my boss drunk before, at after-work gatherings and holiday parties and such, but I'll never get used to it. "Come on, Flynn.

Places to go. People to see." He winks in an exaggerated manner, and I wonder just how many he's already had. Not that I care, really. He's not driving, that's for sure. Not with this lovely vehicle to chauffeur us around.

Two more steps forward and a woman's high-pitched giggle comes from inside the giganti-limo. I experience a moment of pure panic, thinking they've already got a stripper in there, ready to… I don't know what, but I'm certain it will be mortifying. Then she laughs again, and I recognize Allie's voice and relax.

I lean my head inside—the interior is exactly as I imagined, including the mini disco ball—and spot her in her boyfriend, Steve's, lap, chatting up the rest of my construction crew guys while pausing to chug a Budweiser. Leave it to the completely straight girl to fit in better than I will. But maybe with another woman along, this won't get as raunchy as I thought it might.

Then again, this is Allie. She's a cocktail waitress and can get plenty wild when she lets her hair down.

I think I might be in serious trouble.

"Hey, girl," she calls to me over the dance music—Maroon 5. "Get your ass in here and have a drink."

I do as she commands, pasting on a smile and accepting the sweating bottle Tom hands me from a built-in and fully stocked fridge. There's a wet bar, too, complete with sink and some

complimentary toiletries and towels in case anyone wants to freshen up. I blink at the label on
the beer. Breckenridge Vanilla Porter, my favorite,
and not common, so they must have had it brought
in special. At least something is going right.

I plop into the red velvet cushioned bench
seat across from Allie and Steve, between Joe and
Alex, and try not to drink the entire beer in one go.
Joe, Alex, Tom—my entire construction team…
minus Diego.

His absence hits fast and hard, a physical
punch to my emotional gut that makes my next
swallow difficult to work past the sudden lump
in my throat. It's been months since we lost him
to that heart attack, months since I lost my grip
on him and he fell from that rooftop. It feels like
yesterday.

*Not your fault. Not your fault. Even Diego's
ghost told you that, so let it go.*

And I have. Mostly.

His death is the reason why Tom and Chris
ended up sharing the bachelorette party duties. It's
why Tom is giving me away tomorrow, instead of
Diego, who was like a second father to me. Can't
exactly have my real dad do it, since he's, well,
insane three days out of every week and spends
much of his time as a homeless guy.

Diego would never have made me ride around
in this ridiculous thing.

"So," I say, taking another long pull on the
beer, "whose idea was this?" I wave a vague hand

around the inside of the Hummerlimo while someone outside, the chauffeur, presumably, shuts the
door. A few seconds later the engine starts up and
we're moving toward God knows what.

Chris and Tom exchange looks and shrug. "It
was kind of a group decision," Chris says.

Right, Chris. That way I don't have one person to blame. Smart.

"You like it?" Tom's got a wicked grin on his
face, totally teasing, but I still nearly spit my beer.

Before I can come up with an appropriate ver-
bal response to that, or put up both middle fingers,
which is my first inclination, Chris interrupts, saying, "Come on, Flynn. You know the rules. Get the
groom wasted and embarrass the hell out of him.
And since you're the one wearing the tux...."

I roll my eyes.

"You wouldn't want us to break with tradition,
would you?" Joe says, clinking his beer against
mine.

"Heaven forbid," I mutter. Everyone laughs.

Glad I'm so entertaining.

Seated across from me, Chris catches my eye,
and a flicker of worry crosses his expression. I
manage a smile for him and shake my head, like
I'm resigned and accepting of whatever they want
to throw my way. Joe's right. It's customary to
humiliate the groom, and bride for that matter, at
bachelor and bachelorette parties. I'm not trying
to be a poor sport.

But I'm also not a typical bride or groom. I'm something in between, and as much as I act like one of the guys when I'm at work or bowling with the company team, part of me is still a girl, and an introverted one at that. Add in the intense arousal I'm desperately trying to drown with beer and I have good reason to be legitimately concerned.

"Don't worry," Allie says, leaning back against Steve's chest. "I'm your self-designated alcohol intake monitor. I won't let you be too hungover for your wedding tomorrow." She winks at me. "Speaking of which, you might want to slow down on that bottle. We have a long night ahead of us."

I nod and set my beer in the handy cupholder to my left, only realizing when everyone laughs that she was teasing.

Sigh.

Chris takes pity on me and starts a round of small talk that is of interest, but mostly leaves me out of it so I can regroup. He asks about the latest construction project on Festivity's outskirts, how the building is going, when they plan to finish, and what's next.

I shake off a pang of jealousy and remind myself that I'm healed. Cassie healed me. I can give up bartending for Chris and go back to that job anytime I want to.

Except I like bartending. And I like construction. Tom promised me a foreman position in my future.

But if I take up that rather dangerous line of work again, Gen will hate it. She worries so much....

I almost laugh out loud as the ludicrousness of that thought hits me. I'm a freaking psychic succubus. Gen and I just battled a dark-magic-using bitch from hell and nearly got ourselves killed, and I have no doubt I'll be going up against Tempest Granfeld again. Construction risks can't begin to compare.

I'm still chuckling to myself when I feel the Hummer turn off a road and into a parking lot. We're coming in on the side of a nondescript warehousey-looking one-story building, but I think I can make out some neon lights and other decor around the front.

"Welcome to the Pink Pussycat," the chauffeur announces over the intercom.

"Oh... shit."

Chapter 19
Turning up the Heat

"PLEASE TELL me this is a joke and we're really heading to a bar someplace, or a concert, or anything other than a strip club." I'm groaning and burying my face in my hands, while Chris and Tom, each holding one of my elbows so I don't make a break for it, half escort, half drag me toward the front entrance.

Honestly, I thought I was kidding when I suggested to Gen that Chris might have hired a stripper for this party. And even if he had, I figured on maybe one at most, in the privacy of one of the hotel suites.

Not a roomful of them and a very public audience of friends and strangers watching for my every reaction.

Deep inside, a part of me perks up with interest, like a snake uncoiling after a heavy meal to seek out its next bit of prey.

Now there's a mental image I'd prefer to avoid.

It occurs to me that Chris has no idea about my current little "problem." I guess I figured Gen had told him about the succubus side effects. I'm certain Gen talks to him about our sex life. I've walked in on that line of conversation more than once, much to Chris's embarrassment and Genesis's amusement. But she's kept this secret for me.

Right now I'm really wishing she hadn't, because if Chris knew, there's no way he'd be doing this to me right now. His grip tightens as we turn the corner.

The place is a lot gaudier in front. Lit signs in neon pink, of course, one depicting a winking hot-pink-and-black cat with long lashes and a swishing tail blinking on and off over the main entrance flanked by a pair of burly male bouncers. There's a line in front of the double doors that runs halfway down the block, so we must have arrived just before opening time, but we don't get in it. Instead, the guys haul me to a much shorter queue sectioned off from the other one with a red velvet rope. This line leads to a single door marked VIP Entrance.

Oh joy.

"Don't worry. It'll be fine," Allie says from somewhere behind my right shoulder. "It says, 'Couples Welcome.' We're not the only women here. Not even close."

I spot the small sign to the side of the door that she's referring to, and she's right, but the knowledge doesn't ease my nerves much. Women who are part of male/female couples aren't here for the same reason the guys are. At least most of them probably aren't. I honestly have no idea what enjoyment they would get out of a place like this, and I turn and voice that confusion to Allie.

She laughs, as I was afraid she would. "Are you kidding? Watching your guy get all hot and bothered? And knowing he's going home with you? It's a serious turn-on." She winks again. "Besides, the sex after going to a strip show is amazing."

Steve claps a playful hand over her mouth and gives me a sheepish grin.

Oookay. Way more than I needed to know.

Once again, I'm reminded of how very little I have in common with most women. Even Genesis would probably be all over something like this. She's a total extrovert, my exact opposite in some ways. I can picture her, hooting and hollering, waving some bills in the air to attract the girls' attentions, tucking ones and fives between breasts and under G-strings....

A dampness forms between my legs. I need another beer.

The VIP door opens inward, and a shapely brunette steps out wearing a fringed black leather miniskirt, thigh-high boots, and a blue satin bustier. I can't help it. My gaze travels from her footwear up to her cleavage, lingering a little too long before I can focus on her face, and I feel the heat of a blush starting at the neckline of my T-shirt.

Don't get me wrong. I'll look at an attractive woman. I'm just not usually so obvious about it. Tonight, it's like I'm on autopilot. Not quite in control of my own actions. And that scares the shit out of me.

She takes the attention in stride, smiling broadly at me before Chris moves over to whisper some instructions in her ear. Her smile in my direction grows broader. And a little wicked.

Great. More surprises. I force my feet to follow the rest of our party inside.

Though it's night outside, the exterior lights keep the parking lot well-lit, so it takes a minute for my eyes to adjust to the darkened interior of the club. It's a tad more tasteful than the "Party Express," but that isn't saying much.

Dark pink carpeting, some secluded booths done in black leather with pink tabletops lining the walls, several bars already crowded with men in business suits and young guys wearing jeans and button-downs with the occasional wife or girlfriend tossed in the mix. I even spot a couple of girl/girl pairings, but lesbians, while apparently welcome, aren't common here.

I'm really hoping for one of those dimly lit private booths, but I'm not that lucky. Nope. The hostess in the blue bustier leads us across an open space for servers and patrons to navigate the different areas of the club, past clusters of separate tables with swivel chairs, right down to the stage, front and center, and a long table with seven seats all facing the performance area.

It's got black and silver balloons tied to every seat back, a "Reserved" sign plunked in the middle of the pink-topped table, and the hostess turns the center swivel seat around for me.

I'd much rather crawl underneath, but I sit my ass down and try very hard not to notice the gold pole in the middle of the stage or the scantily clad waitresses making their way from party to party. My efforts are unsuccessful.

"Try to relax and enjoy yourself," the hostess says, leaning down and speaking right next to my ear. I'm not sure if that's to be heard over the rave music blasting from the club speakers or to raise all the hairs on my neck and make my breathing pick up pace, but it has the latter effect, regardless. "Congratulations on your upcoming wedding." Then she's gone, and I have to close my eyes and count to keep from panting.

Nothing I do will stop me noticing all the exposed female flesh in the room or the way the guys and even Allie study me, some from the corners of their eyes, some more obvious, for my responses to everything. When a waitress taps my shoulder to get my drink order, I nearly jump out of my skin.

Joe and Alex laugh, Allie smiles, and the waitress herself, a buxom blond with nothing more
than pasties covering her nipples and a pale pink
bikini bottom tries, and fails, to hide a grin. "I'm
Candy, and I'll be taking care of you tonight."
The tone of her words suggests that could mean
more than bringing me drinks. And why do girls
like this always seem to have names like that?
"What'll you have, hon?" She leans down so her
breasts brush the fabric of my suddenly too tight
T-shirt.

"Whatever beer you've got on tap," I force out.

"Sure you don't want something stronger?
You look like you could use it."

"Bring her a shot too," Tom puts in when I fail
to respond fast enough. He points at Chris. "Everything goes on his tab. The rest of us will divide
it later."

"You got it," Candy says, boobs bouncing as
she steps back.

I swipe a hand across my brow, where a thin
sheen of sweat has formed. It's not hot in the club.
With smoking allowed, they've got fans blowing
through the vents, circulating the air pretty de-
cently. Good structural planning, there. That isn't
stopping my response to the waitress, and the floor
show hasn't even started yet.

If I'm going to survive the night and get back
to Genesis with my integrity intact, I need a better
game plan.

When Candy returns a few minutes later with everyone's order, I gesture for her to crouch down next to me, a bad move considering I'm now on level with her full red lips and enveloped by the orange-blossom perfume she's wearing. Shaking my head to clear it, I pull out my wallet and lean toward her. "Listen," I say, passing her a twenty and wincing when she insists I slip it into the pink bikini bottoms, giving me a quick flash of her shaved... um, yeah, that... when I do so. My whole table erupts in cheers and applause. I swallow hard and try to remember what I was saying. Oh. Right. "I don't know what these guys have planned, but if you could give me a heads-up, I'd appreciate it. Maybe pass the word along that I don't need any special treatment. I know I'm not your usual clientele," I add.

Her expression fills with sympathy. "Aw, honey, is that what's got you so nervous?" She's so close, her lips are maybe an inch from mine. Her breath is a sweet combination of spearmint gum and strawberry lip gloss.

Taste them. Kiss her.

Uh-oh.

"Don't you worry about that one bit," Candy continues, oblivious to my inner battle of wills. "We see plenty of ladies just like you. And for the record," she adds, laying a hand on my thigh that sends heat searing through my jeans, "we have quite a few girls on staff who share your interests or have broader tastes than you might expect." Her hand strokes once, almost all the way up to my crotch, before sliding back down to my knee. "Including me."

"I… um… I didn't mean…."

But she's already standing and moving away between two tables of Japanese businessmen, sidestepping agilely to avoid a pinch on her gorgeous ass. I have no more warning about what to expect than when I got here.

And I'm out a twenty.

I down the shot Candy brought me in one gulp, then pick up the beer.

Part of me tells myself it was a twenty well-spent. I don't have the strength to tell that part to shut the hell up.

Chapter 20
Life of the Party

BY THE time the house lights dim and the stage spots come up, I'm riding a strong buzz, my skin feels superheated, and the dampness has become a puddle. Okay, that's exaggerating things, but it's bad. Really bad.

Worse... I don't care.

The first two dancers, one with sandy brown hair about my own color in a cowboy hat, jean skirt, and nothing else, the other wearing a military uniform she strips down to a camouflage-colored bikini—as if that would camouflage anything—are sexy and seductive, but not my type. Oh, I'm turned on. No doubt about it. My nipples strain against my bra, protruding through the front of my T-shirt, and I'm glad I wore black and it's dark in here. But these girls are too skinny, like almost meth-addict skinny, and they play exclusively to the men around the stage, collecting more and more bills in the miniscule strips of cloth they retain by the ends of their numbers.

My guys are loving every minute of it, adding to the financial well-being of the performers, but I'm leaning back in my chair, sipping my third beer—or is it my fourth?—since we arrived, just taking everything in.

The next dancer arouses a little more of my interest. Long black hair, nice rounded breasts, firm ass. When it appears she intends to ignore me, too, I pull out a ten and crook my finger at her. I tuck the bill between those breasts while she leans down to plant a kiss on my burning forehead.

A tiny voice whispers that I should be ashamed, that the only girl heating me up should be my Genesis, but I remind myself that Gen would love all this. Chris shoots a concerned glance in my direction, but I shake it off and signal Candy for another shot.

You wanted me drunk and rowdy, my soon-to-be brother-in-law? Well, you've got it.

There's a quick break after the dark-haired girl finishes, and I push up from my seat to hit the restroom, dropping back into it when the room spins.

Two seats down, Allie laughs, stands, and pulls me up by my elbow. "Come on, I'll help you."

"Weren't you supposed to be making sure I didn't get this wasted?" I scold as we weave our way between tables to a short hall leading to the bathrooms. "I've gotta walk a straight line down that aisle tomorrow." The thought of which releases an entire swarm of butterflies in my stomach. Or maybe that's the whiskey shots catching up with me. With everything else demanding my attention, the wedding got bumped down on my list of things that panic me.

"Yeah, I've been remiss," she admits.

"'Remiss'? Good word."

"Thanks." She catches me as I misjudge the distance between myself and the wall and nearly crash into it. "Don't order any more shots, though. Stick with beer for the rest of the night. You're not a lightweight, but you look tired, and they're hitting you harder than they normally would."

"Good advice."

We manage the ladies' room without further mishap, though once I'm alone in a stall, I'm really wishing I hadn't needed an escort. Here with some relative privacy, I could do something about the aching need, that is, if I didn't know Allie was standing right outside, checking with me every few seconds to make sure I'm okay.

Forget about her. Do it anyway.

My fingers creep to the juncture of my thighs, brushing the top of my sex. The jolt the contact sends through me has me jerking my hand away as if I've been scalded.

In a way, I have.

What the hell am I thinking?

Don't think. Just do it.

It's my voice in my head… and yet not. Not quite. Like an echo of myself.

It's the you you've always been. The one you've wanted to be. Don't suppress the side that gives you power. Embrace it.

Oh my God, I'm hearing voices.

It's the alcohol. Gotta be. I'm tired and drunk and horny as hell. Of course I'm not thinking straight.

And now I'm talking to myself.

"Flynn? You still all right?"

"Fine," I growl, then clear my throat. My hips jerk. Startled, I look down to find two fingers buried deep inside myself.

Oh holy hell.

"Out in a sec."

Fumbling, I zip my jeans and unlock the stall door on the third try. At the sink, I wash my hands and splash cold water in my face, trying to regain some measure of control. At least it's just the two of us in the bathroom. The overwhelming ratio of men to women ensures there's no waiting for a stall or sink.

Allie hovers at my shoulder, watching me in the mirror. "You sure you're okay? You're not acting like yourself. I mean, we all kinda figured you'd blush a lot and spend most of the night studying your fingernails while sneaking a glance or two, not tuck bills down the girls' G-strings."

"You mean I'm supposed to be humiliated," I say, unable to keep the edge out of my voice.

She takes a step backward. I'm scaring her.

Good.

"Only in fun." Her lips pout at me. Full pink lips with a sheen of gloss. "It's just a game, like Chris said."

"A game you didn't expect me to play." I try to rein in the sudden bursts of lust and anger, but they're running through me headlong, my mood shifting with the writhing snake of unsatisfied power within me.

"No," she says, all seriousness now. "We didn't."

"So sorry to disappoint you." I push my way past her out of the restroom.

Get away. Get away from her.

Or I might just try to take her right there on the bathroom counter.

I make it all the way to my seat without further mishap and drop into it, panting. Deep, even breaths. The anger recedes as fast as it came. But not the lust. Of course.

Allie isn't my type. I mean she's hot and sexy as hell, but she's into practiced appearances, like the Catholic-schoolgirl-style skirts and knee socks she wears to work the bowling alley bar where I hang out back home. I enjoy the show, but I prefer Genesis's more organic approach to female beauty.

And if I hit on her again, after that one time when I was possessed, I know I'll lose Allie's friendship forever.

Dammit, this isn't how I wanted tonight to go.

Down the table, Allie crouches next to Chris's chair, carrying on a rapid whispered conversation and casting nervous glances at me. The rage threatens to rise again.

The power curls beneath my skin. My vision tinges with green.

I have no idea where that's leading, and I'm glad I don't have to find out as the stage lights come back up, revealing the next performer—long red hair, gorgeous green eyes, and a body that....

My heart nearly stops.

She looks like Genesis.

It's not, of course. Gen is back at the casino hotel, probably unwrapping sexy little negligees, sipping wine and laughing with Rosaline and some of her psychic friends. But the resemblance is uncanny, and if I was hot before, I'm on fire now.

Even more coincidental, she's dressed as a classic fortune-teller, complete with a skirt comprised of dozens of veils which she pulls away one by one to reveal calves, thighs, hips, leaving one last veil covering her sex. Her top is a bra decorated in gold coins that jangle as she sways from side to side in hypnotic seduction.

And she's staring directly at me. Her gaze locks with mine, and it's as if we're the only two people in the room. I cannot look away.

I'm not trying very hard.

To my left, I hear Steve lean over past Allie to ask Chris, "Did you set this up?"

And to my surprise, Chris's answer is, "No."

The music, a combination of violins and tribal drums, swells to a crescendo, and the girl leaps from the stage to land in a predatory crouch beside our table. She rises, never breaking eye contact, and comes around the table's side, past Joe, Alex, and Tom to stand beside me so that I'm craning my neck to watch her.

In one quick move, she grabs my chair and spins the swivel seat around so we're face-to-face, then places both her hands on my shoulders, giving me a perfect view down her perfect cleavage.

And it finally dawns on me.

I'm about to experience my first lap dance.

Chapter 21
Sensory Overload

AT FIRST, I'm too startled to do anything except sit there, letting her curves sway against me. She presses one leg between mine, parting them and slipping into the space she's made. Her thighs brush back and forth against the juncture of mine, and I catch my breath in a quick gasp that I hope only she notices.

From her smile, I can tell she knows exactly how she's affecting me, and if she wasn't a stripper making her living off this, I'd swear she was enjoying it too.

"I hear you're getting married tomorrow," she says in a sultry purr.

I nod mutely.

"What a loss for the rest of us."

All around us, men, and women as well, are catcalling the performance, but my table has gone utterly silent, my friends holding their collective breaths as they wait to see what I'm going to do.

Wish I knew that myself.

Touch her. Feel her. Let it build.

Let what *build?* And then I feel it, a pressure, growing and growing like a geyser preparing to erupt inside me. Not an orgasm. The power. Pure, unfettered power, exhilarating and terrifying.

And pissed at being left unsatisfied for so long.

"You can touch me, you know," she says, as if reading my thoughts—or hearing the voices. I'm not sure which. She slides her hands down my arms, then back to my shoulders. "It's not against the rules."

You want to. You want this.

Before I realize they've left the chair's armrests, my fingertips encounter the soft flesh of her hips. She lets go of me long enough to reach back and unclasp the coin-covered brassiere, then toss it onto the stage and out of the way. I pull her in close—close enough that her hard nipples rub against mine through my thin T-shirt. A groan escapes my throat.

"Flynn," Chris says beside me, "what are you doing?"

Whatever the fuck I want.

The dancer leans close to my ear. "You really know so little about yourself, don't you? What happens if you deny your needs. It's what drives us crazy, the denial, the resistance." She shifts her body back and forth, rubbing between my legs, rubbing against my breasts, the friction bringing me so very close to that explosion I've been fighting since Gen and I returned to our bodies in the hotel suite.

"You can't escape your nature," she whispers, "succubus…."

On the last word, she presses her knee hard against my center. My hips jerk.

The room sideslips.

One second I'm in the chair. The next, I'm so disoriented, I have no idea where I am or when, what day, what year.

I'm not out-of-body. It doesn't feel the same. But I'm not entirely *in* it, either.

She called you "succubus."

I slam back into myself, heart thudding, pulse racing, and push her away with a strangled moan. Then I'm shoving myself from the chair and bolting for the Pink Pussycat's exit while the name *Tempest Granfeld* shrieks in my ears and the rival succubus laughs and returns to the stage.

Chapter 22
Payback's a Bitch

TOO EASY. All too easy. Perhaps Tempest had worried about that other succubus, Flynn, for nothing.

How simple it had been to find a psychic at the Registry conference with the talent of possession, a dark magic but latent within several individuals in attendance. Using her succubus skills to *pull* the ability from one of them, Tempest stepped into the body of the fortune-teller stripper, altered her appearance to better suit Flynn's taste, and then she had her.

The power had practically radiated from Flynn unchecked, untempered. And the only explanation for her allowing herself to get that way, to be so out of control....

Flynn was untrained.

Or barely trained. The woman had used some skills in their fight at the hospital. And as a team, she and her girlfriend had proven formidable. But to not satisfy her sexual needs… the woman was risking insanity.

If Tempest hadn't pushed her to it already.

She continued her dance on the stage while the rest of Flynn's party carried on a hasty conversation. Then a good-looking young man who bore some resemblance to Flynn's girlfriend stood and headed for the door, a deeply concerned expression on his face.

Tempest smiled.

Perfect.

Chapter 23
Mistakes Made on all Sides

CHRIS FOLLOWED the sounds of incoherent shouting and wailing around the side of the Pink Pussycat and prayed they weren't coming from Flynn. But he knew his prayers were in vain. He'd heard those sounds before.

Not often, that was for damn sure. Flynn was tough. One of the toughest people he'd ever known, male or female. She didn't fall apart easily. Once, when she got possessed by her ex-lover's spirit, she'd freaked out so badly the screams had brought him running from the Village Pub's kitchen all the way upstairs to Genesis's old apartment above the restaurant. And even then, she had gotten herself back together with a speed that surprised both him and his sister.

Gen had told him about a couple of other times, too, but Flynn always rebounded.

Chris rounded the corner. Flynn had one of her palms braced against the exterior wall; the other was clenched in a fist as she pounded the concrete structure again and again. Looking at her now, he wondered if she'd finally reached her breaking point.

And it would be his fault.

Chris slowed his pace, approaching with a caution like a hunter would use closing in on a wounded but dangerous animal. Allie had warned him inside that Flynn's temper was flaring. A drunk and angry Flynn might be more than he could handle alone, but he'd discouraged the others from coming with him. She'd been embarrassed enough for one night.

And that had been his intention.

Dammit, he hadn't meant anything malicious by taking her to the strip club. Just a source for some good-natured ribbing he and the construction guys could trot out when they were all old and gray and hanging around the bar watching a baseball game. They'd tease her, like they all teased each other about a million different things, and she'd laugh along with them….

He'd never expected anything like this.

She'd quieted some by the time he got within arm's reach, her back heaving as she struggled to catch her breath and control the ragged sobs. And God, didn't that just make him feel like utter crap. Even though they were about the same age, he'd always thought of her as a kid sister. What kind of a big brother had he been for her tonight? Blood stained the pale pink stucco of the building, and Chris realized she'd split the knuckles of her right hand.

"Jesus, Flynn, I'm sorry," he said into the chilled night air.

Flynn whirled, throwing her back against the wall, eyes wild, hair whipping about from a ponytail come half loose, her bleeding hand now cupped in the opposite palm and cradled to her chest. She stared at him and past him, searching the otherwise empty parking lot for... what?

Chris glanced over his shoulder at the rows of parked cars, the Hummerlimo on the far side of the lot, where it took up several spaces with its bulk. And oh, wouldn't it be fun to try to get Flynn all the way over there. But Chris detected nothing threatening. No movement. No sound beyond the distant thrum of music from behind the wall.

But Flynn looked... scared.

A thin trickle of fear ran in an icy rivulet down Chris's spine. Anything that could scare Flynn should absolutely terrify him.

He studied her more carefully, the way her eyes moved, darting from his face to his clothing, like....

Like she didn't recognize him.

"Flynn? You okay?" Stupid question. Obvious answer. But he couldn't think what else to say.

"I don't— I can't— Who are—"

Almost incoherent. And confirming his earlier suspicion that she had no idea who he was. Panic joined his fear. This wasn't drunkenness, though from her swaying, she was clearly that too. And it wasn't embarrassment.

Tonight had done something to Flynn.

Genesis was going to kill him.

She didn't know about the strip club. Chris hadn't told Gen. She had a bit of a jealous streak he hadn't wanted to set off. Now he really wished he'd run his party plans by her.

Chris held out a hand in as nonthreatening a manner as he could. "It's okay, baby," he whispered.

She flinched from him and showed no anger whatsoever at him calling her "baby." His heart sank further.

"Come on, Flynn. Let me help. It's me. Chris. Gen's brother. Soon your brother too." He took a step toward her. She took a step back.

A shudder passed through her. She closed her eyes, exhaled, opened them again. "Soon… soon you'll be…. Chris? I think… I think I'm in trouble."

At least she knew who he was. "Yeah, honey, I think you are. Take my hand. Come on over here. Let's see if we can't get you sorted out."

Flynn moved forward an inch, a foot. Chris held his ground, not wanting to spook her further. When the fingers of her good hand closed around his outstretched one, he tugged her gently to his chest, then wrapped both arms around her shaking figure.

The tremors didn't stop.

"Can you tell me what's wrong?"

"I'm… I don't…. Three times. I'm in three times." Her face pressed against his shirt, but he understood the words. He had no idea what they meant.

"Can you explain that?"

She leaned back, blinked up at him. "What day is it? What year?"

He told her, his spirit falling with each word he spoke. She didn't know the day or year? And she was letting him hold her? Compared to Genesis, Chris possessed precious little information about psychics, their abilities, and the side effects. But he knew psychic succubi had an alarming tendency to go crazy. Had Flynn lost her mind? The day before her wedding?

Was it his fault?

Flynn nodded, processing the calendar information he gave. Her eyes unfocused. "It's also ten years ago. I'm eighteen, and I'm getting ready to experiment with a girl in college. *And* about three years ago. Kat has a few tricks to show me with her tongue...."

Chris's face flushed with heat. Yeah, Flynn was stone drunk if she was discussing sex with him. Then the pieces clicked. Flynn was a time walker. She was walking through time. But.... "You're being literal? You're in three different times, but you aren't out-of-body?" He wasn't entirely sober himself, and this was damn hard to follow.

She shook her head and almost fell over. Chris tightened his grip. "No, I'm still here. And there, and there. I can't focus. I need...."

"What do you need, Flynn?" He'd do anything. Absolutely anything to bring her back to herself and save Gen some serious heartbreak.

Flynn laughed, a sound bordering on hysterics that raised the hairs on the back of Chris's neck. She looked him right in the eye. "I need sex."

Chapter 24
Seeking Clarity

THE INCREDULOUS expression Chris gives me sets me laughing harder. So hard, in fact, that it helps ground me in the here and now a little better. The other times fade a bit from my senses, but not completely. Not enough to function without help.

"I don't mean you," I assure him as he half carries me across the parking lot toward the Party Express. I'm also walking down a dorm hallway. And over a living room carpet in my long-lost condo. It's beyond disorienting. I sidestep a couch and collide with a Buick. I go to climb a step and trip over one of those concrete blocks at the ends of parking spaces.

There's something else I should be telling him. Something important. But I can't focus enough to remember what it is.

"Just a little farther, Flynn," Chris says.

Thank God.

We reach the monstrosity. Chris waves off assistance from the chauffeur lounging in the front seat and opens the door for me himself, then hands me inside. I collapse into one of the bench seats/couch/bed... fuck... and curl into a fetal ball, eyes shut to block out the three sets of different surroundings.

It's better this way. Much less sensory input to sort through, and I can almost grasp the thing I should be telling him. Except that even with my eyes closed, even with me lying down, the seat's still moving. I suspect that's the alcohol rather than the succubus shit, but I've never been this drunk, and I've never had this reaction to using my power, so who the hell knows?

"So," Chris says, taking a seat near my head. "You don't want to have sex with me. That's reassuring. It would have been some switch." He's working hard to keep his tone light, but the strain in his emotions comes through.

"I need Genesis," I mutter into the cushions.

"Kinda hoped that was the case, yeah. Can you tell me why? Beyond the obvious, that is."

A bit of sobriety leaches through my drunken haze. I'm talking about screwing around with Gen. To her brother. Holy mother of fuck.

But I tell him.

And when I finish explaining the intricacies of my power's side effects, the toll I'm forced to pay in exchange for an ability I never wanted in the first place, the loss of control until I *learn* control, which at the rate I'm going might not happen before I go nuts, it's dead silent inside the Party Express.

Finally, Chris says, "Why on earth didn't one of you share that before?"

I laugh. More hysterics that wrench my guts in knots and force more tears from the corners of my still-closed eyes. "It's kinda private, you know? Use my power, crave an orgasm, get it or lose my grip on reality. Not the kind of thing you chat about over a beer." Or two. Or four. Or however many I drank tonight.

"And you're a private person by nature," Chris says sympathetically.

Not so sure of anything about my nature anymore. I run a hand through my hair, and shit, it hurts. Opening my eyes, I sit up and focus on it, cut, bleeding, the knuckles swelling up to twice their normal size. Now that I can see it, the pain doubles, which sets off the nausea, and—

"Chris, I'm gonna throw up."

"Hang on." He dives for a trash can under the sink at the Hummerlimo's minibar and gets it next to me just in time. My stomach heaves. I half fill the can.

Beer and shots are a lot more painful coming back up than they are going down.

Chris has my hair pulled aside—at some point, my ponytail came loose, and he's gathered all the strands, keeping them out of the muck leaving my body. I'm more than grateful for that. When I'm done, I fall backward against him, having ended up on the limo's floor somehow. This is turning out to be one helluva family initiation, but I'm not sure which one of us is getting hazed.

He reaches into a pocket and pulls out one of those minibottles of mouthwash from the hotel suite. "Rinse and spit," he says. "It'll help."

I do it, the minty spearmint taking away the foul taste, though there's nothing to be done about the smell from the garbage can.

On the upside, removing some of the alcohol from my system makes the Hummer stop rocking and spinning. On the downside, I'm sideslipping again.

"Chris—" I strangle out, panicking. "—losing touch."

That's vague, I know, but he gets it, his arms holding me tighter, as if he can keep me with him through sheer force of will. "Hang in there, Flynn. I'm gonna get you back to Genesis."

He risks letting go with one hand, stretching to hit the intercom on the closest bench seat's arm-rest to contact the driver. The chauffeur answers a second later. I can make out the sound of a base-ball game playing on the front cab's radio in the background.

"Go ahead and take us to the hotel," Chris says. "The others will grab a cab."

When the driver clicks off, Chris pulls out his cell phone one-handed. Holding it in front of us both so that he can see the screen, he one-finger texts Tom that I'm sick, he's taking me back, they should get a taxi, and he'll pay them later for picking up the tab.

Way to ruin a party, Flynn.

The engine starts up and we're moving, which is not helping my stomach.

"How you doing?" Chris asks.

"Not. Good." I clench my teeth. The interior of the Hummerlimo blurs, and I'm—

—seated on a twin-sized bed in a narrow dorm room, another bed just like it pushed up against the opposite wall, but empty. Roommate's out, place to myself.

Well, not quite to myself.

A girl in a cheerleader's uniform with a Florida Gator on the front in blue and orange kneels between my jean-clad legs. She's smiling up at me, hands at my waist, working my belt buckle loose.

"I've never seen you blush before," she says, giggling. Long red hair fans across her face. "First time with another girl?"

"First time with anyone," I admit, pushing her hair aside to see her smile. Trish. Her name was Trish. Is Trish.

No, was, I tell myself, but it's not clicking.

And I'm also—

—in the bedroom of my foreclosed condo, well, not foreclosed yet. Or was it? Fuck. Kat's naked body curls around mine, the comforters pushed to the foot of the bed, the overhead fan

whirring, the softer light of sunset glowing around the tan curtains.

She slides down my back, long fingernails scratching lightly on my skin. "I was watching some videos," she begins.

I shake my head against the pillows, grinning. When Kat watches videos, I know I'm in for some interesting sex play.

She rolls me onto my back and parts my legs, letting her face drop between my thighs. The tip of her tongue makes contact and I buck upward.

"Um, Flynn?"

Chris. Hummerlimo.

Shit.

I'm still on the floor of the Party Express, seated between his legs, his arms wrapped around my torso. I have this horrible feeling I just rocked my hips while he's holding me. My face heats up even further. "Talk to me. Ground me," I say. If he can. If that's even possible.

"Sure, Flynn, sure. Um, about what?"

Now he's speechless? "You're an ex-freaking-bartender, Chris. You always manage to make small talk. How about Cassie? How are things going with her?" And how long is this car ride, anyway? We were all talking and drinking on the way out. I have no concept of travel time.

Hah. That's funny. No concept of time, period. The other images hover on the edge of my consciousness, just waiting for me to drift out again.

"She's great. Great. I called her while you were in the restroom at the club and told her what you and Genesis did for Tracy."

I reach over and slap him on the thigh with my good hand.

"She needed to know, Flynn. It's her daughter."

"Yeah, I guess."

"And I think we all need to stop keeping so many secrets from each other."

Right. Because he'd told Genesis all about him and Cassie. Not. Still, he has a point.

"You think I can let you go long enough to grab the first aid kit?" Chris points across the passenger space to the familiar white plastic box with a red plus sign on the cover, hanging next to the mirror above the wet bar.

I consider that. The corners of my vision blur, and I can sense movement in my peripherals that isn't actually there, but for the most part, I'm in the here and now. "If you keep talking," I tell him. He slides out from behind me.

"Actually," he says, pulling the kit from the wall fasteners and coming back to kneel beside me, "things have been getting pretty serious. I know it's fast, but…." He trails off, lifting my injured hand and examining the damage. He pops open the kit and finds some antiseptic and gauze.

"But what?" I urge, partially because I'm curious, partially because some whispered voices are creeping back into my range of hearing.

"I'm afraid you may have broken something," he says, cleaning the splits in my skin over my knuckles.

I suck in a hissing breath. "You're hedging," I say through clenched teeth. My hand fucking hurts, and yeah, it probably is broken. I can't move a couple of my fingers. Gonna be hard to put a ring on Gen with that hand. Just dandy.

For half a second, in my drunken state, I panic. The ring. Did I pack the ring? But no, it's safe, tucked into one of the zippered pockets of my carry-on, the gold band with unusual angles being the other half of the set I bought at the pawn shop all those weeks ago—a pawn shop taken over by my crazy dad. God, I hope he doesn't try to crash the wedding.

The wedding that's tomorrow.

Or maybe today. I have no idea whether it's past midnight.

You're about to get married, and you're an absolute wreck.

Chris finishes wrapping my hand and rocks back on his heels. "I think Cassie might be the one."

Oh. Wow. That snaps me out of my impending wedding freak-out, but the voices in my head get louder, and the movement shifts fully into my line of sight.

"—really? Your first? So, you're, like, a gold star."

"Huh?"

Trish beams up at me. "Gold star. A lesbian who's never been with a guy. Only girls."

Oh. I've never heard that one before. So now I've got a new label. Gold Star Lesbian. Well, Mom always said I was a special snowflake. "Sounds a little offensive," *I murmur.* "Exclusionary. Better than other people. I think I'll pass on taking that title."

Trish pouts a little. "Yeah, sure, I guess you're right. Never really thought about it."

She has gotten my belt open. Her fingers tug the zipper down. At the moment, I'm not thinking much either.

"Come closer," *she commands. I squirm my way forward to the very edge of the bed, raising up for a moment so she can work my jeans over my hips to drop around my ankles.*

Now it's just my black cotton underwear between me and her fingertips, which she brushes lightly over the suddenly-too-thin material. She's so freaking hot. No way I ever expected a cheerleader to take an interest in me, but she said she saw me at the pool during diving practice, and I had such a hard body....

Trish switches from fingertips to nails, and I can't suppress a moan of pleasure.

"—mother? Have you thought any more about paying her a visit?"

Chris's hand rests on my shoulder, gripping hard. Did I moan out loud too? Can this night get any more humiliating?

The Hummerlimo makes a turn, lights glowing by outside the tinted windows. We have to be close to the hotel, right?

"You with me, Flynn?" he asks, peering into my face.

"Barely," I admit, dropping my head back on the seat behind me. We're still on the floor. I don't have the energy to get up. Don't know what I'm gonna do when we reach Harrah's entrance. "Did you say something about my mother?"

Good old Mom. Suicidal, paranoid, and a total homophobe. But a good topic to keep my mind off sex, that's for sure.

"Visit. You. Her. You told Genesis you'd do it, right?"

"I told her we'd try. President Argyle's a real slave driver." But I haven't tried, and I did promise. More guilt to weigh me down.

"You should call and set up a time."

Well, she certainly isn't going to call *me*, even if she wants to, which I know she doesn't. Not long after the Dead Woman's Pond thing, I switched my cell number. The press had gotten my old one, and they kept calling for interviews. Apparently lesbian heroes make for sensational stories. Even though threatening to go to the press helped me keep my construction job back then, I'd gotten tired of the harassment.

At the very least, I should get a hold of the lawyer I hired to handle Mom's finances. Everything gets paid automatically, but it wouldn't hurt to check in. In a few days. After the wedding.

Back come the prenuptial jitters. And out I go again.

"—you like this?"

I like anything Kat does to me. Right now it's swirling her tongue in my belly button while she reaches up to massage both my breasts. My hands clench in her hair.

"Tickles," I say, sucking in a gasped breath.

"It's supposed to," Trish says from the floor between my legs, pausing what she was doing with her lips. "Let the tickling build. Don't pull away from it. Don't be afraid. It feels so good when you can't control it anymore."

"I'm not afraid."

Kat looks up from my stomach with a wicked gleam in her eye. "Maybe we should try a little bondage...."

"Chris. Help." I'm drowning in imagery, Kat and Trish's faces swimming in and out of focus, the pleasurable sensations they gave me in the past overloading my nerve endings here in the present. Voices overlay voices, a rising cacophony impossible to separate any longer.

There's movement around me, scrambling across the floor of the Hummerlimo, the rustling of clothing, a few beeps. More voices, adding to my confusion—Chris, I think, and another more distant but vaguely familiar. I strain to hear. I want to hear. I *need* to hear. Because instinct tells me that familiar, distant voice is my only hope of holding on to my sanity.

"You took her *where*?" That sentence comes through loud and clear from the cell phone's tiny speakers. More rapid conversation, explanation.

Smooth, cold plastic presses against my ear. Then, "Flynn? Flynn, talk to me."

"Genesis!" The word comes out in a gasp of relief. "Keep talking, Gen. Don't stop. I'm losing it, here. Please… don't let me slip…." I have to be terrifying her, but I'm too scared to hide my fear. The tremors come back, more violent than before. Chris has me, I think, but the arms around me could be Trish's or Kat's or—

"I'm right here, Flynn," Gen says in my ear. "It's okay. You're five minutes away from me. Five minutes. You can hang on for five minutes. I know you can."

What follow are five of the longest minutes of my life.

She keeps talking, giving me a play-by-play of her progress from Rosaline's hotel room, down the hall, waiting for the elevator, then riding it down, crossing the lobby, and waiting outside for our arrival. Throughout it, all I can manage are a few noncommittal grunts of acknowledgment, but they're enough to satisfy her that I'm at least partially in the here and now.

And then, "I can see your limo pulling up… damn, that thing's an eyesore."

And I'm laughing and crying and wondering what the hell I'm going to do now.

Chapter 25
Breakdown

WE ARRIVE in the valet lane. Chris helps me out and hands me off to Genesis while he settles accounts with the chauffeur. I blink into her blurred face. "Can't focus," I mumble.

"Chris told me."

I think she studies me. I can't be sure of anything.

"You're also really drunk," she concludes, a slight note of disapproval in her voice.

I'm weaving where I stand, so yeah, probably. "Stressed out," I give by way of explanation and apology.

She brushes some hair from my face and tucks it behind my ear. "Flynn, I'm sorry. I had no idea what Chris and Tom had planned for you. If I had, I would have told them what a bad idea it was." Her words get lost a little in the chorus of voices in my head, but I nod. It comes off more like a loll.

"She was more coherent in the Hummer," Chris says, grabbing one of my arms and throwing it over his shoulders while Gen does the same with the other. It jars the hell out of my injured hand, and I cry out before clamping my jaw shut. Last thing I want is to worry her more, but it's too late.

She peers at the bandages. "What happened to your hand?"

"Punched a wall," I tell her.

Her eyebrows go up.

"A lot," I add. "Helped keep my head clear. For a little while."

"Pain will do that. We need to get her up to the suite. Her energy's all over the place, and her aura's scattered. I can barely make it out, and it's usually distinct."

Gen can see auras? That's a new one on me, but I guess it makes sense. She earns her living from seeing spirits.

And speaking of spirits… "Shit! Granfeld!" In all the confusion, I'd forgotten about her being that dancer in the Pink Pussycat. Or maybe she spelled me not to remember. My good hand clenches on Chris's arm. "Call the guys. Call Allie. Make sure they're okay."

"Flynn," he says, in a tone used to soothe a frightened child, "I'm sure they're fine."

"Call. Them." I plant my feet, refusing to take another wobbly step until he does it. We're halfway through the lobby. Even at this late hour, there's plenty of foot traffic. The incessant dinging of the slot machines carries from the open casino archways. Glasses clink, and laughter erupts from the off-lobby bar. I'm aware of people stopping to stare at me, the unruly drunk girl, and a couple of hotel security guards meander in our direction, but I'm no petite princess, and if I don't want to move, they're gonna have a hard time moving me.

Chris pulls out his phone, dials, and has a quick conversation. He clicks off. "They're all fine. Worried as hell about you, but fine. They're in a cab, on their way back. Wanna tell us what that was all about?"

"While we're walking," Gen adds. "Drawing a lot of attention here." She smiles and finger-waves to one of the guards. "Bachelorette party," she calls to him. "Big day tomorrow." The guard grins and moves off, rolling his eyes and shaking his head.

The stress returns. The faces blur. The voices swell to a deafening crescendo. I lose my balance, but Chris and Gen keep me from hitting the tiled floor. In the elevator, I fill them in, pausing to chat a few words with Trish and Kat, which has them exchanging a lot of concerned glances.

I know my old flames aren't here. I know it. And yet, part of me is with them.

And ignoring them would be rude. Especially while they're making love to me.

Both of the past scenarios have me on the edge of orgasm. So wet. So close. They whisper to me to relax, let go, soft, encouraging moans and murmurs. But I can't reach that pinnacle. Maybe because right here, right now, I'm not having sex. I'm standing in a fucking elevator.

Instinct tells me I've denied the need for so long, if I want to pull all my selves together, I'm going to need a three-pronged sexual assault: Trish, Kat... and Genesis.

I don't even want to consider what the elderly couple and the pair of teenagers riding with us make of the conversation. Or my insane behavior.

"How did Tempest pull that off?" Chris asks when we're heading down the short hall to the suite's door.

"She *pulled* from a psychic who can possess people," Genesis says, shrugging. "That's my guess. It's a dark skill, but even kept dormant, the power can be drawn by a succubus. Then she used that talent to temporarily take over that dancer."

Temporary. Right. As soon as the power wears off, the redheaded dancer should be fine. I hope.

"And everyone else could see her because she was within a living body, but they couldn't recognize her for who she was. Clever." Chris helps Gen prop me against the wall while she pulls a room key from her skirt pocket and opens the door.

Yeah, clever.

"I would have known," Gen says, "if I'd been there. Possessed people give off weird vibes. The spirit inside causes a kind of double vision if I look at them the right way."

I swallow a very uncharacteristic giggle which comes out more like a drunken snort. I've got double vision, too, and it has nothing to do with spirit possession.

We move into the suite. Cassie's inside, waiting on the couch, but she jumps up to assist in getting me to the master bedroom, where I collapse, facedown, on the bed. Someone pulls off my boots. Another pair of hands helps slip me out of my jacket, being extra careful getting it over my injured hand—Genesis, probably. They roll me onto my back, and a cool cloth drops across my forehead.

"She's burning up," Cassie says. "I think the fever's proportional to the amount of time she goes without satisfying her… need. So is the disorientation, if I had to guess."

I wonder how Cassie even knows what's going on. Then again, I was in and out back in the Hummer, so Chris probably called her. And she has a key to this suite. Which Genesis hasn't noticed yet. I'm surprised I've picked up on that little detail, but I'm not going to clue Gen in. I'm just glad the healer is here.

"Wait, you knew about this too?" Chris says, sounding hurt.

"Because I work for the Registry," she reassures him, "and I'm helping with her training. Keeping Flynn healthy is partially my responsibility, so I researched as much as I could. Not because I was keeping secrets. Besides, we know so little—"

"I'm not a test subject," I mutter.

"Sorry." Cassie lifts my bandaged hand, taking it gently between her own and closing her eyes for a long moment, then opening them and resting my hand on the blanket. "This is broken. In several places. I can give her something to mend the bones, but it won't go down easy."

"Nothing ever does," I say. No one seems to hear me. They're too busy arguing.

"—keeping her healthy? Oh, you're doing a great job of that," Gen growls.

Cassie points an unsteady finger at her. "*You* of all people should have known better, letting her leave after all the power she'd used today. It's not like *I'm* going to sleep with her."

"No, you'd just get her more hot and bothered and then walk out." Like Cassie had done to Genesis all those years ago.

Ouch.

Chris swivels his head back and forth from one to the other, looking like he has no idea how to stop any of this, but I do. Gen loves me. Cassie owes me. Get them focused on a common goal.

"Hey!" I shout, getting everyone's attention, though it's not much of a yell. The weakness of my voice startles me. "Fight later. Help now." I groan, then yelp as an intense wave of need washes through me, followed by a jolt of pain from my hand.

"Sorry, Flynn," both of them say together. Cassie runs a hand through her blond hair. Gen studies the carpet at her feet.

Cassie leaves the room, presumably to fetch whatever she needs to mend my broken bones. The outer door to the suite closes a minute later.

The shaking returns with a vengeance, making the king-size mattress tremble beneath me. Gen slides onto the bed and wraps me in her arms, but it doesn't help.

"Don't worry, Flynn. Soon as Cassie fixes your hand, I'll fix the rest of you." Her lips brush mine, warm and soothing, her voice sultry and promising pleasures I haven't imagined yet. The trembling doesn't ease, and it's not just coming from my succubus issues.

None of them seem to have realized what *I* have, even in my drunken, half-crazed state.

Tempest isn't just clever. She's fucking brilliant. And we've all underestimated her yet again.

Because with power drawn from a psychic who can possess others, she can become anyone.

Anyone at all.

Chapter 26
Sexual Healing

A HALF hour later, Chris watched the door to the master bedroom open, then close behind Cassie as she emerged. He'd left the healing to the women, knowing Flynn would prefer as little of an audience as necessary. The moonlight shining through the open living room curtains caught Cassie's white skirt and blouse, turning her into something ephemeral and angelic. But as she drew closer to him, the paleness of her face proved Flynn wasn't the only one having a rough night. Almost losing her daughter and then pouring her energy into a healing potion had taken their toll.

He hadn't bothered turning on the lights. A headache pulsed behind his eyes, the result of about half of what Flynn had drunk. Chris didn't envy her when morning came.

"She manage to swallow it?" he asked, taking Cassie's hands. He rubbed the cold skin, warming them with his own.

Cassie's nose wrinkled in disgust. "Yes. Not without gagging a few times. It's foul. But it works. The bones will be good as new by the wedding."

"And the rest of her?"

She frowned. "No idea. She's the first psychic succubus we've seen in generations… the first the Registry has been aware of, anyway. And the old records are incomplete. No one quite knows how to deal with Flynn's… idiosyncrasies. But Genesis is working on her now. I think she'll be fine."

As if to punctuate Cassie's words, a cry of pleasure carried through the closed bedroom door, followed by some softer murmuring, then steady, rhythmic moans.

"Um… yeah." Chris shifted his feet on the plush carpeting. Too weird, standing outside their bedroom, listening to his sister have sex with his soon-to-be sister-in-law. He hadn't even eavesdropped on Gen with her boyfriends and girlfriends when the two of them lived under the same roof, though he suspected Genesis hadn't extended the same courtesy to him and the few girlfriends he'd brought home. "Listen," he said, glad Cassie couldn't see his blush in the shadows, "Flynn would flip if she knew we were out here. I'm gonna give them some privacy." He nodded toward the door to his own bedroom on the opposite side from the master. "You, um, wanna join me?"

Chris didn't make the offer lightly. He and Cassie hadn't slept together yet, though they'd made out quite a few times on the couch in his apartment back in Festivity. After the disaster of her first marriage and a series of unsuccessful relationships, she'd wanted to take things slow, and he hadn't pushed her. From the sad smile she gave him, tonight wasn't going to be the night either.

"Actually, I just want to use your guest bathroom and then go to bed. My bed," she added for clarity. She leaned in and kissed him, her lips tasting of the coffee she'd drunk to stay awake this long. "It's not that I'm not interested...."

"No, it's fine." And it was. Really. Even if it had been a while, a long while. Even if his body was responding, just a little bit, to the sounds coming from the master bedroom. (And oh, wasn't that awkward?) But he wouldn't push her. When she did agree to stay with him, he wanted it to be because she had absolutely no doubts.

"Thank you. You make it easy to want to say yes, soon."

Thank God.

Because despite being a gentleman, despite wanting to give her the time she needed, watching the sway of her hips in that tight white skirt as she walked to the entry hall half bath nearly undid him.

Chris took a deep breath and let it out, then went to his own room. Inside the doorway, he hesitated. Open or shut? Open made him feel like the voyeur he was trying to avoid being. But shut....

Shut meant he wouldn't be able to hear Genesis if she called for help. And while he loved Flynn and trusted her when she was in control of herself,

Chris had to admit he didn't entirely trust the psychic succubus in her current state. That desperate need for sex she'd displayed at the Pink Pussycat had him worried she might be rough with Genesis, might hurt her without meaning to, perhaps without even realizing she was doing so.

So he left the door open, changed into sweatpants and a white T-shirt, and went to bed, the sound of Flynn crying out Genesis's name ringing in his ears.

Other than that, the room lay silent, the bed cold, the second double bed empty, lonely.

Like him.

All his waking hours went into the Village Pub. Only in the last two years had he felt comfortable when he left his managers to run it on his days off. His parents had entrusted the family business to him. Gen, who could still speak with them through her gift, said he'd made them proud.

But the sacrifice….

The door creaked as someone pushed it open a little farther than he'd left it. A shadow crossed the room on silent feet, then slid into bed beside him, soft skin and toned muscle curling against his back. Cassie's perfume settled over him in an intoxicating haze.

"Change your mind?" he whispered, afraid louder speech might break this spell, chase her away.

"Mmm," she purred, sliding her hand beneath his shirt, skimming fingers down his spine.

A wave of tiredness swept through him—not the response to her touch that he'd expected. Too much alcohol. Too many hours awake. Too much stress.

Chris forced it all aside.

If it meant making love to this beautiful woman, he'd find the energy somewhere.

Even if it drained him dry.

Chapter 27
Daddy Issues

ROBERT DALTON, aka Ferguson, stepped out of the taxi in front of Harrah's hotel and casino and scanned for anyone who might know him. Even in the predawn hours, plenty of people frequented gambling establishments, so he couldn't be too careful, but he saw no familiar faces. No sign of Genesis McTalish, who only knew him as the homeless man who loved Starbucks, or her brother, who could recognize him in either of his personae.

Or his daughter, Flynn.

Not too surprising. On sane days, his seer skills could usually predict when she would approach and where she would be, even if that wasn't the strongest of his talents. Right now, he saw her in the top floor of this building, which was what led him here.

Fate knew he hadn't been invited.

She was in a spot of trouble at the moment, but the emotions surrounding his seeing said she had it under control.

Robert supposed there was a first time for everything.

He paid the driver, with half a mind to climb back in the cab and return to the airport. Bad idea, coming to New Jersey. Flynn wouldn't want to see him. The one time she'd tried, he'd been in one of his mad days, unable to communicate coherently or comprehend half of what she said. She'd left in disgust. She could barely stand the sight of him. And who could blame her?

He'd run off, left her and her mother. Not like he'd had a choice. Self-preservation and all, but Flynn didn't know that. Didn't know that she'd be safe where he... wouldn't. Besides, after he'd tapped into the dark magic to protect himself, they should have been better off without him.

He couldn't have known Caroline would fail to find new partners, that she'd remain alone... out of guilt? To protect her image? To set a good example for their daughter? He had no idea. He'd checked up on her and Flynn, of course, left copious amounts of money for their care and comfort, which Flynn did her best not to touch on her own behalf. Stubborn girl. But it wasn't total abandonment. Robert Dalton was no deadbeat dad.

Just a coward.

And without companionship, Caroline had fallen into depression and madness, much like his own insanity, forced upon him three days a week by the Psychic Registry for touching the dark. He chafed at the unfairness of it. There ought to be some kind of self-defense clause in their black-and-white book of rules.

Robert shook off the wave of anger, picked his overnight bag up from the pavement, and headed into the lobby, still wary, still watchful. The majority of activity centered around the casino and the folks waiting for the valet to bring their cars. No guests stood at the check-in desks, manned by a single clerk at this hour.

"Can I help you?" the dark-suited gentleman asked, flashing a model-worthy smile.

"I'd like a room for the rest of tonight, and possibly through tomorrow night as well." Depending on how things went when Flynn spotted him at the wedding. He wasn't missing his little girl getting married, no matter how she felt, and he definitely intended to show himself to her there. Thank fate, he was in his "sane days" for the rest of the week.

But he couldn't take her on if she started a fight, either. It would rouse his dark magic. Under those circumstances, he'd have to leave.

The clerk frowned at his computer screen, moving the mouse and clicking a few keys. "We're pretty full up. There's a large wedding, and a psychics convention, of all things."

Robert grinned. "Psychics, eh? Imagine that."

"I think we can accommodate you, though. If you don't mind a parking-lot view?"

He passed over his credit card in response and took the room key handed to him. Third floor, well away from the penthouse honeymoon suite. Perfect. He headed for the stairs. Wouldn't do to run into one of them in the elevators.

Trudging upward, listening to the steps clang under each fall of his dress shoes, he steeled his resolve. Maybe he was a coward, but he still cared. Nothing to be done for Caroline, but he watched out for Flynn as best he could, used his minimal precognitive skills to predict her movements, at least when he was sane, and his much stronger eraser talent to clean up after the murder she'd involved herself in, the same way he'd used it to remove her mother's name from the Registry records. The bastards wouldn't be bothering Caroline. Poor woman had enough troubles.

He'd warned Flynn when the Registry began interfering in her and her girlfriend's lives. And he'd guided Flynn home when she'd time walked too far. Because that's what fathers were supposed to do. Provide guidance.

If she'd talk to him, he'd give her more guidance after the wedding.

Now that her powers had manifested, there was much Flynn needed to know.

Chapter 28
Down the Drain

"COME ON Chris, wake up. I know you have more to give." Cassie straddled his hips, his semi-erect member buried within her, rocking against him in a slow, steady rhythm that tortured as much as it pleased.

He blinked at her, rousing himself to her obvious need, surprised by the demanding tone she'd used. Hadn't he already given her satisfaction, and more than once if his fuzzy memory served him correctly? Tired. So tired. More tired than he could recall ever being. He knew he'd found his own release at least twice since she'd joined him in bed, but that didn't fully explain the lethargy weighing him down, the heaviness in his chest, the effort to draw each breath into his lungs.

Chris forced a laugh that came out more like a strangled groan. "Guys can't keep going the way women can," he reminded her. She shouldn't need reminding. She'd been married, and he knew she'd had other partners over the years, more casual ones. She ran Orlando Match, a very successful dating service, and she practiced love magic. Cassie knew how men and women operated.

Her fingertips caressed his cheek in the moonlight. She glowed with it, naked and beautiful. Worth waiting for.

Worth dying for.

His muscles jerked beneath her, going taut and then relaxing. Where had that thought come from? Not that it wasn't true. With all Flynn's hero activity, and Genesis's now, too, the impulse was kind of contagious. But that thought hadn't felt like his own.

Could she be using her ability on him?

"You have to know I want you, right? That when I have more to give, I'll give it," Chris whispered. "You don't need to use magic on me." Unless she worried that he didn't truly care for her. Some kind of test?

Cassie laughed. "You have more right now. I can feel it."

Her hips rocked again, drawing a sigh from him. To his amazement, he stiffened within her. Her eyes closed with pleasure.

"Much better," she purred. "I knew you wouldn't want to disappoint me."

No, not that. Anything but that. He never wanted to disappoint her. The consequences would be—

Not his thoughts. Not his thoughts. But whose were they if not his own?

She rode him hard, driving away confusion and concern. And when he came, his voice hoarse from earlier shouts he couldn't quite recall, she began again. And again.

A dull pain replaced the pressure in his chest. It throbbed in time with his racing heart, growing and spreading with each frantic beat.

You have to stop her. Stop it.

Run.

Fear forced its way through pleasure. As with Flynn and her broken hand, pain brought some clarity of thought. Chris tried to roll Cassie off him, just to catch his breath, regain his stamina, but he'd grown too weak. And she was so strong.

She shouldn't be.

The realization terrified him more. She'd used her power, pouring it into a healing potion for Flynn. That always drained her. She'd been so tired when she left the master bedroom. No sign of that weariness now.

Cassie brought him to another climax, her body glowing with more than moonlight. Chris's chest exploded in agony, pain greater than he'd ever known, greater than the injuries he'd suffered in the car accident that almost killed him.

In that torturous moment, he knew two things with absolute certainty.

He was dying.

This wasn't Cassie.

As the first rays of dawn came through the open curtains, she began again.

Chapter 29
Bitch Slapped

SATIATED. IT'S the only word I can come up with to describe my current state. Actually, "wrung out" might also apply.

Genesis has always been a patient and enthusiastic lover with an extensive repertoire of positions and variety. Last night I needed each and every one of those skills. I think she may have even invented a few new ones. Whatever methods she used, she brought me over that edge again and again, and I'm really glad we occupy the only room on this floor, because I was more than a little vocal.

I hope Chris had his door closed.

No more sideslipping, visions, or voices not in the present. The snake of power I sense when I'm stressed or using my talent curls dormant within me. It's the most peace I've known in a very long time.

My body complains when I ask it to move, loudly and achingly in the form of creaks, joint pops, and pulled muscles. I flex my hand at my side, the fingers sore but responding, the cuts already closed over, leaving only the faintest hints of pink scars behind.

It occurs to me to wonder what woke me.

Maybe the sunrise peeking through the mostly closed curtains, separated just enough to let in a thin and somewhat painful beam of light that lands squarely on my face. I shut my eyes against the impending hangover headache, preparing to roll over and go back to sleep.

Beside me, Genesis groans.

A pang of guilt rouses me further. I kept her up for hours, dozed off, then woke her again when the heat returned. She never complained, just eased me through each successive rise and fall. And while, at the end, I returned what I'd been given and I know she enjoyed it, she has to be exhausted.

It's her wedding day. Mine, too, but not as big a deal to me. I'm hers. She's mine. I don't need a ceremony, fancy clothes, and a ring to prove it. Not saying she does, either, but she'll be the focal point of dozens of pairs of eyes. She's got hair appointments, a final dress fitting, God knows what all to do before the 6:00 p.m. ceremony.

Shifting onto my back, I check on her in the mirrors embedded in the ceiling over the bed. Yeah, mirrored ceiling. Atlantic City. Honeymoon suite. Kind of a given.

My heart stops.

She's clutching at her chest, skin whitewashed, eyes squeezed shut, face contorted in pain.

"Gen!" I sit bolt upright, my back and legs screaming in protest, a lance of pain piercing my skull. My hands find her shoulders, and I'm shaking her, willing her to look at me. If this is something I've caused....

Her fist slowly releases the front of her negligee. I have no idea when she put that back on. I'm still naked. Her face muscles relax, her eyelids flutter, then open, and she's peering up at me. "Don't tell me you need more," she says, lips curling in a sleepy smile.

A nightmare? "You were... I thought.... Are you okay?" The color hasn't returned to her cheeks.

A second later, her eyes go wide, as if everything is rushing back. She twists free of my grasp, throws off the blankets, and lurches to her feet. "Not me," she shouts, racing for the door and slamming it against the wall in her haste to open it. "Chris! It's Chris!" And she's gone.

Shit.

I move to follow, tangle my bare legs in the sheets, and face-plant into the carpet, one foot still on the mattress above the rest of me.

Yep, that's me. Hero Flynn to the rescue. Sigh.

While I'm untwisting my ankle from the linens, shouting erupts from the suite's other bedroom. Much of it I can't make out, but then—

"You fucking *slept* with *her*?" Genesis. And if she's using the f-word, she's pissed.

At least for once, it's not directed at me.

My heart rate slows a little, the adrenaline rush ebbing as the pieces fall into place.

After healing my hand, Cassie spent the night. With Chris. And Genesis just caught them.

But could she really have mistaken sex for a threat to his life? I suppose it's possible. Increased heartbeat, faster breathing, pulse racing. They don't call it the "little death" for nothing.

Gen felt it when her parents died. She also knew when I almost drowned in Dead Man's Pond. I'm not doubting her sensitivity to her loved ones, just her interpretation of it.

More incoherent shouting from the other room. I find where Gen tossed my black jeans and pull them on, the smell of secondhand smoke from the Pink Pussycat rising off them and making me sneeze. Gonna need to get these washed.

Something crashes, maybe a lamp.

Yeah, I know I should be in more of a hurry, but really, this is none of my business. If Gen and Cassie want to get into an all-out catfight, well, they need to work through this somehow. And I don't want to take sides. I love Genesis, but Cassie has also had my back since I signed on with the Psychic Registry. She healed my leg and shoulder.

And between me and the wallpaper, I believe Gen is being unreasonable.

More shouting, more crashing. Housekeeping's gonna love us. I hook my bra and hunt for my T-shirt. My headache pounds behind my eyes. How much did I drink anyway?

"Chris? Wake up. Please wake up!"

Uh-oh.

Still in only jeans and the bra, I hit the other bedroom at a run and come to a dead stop in the doorway.

I find Genesis first, standing at the foot of the closer double bed, hands raised, green sparking energy crackling between them, her eyes lit up like two emeralds in the sun. Never thought she'd go for the dark magic, not over something like this.

But *this* isn't what I thought *this* was.

Cassie's on the bed, literally on it, standing at the head, her feet planted on either side of Chris's shoulders. She's naked, her face a mask of fury and her own eyes glowing green. And Chris is....

My breath catches.

He's not moving. Gray skin, absolute stillness. If he's breathing at all, I can't see it.

Gen raises her hands higher, over her head, preparing to throw.

"Stop!" I shout, not knowing what else to do.

Gen swivels her head toward me, gaze seeming to go right through me, but she hesitates.

Cassie, not so much. She lets loose with her blast of dark magic, the ball of green fire hurtling at Gen, who ducks just in time. The sphere hits the mirror above the dresser behind her, shattering the glass, but not before it bounces off at a weird angle. It circles around as if seeking a new target and finds—

Me.

The blast throws me backward, out the door and halfway across the suite's living room to land in the center of the empty ten-person jacuzzi. My head cracks against the marble inner edge of the tub, and I slide down it to the tiled bottom.

"Oh, fuck me." I crawl toward the rim, seeing stars and feeling for the cell phone I left in my back pocket last night. The screen's fractured, and little green sparks come off it, but it lights up when I hit the on button.

I've got Nathaniel, President Argyle's spy/lackey and my personal trainer, on speed dial, so I call him.

He answers on the first ring, like the good little lackey he is. One point for you, Nate. "Mmm?"

Right. It's early. According to the phone, it's 6:45 a.m. Too fucking bad. "Nate, it's Flynn. Wake up and wake everyone else up. I don't know what the hell's going on. Chris is hurt." Not dead. I won't think dead. "Cassie and Gen are going at it. They're both using dark magic, and—" I break off.

Cassie doesn't use dark magic. At least, there's never been any indication of it.

"Not Cassie. Granfeld. Granfeld's in the honeymoon suite. We're under attack, and—" A zap of energy arcs out of my phone, shocking my hand so bad that I drop my cell on the tile. When I grab it back up, the screen's dark, the phone smoking.

"Dammit!" I throw the thing across the room to smash against the wall. It lands on the carpet in pieces.

Gen's furious shriek echoes through the bedroom.

I dart for the front door to our suite, throw it open, and leave it that way. My head pounds, my vision swims, and my middle, where the energy ball hit, burns like I've got the worst sunburn ever. When I look down, the skin across my stomach is red and blistered.

Back into the war zone. Gen's crawling on the floor behind the farther bed. I just make out her bare foot disappearing from my view. Granfeld still holds the high ground in Cassie's body. A new ball of wicked energy forms between her hands, but it's small, recharging. Chris hasn't moved.

"It's Granfeld!" I shout for Gen's benefit, then swing the bedroom door around to use as a shield. "*Look* at her." Gen said she could see if someone was possessed by looking at them the right way.

Her head pops up from behind the other bed, her eyes still that freaky green but a little dimmer. Has she used the dark power she was holding? Does she still have it? I don't see any damage beyond some broken lamps and the shattered mirror. No scorch marks—other than the one on my abdomen. But I have so little real-world experience with this shit.

Real world. Right. I'd laugh if I weren't about to get my ass kicked again.

Gen nods, cocking her head at Cassie first one way, then the other. "You need to get her out of there."

Uh-huh. And how exactly do I do that? I can pull other psychics' power, but I can't....

Hell, why not? I focus my energy and aim it in Granfeld's direction. Then I *pull.*

Chapter 30
Backup

IT'S A quick tug, not a full draw. I sure as hell don't want to risk ending up with Granfeld inside *me*. Cassie's unconscious body drops to the bed, landing next to Chris with a bounce of the mattress. There's no sign of Tempest Granfeld.

Terrific. Unless it's someone close to me, or I'm out-of-body, or I've drawn some of Gen's energy, I can't see spirits. I have no idea where Granfeld is or if she might be playing possum.

Maybe this wasn't such a great idea.

"Did it work?" I call to Genesis.

"Flynn, watch out!"

I'll take that as a yes.

I duck down behind the door, peering around the edge while trying to make myself as small a target as possible, having no clue where the attack is coming from, but it does come. Green fire erupts as if from thin air and pounds me and the door against the inner bedroom wall. I end up on the floor.

Getting really tired of that.

I rock from flat on my back onto all fours, the breath gone from my lungs. Gen's beside the bed, checking her brother, her expression grim. "He's barely breathing," she says. The glow in her eyes intensifies. Dark magic can heal as well as harm. Only problem is someone else will suffer for it if she uses it.

"Don't... do it," I tell her between gasps. "He wouldn't want that." Neither would I. I live and an innocent person dies? I'd have a hard time going on with that knowledge and guilt. Okay, she did it for me once, and Leo VanDean died. But Leo was far from innocent. I haven't lost sleep over that one.

But Genesis has.

"I don't care. I'm not letting him go."

I get it. I do. He's her only true family. If our positions were reversed, I'd do the same. But they aren't. And even though she'll probably never forgive me, I can't let her addict herself more than she already has, can't let her sacrifice one life for another again.

Footsteps approach from the living room, thudding across the carpet. Voices call our names; it's Nate and Madame President Argyle herself. But there's no time. I don't know where Granfeld is, but she's here, somewhere, recharging for another attack. And Gen's got her palms over Chris, about to let loose to try to heal him....

Reaching forward with all the power I can muster, I grab the dark energy from Gen's hands and *pull.*

I'm not so careful this round, partially because I don't have time to finesse and partially because I don't know where that magic will go or what it will do if I release it into the ether.

It slams into me, a powerful, steady blast that ignites every nerve in my body.

"Flynn!"

Muscles go slack. I collapse onto my side, writhing with not pain but pleasure. Tingles course through me. So good. So fucking good. Part of me wonders if everyone messing with the dark feels this way, or if it's just my succubus side coming out to play.

Not my first taste of this sort of energy. The night we got engaged, Gen lost control during our lovemaking and hit me with a touch of it. That was nothing like this.

Two figures burst through the doorway, splitting up to take opposite sides of the room. Argyle shouts orders, though the roaring in my ears keeps me from understanding them. She uses her limited *seeing* skills to point to the corner where I'm assuming Granfeld's spirit stands. Nate, who can read power usage, confirms the location.

And me? I'm invincible. I can do anything... if I use what I've absorbed. It pulls at me, whispering encouragements in my ear. I want... I want to use....

"Don't," says a voice to my left. A hand grips my shoulder.

Confused and disoriented, I blink up into Nate's face.

"Don't use it. Push it out of you, but don't pick a target. Without direction, it won't harm anyone. It will simply return to whatever its source was and you won't suffer consequences."

Unable to form words, I shake my head, then take a stuttering breath. "Feels good," I manage.

He offers a grim smile. "Bad things often do. Come on, Flynn. Where's the hero we've been training? That was an inspired move, pulling it into you. You saved Gen from further addiction. Finish the job."

There's movement all around me, but I'm too centered on myself, the power, the pleasure.

Gen... is she all right? Can't focus. My green-tinged vision blurs and shifts. I can't see her.

This is not okay.

With a growl of frustration, I *push* the dark magic from my core. It fights me, wrapping around my own power, infusing itself with mine, wrenching and tearing. Forcing it out feels like removing a thousand Band-Aids a millimeter at a time. When it finally goes, it takes a good portion of my own with it so that I flop onto the carpet, drained and exhausted.

My perpetual state these days.

At least I can see without the green, and most of what I make out isn't good.

Cassie's regained consciousness, which is the one positive. She and Genesis kneel on the bed on either side of Chris. They've got all four of their hands on his chest, eyes closed, and, I assume, pouring healing magic into him.

Cassie's still naked and worn. She can't have much power left. And healing is just a minor talent of Gen's. Without dark magic, she can do little more than keep him breathing.

On the far side of the room, President Argyle stands with her hands raised and her eyes closed, focusing on a shimmering column in the corner of the bedroom. I must have gotten some of Gen's power when I took the dark magic from her and it's coming through now. Otherwise, I'd still have no idea where Granfeld is.

I'm guessing Argyle's using her dampening skills to keep Granfeld from continuing to attack us. It seems to be working. I'm not getting slammed around anymore. And I'm reminded that other than untrained me, Linda Argyle is the most powerful psychic in the Registry.

"I can't keep holding her, and I can't destroy her. Flynn!" Argyle shouts, never turning from Granfeld.

I try to respond, but I can't even lift my head.

"She's drained," Nate answers for me.

"The dark magic. Use it," she commands.

Everyone conscious turns to stare at Madame President.

Chapter 31
Opposing Views

NATE'S GRIP on my shoulder tightens. "Madame President...," he says, shock clear in his voice.

"This is not the time to quibble over right and wrong. You might not get another chance. Use it. Now."

And to hell with the consequences. So much for all the rules and the punishments. Don't touch the dark. Unless, of course, it's for their benefit.

I should have known. Even after all I've been through, I'm so naive when it comes to Madame President.

I push myself up on both elbows. My blistered midsection screams in protest, and I swallow a groan. Nate slips an arm behind me for support. "I can't," I say evenly. "I let the power go."

Interesting, a small corner of my brain notes. It seems to have taken the sexual side effects of my power usage with it. So, touching the dark negates my sex drive.

I shake off that niggling thought. Not worth it.

President Argyle makes a frustrated, almost strangled sound. There's a loud pop as Tempest Granfeld's spirit vanishes from the corner in a brilliant flash of light, her laughter echoing, then fading in her wake.

Not as loud or bright as the last time. I wonder if the exit effects are proportional to the amount of power she has left.

"We need another healer," Gen calls from the bed.

"On it." Nate tugs out his cell phone and glances to me to make sure I'm stable enough to sit up without his help. At my nod, he lets go and makes a call, talking rapid-fire to someone on the other end and directing them to our suite.

I roll onto all fours, then use the door to pull myself to my feet. My first instinct is to go to Genesis, but I have zero healing ability, and I don't want to break her concentration. Besides, she may hate me for preventing her from using the dark magic on Chris.

Argyle's still in the same spot, eyes open now, staring at the corner where Granfeld had been. Nothing for me to do there either.

I let go of the door, testing to make certain my wobbly legs will bear my weight, then head across the living room to the master bedroom.

Two more psychics I vaguely recognize from the conference rush in as I pass the open front door, and I point back in the direction I came from. They nod and disappear into Chris's room.

I'm numb, I realize as I enter the master, finally locate my T-shirt, and tug it over my head. I should be caught in a whirlwind of emotion—anger, fear, worry. Instead, I'm moving by rote.

Gen brought a robe. I yank it off the hangar in our closet, head back into Chris's room, and toss it to Cassie, who pulls it on and absently thanks me. She still has a lot on display. Thanks to the dark magic, I hardly notice.

Good.

She and Gen stand off to the side now that the other two healers have taken over the process. Chris moves a bit on the bed, groaning, and his color's better—a positive sign. They've got his nakedness covered with a sheet up to his waist. I can't imagine what's going through Genesis's mind regarding her brother and Cassie. Maybe nothing right now. She's probably too worried to be angry.

Cautiously, I touch Gen's shoulder, my eyebrows raised in silent question. She throws herself into my arms, burying her face in my shirt while I rock and hold her.

One of the healers, a dark-haired man with a goatee, looks to us and says, "He'll be fine. She didn't drain him completely, and we'll be able to replenish what he lost within a few hours."

Genesis sags against me, and I have to move us both to lean on the closest wall or she'll drag me to the floor. Cassie does sink to the carpet, tears streaming down her face. I feel terrible for her. Even if Granfeld controlled her, she must be blaming herself.

I'm about to offer some sympathy, though I have no idea what to say, when President Argyle suddenly whirls on me.

"You idiot!" she says, stalking across the room until she's well within my personal space.

My jaw sets in a hard line. My muscles tense. As gently as I'm able, I disentangle myself from Genesis and move her to the side.

"Flynn," Gen and Nate both warn, but I ignore them.

"You might want to rethink that comment," I say, soft and low.

Cassie stares up at me from the floor, eyes wide. Even the other two healers shift a bit farther away across the comforter.

Now I know where all that emotion was hiding.

"You had her. She was helpless. All you had to do was use the dark power and destroy her, or better yet allowed Genesis to do it," she says, sweeping out an arm toward Gen. "The Registry wouldn't have punished her. Our contract forbids it."

"What?" Gen squeaks beside me.

Right. Gen doesn't know about my extra little arrangement with the Registry, the trading of my services for her immunity to their dark-magic laws. But she knows now, and I'll have some explaining to do later, not to mention that Argyle's basically just given her carte blanche to use evil as she pleases without fear of repercussions.

Great. Just fucking great. Like resisting the dark power's pull isn't already hard enough for her.

"She still would have suffered," I growl. It would have addicted her further. More temptation to keep using it. More nightmares. "And who knows who would have died in exchange? Were you willing to risk Chris's life in trade, or Cassie's, or yours?"

Argyle draws herself up to her full height, maybe an inch shorter than me in her heels. "If it meant the end of Granfeld and the protection of everyone else in the Registry from her insane revenge, then yes."

I take a step forward so we're practically touching. "How nice for you."

"Move back," Argyle says.

I assess my position. If it comes to a battle of powers, I've got next to no energy left in my core. But considering she'd been holding Granfeld at bay until she lost her magical grip, I'm betting Argyle may have even less. And in a purely physical fight, I can take her, no contest.

"Make me," I say.

"Whoa, whoa," Nate says, waving his hands and attempting to step between us. "We're all on the same side, here."

I throw out an arm to block him and point a finger at Argyle's chest. "No. We're not." I glance around at the other psychics in the room before returning my attention to Madame President. "I care about you people. Hell, I've finally figured out that I'm *one* of you people. And I'm glad to help… on my terms. But when it comes down to sides, the only side I'm on is Gen's."

Genesis smiles beside me, though she still looks terrified.

"After Gen, I'm in this for Chris, who's about to be family, then my friends, like Cassie and Peter and, yeah, even Nate." He's a toad, but he does care about my training, my success, and even my well-being. I have to admit, I've grown grudgingly fond of the obsequious little shit.

Nate turns to stare at me, stunned, before a small smile creeps across his face as well. He offers a slight nod.

"I'll do the job you've given me. But I *will not* do it in a way that involves dark magic or puts any of them at further risk. They're all family, the only family I've really got." I fix Genesis with a hard stare, hoping she understands my next words are non-negotiable. "And I will do anything I have to to protect them."

President Argyle's scowl remains firmly in place. "Then you may have doomed us all." Turning on her heel, she stalks from the room. A moment later, the door to the suite slams shut.

Everyone lets out a collective breath, including me. I'm shaking with rage and exhaustion.

"I really thought I might have to slug her," I mumble, letting Genesis grab one of my arms while Nate takes the other. They help me to the master bedroom and lay me out on the bed.

"Never seen anything like it, I'll admit. Almost no one stands up to Madame President."

Nate pauses, considering. "And she never backs down when they do."

Genesis tugs my shirt up, sucking in a breath at the sight of my blisters. "Flynn will need one of those healers when they're done with Chris," she says.

"If they have any energy left. Looks like he took quite a hit." I pull the T-shirt back over my injuries. If they can't heal me, that's gonna feel great in a tux and cummerbund. And shit, I still have to get married today.

"He would have died if I hadn't interrupted what Cassie was—" Gen pauses, clears her throat. "—what *Granfeld* was doing to him. Which reminds me—"

"You know you've made yourself a powerful enemy, Flynn," Nate interrupts before Genesis can question either her brother's relationship with Cassandra or my preventing her from using dark magic to save him. I don't think he's only speaking of Granfeld.

Regardless, I'm grateful for the distraction. "Yeah, I figured." I close my eyes, weary of everything and pretty much everyone. Except Genesis. I'll never tire of her.

"I consider Linda Argyle a friend, but she's changed much over the years," he clarifies. "Her moral compass may have become a bit skewed. I do her bidding because she's been a good leader. However, you have demonstrated some impressive leadership qualities of your own."

I crack one eye open at that, eyebrows rising.

"Indeed. You're a woman of integrity, intelligence, and fierce loyalty to those close to you, and you extend those qualities to people beyond your inner circle, if the need arises. You are to be admired, even if you do have an annoying tendency toward hardheadedness and rash action."

Of course he couldn't have let it go at the compliments.

"In short, whether you like it or not, you are the Registry's champion. Our hero, if you will, and I'm not the only one who thinks so. So I will warn you," Nate continues. "President Argyle might claim her first concern is the members of the Registry, but that is only partially true."

I connect the dots. "Right. Her first concern is maintaining her position."

Nate nods. "And if she sees you as a threat, well, just be careful once you've completed your mission. When Tempest Granfeld is removed from the equation, President Argyle will no longer have a use for you."

And I'll be fair game.

I'm betting it wouldn't be hard for the Registry president to manufacture some negative evidence toward someone like me, yet another psychic succubus with the potential to do as much damage as Granfeld has. From the serious expressions on my companions' faces, they're thinking the same thing.

Terrific.

Chapter 32
Succession

"I DON'T know what happened!" the orderly whined, swiping a hand through disheveled hair and scrambling to get out of the way of those with a lot more years of college than he had. "I did rounds an hour ago. She was fine. But the surveillance cameras went down...." System glitch, maintenance said. Don't worry about it. But it had knocked out his view of the high-risk patient rooms for about thirty minutes. And when they came back on....

His gaze went involuntarily to the woman gently swinging from the sprinkler system, her neck constricted by her own sheets. Gray skin, blue lips, bulging eyes.

He looked away and swallowed hard.

What were the odds? Could she have known somehow that he wasn't watching? Had she really been paying that close attention to the little red light on her room's camera?

Could she have caused the camera's glitch?

The orderly shook his head.

Ridiculous. And yet.... There'd been rumors for years about this one. Lights flickering, malfunctioning equipment, every time she had one of her fainting spells, like they were connected.

Cursed, the other orderlies said. Possessed.

Two of his friends had gotten themselves fired for whispers like those. He clamped his jaw shut. A patient had died on his watch. He had enough problems without making more.

"Need to get in touch with the next of kin," one of the doctors said. "She had a daughter.... Lynn?"

A much older nurse, one who'd worked in the facility for as long as he could remember, shook her head. "Flynn. And they're estranged. Her mother drove her away. Haven't seen her in years and years." She wiped her hands on her uniform. "I'll see if I can pull up her number."

Chapter 33
Family Ties

I HAVE come to the conclusion that wedding venues aren't all that different from construction sites—controlled chaos populated by a myriad of professionals who specialize in a dozen different areas all working together to create something functional and hopefully, beautiful.

In my case, I'll settle for functional.

Somewhere during having my burns healed, I zonked out, to awaken several hours later, starving, groggy, and alone. Cassie showed up within minutes bearing a tray of room service, and after overseeing my meal and dragging my sleepy ass through a shower and into clothing, she hustled me into a limo to drive me to One Atlantic—the wedding location Genesis picked.

I did rouse myself enough to ask about Chris. Cassie's smile is tight when she tells me he's fine.

Damn. I hope they work out the awkwardness after this morning. They both deserve a little more happiness than they've been getting.

So now I'm here, in a pleasant and intentionally soothing dressing room, one wall made up of full-length mirrors and another with a floor-to-ceiling window overlooking the gray October waves below. The building extends out over the Atlantic, and we're about two stories up, so it's quite the view and a nice piece of architecture. The steady crashing of the surf and cries of seagulls do nothing to calm my frayed nerves, nor does the soft lavender-blue hue of the walls or the recessed lighting. I'm a wreck, and that's not going to change until well after we've said "I do."

Gen's in another room similar to this one, somewhere down the hall, or so I'm told. I have half a mind to slip out the door and find her, if for nothing else than to have her tell me to get a grip, but she's got to be busy with hair or makeup or the dress or, well, something.

Besides, if I leave, I'm liable to miss an important visitor. I endure the nondenominational minister who's performing the ceremony, along with answering his twenty questions on why I feel I'm ready for marriage. Despite my initial deer-in-the-headlights look, I guess I pass the test, because he leaves with a smile on his grandfatherly face. Then comes the caterer, double-checking that I had indeed ordered blueberry champagne for the wedding couple toast.

Next, Rosaline arrives to make adjustments to my tux. I pull it out of the garment bag I brought. The final choice/compromise was black with a pink cummerbund, though I'd hoped the Barbie-colored accessory might have gotten lost in transit. She fusses and fiddles getting it on me, tsking over the weight I've lost in the past couple of weeks and doing what she describes as an "emergency tuck" about the waist. I have to admit, though, it looks good. Masculine enough that I don't feel like it's trying, and failing, to make me dainty or delicate, yet with a cut to the jacket similar to those found in women's military dress uniforms that shows off my nice-sized chest.

Rosaline flutters out, headed back to Gen's room, and lets in the florist with my corsage. He pins the pink rose to my lapel, offers me best wishes, and off he goes.

The photographer and videographer come as a pair, but I glare them into fleeing after only a few shots and a handful of minutes of footage.

And I'm alone. For the first time in almost two hours.

The clock on the wall tells me I have about twenty minutes before they fetch me for the big moment.

I think I'm going to throw up.

I perch on the edge of my paisley-covered armchair, too tense to lean back, hands pressed together in my lap to try to keep them from shaking. My power, having renewed itself during my nap, tugs at me to escape out-of-body, but I lock it down using the techniques I've learned in my training. I can't think of a worse time to abandon Genesis because my nerves got the better of me. Vaguely, I wonder where my boss, Tom, is. He's giving me away, and he's got the ring, which I remember passing to him earlier in the hotel lobby because I was terrified of losing it. If he doesn't show up….

The door behind me creaks open. I let out a sigh of relief and turn to—

My father.

We stare at each other for a long moment, neither of us saying anything. Why am I really not all that surprised to see him? He's wearing a black tuxedo, shiny black shoes, and a pink rose on his lapel that matches mine. His cummerbund also matches, so he's planned this. Somehow.

I really can't take anything for granted when it comes to Robert Dalton, aka Ferguson, aka Dear Old Dad. Not.

"You clean up pretty good for a homeless guy," I say.

"You clean up pretty well for a construction worker," he replies, taking up a position against the door frame. "Your invitation must have gotten lost in the mail. But I wouldn't miss giving my daughter away at her wedding unless I had no choice."

I suspect he's referring to his intermittent madness, the one imposed upon him by the Registry for using dark magic. Must be one of his good days. He seems perfectly sane at the moment. And yet he must be crazy, coming here, now.

"You gave me away a long time ago," I say, rising from my seat, willing away the traitorous part of me that wants to welcome him with open arms. A flash of memory rises from buried depths, him spinning me around as we dance across our living room, calling me "Daddy's girl," and I'm laughing and laughing. I squeeze my eyes shut and push the image away.

"Flynn...."

"Don't," I say. "Just don't. Go back to Festivity, or better yet, disappear for another twenty years. You might have saved me when I was out-of-body and out of time—" He had. He'd told me how to get back home to Genesis. "And you kept me from getting arrested for murder, but that doesn't even begin to balance the books."

"You don't understand." He reaches for me, but I step beyond arm's length.

"You're right. I don't. Don't do this now. Not today. You want to make things right with me? You can start by not ruining this." I go to push past him, determined to locate Tom and wait somewhere else, maybe with the rest of the guys.

Before I can escape, he grabs both my arms and something... happens.

His power surges into me, a crackling wave unlike any force I've touched before. I've tasted spirit seers, telekinetics, clairvoyants, healers...

another succubus. His talent is none of those, which doesn't make sense, because I got my abilities from him. I guess, being male, he'd technically be a psychic incubus rather than a succubus, but still, it should be similar, right? I should recognize—

Whatever he is, he's doing something to me.

I fight it, not knowing what "it" is, but his energy envelops mine, twisting and wrenching and *pushing.*

Fuck.

Too late, I realize his intention.

He's forcing me out-of-body.

We fall together, our physical selves collapsing to the dressing room carpet, his atop mine, in an unconscious heap. Then I'm diving down that dark tunnel, aware that I'm not alone, that his energy is dragging mine, propelling itself in a direction of his choosing, one over which I have no control.

Chapter 34
Power Play

OUR SPIRIT selves land in a second heap, not unlike the one we just left, on a carpet more familiar than the lavender blue of One Atlantic. Brown pile, a little musty, not having been vacuumed in a while. A carpet I'd just been dancing across in my memories.

I'm home.

Robert—I refuse to call him Dad—lies to my right, groaning and gagging, experiencing the usual aftereffects of out-of-body travel. Good. I hope he stays sick for a long, long time. Gen's going to kill me, and it's not even my fault.

He's still wearing his tux, so I glance down at myself, half expecting to find I'm in my four-year-old form, but no. I'm in the badass leather pants, black T-shirt, boots, and black fingerless gloves I wore when I fought Granfeld at the children's hospital.

Huh.

I wonder if this outfit has become my subconscious go-to for when I'm on the defensive.

Not doing much better than Robert, I swallow bile and look around. Once nice but now worn coffee table with circles left behind by coaster-less cups, patchwork fabric couch and easy chair, a build-it-yourself stand supporting a two-foot-thick TV that seems huge compared to modern flatscreens. Bright-colored plastic toys litter the carpet: blocks, Legos, along with an elaborate castle-like structure off to the side.

A tiny smile curves my lips. Guess I was into construction even then. No dolls or pretend kitchen stuff. No dress-up costumes or jewelry.

At that age, Mom called me a tomboy. How little she knew.

Robert rises to his knees, then his feet, offering me a hand up, which I refuse. I stand and put the coffee table between us. He looks me up and down.

"Interesting wardrobe choice."

I shrug. "Genesis likes it."

"Yes, I'll bet she does."

I want to wipe the smirk off his face with my fist, but Gen doesn't know what's happened, and she's not likely to find out for a bit. The bride and groom, or in our case, bride and bride, aren't supposed to see each other before the wedding.

Tom should find our collapsed bodies eventually, but in the meantime, my father might be my only means of getting back.

"You wanna tell me why I'm here? And how you did it?" I remember the odd taste of his power. "What are you? You don't feel… right to me."

Robert's turn to shrug. "You've never felt an incubus's power before. A good thing too. Few women do so and survive."

What the hell does that mean? According to Genesis, succubi, and I'm assuming incubi as well, aren't inherently evil. They only become so if they start using dark magic.

And okay, Robert's messed around with the dark stuff, but I don't get the sense he intends to harm me, so….

"You really know so very little about what you are," he says, shaking his head.

I suppress a shudder. It's too close to what Granfeld said to me in the Pink Pussycat.

"I'm learning. Maybe I'd know more if you'd stuck around to teach me." I cross to the castle structure, circling it to examine it from different angles. It really is impressive for the age I'm guessing I was when I built it.

"Maybe their records really are that incomplete. And that's partially my fault. I suppose they might have left off the 'deadly' bit," he goes on, ignoring my jab, "since you're a lesbian and all."

I twist around to stare at him. "Getting a little personal there, aren't you?"

He opens his mouth to respond, but at that moment, my four-year-old self comes wandering into the living room, dragging a battered teddy bear with one hand and sucking the thumb of the other.

Yeah, I sucked my thumb until I was well past seven, probably why I have a slight overbite I never bothered to get fixed.

I freeze where I stand, waiting for my young counterpart to scream or stare or say something, but she just heads over to the castle and takes a few blocks off the top, rearranging pieces to make a seat for the bear.

"You're not dead. She won't see you," Robert says.

"*You* saw me when I went out-of-body back in Festivity."

"My talents were more developed than yours were at that age. And spirit seeing is one of my other skills."

Well, that clears that up. Like so many psychics, Robert possesses multiple abilities, just like Genesis and Cassie, with some stronger than others, whereas all my strength seems to be centered around tricks connected with the *push* and the *pull*.

Another bit of a surprise, little kid me is wearing a dress, though it's stained with dirt and grass, and it's been patched in several places. The bow in my hair is half-untied. Mom tried to girlify me. She really did. And she never gave up. But it didn't take.

A low groan from outside the room draws our attention, and both I and my younger self turn toward the sound, cocking our heads and listening in an identical manner.

So freaking surreal.

Mini Me ignores it after a moment and goes back to playing, like it's something she's heard many times before, but I have no memory of it, and I follow it out of the living room, down a short hallway to my parents' bedroom. Robert trails close on my transparent heels.

More moans and groans carry through the closed door. I reach out my hand to open it, then stop, a flush of heat suffusing my cheeks. I glance over my shoulder. "You didn't seriously bring me all the way back here to watch you and Mom doing the nasty, did you?"

"Open the door, Flynn." He's dead serious now, all hints of snarkiness and sarcasm gone.

Really hoping I'm not about to see it doggie style, I square my shoulders and grip the knob in my ethereal hand.

There's movement inside, a squeaking of mattress springs and a rustling of sheets as if somebody is climbing out of bed—two somebodies, judging by the number of footfalls on the carpet.

"I'm sorry, I'm sorry," comes a voice I recognize as my mother's.

Followed by, "It's all right. I'm all right." Dad.

What the hell? I turn the knob and push the door slightly open.

Neither notices the moving door as I slip through the opening. The entrance sits back in a little alcove that opens into the master bedroom. It's a good hiding place and a good sneaky spot, a memory from my past tells me.

Okay, so I *did* spy on them from here. Just not today. Well, not as a four-year-old, anyway.

I peer around the corner of the alcove, then stumble fully into the room when Robert's spirit-self gives me a shove from behind. "I'm too drained in this moment in time to see you, and she doesn't have the skill," he explains.

They can't see me. Right. It's still weird, and I keep expecting one of them to turn and yell at me for peeping and eavesdropping.

But when I get a closer look, I realize they've got bigger problems than worrying about being observed.

Younger Dad's barely keeping his feet. He's trembling, one hand gripping the edge of the dresser to remain upright. His eyes flicker briefly with the green of dark magic. The ashen color of his face reminds me of....

Of how Chris looked after Granfeld had her way with him.

But that didn't make sense unless....

"You're both... you're both...."

"Incubus and succubus," my father's spirit form confirms from just behind me. "Two of the most powerful magical beings in existence." He pauses, a note of sadness tinging his tone. "Though one was considerably more powerful than the other and unable to control it."

Mom turns from Dad, throws open the walk-in closet, and disappears inside. A few seconds later she emerges with a suitcase. She flings it open on the bed and starts emptying drawers, haphazardly tossing in Polo shirts, slacks, boxer shorts.

"You're leaving," she says. "Before it's too late."

Dad tries to stop her, grabbing for her wrists, but he's too weak and she jerks away easily. "I can handle it," he says, using words instead. "I'm not running out on you and Flynn."

"No, you're not," she says, never pausing. "I'm *throwing* you out."

No. This isn't the way it happened. Dad left us. Didn't he?

"It's a trick," I whisper, wanting to believe it. Everything I thought I knew is getting turned on its ear. This man could erase evidence from a crime scene. He'd done it to protect me, Chris, and Genesis from being accused of Max Harris's murder. He could be influencing my perception now, making me see things that aren't true. But he's not.

In my heart of hearts, I know what I'm seeing is real. *Was* real.

"Every time, you get a little bit weaker, use the dark magic a little bit more to protect yourself. From me. Either I'll kill you, or you'll become so addicted that the dark will do it for me. Either way, it will be *my* fault." Tears stream down Mom's face, her eyes stricken.

Dad just looks defeated.

"We thought our powers would cancel each other out, that we could be together, be happy, without risking draining each other's life force," Robert says in my ear.

His ephemeral hand falls on my shoulder, transferring his pain, sadness, and yes, love to me and through me. "It's what happens, Flynn, when one of our kind mates with the opposite sex. The classic tales are partially true. We drain them of all their energy, psychic and otherwise. We just don't have to be in spirit form to do it. The Registry's records are rather incomplete about our nature, but they know some of it. If we pull power from the opposite sex, we run the risk of rendering them permanently null. And if we mate with them, the stronger one could kill the weaker."

I let that sink in while Dad continues trying to convince Mom that he's got it all under control, but she's not having any of it. He starts pulling on some clothing, slacks and a button-down.

Is this why almost all my training partners have been women? And why they watch me so closely when I'm working with a male psychic?

"You're lesbian. You're marrying Genesis. She's not at risk. They probably didn't want to scare you by telling you."

"Does Gen know?" I ask as Mom zips up the suitcase and shoves it at Dad.

"I have no idea. Likely not."

We clear out of the way as Dad accepts the suitcase and heads for the door. He pauses a moment in the alcove. "I love you," he says. "You and Flynn. Tell her I left. It will spare you any resentment from her, and it will be easier for her to understand." And he's gone.

"We were each other's one chance at finding happiness," Robert says beside me. "But she was so very much stronger. It's why you're the most powerful psychic the Registry has ever known, this combination."

My mother collapses onto the bed, sobbing uncontrollably. And she's not the only one.

My vision blurs, but I will the tears away. I'm a freaking spirit. I don't have eyes or tear ducts or, hell, a real face. For now, mind over spiritual matter works.

"Let's go back," Robert says, and I feel his power wrapping carefully around mine.

Chapter 35
Truce

"TRY TO pull yourself together, Flynn. You're walking down the aisle in less than ten minutes." Dad passes me yet another tissue from the box the dressing room staff provided.

I wipe at my eyes, the minimal makeup I'd applied at the hotel coming away with my tears. Since recovering from our return, which apparently occurred mere minutes after we left our bodies, I've done nothing but cry, twenty-four years of anger and hurt coming out in one long, humiliating outpouring of emotion that I can't help or stop.

Eventually, Dad reaches out and gives the sleeve of my tux a tug. Then I'm in his arms and he's holding me and I'm hugging him for all I'm worth.

"Why didn't you tell me sooner?" I choke out, voice muffled against his white shirt.

"I wasn't going to have you hating her. After your grandmother passed, she was all you had. You couldn't come stay with me. I was already in some trouble with the Registry, even if I had managed to keep both my and her true natures hidden." He pats my back awkwardly. "Even after the falling-out between the two of you, I kept hoping she'd accept you for the amazing person you are and guide you through learning how to handle your awakening abilities."

So, the Registry didn't know I had a succubus and an incubus for parents. Well, they had to suspect one of them now, probably Dad, but he'd kept that hidden from them all these years. Impressive.

"Yeah," I say, managing a little laugh and pulling away from him, "having a heads-up on the side effects would have been helpful. And speaking of which…." I'm not hot, not running a fever, and the usual rise in my arousal levels is conspicuously absent.

Dad smirks at me. "We mostly used *my* power for our little side trip. I can't time walk as you can, so I had to draw on your strengths a bit for that, but the rest was mine. So you shouldn't have to worry about any effects beyond your natural responses to your life partner."

Huh. I'm tempted to ask him about himself, but if my dad has ways of dealing with the sexual side effects, I decide I really don't want to hear about them.

And I realize, with a bit of a start, that I'm thinking of him as my dad again.

"Anyway, once I understood your mother wasn't going to change her views, I started

keeping closer tabs on you. And when I discovered you were getting married, well, I decided I'd
missed enough. I wasn't going to miss this." He
grips me by both shoulders and forces me to meet
his eyes. "Make no mistake, Flynn. I'm no angel.
I've done many things I'm not proud of and used
more dark magic than you can fathom. I'm *still*
using it from time to time. But for today—"

A knock on the door startles us both, and Tom
opens it to poke his head inside. "Flynn? You
ready?"

The opening measures of "Pachelbel's Canon
in D," the piece I picked out for my entry, drifts
through the open door.

Tom steps all the way in, looking from me to
my father and back again. His eyes linger on my
tearstained cheeks and the wad of tissues in my
fist. "Everything all right in here?"

I find my voice. "Fine, Tom. I'm fine. But if
you don't mind, there's been a change of plans."
I nod to my father. "Could you give him the ring?
My dad's going to give me away and handle the
best man duties. I don't want to hurt your feelings," I hurry to add.

"No! No," Tom says, grinning from ear to ear.
He pulls the ring from his vest pocket and passes
it to my father, who looks like he might fall over if
I breathe on him too hard. "No hurt feelings. None
whatsoever." Tom gives me a one-armed hug. "So
happy for you, Flynn. So very, very happy." Then
he's gone, and it's just the two of us again.

"Well," Dad says, a little choke making him stop and clear his throat. He crooks his elbow, and I hook my arm through it. "Let's get you where you're supposed to be."

Funny. For the first time in days, I feel like I'm already there.

Chapter 36
Opportunity

THE MOMENT Flynn appeared in the doorway on the stranger's arm, Nathaniel knew the man with her had to be her father. Same hair color. Same eyes. Same stubborn set to the jaw, even if Flynn was currently smiling. No. Not smiling. Beaming. He didn't think he'd ever seen the woman so happy. Nervous, too, but that was to be expected. This was Flynn, and he'd learned enough about her in the past days to know she hated being the center of attention.

And, Nathaniel was surprised to discover, he was happy for her. She deserved this—a peaceful wedding, free of magical interference, her father, whom he'd heard she was estranged from, now escorting her down the aisle. She'd worked hard for the Registry, and Nathaniel's investigation into the rest of her life told of numerous family difficulties, though he still hadn't managed to locate Flynn's mother.

He slipped a hand into his pants' pocket, his fingers brushing his cell phone, and stopped. Guilt nagged at him. He had a duty to President Argyle. She'd asked him to find Robert Dalton, also known as Ferguson, and here the man was, dropped right into his lap. If he didn't contact Linda and she found out about Dalton's attendance at the wedding, well, to say she'd be angry would be putting things mildly.

On the other hand, he had a loyalty to Flynn as well. She'd named him friend. Despite everything: the testing, the spying. She knew it all, and she still counted him as one of her own. And she was a woman he'd be willing to follow.

Oh, she needed more training, a lot more, and refinement, polishing. Her diplomacy skills were sorely lacking. Flynn tended to throw a punch first and talk afterward. But he and the other board members could work with that.

He couldn't deny Flynn's strength or integrity, not after today's earlier display.

Or Linda's shifting of policies and politics toward things that made the board uncomfortable.

He shook his head. Flynn wasn't Registry president, nor did she give any sign she wanted to be. Her ambitions lay elsewhere, and she spoke often of wanting to resume as much of a normal life as possible once the Tempest Granfeld matter became settled.

Nathaniel pulled the phone onto his thigh and typed in a text message, though he didn't hit Send.

Let Flynn have a little more peace, a few more
minutes of pure happiness. He'd transmit the text
midway through the ceremony, ensuring they'd at
least get *through* the ceremony, and suffer whatever consequences Madame President chose to dish
out for his delay.

Chapter 37
Processional

I LEAN a little more heavily on Dad's arm when the One Atlantic staff member throws open the double doors to the wedding hall. My knees threaten to buckle, and I have to wipe the palm of my free hand on my trousers.

"Nervous?" Dad asks me out of the corner of his mouth, his smile never faltering.

"I didn't realize she'd invited so many people."

There have to be over a hundred, seated in white folding chairs arranged in dozens of neat rows flanking a central aisle. And every single one has turned to stare at my father and me. Smiling faces, some familiar, many not. I spot my construction guys with their wives and girlfriends, Rosaline sitting with her daughters, the gang from the Village Pub, Allie and Steve from the bowling alley, and Cassie, Nate, and a number of the other psychics who've worked with me these past days. The rest must be Gen's friends—some clients I've seen in passing, a lot of psychics from the conference who seem vaguely familiar.

And Genesis describes this as an "intimate gathering." The reception is supposed to be three times bigger. Holy crap, how am I going to get through that?

"They're all here for you," Dad says, "whether they know you or not. Everyone here wants you to be happy."

I am happy. I'm marrying Genesis. I'm with my father. I couldn't be happier. I'd just rather there not be so many people watching. My knees lock, and I can't make myself take a single step down that damn aisle.

"Flynn." One word, in the sweetest voice I've ever heard.

I turn and spot my Genesis, peeking around the corner just down the hall outside the main room. She's got her gorgeous red hair flowing across her bare shoulders. Off-the-shoulder dress, I remember, though I can't see any of it from where she's positioned. Just the right amount of makeup to accent her brilliant green eyes. I'm gaping, and I force my mouth shut.

She's smiling, and I know she understands exactly why I haven't moved.

"You can save a woman from a sinking car, stop a murderer, survive three snakebites, and chase off an evil succubus," she whispers. "Not to mention proposing to me in front of a room full of people in the first place. You can do this."

I give a shaky nod and swallow hard, turning back to the assembled gathering.

"Besides, if you don't, I'm going to kick your ass," comes her final pronouncement.

That startles a laugh out of me, and before I know it, my father and I are halfway down the aisle and the smile on my face is genuine, not forced.

We pass row upon row, pink and white balloons tied to the end chairs, matching streamers hanging from the ceiling. Gold and glittery chandeliers cast soft light over the room, and the setting sun turns the Atlantic Ocean outside the floor-to-ceiling windows a dozen shades of red, orange, and lavender.

We step onto the temporary stage where the reverend waits, Dad taking a place to my left with his hands folded in front of him. I remember this is the "fig leaf" position, that I'm supposed to stand the same way. The Registry couldn't spare me long enough for a rehearsal, and with everything that's happened over the past few days, I wouldn't have been up to it anyway. It's a wonder I'm upright at all. But the venue staff emailed me a helpful video, and I watched it a couple of times between training sessions.

I hope I have everything right.

The music changes, "The Wedding March" beginning its familiar tune. Chris, looking a bit worn but generally none the worse for wear, appears in the entry with Genesis.

My world stops.

If she looked beautiful when I walked in on her fitting session with Rosaline, she's beyond stunning now. The dress hugs her perfect curves in all the right places, dipping at the neckline to reveal the tops of her gorgeous breasts, a long train in the back, but shorter hemline in front to show off her fabulous legs, and that shining love in her eyes is meant only for me.

Yes, I have everything right.

Chapter 38
Ceremony

GEN'S HALFWAY down the aisle heading toward me when her radiant smile falters. Her eyes flick between me and my father and back again. Guess one guy looks pretty much like another in a tux from behind, but now that she can see him head-on....

Chris notices her hesitation, spots Dad, and makes the connection. He raises his eyebrows at me. I give them both a slight shake of my head and a reassuring grin.

They keep coming.

A moment later, Gen's standing beside me, her warm hands clasped in my ice-cold ones. I'm still nervous, no doubt about it, but it's manageable now, with her at my side. I think I could handle anything if she's my partner in it.

My mind flashes back to the two of us, taking on Tempest Granfeld at the children's hospital. We made quite the team. And though I wouldn't want to put her in further danger, her skills might be essential in—

"The ring?" The reverend watches me, that grandfatherly smile patient and expectant.

"Hmm?"

Genesis rolls her eyes. Dad pokes me from behind. He reaches around my shoulder, the wedding ring I bought all those months ago sitting in his palm.

"Oh, right." Our guests chuckle good-naturedly. I pluck it from his hand, the band jagged and unusual but so very cheap. I wanted to get her something better, but Genesis wouldn't let me upgrade her engagement ring, and they're a set.

I retake Gen's hands in mine. Our officiator launches into a lengthy recitation about the history and significance of wedding rings, and again my mind wanders. I scan the crowd, making eye contact with friendly faces, until my gaze falls on a woman standing in the very back by the double doors.

A woman who looks a helluva lot like my mother.

Shorter than me, slighter build, same hair color, and a terrifyingly familiar stance, with her arms crossed over her chest and what looks like a scowl on her face. The aisle is long, and she's too far away for me to make out details. The lighting back there is poor. I can't be certain.

Genesis squeezes my hands, jerking my attention to her. She raises her eyebrows. I guess

I must look pretty freaked because she mouths, "You okay?"

Not sure how to answer that, I take another glance toward the woman who could be my mother… and is now gone. Turning my head from side to side, I search the crowded room, but there's no sign of her.

My muscles untense. Not her. It couldn't have been. Probably some staff member thinking of the amount of clean-up she'd have to do after the ceremony.

I look to Genesis. "I'm fine," I mouth back.

The reverend wraps up his history-of-jewelry lesson. "Do you, Flynn Dalton, take Genesis McTalish to be your lawfully wedded spouse?"

"I do." With those words, I slip the gold band on Gen's finger.

Chris passes Genesis the ring she's chosen for me.

"Do you, Genesis McTalish, take Flynn Dalton to be your lawfully wedded spouse?"

"I do," Genesis intones.

Hard to believe a few years ago this union would not have been legal, that our own government, to whom we pay taxes, pledge allegiance, and so forth and so on, would have forbidden us this basic human right to formalize our bond and our happiness.

She slides the ring onto my finger. Titanium, if I don't miss my guess, sapphires that match the new color of my inherited McLaren deeply embedded in its surface at even intervals. It's perfect. Not delicate or especially feminine, durable material, no protruding stones to catch on anything, whether I'm working at the Pub or I decide to go back to construction.

"I love it," I tell her. "And I love you."

"I now pronounce you partners for life."

Partners for life. I like it.

"You may kiss your spouse."

I intend to place a chaste kiss on her lips, nothing showy, but Gen pounces on me, pulling my head down and pressing her mouth to mine. Her tongue parts my lips, slides inside, and I lose myself in it, the cheering of our friends fading to a dull roar in the background. My cheeks are flaming, and I'm out of breath when she lets me go.

We process out, Chris and my father not too far behind us.

I'm walking on air, my heart lighter than it's ever been. We did it.

Considering all that's happened in the last two weeks, I wasn't sure we'd make it to this point.

"There's a limo waiting to take us back to Harrah's, so we'll beat the traffic and have time to relax a bit before the reception." Gen places a hand on my dad's shoulder. He looks down at it in surprise. "Chris is riding with us. Would you care to join us as well? And I'm sure we can add a chair to the head table."

His eyebrows rise, and I swear there's a glistening to his eyes that wasn't there a second ago.

He pulls Genesis into an impromptu hug which she returns, but says, "I'm afraid I won't be able to attend the reception, my dear."

My spirit sinks. "You're leaving again?" Damn, hadn't meant for that to come out quite so bitter.

He lets it roll off. "Indeed. Not a decision of my choosing, but necessary nonetheless." He directs his gaze meaningfully over my shoulder.

Gen and I turn to look, spotting President Argyle and one of her more aggressively gifted followers—a psychokinetic—coming in the front entrance. They pause, scanning down the hallway to where we stand, but we're blocking their view of Dad.

"Sorry," Genesis says to me. "I didn't think she'd be here. After your argument this morning, she sent a message saying she'd be unable to attend."

"Yes, well, be that as it may, I must take my leave." Dad smiles at Gen. "Your invitation to dinner means more to me than you'll ever know. And Flynn," he says, taking my hands, "you are beautiful in any way you choose to express that beauty. And while you might not appreciate my choice of words, you look lovely today."

And with that, he slips through the nearest door, one marked Staff Only, and he's gone.

Having turned my entire world inside out and upside down.

Chapter 39
Round Two

GENESIS AND I escape with only a glare or two from President Argyle and her lackey. I suppose even she isn't rude enough to stop a wedding couple from going to their own reception.

Chris opts not to ride with us after all. He's got Cassie with him, and I'm betting he knows bringing her along wouldn't go over well with Gen. I'm glad he and Cassie are still together. Hopefully they've sorted things out, though I'm betting they won't be having sex again for a while.

Once our limousine starts moving, I fill Gen in on all that transpired with my father. She listens, eyes widening the more I speak, but she never interrupts. When I finish, she wraps her arms around me.

"I'm not sure if I should be happy or sad for you," she says. "Finding out your father didn't leave, but learning your mother kept it all a secret. Quite a shock."

I nod, not sure what to say either. She won't appreciate knowing that I hate my mother more than ever for not telling me the truth.

"You're still going to go see her, though, right?"

Ah, that's where she's headed. Gen's got it in her head to make my family as happy as her own, even if her parents are dead and she can only speak to them through her gifts. I don't have the heart to tell her that my mother's a lost cause.

Reaching out, I tap the shiny ring on her finger. "I keep my promises," I tell her.

She smiles and kisses me on the cheek. "I thought we might go tomorrow."

I straighten on the seat. "Not much of a honeymoon." The Registry gave me today and tomorrow off from my training. So very generous of them, but I do understand their urgency. I'd planned to take Genesis on a whirlwind tour of all the Atlantic City casinos, play some slots, see a show (the Blue Man Group is in town), have a nice dinner. We'll go away somewhere over the winter holidays and celebrate properly, once Granfeld is long gone. For now, this is the best I can do, but she wants—

"Please?" she begs, slipping her hand inside the jacket of my tux and curling it around my waist.

I close my eyes. "I promised. We'll go."

Needless to say, I'm not in the happy, celebratory mood I should be when we return to the hotel for the reception.

Gen's arranged two venues for the party. The majority of the guests, about two hundred, are seated at tables in a large ballroom, decorated like One Atlantic in balloons, flowers, and streamers in pink and white with glittery silver accents. Adjacent to the rather typical ballroom is an extended balcony overlooking the indoor pool and holding tables for another hundred people. The entire space is like a gigantic greenhouse, with glass walls and ceiling offering fabulous views of the star-filled night sky and the Atlantic Ocean. Indoor trees and other greenery add to the effect.

The head table sits at the very edge of the balcony where we can see everyone—those on the balcony with us and through a set of folding doors into the other ballroom beyond. Music plays. A DJ has his gear set up on a side table, and some of the early arriving guests dance on the central floor in the interior ballroom. We've got two open bars in opposite corners, and I grab a bottle of Breckenridge Vanilla Porter from the first one Gen and I pass. A smaller table off to the side holds the cake, a giant four-tiered affair, strawberry with cream cheese icing—my favorite. I pause to peer at the miniature wedding couple on top—a bride in a gown and a figure in a tux with decidedly female curves and long light brown hair. Despite my mood, it makes me grin. I bet Gen had it custom-made.

We make the rounds, nodding and smiling, exchanging introductions and hugs and shaking hands. I'm so preoccupied with the thought of going to my mother's asylum tomorrow that the nerves about the crowd take a back seat.

That is, until I see President Linda Argyle arrive at the ballroom's entrance with the same telekinetic I saw at One Atlantic.

"Excuse me for a minute," I say, disengaging myself from Genesis and striding toward the door. She never glances back, too involved in receiving congratulations from a table full of her old high school friends.

Good, because I don't think I want her to see what happens next.

I'm pissed. Really and truly pissed. Why can't they leave us alone for one fucking day? The day that's supposed to be the most important one in our goddamn lives?

I force the anger down with great effort, but it's still there, bubbling just below the surface. If I'm not very careful, it's going to overflow.

"Madame President." I block the doorway with my considerable bulk, feet apart, arms crossed over my chest. And yes, the similarity to my mother's favorite imposing stance isn't lost on me.

"We want Robert Dalton," she replies without preamble. The telekinetic nods in agreement.

I grit my teeth and smile, though it probably comes off more feral than friendly. "He chose to decline our invitation," I tell her. "Something about not liking some of the company. From what I hear, you also chose not to attend."

She takes a step, attempting to push past me. I'm not budging.

"I was invited. I'll see for myself that he isn't here."

And now she's calling me a liar. My smile vanishes.

"Consider yourself uninvited," I say evenly. "I work for you. I don't have to have you here."

I sense movement behind me, and murmuring from the nearest tables, all of which are filled with psychics Genesis knows. Psychics loyal to Linda Argyle.

"Problem, Flynn?" Tom, accompanied by my construction guys, Steve, Chris, and a couple of waiters who worked with me at the Village Pub.

I grin. They have my back. They always do.

"*Is* there a problem?" I ask Argyle. At her side, the telekinetic raises a hand, palm aimed at me. I sense the build-up of his energy and fix him with a hard stare. "Are you really going to make a scene in front of *these people*? They're not all with the Registry, you know."

In other words, a good third of our guests are nulls with no psychic ability and no awareness of the magical world around them. A world the Registry wants to keep secret at all costs.

President Argyle reaches over and presses the telekinetic's hand back down to his side, ignoring his blustering. "No, no problem," she says. "We'll speak in two days, when you return to training."

I shake my head. "No. Not about this. I'll do the job I signed on for. I always fulfill my contracts. I'm not helping you find my father. That's not part of the deal. Push me and I'll consider it a breach of our agreement."

"And then what? Would you really let Granfeld continue running loose?" She's got her hands on her hips, completely, utterly, entirely sure of herself.

"No, I'd never do that." Granfeld has to be stopped, and I'm the one to do it.

"What then?"

I fix her with a hard glare. "Then maybe we see which of us really holds the power." The words are past my lips before I can stop them. A threat. A direct challenge. Holy Mary mother of fuck, what the hell did I just do?

Audience or no audience, the telekinetic can't restrain himself any longer. His palm comes back up, the power gathered at its center.

Without even thinking, I coil my own power, reach out, and *pull* the energy straight from his hand. It's a beautiful move, something Nate has had me working on for days. Sadly, my follow-through isn't quite as lovely. The stolen magic goes wild. Instead of being drawn into my own core, it shoots upward in a brilliant arc of blue fire only I and a handful of others in the ballroom can see.

The chandelier over our heads explodes in a fireworks display of sparks, raining bits of glass and metal down upon those of us gathered at the door.

Several people at nearby tables scream, while everyone scrambles out of the way. The dance music stops, and the DJ gets on the microphone, telling everyone to calm down. Hotel staff members come running, asking if anyone is hurt while of-fering profuse apologies for the "odd electrical surge." But I ignore them, all my attention on Ma-dame President and her pet.

Something niggles at my senses, and I rec-ognize the dampening ability Argyle used on my power when I first arrived in Atlantic City. But then I was exhausted and weak. Tonight… tonight I feel more alive and energized than I ever have. Adrenaline and terror—the two boosters to my magic-wielding ability. Well, I've got plenty of adrenaline, and I'm more than a little bit terrified. And I've been learning. Fast. Without any effort or thought, I *push* it aside like it's nothing.

Argyle's eyes go wide. She doesn't say a word, just grabs the telekinetic by the arm and leaves.

But the damage is done. This didn't go down in front of a circle of close friends.

A couple hundred members of the Psychic Registry just watched me defeat their president in a battle of magical wills.

When I turn back to the room, a lot of folks at the surrounding tables are studying me intently, appraising me.

And Genesis? She's staring at me, her face gone completely pale.

Chapter 40
Venting

"DO YOU have any idea what you've just done?" Gen hisses, and it registers that she's not scared, or at least not only scared. She's also furious.

With me.

Again.

"You're mad at *me*?" I growl back, then note the curious looks we're getting from the tables to our left and right. The music has started back up, a rocking number by Pink straight off the playlist I had Gen give to the DJ, but it's not enough to cover our argument and definitely not loud enough to cover where I think it's going.

I catch her arm and walk her to the one corner not holding a temporary bar or a cake. A couple making out there catch one look at my face and decide to find a better place to swap spit. When I've got Gen as far from prying eyes as I can get and still remain in the room, I look down at her.

"Seriously? Did you want me to let her walk all over us again? Tonight? Here?"

"She would have made the circuit through the room, seen your father wasn't here, and left us alone. Instead…."

"Instead what? Look, Gen, she's called the shots since she got me here. She's used coercion, blackmail, and brute force. And I've let her, for my sake and yours. But showing up at the wedding and then here? That's too much, too far." My power rises, a fierce crackling sensation in my core unlike anything I've experienced before. I feel it. I know it's the precursor to something bad, but I'm beyond trying to control it.

Genesis opens her mouth to speak, but I'm not done.

"From the moment all this magical shit came into my life, everything's gone to hell. I've been possessed, attacked, snakebit, controlled. Fuck, I can't even remember the last time I made a decision without someone from the Registry influencing my choice. Why? Because I've *had no choice.* Do this or I won't heal you. Do that or we'll punish the one person you love most in the world. The one person who's supposed to understand me and support me. You once told me you and Chris thought I'd break months ago. Well, guess what? I've hit my breaking point. So the only question is, whose side are you on?" I'm shouting. I know I'm shouting. And people are staring. I don't think they can make out my words, but they know something is very wrong.

Across the room, Chris and Cassie head in our direction.

"Flynn, I'm sor—" Genesis begins, but I'm done. I'm more than done. I've had it.

I'm next to an exit, and I push through it, slamming the opener bar so hard the door bangs against the exterior wall. Down an empty hall, through another door. I don't know where I'm going, and I don't give a flying fuck, so long as it's away from anyone and everyone who has any connection to the National Psychic Registry.

When I come back to myself, I'm standing in the dead center of an empty ballroom identical to the one I left, the red glow from the exit signs providing the only light in the darkness.

It's silent and surreal, my pounding heart and heavy breathing the only sounds. For half a second I wonder if I'm in the same ballroom and Tempest Granfeld has somehow managed to wipe every single one of my friends and family from existence. But I alone would remember them.

I'd remember them all.

A scream builds in my throat, closing off my air in its efforts to escape. I swallow hard, but the pressure increases, all my pent-up rage and power behind it.

My energy urges me to *push*, to sideslip, to leave my body and escape to… anywhere. I don't know. I don't care. It would be so easy… so much easier than all this….

Dear God, is this what happened to Granfeld?

Scrambling internally, I clamp down on the power as best I can, hands pressed to the sides of my head, turning in endless circles, a partnerless dancer without any sense of direction. Nothing in my training has prepared me for this, but I have to stop this surge. Because I know with absolute certainty, if I go out-of-body now, I'm never coming back.

While I cling to my power, I let the rage tear free, my deafening shriek echoing through the huge empty space, bouncing off the high ceilings and roaring back at me.

The dam's burst, and there's no force on earth strong enough to reseal it.

Physical stress, relationship stress, work stress, wedding stress, family stress, they all pour out of me in scream after throat-tearing scream until I'm on my knees and pounding the carpeted floor with both clenched fists.

And Granfeld. My responsibility to stop her. My responsibility to end her. And I have no idea how or when or where.

A second wave of anxiety and inadequacy hits, but I'm too hoarse to scream anymore. So the pressure seeks, and finds, a new outlet.

The exit sign above the door I entered through explodes in a shower of red sparks and plastic shards. Then another and another, like a chain reaction going off in sequence all the way around the room until I'm plunged into pitch-blackness.

I don't know how long I kneel in the middle of that room, listening to my gasping, heaving breath, my arms wrapped around myself to hold the shaking in. What feels like an hour is probably only a few minutes. Long enough for the energy surge to ebb and recede. Too close. Too fucking close.

The tiny remaining rational part of my brain reminds me that Tempest hasn't attacked, that I'm not the only one left, and that my friends are down the hall somewhere, probably panicked and worried sick about me.

Not to mention Genesis, who I left standing alone at our wedding reception.

I really am a total screw-up.

"Fuck." The oath comes out as a whisper, all I can manage right now. I press my palms flat on the floor, preparing to push myself up and go back to face the music.

One of the ballroom doors opens, casting a wide beam of light across the room that lands squarely on me. I raise my head, blinking in the sudden brightness.

Genesis.

Even back-lit, I'd recognize her anywhere.

Her eyes find me, and she turns to shout something down the exterior hall.

Another door opens, then another and another all around the room until I'm emblazoned at the center of six separate beams forming a star pattern across the floor.

As upset and embarrassed as I am, I have to admit, that's kinda cool.

Someone finally has the wherewithal to reach in and flip some light switches, and the overhead chandeliers come on, dispelling the remainder of the dark.

My friends stand in the six separate doorways, looking down at me. Flushing, I push to my feet and face Genesis as they all enter: Gen, Chris, Cassie, Nate, Tom, Steve. And behind them, Allie and Rosaline, her daughters, and my other construction guys.

Genesis comes to a stop a few feet in front of me, the others making kind of a loose protective circle around me like elephants defending an injured member of the herd. Only I'm supposed to be the protector here. I hang my head.

She reaches out and pulls me to her, holding me tight and close, my tremors rocking us both. "I almost went out-of-body, Gen. For good." I'm whispering in her ear. No one can hear me but her. It kills me to admit that kind of weakness, but she needs to know. And dammit, I'm terrified of it happening again.

Gen says nothing, but her grip gets tighter. She knows, if I'm saying these things out loud, that I'm good and scared. That she just came this close to losing me.

"I'm sorry," I whisper. "I lost it."

"No," she says. "*I'm* sorry. I wasn't thinking about the big picture, what you've gone through. You asked which side I'm on." She leans back to look me straight in the eye. "I'm on yours, Flynn. I'm always on yours. No matter what or who we're up against, I'm on yours. You should never have had to ask."

"That goes for us too," Tom, my boss, chimes in before I can totally break down sobbing. He lays a hand on my shoulder while the others nod their assent. "Don't know exactly what went down between you and the bitchy lady at the door, but we've all got your back, Flynn. Whatever's going on, we support you."

I smile my appreciation. No way can I speak coherently right now.

"And whatever dissension you've added to the Registry," Gen says, "we'll weather that too."

"Added to?" I croak. I thought I'd started the problems.

She nods. "I've been hearing a lot of rumblings while I've attended the conference. People aren't happy with Argyle. Those who've noticed the disappearances—"

Meaning Granfeld's victims.

"—don't think Madame President is doing enough to stop the threat. And at the reception, I gathered someone leaked the info about her condoning the use of—" Gen pauses to glance at Tom and the other norms in the room with us. "—unauthorized tactics this morning."

Meaning the dark magic.

Cassie gives me a little wave from where she stands beside Chris, his arm around her shoulders. "Guilty as charged," she says.

Nate steps forward. "People are tired of her bullying, her willingness to risk the people under her, even if she does claim it's for the greater good. Friend or not, I will confess, I'm tired of it as well."

"The tide's shifting, Flynn," Genesis says. "They're looking for new leadership. When you showed your hand tonight, well, you may have just given them what they're searching for."

And there it is, that fear I saw earlier. She's scared. For me. And it came out as anger.

I take a deep breath, let it out slowly, and shake my head. "I don't want to be a leader. I'm not leadership material. Hell, I can barely lead myself."

Tom and Chris both start to protest. Tom's been trying to get the company to promote me to foreman for over a year, and I've suspected Chris has considered bumping me up from bartender to manager at the Village Pub. If he does, I'm turning it down. I'm turning them both down. If I ever get the chance to have some say in my life again, I want it to be simple: build things, mix drinks, love Genesis. I don't need more than that.

"I'll try to keep it together better," I say.

Gen smiles. "I know you will. You always try so hard. And when you can't, because no one can, not under this kind of pressure, I promise I'll be your support, not part of the problem."

Fair enough.

"So," Rosaline says, clapping once. "Now that we've worked this out, whatever this was…." She's grinning, not pressing for more information, bless her. "How do we explain your prolonged absence to the other guests?"

Joe and Alex from my construction crew nudge each other and exchange looks. "I think we've got it covered," Joe says.

Gen and I follow them back to our ballroom. I hesitate to leave my borrowed venting space without letting someone know about the damage I've caused to the exit signs, but hopefully it will be explained away by another electrical surge. Even if there are cameras somewhere, security won't see me harming anything. At least not in a way they can prove.

And hell, given what the hotel is making off us tonight, they can afford to replace a few signs.

The guys let us go in first, all heads turning and faces confused and questioning. Gen and I take up a position along the wall, waiting. Everyone except the construction crew returns to their seats. Tom whispers a few words to the DJ and takes the microphone from him.

"Ladies and gentlemen, please excuse the interruption in the festivities. We had a little last-minute preparation to do before my boys and I present the happy couple with our group gift." He nods to the DJ and hands back the mic before joining Alex and Joe on the dance floor.

The three of them strike identical poses, one hand in the air, the other on a cocked hip. The first strains of Beyonce's "Single Ladies" pour from the speakers set up around the room.

Oh dear lord.

They launch into a perfect lip-synch of the song, complete with all the video's dance moves.

Before they're halfway through it, everyone in the room is on their feet, cheering, hooting, whistling, clapping along, and aiming their camera phones.

I'm laughing my ass off, Gen leaning on me because she's giggling so much she can't stand upright without support.

The rest of the reception passes in a happy blur of strawberry cake, tossed bouquets and garters, blueberry champagne toasts, and dancing with the most wonderful people in the world.

If only it would last.

I know it's not going to when, toward the end, I notice several empty seats at what had before been full tables of guests. They might have left early. It's pretty late. But a twist in my gut tells me that's not it. When I ask, the others sitting there say those seats have been vacant all night.

I know they haven't been.

I don't let Genesis know. No reason to ruin her evening more than my earlier tantrum already did. But I'm absolutely certain of it. A shiver runs the length of my spine, the anxiety-induced horrors I experienced in the other ballroom coming true.

Tempest Granfeld has taken more victims.

She's chosen carefully, picking targets who apparently came alone, those still seated nearby being friends, not family. They forget their missing companions quickly. And without any idea of when in their lives they might have been wiped out, there's nothing I can do to save them.

Nothing at all.

Chapter 41
Memory Lane

OUR WEDDING night isn't the raucous, sex-filled extravaganza all the stories talk about. By the time Gen and I crawl up to our suite around 2:00 a.m., Chris right behind us, we're so exhausted and champagne-buzzed that we go straight to our rooms and crash. I do pause long enough to hear Chris mention that his room's been straightened up and the broken furnishings replaced, so that's good. Don't want to think about the bill for all that.

I strip out of my tux and drape it over a chair to have dry-cleaned in the morning. Weird to think I actually own one. Not sure when another occasion will arise to wear it, but I'm sure there'll be something.

Like when they appoint me against my will to be the next president of the freaking Registry.

Gen's attire requires a little more attention, and I spend the next ten minutes unhooking hooks from eyes and undoing the bustle Rosaline tied up in the back so she could dance without tripping. Gen urges me to move faster. She's desperate to use the bathroom. Apparently doing so in that dress was more trouble than it was worth, and she hasn't gone in hours. Then the next fifteen minutes pass with me searching through her beautiful thick hair for stray bobby pins so she won't roll over and stab herself in the skull during the night.

"Next time," she laughs, "*I'm* wearing the tux."

Yeah, like I'd ever put on a wedding gown. The dress I wore for the cocktail party that first night had been uncomfortable enough, even with Rosaline tailoring it to my exact measurements and specifications.

We slip on pajamas—shorts and a T-shirt for me, a sexy little green satin negligee for Genesis, but I barely have time to admire it on her before I'm dozing off. Neither of us got much sleep last night. I stay awake just long enough to register her good-night kiss and her soft "You okay?"

I mumble affirmative noises. Then I'm out.

The ringing of the bedroom phone wakes me from the sleep of the dead. I fumble for it, almost knocking it off the nightstand before grabbing the receiver and pressing it to my ear. "'Lo?" Great. I'm still hoarse, my voice croaking like a frog chorus.

"Ms. Dalton? The rental car you ordered is waiting for you at the valet downstairs."

"Rental car?" I glance at Genesis. She gives a sleepy wave. "Right. Rental car. We'll be down in about fifteen minutes."

Genesis groans and rolls over, pressing her face into the pillow.

"Better make that twenty," I say and hang up.

It's late, after ten, but we're dragging when we hit the shower together, neither of us awake enough to play with the dozen showerheads. I emerge first, ducking into the closet to worry over what to wear. Mom's not going to approve of anything except a dress, but I tore the one and only one I brought (and own) during the Registry board's initial testing of my abilities. Jeans and T-shirts are right out, so I end up opting for black slacks, a dark blue button-down, and my black vest with my black leather boots.

Gen appears a few minutes later, hair flowing in perfect red waves, tasteful makeup, her standard peasant blouse and tiered skirt replaced by white slacks and a fuzzy gray sweater and gray suede boots. I'm still wiping sleep from the corners of my eyes and she's cover-model quality. How the hell does she do that?

"You look nice," she comments, grabbing a white purse I haven't seen before. Maybe she bought it here.

"Not nice enough." I'll never be nice enough. Not for my mother, not with a girl on my arm.

We find our rental car still waiting for us in the valet lane, even though it's been more like forty

minutes rather than the promised twenty. I'm not
surprised it's a Dodge Charger, black. I hold the
door for Gen and then slide in behind the wheel
myself. Gen takes out her phone and plays naviga-
tor, which I appreciate, since even though I grew
up in New Jersey, I'd never been to Atlantic City
prior to this trip and I don't know my way from
here.

She gets us on the causeway, then, eventually,
the infamous turnpike, and finally, I-95. Yeah, I've
heard the joke a thousand times: "You're from
New Jersey? Which exit?"

In my case, it's exit four.

Contrary to popular belief, New Jersey does
have good reasons to be called the Garden State.
It's not all cities, highways, and pollution. Farm-
land stretches out as far as the eye can see. Not
much growing this time of year, but in spring and
summer we produce some of the most delicious
corn, tomatoes, and of course, blueberries.

But as landmarks become more and more familiar, the remembered taste of luscious fruits and
vegetables turns to dust in my mouth. Kupek's
Mowing Service, where I worked three summers
mowing lawns and trimming hedges, Pennington
Pizza, where I broke up with my high school girlfriend after only a couple of dates because Mom
got herself committed and I had to take care of
everything, the Presbyterian church I left due to a
strong suggestion from the minister that I "wasn't
what God was looking for."

"Flynn, pull over."

"Huh?"

Gen lays a hand gently on my thigh. "Pull over. Right now."

"Sure, okay." I figure she's sick or something, so I turn into the parking lot of the town's one major grocery store, Pennington Market, and stop.

"I'm driving from here." She gets out, coming around to my side of the Charger, and opens the door for me.

I blink at her in the early-afternoon sunlight. "Why?"

"Let go of the wheel."

What? I go to get out, to figure out what she's going on about, but my hands are glued to the steering wheel. I've got a white-knuckled grip on it that won't release. "Um…."

Genesis crouches beside my seat. "Exactly. Your grip's gotten tighter and tighter since we left I-95. And you've been hyperventilating on and off." She covers my left hand with her own and pries my fingers off the wheel one at a time, then does the same with the other one. "Come on. I'll drive the rest of the way. I memorized the directions."

Chapter 42
Moral Compass

"THIS MAY have been a mistake, setting a succubus to catch one." Linda Argyle paced the sitting area of her Harrah's Hotel and Casino suite, nowhere near as large or luxurious as Flynn Dalton's, but she supposed allowances had to be made for a wedding couple. Next time, single or not, she wanted the honeymoon suite.

Cassandra and Nathaniel stood behind her, in front of the sea-green couch, looking more like soldiers at parade rest than business assistants.

Good, because this was turning into quite the war.

"She's the only one with the appropriate skill set to complete the task," Nathaniel said. "Though, if I might add, antagonizing her at her own wedding reception may not have been the best move."

Linda whirled on him, glaring until he took a step back and almost fell onto the couch. "You may *not* add," she snapped. "Finding her father and bringing him in is a priority, wedding or no wedding. From what the archivist has managed to ascertain, Robert Dalton is responsible for erasing much of the information about succubi and incubi from the Registry records. Those working with Ms. Dalton have told me they've reached an impasse. They don't know enough about her or her strengths and weaknesses to decide in which direction to take her training. Her father might be the only one alive with that information." And knowing Flynn's weaknesses might become very valuable later, when all this ended. She needed a way to put that woman back in her place.

"She's not your enemy, Madame President," Cassandra said softly, as if she'd read her mind.

Stiffening, Linda sorted through her memory of Cassandra's skills. No, she wasn't a telepath. Her shoulders relaxed. Her frown didn't.

"I've gotten to know her rather well these past weeks," Cassandra went on, her eyes flicking to Linda's face, then quickly away toward the calmer view of the Atlantic outside the windows. People didn't voice their disagreements often in Linda's presence. "She wants nothing of power, magical or otherwise. She'll do what's right, what she's promised, but after that, really, all she wants is to be left alone."

"Hmph." Linda strolled to the minibar, removed tiny bottles of gin and tonic, and fixed herself a drink, even though the hour was barely past noon. She tossed back half in one go. "Everyone wants power." And Flynn had plenty to spare. "She'll show her true colors soon enough. In the meantime, find me Robert Dalton. Flynn must have another succubus or incubus in her lineage. I'm betting it's him. That would explain why he'd erase the archive entries, to hide himself from us."

"Unless he was merely protecting Flynn," Nathaniel suggested.

"Nonsense. I remember the man. Self-centered and as egotistical as his daughter. But regardless, I want him. He knows things we don't. We've already got him on madness punishment three days a week. Perhaps we could offer to rescind that early in exchange for his cooperation."

Or threaten his daughter. Whichever worked.

Though she wasn't sure what threat she could bring to bear on a psychic as strong as Flynn. She downed the rest of her drink and slammed the glass on the coffee table. "You've checked the Festivity address?"

Nathaniel pulled his phone from his pocket and scrolled through several screens of information. "Vacant for four months. Realtor has it listed for rent, but no one's taken it, so I can't even trace payments. I have no idea where he's staying now."

She studied him, certain he had to be withholding information, but her old friend gave no outward sign. Still, he'd grown too chummy with the Dalton woman. He'd bear closer watching in the future.

"Keep searching," she told him. "If he'll work with us, fine. Better still if he's a time walker himself and we can dispense with Flynn altogether."

"Dispense with?" Cassandra asked, eyes fixed on Linda's face.

Linda forced a pleasant smile. "Of course. Releasing Flynn to go back to her 'normal' life would make everyone happy."

Cassandra nodded once, slowly. "Yes, it would."

And if Robert wouldn't take his daughter's place, well, threats could work both ways. Linda wondered just how close the two of them had recently become and what Hero Flynn might be willing to do to protect her father in addition to her new spouse.

Family connections were dangerous things—weaknesses to be exploited. For once, Linda saw an advantage to having lost her parents long ago, despite how much it had hurt her at the time. She headed for her bedroom to change before going downstairs to the conference wrap-up luncheon.

Her steps faltered at the bedroom doorway, frozen by a flash of memory of her mother and father, much older than they'd been at the time of the car crash that took both their lives. Mom pulling a turkey from the oven while Dad struggled to work free the cork in a bottle of Dom Perignon. They stood in Linda's kitchen, at her Point Pleasant Beach house. And it was Christmas Eve... last year.

Last year.

Impossible. They'd died when she was twelve.

Hadn't they?

Strong psychics, possessing several talents apiece, they'd preached a code of morality that embraced helping others, never abusing power, finding value in everyone regardless of level of talent.

Linda blinked away the sudden and surprising tears, careful not to let her two underlings see. She continued on into the bedroom.

But it occurred to her, she might have been a very different sort of leader if her parents truly had survived.

If she'd even chosen to pursue the presidency at all.

Chapter 43
Double Agent

WITH A nod to Cassie, Nathaniel slipped out of President Argyle's suite the moment the woman left their sight. He waited until he'd taken the elevator to the noisy lobby three floors below before taking out his cell phone and dialing his connection at the Festivity Starbucks.

"Bloom Street Starbucks, Anthony speaking," said a pleasant male voice. From the background came sounds of hissing foam, smooth jazz, and congenial conversation interrupted by occasional drink orders.

Nathaniel could almost smell the espresso. His steps turned toward the lobby coffee shop while he talked. "Is Carmen working today?"

"Yeah, hang on a sec." The phone clattered as Anthony set it down on a counter or table.

A few moments passed, then, "Hello? This is Carmen."

"Nathaniel here," he said, stepping into Harrah's own coffee shop and getting in line. "The old man in today?"

"Old man" was their code for Ferguson, aka Robert Dalton. Yes, he knew where the man spent his "mad" days. And there was no way he was going to persecute him during one of those, no matter what Madame President ordered. The fellow had enough troubles. She'd have to wait until Nathaniel located his sane day hideaway. To do otherwise would be cruel, and no matter whom Nathaniel worked for, cruelty was not his style.

"Not today," Carmen reported. "He's usually here Saturday to Monday, remember?"

With the Psychic Registry conference blurring one day into another, Nathaniel had lost track. He'd thought today was Saturday, but it was only Friday. "Right. Any luck following him?" He'd had Carmen tailing Ferguson on and off, hoping he'd lead her to his hiding place, but crazy or not, Flynn's father always gave her the slip. And more impressive, Carmen's primary talent was a finding ability.

"None," she said. "I swear he's got more going on in his head than anybody realizes, even mad."

"Let's hope so," Nathaniel murmured. He'd reached the front of the line and covered the cell's mouthpiece to quickly order a double espresso while swallowing a yawn. That much caffeine should keep him going a little longer. No one had slept much on this trip. He returned his attention to his phone. "When he comes in tomorrow, I need you to give him a message."

On the other end, Carmen snorted. "A message? Are you serious? He can barely say 'coffee.' You want him to read and comprehend?"

"Just do it. Write my name and cell number on a slip of paper and tell him not to throw it away or try to read it until Tuesday. And make sure he puts it in his pocket. Be convincing, Carmen. Bribe him if you have to. Lives might depend on it." Ferguson's and Flynn's.

"I'll do my best. Gotta run. Line's getting long." She cut the call.

Nathaniel sincerely hoped her best would be sufficient.

Chapter 44
They're Coming to Take Me Away

WE PULL up to the Pines & Meadows Sanitarium at the end of a long circular drive of cobblestones. I'm sure the old-fashioned paving evokes a sense of wealth and countryside for most of the well-to-do clientele of this private facility, but for me, it jars my already throbbing head and sets my teeth on edge.

Pines & Meadows itself resembles an overly large country farmhouse more than a hospital. Two stories, painted white with blue-flowered curtains in all the lower windows, treatment rooms and offices downstairs, patient living areas upstairs, an out-of-place modern elevator hidden at the back of the main "house" to aid those in wheelchairs and move gurneys and such. Outbuildings designed on the outside to look like a barn and stables actually house staff quarters and recreational facilities, including a full spa, gym, indoor pool, and single-screen theater.

Those receiving care have access to every modern amenity, and the price tag is exactly as high as anyone might expect.

Good thing Dad is loaded.

Visitors have the option of parking in a small grassy side lot for prolonged visits or remaining in the turnaround if they intend to stay less time. I point to an open space on the driveway by the "One Hour Parking" sign. Gen frowns but pulls into the spot.

"Deep breaths, Flynn," she says, patting my thigh and opening her door. I follow suit, planting my boots on the stones in the crisp, now overcast, October air. A pair of crows perched on the front steps announce our arrival with loud, hoarse cawing.

Around us are acres of just-starting-to-turn-brown-for-winter, freshly mowed grass, cut off in the distance on all sides by pine trees, hence the facility's name. I've always had a sneaking suspicion the cleared land around the buildings is by design. If a patient escapes, there's nowhere to hide before reaching the tree line, hundreds of yards away.

As often happens when I'm stressed, I'm having a hard time making my feet move, but Gen takes my hand and pulls me toward the entrance, up five wooden steps to a wide wraparound porch full of empty swings and rocking chairs.

Don't wanna. Don't wanna. Don't wanna. Don't wa—

"Flynn."

"What?" It comes out a little sharper than I intended.

"You're grinding your teeth."

"Sorry." I squeeze her hand once in apology.

"It's quiet," Gen murmurs, studying a creaking rocker moving back and forth slowly in the breeze. Given what I know now, I wonder if there's a ghost in it. Posh or not, this is a hospital after all, and ghosts tend to linger around places where larger numbers of people die.

"Friday," I answer. "Most visitors come on weekends." At the moment, the parking area only holds two cars, and most of the circular drive is empty. But I remember whole families coming on Saturdays and Sundays to be with their mentally ill loved ones, back when I was in my senior year of high school and visiting regularly.

Back before I came out to Mom and she threatened to have *me* committed.

I drop Genesis's hand before pushing through the front door. She gives me a hurt look, making me feel like a total shit, but I'd rather not provoke my mother from the get-go. She'll work herself up to her usual self-righteous intolerance soon enough.

A little bell over the door rings as it closes behind us, and several patients look up from around a large sitting room, two playing checkers by the front windows, a third plucking out the same tune over and over again on a baby grand piano in the corner.

"Good afternoon!" calls a cheery voice from behind a polished desk in some light wood—maple maybe. A woman in a nurse's uniform beckons us to the far-left corner of the room, opposite the piano. When we're standing in front of her, she asks, "How may I help you?"

"Hi, I'm—" The sound of an opening door interrupts my introduction, and I glance aside to see an older nurse with graying hair come bustling into the room, clipboard in hand. She looks up, makes eye contact with me, then does a double take. The clipboard drops from her fingers, clattering on the wood flooring. The noise startles the piano player, who bangs several keys at once in loud discord.

"Here," Genesis says, stepping over to the nurse and retrieving the clipboard and an escaping pencil that's rolling across the floor. She hands them back, and the woman murmurs a thank-you, but she barely seems to notice Gen's presence. She's still staring right at me. Genesis looks back and forth between us, shrugs, and returns to my side. The nurse behind the desk seems equally confused.

"Do I know you?" I ask. I have the strangest feeling I do. The woman is vaguely familiar. It's been ten years. Her hair was darker then, a rich brown, but I think she might be the woman who'd been assigned to the evening shift when my mother first arrived here.

"You're Flynn, aren't you?" she asks, voice wavering a little, though whether that's from age or something else, I can't tell.

Behind the desk, the other nurse sucks in a quick breath.

I nod once, frowning. This woman remembers my name? That's one helluva good memory. Unless there's some other reason....

"What're the odds?" the older woman mutters. She turns her attention to the younger nurse. "I've got this, Angie. Buzz Patrick and have him bring me Caroline Dalton's file. We'll be in my office if there's any emergency."

"Yes, ma'am." She picks up the desk phone, shifting her rolling chair toward the windows while she speaks into it.

"Ms. Dalton," the older nurse says, "I don't know if you remember me. I'm Lydia Rowland, head nurse now, but back when your mother first came here, I worked night shift."

Well, I was close.

"Why don't you and...." She looks questioningly at Genesis.

"Oh. Right. This is Gen. She's my—" I break off. This is the first time I've had to introduce Genesis since the wedding, and I'm not sure what the proper title would be. I glance at her for help.

Gen laughs. "Life partner," she answers for me. "As of yesterday."

To Lydia's credit, it only takes her one blink before she gets it. Her smile is genuine, though a bit sad, and that sadness has my heart sinking and my gut twisting. What the hell is going on?

"It's a pleasure to meet you. Since you're family too, now, why don't you both come with me to my office. We have a lot to talk about."

Chapter 45
In Memoriam

WE FOLLOW Ms. Rowland first past a large communal kitchen manned by a pair of white-jacketed orderlies with several patients preparing snacks for themselves under their watchful care. I notice the sharpest implement any of them seem permitted to handle is a butter knife, but it's nice that they get so much autonomy. We turn down a long carpeted hallway with a number of doors on either side. Some rooms stand open, revealing comfortable treatment areas with cushioned armchairs and teapots waiting on side tables. No reclining couches and straight-backed doctor seats for these people. Having a consultation with your shrink here is like tea and cakes at a ladies' society club meeting.

Meanwhile, I'm running over every possible scenario in my head. Did an e-payment not go through? I changed my number a while back, but I made sure to let the lawyer handling Mom's affairs know about it. Surely he would have contacted me if Dad's well had run dry. Maybe she'd been discharged? Or could she have escaped? That would surprise me. Mom always seemed to like it here. Back when I was visiting, she'd been a bitch to me, but she wasn't a problem patient. She knew she needed help.

Ms. Rowland opens the last door on the left, and we enter a more traditional office. Not a patient area, it's clearly her workspace, desk covered in scattered files and forms, a laptop closed and waiting. "Sorry to meet here," she apologizes, taking the chair behind the desk and gesturing to the two in front of it. "But afternoon consults are about to start, and the treatment rooms will all be in use."

Gen seats herself, but I remain standing, eager to get this over with, visit with Mom, take the expected abuse, and hustle ourselves back to Harrah's. It's a long drive, a couple of hours, and I've got training in the morning. Besides, I'm still hoping to take Gen to a late performance of the Blue Man Group tonight and salvage something of this brief honeymoon.

When Rowland figures out I'm going to keep leaning against the wall, she sighs and clears her throat. "Well. It's been a long time."

My posture stiffens. If I'm in here to get a lecture on what a bad daughter I've been, she can stuff it. Supportive, loving mothers get supportive, loving daughters. Crazy, I can forgive. Crazy is no one's fault. But the homophobia? The disgust at the person I am? Those have nothing to do with her succubus insanity. She'd been that way well before she tried to off herself, and quite honestly, if not for Genesis, I wouldn't be standing in Pines & Meadows now.

The head nurse must sense my defensiveness because she hurries to add, "You're not here for me to guilt you, Flynn. I remember the volatile relationship you had with your mother. Under the same circumstances, I probably would have stayed away too. But we've been trying to reach you. Normally, your mother's psychiatrist would be having this conversation, but he's out today, and he's authorized me to speak with you… if I was able to contact you. Your number's been disconnected, and when we called your lawyer, he said your new number wasn't working either."

My hand goes instinctively to my back pocket where I always keep my cell phone—empty, of course. Because it got fried and then shattered in yesterday morning's battle with Tempest Granfeld. God, was that only yesterday? "My phone… broke," I say for want of any explanation that the head nurse can comprehend. "Why don't you just tell me what's going on?"

Rowland folds her hands on the desk, a sad but sympathetic, grandmotherly smile on her face. "Really, I think you should sit down."

In the chair beside where I'm standing, Genesis suddenly gasps. She's not looking at me or Rowland. Instead, she's focused on the corner behind Rowland's desk. "I think she's right, Fly-nn. You should sit."

I stay where I am, not moving a muscle as a column of light forms in the corner that holds her attention. It shifts and undulates, taking on female characteristics that coalesce into a figure I recognize.

My mother.

And since I can't see spirits of people I'm related to out of their *living* bodies unless I'm in spirit form myself, there's only one reason she could be appearing to me now.

My knees buckle, Gen jumping up to catch me and ease me into the chair she's vacated. I press a hand over my eyes, not wanting to look, not wanting to *see*.

Genesis finally asks the pertinent question. "Ms. Rowland, when did Caroline Dalton die?"

Chapter 46
Once a Bigot

"So, is that really a wedding ring on your finger? Not disgraceful enough that you've sinned with your body and soul, you had to desecrate the sanctity of marriage as well?"

Any guilt I might have felt about not getting to see my mother alive one last time fades at her scathing tone. I remove my hand from my eyes. She's got her arms crossed over her chest, and she's glaring at me down the length of her nose. Her hair is done up in a neat chignon—a word I learned from her—her knee-length straight skirt and blouse free of any wrinkles, her makeup impeccable. But then, she can look any way she wants to now, I suppose.

"How did you know?" Nurse Rowland asks, stunned.

It takes me a minute to process that she can't see or hear the ghost behind her, and she's engaged in a completely different conversation.

Gen comes to my rescue. Again. "Given all the secrecy and urgency, it seemed like a logical guess." She shifts her body away from Mom, ignoring her for the time being.

Mom does not take that well. "And *you*," she spits, striding across the tan carpet to stand between Gen and the desk. "What sort of slut are you, hmm? One of those—what do they call them?—lipstick lesbians. Immoral, worthless whore. Did my daughter corrupt you? Or were you already an experienced dyke when you met?"

"She passed yesterday, early in the morning," the nurse says. "We had a technical malfunction in the surveillance system. She must have been watching the camera very closely to notice. As soon as it stopped working, she... hung herself."

Oh fuck.

Succubi and insanity walk hand in hand. I've thought about my mother a lot since Dad's revelations. She had few sexual partners after he left, and I know firsthand what that can do to our minds. I've got Genesis. I only hope it's enough to keep me balanced, because I'm terrified of ending up like Mom.

"It might have been fifteen minutes at most," Rowland hurries on. "You know we have state-of-the-art equipment here, and the orderlies were in the process of double-checking patient rooms when they discovered her. Resuscitation attempts were unsuccessful." She seems concerned. I quickly figure out why.

"I'm not going to sue you," I mutter, still watching dear old Mom berate my Genesis and knowing there's not a damn thing I can do about it without looking like a raving lunatic myself.

Gen's pale, and I can tell she's fuming, fist clenched on the armrest of my chair, but anyone not knowing her as well as I do wouldn't notice. Other than her pallor, her face projects the perfect picture of calm. She's had to deal with angry spirits before, I'm sure. And even if this one is her mother-in-law, Gen's a professional.

"What do you need from me now?" I ask, tone fatalistic. The nurse passes over a sheaf of paperwork I'm going to have to complete while ignoring Mom's raving.

Worse, as I fill in blanks with instructions for handling funeral arrangements, names and numbers of people to contact and so forth, I realize from now until eternity I'll be connecting my wedding anniversary with my mother's suicide.

Even after death, she manages to fuck up my life.

Chapter 47
Temporary Block

IT TAKES considerable time to fill out everything. Mom eases up a bit on the insults, instead using the opportunity to interject her funeral preferences in detail: red-velvet-lined coffin, open casket service at the Nassau Street Funeral Home, red-and-white floral arrangements, specific Bible passages to be read, Reverend James performing the ceremony, burial plot 972 at Oak Creek Cemetery. And when I spell "cemetery" wrong, she's right there to correct me. Oh, and I'm not invited. That's fine. Pines & Meadows has a company they recommend to me to handle everything, even in my absence.

"I'm impressed you have so much information," Nurse Rowland comments. "People who come to visit patients every day don't know their wishes as comprehensively as you do."

I accept the compliment with a noncommittal sound. After all, it's not like it's my doing.

Mom sneers something under her breath, though whether it's directed at the nurse or at me, I can't tell and don't care.

Oh, it's not like I don't feel anything. Deep down, buried beneath the years of her hatred and dissatisfaction, a few fond memories bubble up: birthday parties, trips to the zoo and Great Adventure amusement park, baking cookies. But they're all before I hit puberty and started putting my foot down about my hair and clothing choices, and most occurred before Dad left.

I'm twenty-eight. Fifteen years of negativity is hard to overcome.

I'm almost grateful for the close-to-endless pile of forms, because as soon as I sign on the final dotted line, she starts up with the criticism again.

We head back the way we came in, Ms. Rowland our constant guide, issuing final condolences for my loss.

"At least you look like a girl," Mom says to Genesis, keeping pace with us on Gen's left. "You couldn't have taught Flynn a thing or two about hair and makeup? Gotten her in a dress so she could *pass* for normal?"

"Normal is boring," Gen says under her breath, clearing her throat when Rowland gives her a curious look.

I take and squeeze Gen's hand, trying to convey the "don't engage her" message, but I can tell her patience has reached its end.

We leave Rowland in the main sitting room by the welcome desk. The ghost follows us out the front door, all the way to the car, and it suddenly occurs to me that if she wants to trail us indefinitely, I have no idea how to stop her. Ten years I've run from this. There's nowhere to run now. Instead of getting back in the rental, I sink onto the grass beside one of the front tires, prop my elbows on my knees, and rest my face in my hands.

Anyone viewing my actions from inside Pines & Meadows would assume I'm finally having the emotional breakdown expected of a child who's lost a parent. And I am. Just not for the reasons people would think.

Mom proceeds to pass judgment on my boots, my slacks, my "ragged" ponytail, my choice of professions, both construction and bartending—the latter reserved for those secretly hiding their alcoholic natures, the former too butch. Of course.

"You have a perfectly fine degree from a perfectly fine university. Why on earth would you choose to do menial labor?"

Because a bachelor's degree in English Lit. gets you two things: a pretty piece of parchment and an unemployment check. Not that I did much better in construction during the economic crisis, but I don't mention any of that.

"And Dear Lord, look at your fingernails!"

I do it, surprised by that one. I haven't worked the site in a while. Tending bar isn't as hard on my nails. But I'd forgotten all the rough training the Registry's been putting me through. They aren't dirty or anything, but they're all broken and chipped. And unpolished, which to Mom might be a greater sin than lesbianism.

"Oh, for fuck's sake," Gen says, startling me with her use of profanity. Yeah, she's really pissed. And defensive. Of me. It's really cute, actually, her standing up for me, and I love her for it. "If you didn't want her to be a tomboy, why did you give her a typically boy's name?"

They both stand in front of me, Gen with her hands on her hips, Mom with arms crossed over her chest. It's a showdown. And me without popcorn.

Mom blows out an irritated and utterly useless breath, for a ghost. "I didn't," she says. "We named her Farah Lynn. She couldn't say it properly when she was a toddler, kept running the words together. Her father let it stick."

"Right. Because everything that went wrong for you was Dad's fault," I mutter. I don't want to get into it, not here and not now, but I'm also not allowing her to keep blaming him when she was the one who threw him out. She's told all the lies about him that I'm willing to hear.

Genesis covers her mouth with her hand, suppressing a giggle despite her anger. "Farah Lynn?"

I shrug. Flynn's the name I've had since I was three. At eighteen I had it legally changed. I'd almost forgotten that I'd been called anything else.

Our mirth prompts a whole new tirade from
Mom. "What's wrong with heterosexual sex? Can
you explain it to me? Does it disgust you? Scare
you? Have you ever even tried it? What, exactly,
do you think would happen if you let yourself be
with a man?"

Okay. That does it. I get up and in her face, not
caring what this looks like to anyone in the mental
hospital who might glance out a window.

"What I think," I say in even tones, "is that
it's a damn good thing I prefer women. Because if
I ever *had* tried to sleep with a guy, since neither
you nor Dad ever saw fit to tell me a goddamn
fucking thing about myself or give me *any* kind of
warning whatsoever, there's a really good chance
I could have accidentally *murdered* any man I actually cared about!" I turn and throw open the car
door, get inside, and slam the door shut behind me.
I recline the passenger seat all the way back, close
my eyes, and press my palms over my ears.

It's not enough to block out all the shouting,
even inside the car. I can make out bits and pieces,
Gen's voice telling my mother everything she's
been missing not sleeping with other girls, in detail, complete with positions, finger and tongue
maneuvers, and sound effects, while my mother
quotes scripture at the top of her lungs.

Then silence.

I crack open an eye, a little worried. Mom's a
powerful succubus. I don't know what other talents she might have, like Dad's eraser ability, but

she could *pull* power from Genesis if she chose to, if she's figured out that she still has her skills, even after death. I'm thinking she hasn't grasped this yet, since she hasn't tried it, or maybe she doesn't want to alert the nulls to her paranormal presence, but I'm still concerned.

I sit up in the seat. Gen's just disappearing back through the Pines & Meadows front door, Mom right on her heels.

I reach for my phone to call Gen and ask what she's up to or if she needs backup, then punch the dashboard when I remember, again, that my cell is broken beyond repair. Gonna need to replace that soon.

Several minutes pass. I'm about to go after her when Gen reemerges at last, a brown paper sack in one hand, waving at someone over her shoulder with the other. She heads for the car at a brisk pace, my mother's ghost nowhere to be seen.

Genesis climbs into the driver seat and passes the bag over to me. "Here," she says with a grin, "have a peanut butter and jelly sandwich."

"Um, okay. Really not hungry. Kinda queasy, actually. I'll save it for later." I tuck the bag by my feet while Gen rubs my shoulder.

"Eat it or don't eat it. It's just an excuse. I told the staff you were light-headed from the shock and that you hadn't eaten, and they let me use that communal kitchen of theirs." Reaching into her pocket, she removes a smaller plastic baggie and drops it on my lap. "Open it."

I hold up the bag and shake it. White and yellow powders, maybe some red in there, too, some dried leaves. "What is it?"

"Salt, baking soda, cumin, oregano, bay leaves, and a few other common ingredients."

"And it's for?"

"Nothing until I add the final bit."

I turn back to her. She's got her purse open and a needle in her hand. I recoil backward. "What're you planning to do with that?"

Genesis rolls her eyes. "Don't be a big baby. Give me your hand."

I hold it out and close my eyes. Yeah, needles. Don't like 'em. I won't faint at the sight of blood, but my own squicks me out, and it's even worse when needles are involved. The bite of the pinprick mixed with a tiny jolt of her power startles me, and my arm jerks.

"Quit it," Gen admonishes, slapping my leg. "You're going to make me stab you deeper." She lets me go and fiddles around a bit more. The clasp of her purse snaps closed. "You can open your eyes now."

When I do, she's got my baggie and a second identical one out and open. The pungent scents of the mixed herbs and spices fill the car. Taking my hand again, she squeezes my pricked finger over first one bag, then the other, until a drop of blood falls into each. Then she seals and shakes them, mixing my blood with the herbs. My nausea increases.

Gen cocks her head at me. "You're not going to puke, are you?"

"No." Maybe.

"Do it out of the car. It's a rental, remember?"

I swallow hard and close my eyes until it passes. After a moment, Gen hands me back my bag and tucks the other into her pocket.

"Keep that on your person. I call it 'Mother Repellent.'"

Huh. Okay. I double-check the bag's seal and put it away. "Hey, could you do something like that about Granfeld?" Having every psychic on the planet carrying around little baggies of herbs might be inconvenient, but if it kept everyone from being erased from existence....

But Gen's shaking her head. "Sorry, no. I need the familial connection. Your blood, mixed with the other stuff, keeps your mother's ghost away. It won't work for other spirits. Now if we could find a living relative of Granfeld's, then maybe, but that's a huge long shot." She pauses, thinking. "I'll put the archivist on it, anyway. The council keeps lineage records so they can identify new talents as they're born. And while those records might be spotty in some cases—"

Like mine, I think, but I don't interrupt her.

"—maybe there'll be some indication of her descendants."

Descendants of Granfeld, alive and running around today. Now there's something I really don't want to think about.

Chapter 48
Cornered

FROM ORLANDO International Airport, Robert Dalton went straight to his favorite Starbucks in downtown Festivity. He'd been up for almost two full days, having left Flynn and Genesis's wedding to catch a plane out of Atlantic City, only to find himself stuck in Atlanta in the middle of a tropical storm that had unexpectedly veered in from the Gulf. Hotels were packed, and he was in his last "sane" day. He wouldn't be the only one if he ended up in an airport while insane. Personally, he thought airports attracted crazy people. But it wasn't preferable. He opted to rent a car, driving straight through the storm to make it back to Festivity before the madness set in.

He pushed himself hard, stopping only for restroom breaks and coffee, speeding and keeping an eye out for police while desperately trying to stay awake. He had to reach a safe location before his mental faculties left him.

And even though he had little distance left to travel before reaching home, one last cup of Starbucks double espresso would ensure he arrived in one piece.

Robert placed the order, exchanging polite smiles with the young, attractive barista—a woman named Carmen whom he knew from his madness days. As part of the punishment inflicted upon him, he got to recall every foolish, outrageous, socially inappropriate thing he did while insane.

The shirt beneath Carmen's uniform apron revealed a bit more cleavage than usual, and his gaze lingered a little longer than necessary, but she didn't notice. Instead, she'd stopped fixing his drink to stare at his face.

Uh-oh.

Robert took great care to keep his "normal" persona looking nothing like his crazy one, changing into his ragged clothing and casting a beard-lengthening spell the night prior to his three days each week in hell, but once in a while, someone made the connection, like Chris McTalish had at the Village Pub.

"Something on my chin?" he asked, broadening his smile.

"No. Sorry. It's just that… you remind me of another man who comes in here. But…."

"I don't frequent this establishment often." Well, not looking like this.

"No. No, I must be mistaken." She returned to the espresso machine and set it to drip. Strange, but she sounded almost... disappointed.

He wandered over to the pickup side of the counter, watching her measure ice with a scoop and pour it into someone else's drink along with a generous amount of caramel—an abomination. "Is there some reason you'd want to see this person I resemble?"

She glanced up, flustered by his continued interest. "Actually, yes," she said, peering more closely at him. "I have an important message for him... from Nathaniel Spencer."

"Ah." Mr. Spencer, right-hand man to Madame President Linda Argyle herself. Robert had spotted him at Flynn's wedding and strongly suspected he'd tipped Argyle off about his presence in Atlantic City.

"He said it was a matter of life and death." No doubt about her recognition of him now. Carmen knew exactly who he was... on every day of the week. She pulled a slip of paper from her apron pocket.

Robert nodded once, scanning the rest of the coffee shop for any sign he was about to be apprehended by members of the Registry board. No immediate threats revealed their presence. "Perhaps you should give the message to me. I think I may know the man you're looking for."

She dropped the folded note into his outstretched palm and returned to her work.

Chapter 49
Dancing With the Dark

SINCE THE conference has ended but we're staying a couple of extra days in Atlantic City, Genesis accompanies me to my training sessions in the ballroom at Harrah's. I'm glad to have her there. She offers honest, constructive feedback, consoles me when I screw up, and interjects some good suggestions. More than that, when the arousal from my power usage gets too intense, she's right with me, pulling me into a storage closet or an empty convention room for a semi-private quickie. I've never had so much almost-public sex in my life.

There's just one problem—President Argyle. And the increasing tension between her and Genesis.

Madame President drops by at least once every couple of hours to monitor my progress, which is never fast enough or good enough. We only had the space rented for an extra two days. Tomorrow, a pharmaceuticals convention takes over and we all go home to various points across the country. The Orlando psychics contingent will continue working with me, but resources will drastically decrease.

So I'm working around the clock, all day, and sneaking out at night for extra sessions while Genesis sleeps. My opponents are fresh. I'm exhausted. I've caught maybe three hours of rest in the last forty-eight, and meals are whatever I can grab when my trainers swap out. I figure I'll catch up when I get home to Festivity. For now, I want to absorb as much knowledge as possible.

I'm seated on the carpet in the windowless ballroom, Cassie working at healing a dislocated shoulder I got when I misjudged a telekinetic *pull* I took from Mimi, the psychic I practiced with earlier in the week, and ended up throwing *myself* into a wall. Nothing embarrassing about that. Yeah, right. No potions for these injuries. Though they take less of her energy, according to Cassie, they work too slowly and I can't get back to training fast enough, so she's doing it directly, her power to my body. Feels weird, but it doesn't hurt, much.

Gen's on my other side, offering me sips from a chilled bottle of spring water and dabbing at the sweat on my brow and neck with a damp cloth. Outside, it's midafternoon on a Sunday, a million fun things going on in Atlantic City, even if October in New Jersey isn't beach weather. I don't mind hard work and getting banged up if it means saving lives. I just wish certain people appreciated it more.

The squeaky push bar sounds from the main set of double doors. I don't bother looking up.

"Why is she sitting down?" President Argyle demands, striding across the central dance floor to stand over me.

Nathaniel rises from his folding chair off to the side, still texting something on his cell phone. "She took a hit. She needed a break," he says, not looking from his screen.

No apology, no explanation. I do an internal double take. He's gone from slave driver to defense. I'm liking this guy more and more.

"Do you think Granfeld will give her breaks? Or opportunities to get healing? She should be pushing through."

"You're lucky she's helping you at all," Gen starts, but I lay a hand on her arm to stop her.

I've heard this criticism before, but something in Argyle's tone has caught my attention. I look up, swiping some escaped strands of hair from my ponytail out of my eyes. Pale complexion, smeared makeup, rumpled clothing... not like the perfectly put-together leader of the Psychic Registry.

"What's happened?" I ask. I don't mean it to, but it comes out tired and defeated. Because I'm not making further progress. This fuckup with the telekinetic didn't happen because I didn't know what to do. I was just too damn tired to do it. We're treading the same ground over and over again, repeating the same lessons, but no one knows where to take me from here, and I'm no closer to having a clue how to find and stop Granfeld when she has infinite time to hide in. We never know where or when she's going to be. I need a reference point. It frustrates the hell out of me, keeps me up during the few hours I'm allowed sleep. I'm helpless, and I hate it.

Argyle sighs, sounding as worn out as I am, and I clamp down on a pang of pity for her. I'm a tool and a potential threat to her. I know she's desperate to protect her people as well as maintain her position, but until I'm certain which one takes precedence, I'm withholding my sympathy.

"Three more disappearances," she admits. "Or so we think. I try to record them as soon as someone gives me word, but the writing erases itself as time rearranges around their losses. All I have are the blank spaces in my ledger to go by."

I nod. She originally tried keeping computer records, but the deleted lines would shift up, leaving no trace. Handwritten journals, though, don't seem to behave the same way, showing empty lines at irregular intervals in her writing whenever someone vanishes from existence. Weird, since she would never have written their names in the first place, but I guess it's some kind of psychic magic thing.

Mimi, the telekinetic, comes to stand with us. Since she and a few others have been kept past the conference's end, they've been brought into the loop about what's going on. "Flynn's doing her best," she says, earning a grateful smile from me.

"It's not good enough," Argyle snaps, all traces of tiredness gone.

Genesis pushes to her feet. I try to grab her, but I'm too slow, and Cassie's still holding and healing my other arm. The tingling sensation of her power falters and stops.

The ballroom goes silent.

"Are we going to do this again?" Argyle says. "Nathaniel was right the other morning. We don't have time to fight amongst ourselves."

"Then stop starting one."

Gen's voice echoes with the overlay of a hundred others. My gaze jerks to Gen's face. Her green, faintly glowing eyes fix on President Argyle.

Fuck.

Perhaps Madame President doesn't recognize the danger or she's too focused on her own anger to notice, but I and everyone else spring into action. Mimi shouts a warning, while Nathaniel, to my utter surprise, risks himself and grabs Gen's upper arms from behind, his phone dropping to the carpet in the process. Cassie backs off, since she'll be more useful after a fight than in it, but she yanks her own cell from her skirt pocket and begins typing furiously. I lurch to my feet, placing myself in the danger zone between the two furious women, facing Genesis head-on.

"Get out of the way," she says, and I shudder at the words that aren't quite hers. Her eyes look through me, and I wonder if she can "see" Argyle even with me blocking her view.

"Are you going to hurt me if I don't?" I ask softly, gently, putting all the love I have for her into my tone.

"If I have to."

Something breaks inside me. She hasn't had a bad episode in a long time. And she's never, ever threatened to harm me. Not once. Okay, yes, she caused me some damage one time when a dark magic crystal in Leo VanDean's curio cabinet possessed her, but that wasn't her fault.

I'm a little worried, though. Even during her fight with Cassie/Granfeld she didn't sound this taken by the dark. But after that close call, I guess I should have seen this coming. Too damn focused on myself.

My craptastic day's just getting better and better.

"So," I say, pasting a fake grin on my face, "your plan to defend me is to hurt me? Kinda defeats the purpose, doesn't it?"

It's like she doesn't even hear me. "She's insulted you over and over. You're doing everything you can. You barely eat, you hardly sleep."

Guess I didn't sneak out of the suite as well as I thought.

"I heard you in the bathroom last night," Gen finishes.

Oh. Great.

Last night. Yeah. They gave me four hours to crash, but I lay there, staring at myself in the mirrors above the bed, mentally berating my uselessness for over an hour, then furious with myself for wasting the little sleep time I had. When I realized I was gonna crack, I snuck into the bathroom, plopped myself on the tile between the toilet and the shower, and cried it out. I thought I'd been quiet. Apparently not.

Gen knows how much I hate showing weakness. It had to have been killing her, hearing me and being unable to help, especially after my total breakdown at the wedding reception, but she gave me my space. Now her pain is coming out.

But why is it coming out through dark magic? She didn't use the dark in her battle with Granfeld. I pulled it from her before she could. She's been getting better, hasn't she?

Or has she been hiding things from me the way I hid my shoulder and leg pain from her? Worse, has she tapped into the dark magic without me knowing, increasing her affinity for it, her quickness to reach for it?

"Stop her," Argyle says, a little fear creeping in with the indignation. About fucking time.

"Quit ordering Flynn around like she's your personal slave," Gen says. Her eyes flash with the dark barely in check.

"That's exactly what she is, until she fulfills her end of the contract."

I whirl on Argyle. "You think you could be a little more helpful?" That's all I get out before Nate grunts and the dark power slams into my back, knocking both me and Argyle across the carpet and halfway across the dance floor. We slide to a stop on the polished wood, Argyle pinned beneath me in an awkwardly intimate position. She rolls me off her with no apparent damage beyond some bruising.

I, on the other hand, can't move at all.

I took the full brunt of it, and as weary as I already am, there's no pushing it back out. Tingles erupt at the base of my spine, running the length of it like the worst case of pins and needles ever. After each inch it covers, that section of my back goes numb; my legs and arms lie limp at my sides, useless.

God, I hope Cassie can heal this.

The far door opens, and Chris rushes in, eyes darting from me to Genesis as if he's trying to decide where he's needed more. Since everyone except Gen already clusters around me, Nate rubbing his shin where Genesis apparently kicked him, Chris goes to his sister. I turn my head, the only part of me that *will* turn. She's standing in the far corner, arms wrapped around herself and trembling.

"Flynn?" her voice, tiny and terrified, carries across the open space between us. *Now* she sees me.

"I'm… okay," I manage.

Cassie kneels beside me. "You're not," she says so only I can hear.

"I know."

Cassie rolls me onto my stomach as gently as she can, but really she needn't be so careful. I can't feel anything from the neck down. Rustling like she's raising my tank top, the faint whisper of her fingers moving over my skin, a sharp intake of breath. "She's fused all the nerves in your spine."

Okay, that's ominous.

"Call in whatever help you need to fix her, but get it done. She has a job to do," Argyle orders.

Not even a hint of concern or sympathy.

"This would be you if not for me," I remind her, wishing I could sit up and punch her. Actually, I'd be happy with just sitting up. "Shut your mouth or get out."

Yeah, big talk from the paralyzed succubus.

But I've got backup.

"She'll do better without aggravation," Cassie says, pressing along my back. I sense the pressure, but nothing else. Hoping that's a sign of improvement.

"Come on, Madame President. Let's get you something cold to drink." That's Mimi, and two sets of shoes click-clack across the dance floor, away from me. The door opens and their voices fade through it.

"You might want to remove Genesis as well," Cassie suggests, fingers walking up my spine.

"I'm not leaving," comes Gen's voice, teary and broken.

"Let her stay," I say. I'm scared for me. I'm terrified for her. Because she just used the dark magic. Again. And that makes her more addicted to it than she already was. I don't want her out of my sight.

"Flynn—" Cassie's magic hits then, a burning flame shooting from my tailbone to my head, causing every muscle in my body to spasm. I'd forgotten the number one rule—all power has a price. I'm jerking and twitching, out of control. My screams echo back to me from the ballroom walls and the high ceiling.

Gen's screaming too, a high-pitched, sob-ridden wail that I only have to endure for a minute before I black out.

Chapter 50
Tough Love

SOMEONE'S HOLDING my hand. At first I think it's Genesis, but the size is too small to be hers. Too small to belong to any adult.

I pry my eyes open, lids like lead weights, and stare at the tiny bald girl in the chair beside the bed I'm lying in. She looks familiar. I'm not sure why. I'm not sure about anything. I don't know this place—a child's room in lavenders and pinks with white furniture and framed pictures of rainbow-colored unicorns.

I've died and gone to my personal hell.

Potted plants decorate every flat surface. I've seen that before somewhere, too, but my brain's not thinking straight. A pair of cats, one white, one tabby, blink at me from the foot of the bed. One thing at a time. I focus on the girl.

"Um… hi?" I sound like I swallowed sandpaper, and my throat feels about the same.

"Hi!" Too loud and too high-pitched. It's enough to startle the cats, who stand, stretch, and jump off the bed to leave my field of vision.

My head pounds. I squeeze my eyes shut, take a deep breath, and open them again. "You have a name?"

"Tracy. I'm four." She holds up four fingers, two of them smeared with purple and orange marker.

And everything clicks into place.

This is Cassie's daughter, the one I rescued as a one-year-old. I've seen pictures of her, but in most of those, she had hair. Guess they've started back up on the radiation treatments for her leukemia. Poor kid. What a sucky way to go through childhood.

We stare at each other, Tracy studying me like she's taking in every ragged detail. "Mom said you helped when I was sick, so I held your hand. I wanted to help you too."

My chest tightens. My eyes mist over. What the fuck do I say to that?

Tracy's eyes go big as saucers. Crap, I said that out loud.

"Probably not the f-word, Flynn," Cassie says, coming through the door. She motions her daughter out of the chair by my bed and takes it for herself. "I left a snack for you in the kitchen, honey. Why don't you go have that now?"

Tracy gives a little skip, claps, and runs from the room. Adorable.

"Sorry," I mumble.

"No worries. I'm blaming the really awesome drugs I've got you on." She checks the tube of an IV I hadn't noticed yet, running to my left hand. The tug on the needle makes my insides squirm. I hate these things—swear I can feel the metal shifting around in my vein.

I raise my arm to reassure myself it's in correctly, like I'd know the difference, and suddenly realize I shouldn't be able to do that.

Pieces line up in my head: Gen's attack, my injuries, Cassie's treatment, and my blackout. But if this is Tracy's room, presumably in Cassie's house in Winter Park just north of Orlando, how the hell did I get here? How long have I been unconscious?

And where the hell is Genesis?

Cassie reaches out and touches first my forehead, then my chest with her fingertips before she cracks a smile. "Much better," she says, nodding. "Glad to see you awake, though you need a lot more rest. You had us scared for the first day or two."

My eyebrows shoot to the top of my forehead. "The *first* day or two? How long has it been? How did you get me back to Florida?"

"Rented a van," she says, fiddling with the drip rate on the IV and increasing it. "The hotel was kicking us out for an incoming group. We couldn't send you to a real hospital with magical injuries, and no way could we smuggle you onto an airplane, even chartering a private flight. So Nate drove us back here with you and me in the rear of what was really a small motor home. That was about a week ago."

I've lost an entire week. Holy shit.

"And Genesis?"

She pauses just long enough for me to start worrying.

"Chris flew back with her. They're at your place."

I sigh with relief. A haze of calm settles over my nerves, and I'm wondering what exactly is in that IV. I'm betting "drugs" is code for "magical healing potions." If I haven't eaten in a week, that's some impressive stuff. "Need to call Gen," I say, words slurring a bit. "She's gotta be upset." I'm surprised she isn't here now. I can't imagine her letting them drive me home while she traveled by plane.

Another pause. Longer this time. Then, "She's not ready to talk to you, Flynn."

Huh? "Why?" Hard to focus. I blink to clear my vision, but it doesn't improve.

Cassie brushes some strands of hair from my face, her smile sad. "Because she hurt you, *really* hurt you, and she's afraid she'll do it again."

I roll my eyes and blow out an impatient breath, frustration dispelling some of the drug-induced sleepiness. "Bring me a phone."

"Flynn…."

The subtle encouragement to close my eyes and sleep grows stronger. I reach over and yank the needle from my hand.

"Dammit, Flynn!" Cassie wrangles with the loose tubing, liquid medication running from the end and leaving a damp spot on the Barbie-pink sheets.

I swing first one tree-trunk-heavy leg, then the other over the side of the mattress and push up to a sitting position. My back hurts. The room spins, a swirling nightmare of rainbows and sparkles. I groan.

Cassie sighs and grabs my shoulders, pushing me back down and succeeding in doing so, since I have all the strength of, well, a four-year-old with cancer. When she goes to reinsert the IV, I weakly smack her hand away.

She blows out an aggravated breath, disturbing some of her blond curls. "Are you trying to undo all the hard work I've put into healing you? Do you understand that Peter's treatments have had to be put on hold so I could use my power on you?" Hands on hips, stern expression—she reminds me of my mother, and some of the fight leaves me.

Remembering Peter's Parkinson's and early-onset Alzheimer's and knowing Cassie's abilities have limits in usage kill the rest of my will to argue. Time to change tactics.

"I appreciate it. Really. But you know as well as I do the longer Gen's allowed to think that way, the worse it will be. Come on, Cass, get her over here."

She wipes her palms on her pale blue slacks. "I don't exactly hold influence over her."

No, Genesis hates her. But she's taking care of me, and that has to count for something. "Tell her whatever you have to. Tell her I'm refusing treatment and being stubborn. She'll believe that."

"Because it's the truth," Cassie mutters.

I ignore it. "Tell her…." I close my eyes and take a deep breath, let it out. "Tell her how much I need her."

Pity. Works every time, if I'm willing to go for it. Which is only when I mean it. And judging from the slump of Cassie's shoulders, this is no exception.

"I'll call her. You rest."

But I don't. I fix her with a hard stare, cross my arms over my chest, and wait.

Throwing her hands up, she makes a frustrated sound and storms from the room. A minute later she returns with a cordless landline phone in her hand, already pressed to her ear. "Hey, Chris, it's me. Put Genesis on."

A pause.

"She's awake and asking for you. Again."

Again? I've been awake before now? If so, I don't remember any of it.

Another pause.

"She won't rest until she sees you."

Longer pause, this one with conversation coming from the earpiece loud enough for me to make out angry tones. Cassie holds the receiver away from her ear. I reach out a hand, and she drops the phone into it, Gen still yelling on the other end. "—almost killed her. I'm not coming over there. I'm not getting anywhere near her until I can be sure I won't—"

"Gen," I say, breaking into her tirade.

Silence.

Katy starts barking in the background, our husky/German shepherd mix. I miss that dog, haven't been home in over two weeks, and I wonder how long Cassie intends to keep me here.

"I know you can hear me," I continue, getting angry myself.

Still nothing.

Fuck it. "Partners for life, remember? Seems to me you aren't holding up your end of the deal. Now get your ass over here so I can stop worrying about you and get some goddamn sleep!" My voice cracks on the last word. Shouting hurts. Everything hurts. "Please," I add, no more than a whisper.

Silence. Then, "Damn you, Flynn," so soft I can barely hear her.

"People are saying that to me a lot lately."

Genesis laughs. Weak and weary, but still, it's a laugh and I'll take it. I'll take anything I can get right now.

"Close your eyes. Rest. I'll be there in thirty." She clicks off on her end. I hand Cassie back the phone.

A grin spreads across my face as I let myself sink into the pillows and close my eyes.

Sometimes tough love is the only love there is.

Chapter 51
From the Mouths of Babes

I DREAM about the other times I woke up during Cassie's treatments.

"Gen...." My voice so weak I almost don't recognize it. I'm moving. Or rather, I'm in something that moves. The vibrations hurt. Everything hurts so much. "God...."

"Easy, Flynn." Nate. Why is Nate here and Genesis isn't? So confused. Friend now or not, I don't want him. I want Gen.

"Where—?"

"We're headed home. Cassie's driving, spelling me for a bit. But we can stop and switch if you need her."

"Need Genesis. Please...." My back arches as a wave of agony runs my spine's length. I scream. Nate's shouting for Cassie to pull over.

Blackness.

More drifting, people around me. Can't move. Can't open my eyes. Scared. So scared.

"I've got her stabilized. She's maxed out on the potions and drugs, but she's still in a lot of pain. That was a bad hit she took." Cassie.

"Let's not mince words. It was a bad hit I *gave her."* Genesis! My heart leaps. She's farther away, maybe outside whatever room I'm in, but I'd know her voice anywhere.

I try to raise my arm, manage to wiggle my fingers. Pain shoots up to the elbow, and I groan. *"Lie still, Flynn."* Chris. His hand rests for a moment on my forehead, then strokes my hair. It's good and comforting, but he's not Genesis.

"Please. I need...."

"I know," Chris says. *"Cassie's trying. Gen's in the house, but she doesn't want to get too close to you. It's hard for her to see and hear you like this. And... she's afraid of herself."*

I get that. I do. But I'm not capable of caring right now. *"It hurts."* Tears run down my cheeks. *"It hurts so much."*

"I know, Flynn. I know," Chris says. *"I'll stay with you. Shh."*

"She's been calling for you on and off all night. It's putting a lot of strain on her. She'd do better if you'd be with her," Cassie says from farther away.

"She'd do better if I'd never been with her at all." Genesis's footsteps retreat until I can no longer hear them.

My tears fall fast and hard.

THE NEXT time I awake, it's to the sound of whispered conversation broken by the occasional giggle. I crack open one eye, not wanting to disturb whatever's going on, and spot little Tracy, seated across from Genesis at a kid-sized table with two tiny chairs. The kid's wearing cotton pajamas with smiley faces all over them, and when I glance at the window, it's dark past the frilly pink curtains. It was daylight before, I think, so I've been out awhile. Genesis perches on the edge of her seat, probably worried she'll break the thing. They both hold crayons, and from here it looks like they're playing a game of tic-tac-toe.

Relief at Gen's presence washes over me in a soothing wave. Sometimes I wonder if, in addition to the emotional bond we share, there's a magical one too. The way I feel around her certainly feels like magic to me.

For several minutes, I watch them, content to see Gen smile, Tracy too. They both deserve a break. And seeing Gen with the kid… it gives me the weirdest feeling, one I can't quite identify, but it's a good thing, deep and instinctive and—

"I won!" Tracy cries, then claps a hand over her mouth, shooting a worried look in my direction. "I won," she whispers, grinning with triumph.

"You sure did," Genesis whispers back. "You're very smart. But we need to stay quiet if we're going to play some more. Flynn's sleeping."

"No, Flynn's not," I say, smiling to take the sting from my words. "But she'd like to talk to Genesis alone, if that's okay with you. I know it's your room, but could we borrow it for a bit?"

Tracy nods, her head bobbing up and down like one of those bobbleheads they give away at carnivals. The rapid movement makes me a little dizzy. "I don't mind sharing. I'm sleeping with Mommy in her grown-up bed. I get to be a queen!"

I'm guessing she means it's a queen-size bed, but whatever makes her happy.

"Are you gonna have a slumber party?" she asks.

Gen and I exchange looks. "No," Gen says.

"Maybe?" I say at the same time.

Tracy giggles and races out of the room.

No, I'm not thinking about having sex in that little girl's bed. Even if I had the strength, the idea and the decor are total mood killers. But I could use some serious cuddling. Fully clothed, of course. I glance over at Genesis.

She doesn't move.

"Come here," I say, patting the mattress next to me, all seriousness now.

She shakes her head, sun-and-moon earrings jangling.

I gaze heavenward. Maybe I'm not a strong believer in the Almighty, but if he's willing to lend me some strength and patience, now would be a good time for it.

"It wasn't your fault," I try, but she blows out an angry breath, cutting me off.

"Of course it was. So stop it, okay? Who else's fault could it possibly have been?"

Fair enough. Okay. She wants to take responsibility? She can have it. "All right, yeah, it's your fault. All of it. You touched the dark to save Chris's life. You touched it again to save mine. Now you're addicted. It's the price you had to pay for keeping us both around. And sometimes it gets the better of you. That's what addictions do."

For a moment she stares at me, stunned by my bluntness. Then her face falls. "I hurt you. I could have killed you."

"You saved me too. Twice. I never would have survived that fight with Granfeld without you. And yeah, you hurt me. A lot. And I'm not just talking about the dark magic." I close my eyes, take a deep breath that comes out in a shudder, then focus on her. "No, my life would not have been better without you in it."

Gen's eyes go wide. Her hand flutters to cover her mouth. "You heard that?"

"Yeah. And I never, ever want to hear it again. Because without you… I'm not sure I'd be around at all." I was in a bad place when I met Genesis, mostly unemployed, fighting and losing battles against on-and-off depression after my breakup with Kat. I'd walked into this potential relationship knowing somewhere deep inside that it might be my last chance at happiness. "Please come over here. I need someone to hold on to. I'd prefer it to be you."

Her eyebrows rise. I guess it's one thing for me to beg when I'm drugged and out of it and quite another to do it coherently. She pries herself out of the kiddie chair, laughing a little when it topples over backward. After setting it upright, she wanders over to me.

I raise the pale pink blanket, careful of the IV that's found its way back into my hand. Damn, I must have really crashed hard if Cassie managed to get a needle in without waking me. Gen tugs off her ballet flats and slips in beside me, snuggling close so I can feel how much she's trembling. Or maybe that's me. Or both of us.

I smooth her long red hair and make soothing noises until we both calm down. Then I clink my wedding ring against hers. "'Til death do us part, remember?" I whisper into her ear.

She sniffles a little and looks up at me. "I don't want to be the cause of that."

"You won't. Just like with me in the limo, we've learned something."

"Hmm?"

"Well, *I've* learned not to turn my back on you when you're pissed off."

She laughs, as I'd hoped, but her heart isn't in it, so I take her chin in my hand and kiss her.

"Seriously," I say when we come up for air, "I know how to block and *pull* dark magic. You just caught me by surprise. If there's a next time, and I know you'll try your damnedest not to *have* a next time, but if, I'll be ready, and you won't be able to do a damn thing to me, okay? Trust me?"

Genesis sighs. "I trust you. I just don't trust myself."

"Leave that to me." I would like to know what brought her to the dark so fast, though. Madame President is annoying as hell, but her criticism shouldn't have warranted that kind of response. Genesis lost control before I even realized she was on that edge. I'm wondering if she's been using the stuff when I'm not around, but that's a battle for another day.

We lie in comfortable silence for a while, me listening to her heartbeat and her gentle breathing. I almost doze off again, the drugs doing their thing, but now that I'm feeling a little better, all the other stresses come roaring back. "Can't sleep," I grumble when I realize she's not sleeping either.

"Worrying about Granfeld?"

"That and a million other things." Like Gen's addiction, Argyle's paranoia, my father… my *mother*. I reach beneath the blanket, to the pocket of my sleep shorts, finding the plastic baggie within. Whoever changed my clothes knew to keep that on me, at least.

I sigh. Hell, why can't I have a single normal problem in my life?

"If we could figure out how to stop Granfeld, that would go a long way toward ending the insomnia," I say.

"Why don't you just do to her what she tried to do to me?" comes a high-pitched, too curious voice from the doorway.

Chapter 52
Plan of Action

I JERK upright at Tracy's sudden intrusion, wincing when my movement yanks the IV tube in my hand. Genesis pushes me back down. "Stay," she says.

"Woof," I respond. But I obey her. Mostly because sitting up makes me nauseated and hurts like hell. I wonder how much longer I'm going to be laid up.

"Somebody's been eavesdropping again," Cassie says, coming into the room a few steps behind her daughter. She gives the pair of us lying in her daughter's bed a quick raised eyebrow, gathers Tracy into her arms, and turns toward the door. "You're up way past your bedtime."

"Cassie, wait," I call, wheels turning in my head, slogging through whatever drugs she's got me on. "What did she say?"

"You should erase her," Tracy pipes up, squirming around to face me. "Like she tried to erase me. But you stopped her. And you," she says, pointing a finger at Genesis, "made it so she can't hurt me again."

Genesis climbs out of bed, crosses to them, and gives Tracy a kiss on the cheek. "That's right. I warded you when you were a baby. Tempest Granfeld won't bother you anymore."

"She wouldn't bother anybody if you'd erase her," Tracy says.

"Gen...." I exchange thoughtful looks with Genesis, then Cassie, who's finally figuring out exactly what her daughter's been saying.

"Do you think—?" Gen asks.

"We've been going at this all wrong." I glance at the tube running from my hand. "Stop me if this is crazy talk. I know I'm higher than airplanes. But... we keep trying to second-guess where Granfeld will strike, or we wait for her to take someone and try to backtrack from there, except everyone starts forgetting the missing person, and it's almost impossible to get enough details in time to trace her." My excitement has my heart and thoughts racing. With a groan, I push up onto my elbows. Genesis hurries to tuck another pillow, this one neon pink and heart-shaped, behind my back.

Who knew there were so many different shades of pink in the world? And that Tracy's room would contain every single one of them?

Crap, where was I? I scrub my hands over my face, searching for my derailed train of thought.

"We don't have a lot of info on Granfeld in the archives," Gen prompts, earning a grateful smile from me. "Nathaniel gave me everything available. All we know is her birth year of 1879, what some of her abilities were, and that she was punished with permanent madness."

Yeah, that makes tons of sense. Take one of the most powerful psychics on the planet and turn her insane, permanently and on purpose. Sometimes the Psychic Registry's system of rewards and punishments boggles my brain.

"I've been thinking a lot about that," Cassie chimes in. "They must have botched it somehow. Psychics punished with madness can't usually use their abilities. It's part of what makes it an effective deterrent. But we didn't know nearly as much in the late 1800s as we do now."

"All of that aside, we can't do anything without more information. I need a place to go to, not just a year. It's a big world. And I'll have to extrapolate forward from 1879 to find her after she's begun doing some bad things. No way I'm harming a kid, even if that kid is going to grow up to be a dark-magic-using psychic succubus."

Genesis paces back and forth across the carpet covered in rainbow ABCs and 123s. "Then we're really no better off than before."

A slow smile creeps across my face. "Sure we are. Because I think I know who has that missing information." They all turn to stare at me. "And I'm suddenly in the mood for a coffee."

IT'S ANOTHER full day before I can get out of bed, walk around a bit, and eat solid food. I move like a ninety-year-old, hunched over and shuffling my steps, but it beats not moving at all.

When I voice the request to go to Starbucks to hunt for my dad, both Gen and Cassie jump all over me, chastising my recklessness and lack of concern for my own health. So it's yet another day before they'll even consider it.

It seems like they're gonna refuse me again, so I put my foot down—gently, because anything else would hurt like a sonofabitch—and they relent, so long as they get to come along. Funny how two people who dislike each other so much can work together in teaming up against me. Then again, they're talking more, joking about my stubbornness and sharing their frustrations in getting me to do what they want. I wish I weren't the focus of their bonding, but I'm glad they're doing it and Gen is letting the past go at last.

"I still can't believe we didn't think of this sooner," Gen turns around and comments as we ride down to Festivity from Winter Park. Traffic sucks, but that's no surprise on I-4.

"Why should we have? Until Dad got back in touch, we wouldn't have had an information source to go to," I say, trying to make everyone feel better, including myself. "In our subconscious minds, it would have been a dead end."

We're in Cassie's "deep amethyst blue" Chrysler Sebring convertible with a black top. (I know the color's name because I foolishly asked and got a detailed description of how she'd searched the entire state to find this body/top color combination so she could get the off-the-lot discounted price.) I don't mention that she likely spent the difference in gas, tolls, and other travel costs.

Nice car, roomy back seat I'm taking advantage of by lying sideways across it. Gen's up front with her, and my luggage from Atlantic City is in the trunk. After we stop at the coffee shop, I'm finally going home. Chris dropped Genesis off at Cassie's this morning on his way to meet with a craft beer distributor just north of Orlando. I would have preferred Gen to have spent the night with me, but Tracy's bed is tiny, and Cassie's guest room had been converted to an office long ago. So the three of us are all in one vehicle. Tracy's at day care.

It's Monday. I'm guessing, and hoping, that's one of Dad's madness days. He showed up coherent at the wedding on a Thursday, so it's a good bet. Three days out of it, four days sane. God, what a way to live for a year. For his sake, I'm glad it's November and he'll be whole soon, but for now, he's probably more likely to give me the information I'm after if he's not fully aware that I'm after it. That is, if I can make him understand me at all. I didn't have much success last time I tried.

Cassie parallel parks us right in front of the Starbucks courtyard seating area, and I'm in luck because Dad's homeless man persona, Ferguson, sits at the very first metal table, crumpled newspapers spread out before him and a coffee cup off to the side. I always feel sorry for the homeless, having come so close to it myself at one time, but this hurts even more, knowing it's my own father.

"Better let me fly solo on this one," I tell Cassie and Gen. "All three of us go at once and we're gonna spook him."

"More likely he'd make a pass at one of us," Genesis mutters, but she doesn't argue.

As Ferguson, he's not always as polite as when he's sane. I ran across him several times before figuring out our connection, and he's not terrible or anything, but he does appreciate attractive women, regardless of his mental state. He's got a wide moat of empty seats around him now, the wealthy residents of Festivity keeping their distance from the "undesirable."

I get out of the car, pausing to lean on it for a moment and catch my breath before straightening and heading for him. Even though it hurts, I set a brisk pace. Don't want Cassie claiming I'm not recovered enough and wrangling me back in the car… which she could probably do successfully, considering how weak I am.

I drag over a second chair and sit opposite him, resting my elbows on the table and waiting for him to look up from the news. He does, blinking, as if he can't quite place my face.

Insane, I remind myself, trying not to be hurt. He'll know me in a few days.

"Look like shit," he mutters.

I'm not sure if he's referring to me or himself, so I don't respond.

"They're pressing, pressing close, pressing matters. You here to press my buttons too?"

No clue what he's going on about. "Who's pressing you?" I try.

"Button pushers, lackeys lacking, no consideration for an old man."

Lackeys, huh? I wonder if Nate's been in touch with him. Wouldn't surprise me. I can't be the only one who can add two and two. I just hope he's still working on my side.

I cut to the chase. "I need to know about Tempest Granfeld. I know you erased most of her info from the archives, and I need her place of birth." And anything else he's willing to give me, but I figure I'll start slow.

"Tempest, temper, temperamental, temporal. Aptly named, that one," he mutters. "Forgot, forgot to go back and finish, never finished the job, interruptions."

Okay, I follow that. Only some of Tempest Granfeld's information was erased. The partial archive entry is what led President Argyle to suspect the tampering in the first place. We have no idea how many others he removed from the records.

"Just give me a place to start. I need to find her," I say.

He shakes his head, shaggy hair flying from side to side. I wonder at that. How could he get so bedraggled in a few days? Must be part of the

curse. He goes back to reading, or at least looking at, the newspaper, mumbling over whatever's
caught his interest.

Sudden inspiration hits me. "I'll buy you a
coffee."

His head snaps up, a beaming smile spreading
across his face and revealing yellowed, uneven
teeth. "Venti?"

I return the smile. "Whatever you want."

Dad wriggles in his seat like an excited four-
year-old. "Helluva town," he says. "Get to the
core of the matter. Never sleep."

Good thing I'm great at riddles.

Nodding, I get his drink order—given suc-
cinctly and coherently, go figure—and fetch his
coffee, the venti iced upside-down caramel mac-
chiato with extra whip worth every cent. Because
now I know exactly where to start looking for
Tempest Granfeld.

Chapter 53
Trust

"NEW YORK'S a big place, even in the 1890s," Gen says, seated at the opposite end from me at the big dining room table in our inherited mansion. I would have preferred her next to me, but she thought we should take the power positions in this strategic planning session. Chris and Nate are here too, on my right, and Cassie brought Peter, so they're on my left—the entire Orlando contingent.

It's weird seeing so many people in here. Katy keeps circling the table like she doesn't know who to sniff first. We haven't entertained much since we took over the property, and we hardly use this room. I'd like to change that when all this is done. Maybe invite them back for Thanksgiving, something positive. Because if this plan works, we'll have a lot to be thankful for.

"When and where do you propose to start looking?" Nate asks.

"Well," I say, gathering my thoughts, "the way I figure it, I want to get her as close to her death as possible. Don't want to mess up the timelines any more than necessary." If I can find her shortly before she would have died anyway, I can't be changing much by eliminating her, right? I'm not real keen on killing someone who hasn't actually done anything bad yet, but I keep reminding myself that this… person… will die and try to hurt little Tracy, along with who knows how many others she's gotten rid of. I push the nagging guilt into a mental box and shut the lid tight. "We know she was born in 1879, and she looked to be maybe twenty-seven or twenty-eight in spirit form." About my age.

"We can't count on that being accurate," Genesis reminds me, even though we've had this discussion several times in the last few days leading up to this meeting. "She could have died much older. You know from personal experience that you can alter your appearance in spirit form. I'm still waiting for you to buy those leather pants, by the way," she adds with a wink.

I flush with embarrassment, but inside I'm cheering. If she's teasing me, she's starting to forgive herself for my injuries. Good, because it's been a difficult few days.

I'm almost back to normal, working out in our home gym every day to regain muscle strength, and Cassie has reduced the number of vomit-inducing potions I have to drink. Gen's handled me with kid gloves, fretting over every groan, every sign of weakness. It's driven me close to insane, but I take it. If that's what she needs to do to reassure herself that I'm going to recover, then so be it.

Besides, having her baby me once in a while is kinda nice.

The others finish giggling over Genesis's choice of wardrobe for me, and I rap on the table to get things on track. "We have to start somewhere. We'll go under the assumption that she died in her late twenties. So I'll study up on early-1900s New York and pick a place to pop into, like maybe a post office where I can look her up. Or a library. Where were census records kept?" We'd already tried the modern-day ones, but all traces of her are gone. I can only hope Dad's reach didn't extend that far back. He told me at the wedding that he isn't a time walker like I am.

Peter's tapping on his phone. "Libraries would have them. There's also a regional census office in New York City that dates back to that time period. I'll text you the address."

A minute later, my phone (the new one I finally got to replace the one Tempest fried) buzzes and I nod my thanks. "It's as good a starting place as any. I may have to bounce back and forth a few times before I nail it, but if I land too late, the records should also give me her death date, so that will make things easier for the final trip." I turn to Cassie. "Any idea how a series of jumps is likely to affect me?"

"Badly," she says, not mincing words. "The more you jump, the stronger the side effects will be, and I'm not just referring to the headaches, fever, and nausea you've experienced."

She's talking about the sexual arousal, though she's polite enough not to say it out loud. Doesn't matter, I'm blushing again anyway.

"Not something I can help," I mutter, defensive.

"No, but I can," Genesis says from her end of the table. "And by the way, you've been talking like this is a solo mission of yours. If you think I'm letting you go alone, you're out of your mind. Unless, of course, you don't trust me."

Fuck.

Nate and Peter exchange worried glances while Chris and Cassie launch into protests, each trying to shout down the other with their descriptions of how dangerous it will be. They both saw the results of the last time I took Genesis with me. They also know that I wouldn't have survived that encounter without her. Chris is on his feet, pacing the room, and I feel for him. How do you let your sister walk into something like that? How do you let your sister-in-law go into battle alone? I totally empathize.

How do I take the woman I love into that kind of danger?

I let them rant. We're grownups. In the end, we're going to do what needs to be done. The only question left is the one Genesis asked.

Do I trust her?

I let my gaze linger on her, assessing her while searching my own feelings. She meets my eyes calmly and steadily, ready to accept whatever decision I make. If I don't have complete faith that she won't be tempted by Granfeld's use of the dark, I'm risking not only the mission, but both our lives.

If I turn her down, I'm destroying whatever faith she still has in herself and jeopardizing our relationship, because no relationship can survive without trust.

Regardless of any misgivings I might have, there's only one answer I can give.

"I'll be glad to have you along. I can use the backup."

Chapter 54
Trial and Error

I HURRY up the steps of the New York census office, circa 1907, dodging to avoid two men coming out. It's a two-story structure, white brick with brown accents and arched Gothic windows that appeal to the builder in me. Not a large building, but I'm betting the same one stands in my time. Back then, they constructed things to last.

At the doorway I pause to catch my nonexistent breath, or in my current out-of-body state, to pull on my energy reserves. The dizzy nausea gets worse the more trips in a row I take. I'm tired. More tired than I want to admit to myself, and I probably should have waited a few more days to recover before starting my string of fact-finding missions, but every minute that passes is another opportunity for Granfeld to remove more people from existence.

This is my third trip today. The first two I undershot the year, coming in before Granfeld's birth—too early to do me any good. I'm going by old photos of this same building, trying to narrow it down by focusing on small alterations in the landscape: electric streetlights that appeared around 1900, a row of hedges out front that didn't exist prior to 1905, and the disappearance of several outhouses out back when they were replaced with indoor plumbing in 1907—a real luxury considering that private homes didn't have it yet.

Gen's not with me, and I'm missing her presence a lot while I lean on the cool brick exterior. We negotiated a compromise. I do these fact-finding trips alone, since there's no real danger, and she comes with me once I've located Granfeld's home base. It's better all the way around. Gen doesn't take unnecessary risks, and I have her back in my time to act as my anchor and call me home after an hour has passed, because an hour is what we've determined to be the amount of time I can stay out-of-body without feeling too many ill effects.

Except for the arousal. That's been constant since trip two.

How the fuck can I be sexually frustrated when I don't even have a body to arouse?

The door opens, and I slip inside the main entrance as a man steps out. Funny how women's fashion shifts with the breeze, but men's business suits, with just a few alterations, could fit in any era.

I make my way down a short hall to the third office on the left with Census Bureau in bold black lettering painted on the glass door. It's not a popular destination, and I wait longer for this door to open, a secretary in button shoes and an ankle-length white skirt emerging with a pad and pencil in hand.

Inside, I stop, reacclimating myself. I didn't waste my previous visits. I scouted the lay of the land. But a few things have shifted; the filing cabinets, brand-new the last time, sat on the left and are now dented and lined up against the right-hand wall. The calendar has moved to the opposite side. I glance at the date, May 11, 1906.

Perfect. That would make Granfeld alive and about twenty-seven years old, give or take.

I'm not alone. A man in thick glasses sits behind a wooden desk separated from the file cabinets by a low wood partition and a little swinging wooden door leading to his area. I'm in the secretary's area. He's the actual census compiler, in charge of everything in the room.

I peer at him. Yep, same guy I encountered when I arrived in 1877—older, grayer, pencil scratching a bit more slowly, but definitely the same man. I wonder what he'll think of what I'm about to do.

Taking a firm hold on the handle of the second drawer down on the third cabinet over, the one labeled, Gr-Gz, I ease it open an inch at a time. Good thing they don't have locks. Can't imagine why they would. Who besides me would want to steal census records?

The man glances up, frowning. I wait until he goes back to his papers and pull it open a little farther, then farther still until it's about halfway out. He gets up, pushes open the swinging gate/

door thing, and shoves the drawer closed with a metallic clang.

Sigh.

I do it two more times with the same results. On the fourth try, he ignores it, growling something under his breath about poor workmanship and scribbling harder with the pencil. Now the tricky part. Crouching down, I thumb through file after file, watching him with one eye and the names flashing by with the other, careful not to move any of them too much. He can't see me, but he'll notice if papers shift themselves.

Grady, Grafton…. Granfeld. Jackpot.

I ease the file out an inch at a time. He still doesn't look up, so I lay it on top of the others and flip it open so it's lying flat across the entire row of other files.

Flynn? You need to come back, Flynn.

Shit. Seriously? It's been maybe twenty, twenty-five minutes and Genesis is already calling me?

I know it hasn't been long, but Cassie doesn't like your breathing or your pulse rate. She says you're overdoing it. If you can hear me, come back now.

Now that she mentions it, it is getting harder to turn pages. I have to try two or three times for each one, my fingers tending to pass through the paper rather than grab the corners.

A gentle tug pulls at my shoulders. Genesis must be touching me. We've determined through trial and error that her voice and physical contact with my real body transfer to me in spirit form. I'd welcome it if I were ready to return. The stronger the connection, the easier the transference. But I need more time, dammit. I don't want to do this any more than I absolutely have to.

I ignore the urge to snap back into my body and flip another sheet, snagging it on the second try.

Tempest Granfeld. Age 27. Occupation Homemaker.

That earns a snort. She doesn't seem like the homemaking type. I can't see her dusting, folding sheets, and baking cookies. According to this, she lives alone. I wonder how she makes a living.

Address....

"What in God's name?" The voice from right beside my left ear makes me jump. My knee collides with the open drawer, causing a loud bang that resounds through the office with no apparent source for it. The file I'm reading falls off the top and papers scatter everywhere. "How on Earth?"

I backpedal right into the voice's source, the secretary, returning to the office so quietly I didn't hear her enter.

Disorientation and nausea hit hard, as always happens when my spirit passes through that of another living being.

"What's going on, Marie?" her boss asks from his desk. "That drawer keeps coming open."

Cabinets, chairs, pictures on the walls, they whirl around in my dizzy, blurred vision. If I could take a step, I'd break the contact, but I'm helpless and weak, growing weaker the longer we intermix. She seems to feel nothing, but my energy drains in increasing increments as the seconds pass.

At long last, she crouches to retrieve some of the papers, reducing the surface area in direct contact with me, and I'm able to let myself fall, landing on all fours somewhere to her right. My palms and knees sink into the wood floor as if it were quicksand. Pulling them free is like yanking them from vats of molasses.

Not good. Very not good.

Flynn! Now! Come back right now! You're hyperventilating on our end. Please, if you can hear me, you have to come back now. Gen's panicked. I both hear and feel it, so emotions can transfer as well. Good to know. Bad to experience. Her fear and urgency send shockwaves of negativity through me, draining me even further.

Not for the first time, I wish we could communicate both ways, but it's a one-sided conversation I can't answer to.

Scrambling now, I force down the nausea and begin scattering papers, searching for the right one and no longer caring that the secretary is staring at the fluttering sheets in disbelief. I spot it, sticking out from beneath the cabinet, and spend another minute willing my fingers to yank it out.

Address 1021 East 54th Ave.

I commit it to memory, grab the lifeline Gen's voice provides, and let it tug me home.

Only I don't quite make it there.

When the blackness of travel recedes, I'm lying on our front lawn. The sky whirls overhead, the pinks and oranges of the sunset blurring in my screwed-up vision.

Flynn, you're barely breathing. Come on, baby. Please.

Shit.

I roll over, glad to see my hands on top of the grass and not passing through it. Closer to my body, I'm a little more solid. Though when I try to get on my feet, my legs won't support me. I close my eyes and tell myself I don't have any body weight to support, but my mind isn't buying it, and I end up half crawling, half dragging myself to the front walk, the steps, and finally the front door.

Which I can't open.

No matter how hard I try, my fingers won't close around the knob. Even if they did, the door's likely locked. And when I knock, my fist goes through it. So much for better solidity. However, when I try to just push my entire body beyond the barrier, I'm stopped. I jerk back what little of me made it. Definitely don't want to get stuck *inside* the material of the door.

From inside come Katy's frantic barks and the sound of doggie toenails skidding across the entry hall tile. She must know I'm out here. She's been able to sense me in spirit form before. Now if only Genesis will figure it out and open the damn door.

"Problems, Flynn?"

For the second time in fifteen minutes, I'm startled into an almost heart attack (which would be a neat trick, considering) by a voice right beside me. I turn to see the last entity in the universe I want to encounter right now—Leopold VanDean.

Chapter 55
Fee Fi Foe.... Fuck

"I'VE BEEN hanging around, waiting for an opportunity like this." Leo strolls over, jaunty as you please, and kicks me in the spiritual ribs.

Body or no body, it hurts like hell.

"What the fuck, Leo?" I curl into a ball as he kicks me again, landing this one on my upper arms. I'm weak and defenseless, not a damn thing I can do to stop him.

"This is for letting Genesis kill me." He drives his shoe into my shin. "This is for taking my mansion, my car, and my money." A blow to my chest makes me groan and writhe. "This is for convincing the board not to punish Genesis for what she did to me." Vision blurs as he connects with the side of my skull.

Come on, Gen. Listen to the barking. Figure out that I'm outside, getting my ass kicked.

Actually, that's the only part of me *not* getting kicked.

No rescue comes, and I'm fading, literally, my arms becoming transparent as I use them to block my face.

Think, Flynn. Use all that damn training you were given.

And of all people, it's Nate's voice that comes into my head. *"If you're low on energy, draw from Mother Earth. Nothing with a soul. That's dark magic. No people. No animals because the jury's still out on them, but plant life, the sun's rays, they all have power."*

We practiced it a few times, freezing our asses off on the beach outside the hotel while I sucked in solar power like a field of collector panels.

I offer up a silent prayer to whatever entity might be listening and slam my palm flat against the damp grass beside me.

It sinks in several inches, then stops, and I feel it, the flow of natural energy, resupplying my core, replenishing my power. A patch of brown spreads outward from my hand, dry, dead grass replacing the thick, manicured green we pay a lawn service craptons of money a month to keep mowed and healthy. Can't imagine what they're gonna think on their next visit to our house.

Leo doesn't seem to notice, he's so intent on his revenge, and his next blow strikes my face, knocking loose a couple of spiritual teeth. I take it, grunting with the pain, letting my agony continue to distract him from my new purpose.

The circle of brown reaches the base of one of our trees—a fine old banyan that hurts me to take from it. It's got to be older than I am, older than the town itself, having withstood years of droughts and hurricanes.

But it's the tree or me.

Hoping I don't kill it outright, I pull its energy into me and feel an intense surge. Older is apparently stronger. It's all I need and more.

I allow Leo to kick me a few more times, luring him into a false sense of security. Then, without warning, I will myself back to whole, bruises vanishing, swellings returning to normal proportions, transparent parts of me solidifying.

Leo blinks. His eyes trace the brown grass to the tree surrounded in dead leaves, and he swallows hard. "Oh shit," he mutters.

His ghostly image flickers, preparing to vanish altogether, but I extend one hand and lash out with my *pull* skill, snagging his energy with mine. Without letting go, I rise to my feet, noting with mild amusement that I'm dressed in all my badassery: leather pants, steel-toed boots, fingerless gloves, the works.

Well, I'm feeling pretty badass right now.

"You're the cause of everything," I growl, drawing away his power, slowly at first but picking up speed. "Max Harris was a killer, but you made it possible."

Leo's ghost flickers again, but this time it's my doing.

"You cursed the lake. You spelled the snakes, caused my injuries, tried to kill me and Genesis, then ratted us both out to the Registry."

His outline grows hazy, expression shifting to horror as he realizes my intent. Raising both hands toward me in a pleading gesture, he says, "Let's not be hasty, Flynn. Look at what you've gained. You're strong, powerful, the most powerful the Registry has ever seen. You never would have discovered your talent if not for me."

Wrong argument, Leo.

I *pull* more from him, absorbing it into my core, though instead of making me stronger, I'm weakening again, the effort to eliminate him taking its toll. I consider the possibility this might be dark magic, but my vision isn't tinged green, and it doesn't feel wrong or even pleasurable. I barely feel anything at all except a bone-deep weariness, a resignation that this must be done and I'm the one to do it. I guess punishing the guilty gets a free pass.

"Are you really going to kill me, Flynn?" he asks, on his knees now and fading fast.

"You're already dead," I manage between gritted teeth, all my concentration on finishing him off.

This is what I'll have to do to Tempest Granfeld, and she won't be dead already. It makes me a little sick to think about it, but I bury those emotions.

"There's all kinds of dead," Leo whines. I have to strain to hear him now. "This is true death. Do you want this on your conscience?"

Standing over him, I look him straight in the eyes. "I never wanted any of this," I say, and pull the last strands of his spirit from existence.

Leo vanishes. For good.

Taking a deep breath, I let the power go, all of it. I don't want any part of him inside me. It scatters on the evening breeze. Some of the energy touches the grass and the tree. Both resume their healthy green, new leaves sprouting to replace those lost.

Well, at least something good has come from him.

My knees give out and I'm back where I started, lying on the lawn. But the front door opens and Genesis, Cassie, and Chris come running out, Cassie almost stepping through me before Gen grabs her arm and tugs her back.

"She's here," Gen says, pointing at me so the others know where I am. She crouches beside my shoulder. "We saw the tree through the window. What happened?"

I shake my head, too exhausted to speak.

"You have to get back to your body."

I shake my head again. No way am I getting up.

Genesis relays my condition, eyes full of worry. I guess my physical self isn't doing any better than my spiritual one. She strokes my cheek softly, warmth and safety transferring from her to me.

Illusions. "You two can't touch her, and I can't lift her by myself. She weighs too much."

"Actually, she doesn't 'weigh' anything at all," Cassie points out.

But my brain can't wrap itself around that concept, and no matter how I try, I can't *will* myself lighter. Gen's struggles to help me up have no effect.

Beside her, Chris suddenly straightens. "Hang on." He takes off at a run, back into the house. A moment later he returns, carrying my body in his arms.

If I can't get to it, he'll bring it to me. Brilliant.

He lays it down beside where I am, and I'm stunned by my own appearance—paler than Leo's ghost, breath coming in uneven gasps, face contorted in pain. I brush semi-solid fingers against the real, cold skin of my hand.

The pull grabs and wrenches me back, more painful than ever before, like I'm a too wide key attempting to jam itself into a much smaller keyhole, a size fourteen squeezing into size ten jeans.

Physical sensations return in an overwhelming rush of light, sound, and the worst migraine ever. My first ragged breath sets me gagging, and the others roll me over so I don't choke on my own vomit.

I spend the next hour or more puking on the front lawn while Genesis rubs soothing circles on my back. Cassie offers small sips of cold water from a glass fetched by Chris. I tell them what happened, in between bouts of nausea and spikes of headache pain so intense I worry I might black out.

"Well," Chris says when I finish, "at least you got what you went for."

"And you're taking a day or two to recover before you do anything else," Cassie puts in.

I nod my agreement to that.

But as soon as I'm able, I'm going to finish this, once and for all. Then I can get back to some semblance of a normal life.

Fate willing.

Chapter 56
Contact

ROBERT DALTON awoke in an unfamiliar hotel room. He lay sideways across one of two queen-size beds, atop a flower-patterned comforter he hadn't bothered to draw back before falling asleep. The stench of sweat, urine, and garbage urged him to his feet, all of the odors coming off his filthy clothes and unwashed body.

A quick thought and a short incantation removed the homeless man disguise, reducing his long, scraggly beard to three-day stubble and his unkempt hair to its normal neatly trimmed length. But the dirty clothes he kept for his madness days remained, and they smelled as bad as ever.

He stumbled into the bathroom, the labels on the toiletries reminding him that he'd scored the Disney Springs Doubletree Suites on his most recent four-star Priceline search. He switched hotels every week, checking in the night before his days of punishment and hoping his deranged self could locate it at the end of his three mad days. Usually, he could retain that much, though it amused him to think what the front desk staffs thought of him strolling in as Ferguson, complete with room key. And just in case he didn't remember, he always scribbled each address on a slip of paper he carried in his torn jacket.

Other than that cryptic message from Nathaniel, his methods had kept him off the Registry's radar, preventing them from using his skills while sane. Procuring his accommodations through Priceline meant his hotels got assigned randomly, so he didn't risk falling into some subconscious pattern, and his eraser talent removed all traces of his credit card usage.

He stripped out of the smelly clothes, frowning as bits and pieces of his alter ego's memory flickered through his mind: sidewalks, dumpsters, harassment from passersby. He wrinkled his nose in disgust. One and a half more months and his punishment would end, and once it did, he intended to make things up to Flynn, reconnect with her on a more regular basis, find his way back into her life. He turned on the shower with a more violent wrenching of the knob than necessary and waited for the water to heat.

Starbucks.

His mind's eye showed him the outdoor table Ferguson frequented, crumpled newspapers scattered around his feet. Typical. Though Robert abhorred them, Ferguson loved the sickeningly

sweet coffee drinks and could often convince
charitable patrons to buy them for him, since he
always seemed to forget to carry cash while deranged and no one would believe his credit cards
belonged to him, anyway.

Flynn.

Robert froze, half in and half out of the shower.

A flash of her seated across from him at that
same table. Snatches of conversation in his gar-
bled, riddle-filled speech. What had she asked
him? He couldn't quite remember. Something
about... Tempest Granfeld.

A sudden chill having nothing to do with his
nakedness raised goose bumps across his skin.

He'd erased information about succubi and
incubi from the archives for a reason—self-preservation. And even though that damnable master archivist had returned before he'd quite finished with
Granfeld's entry, he knew he'd gotten enough of
it cleared to keep anyone other than an individual
with a very specific skill set from ever finding her.

An individual like Flynn.

If she'd managed to get a starting location
from his mad self....

Forgetting the shower, he returned to the bedroom at a dead run. He had the room phone in
his hand before he realized he didn't know Flynn's cell number. A call to information informed
him that her landline number was unlisted. Which
made sense. He'd kept track of her doings, and he
knew she and her partner had inherited VanDean's

money, as well as Genesis McTalish having considerable funds of her own. And with Flynn's additional notoriety as a local hero, they wouldn't want unknowns calling them.

Next he tried getting Genesis's psychic reading business number, but when he called it, the answering machine picked up. This was not something he could explain in a message anyone might hear. He needed to see Flynn face-to-face, determine exactly what he'd told her so he could reveal as little as necessary.

He slammed the receiver down.

Robert yanked his suitcase from the closet, everything else he owned in a secure storage facility until his punishment year ended, and tore through its contents, searching, searching.

There. The pants he'd worn the day he returned from Atlantic City. The pocket where he'd placed Nathaniel's phone number and his cryptic message to call him.

But when he lifted the handset again to make the call, he hesitated.

This would put him back in the Registry's sights. He'd seen Nathaniel at the wedding, but that didn't necessarily make him Flynn's friend. If the man sold him out to President Argyle....

The reality slapped him across the face. It didn't matter. He had to call.

Because if Flynn caught up to Granfeld, he might very well cease to exist.

Chapter 57
Break Point

"HERE, TRY this. We're testing it out, seeing if we want to get it on tap."

Pleased that my hand barely shakes, I accept a chilled bottle from Chris and settle onto my favorite barstool at the Village Pub. I rotate it until I can read the label: "Liquid Bliss?" I read further. "Peanut butter/chocolate porter." An eyebrow goes up. "Peanut butter beer? Sounds revolting."

He gives me a Cheshire cat grin. "Just. Try. It."

Oookaaay. I raise it to my nose and take a whiff. Hmm. Smells like a Reese's. Interesting. Bracing myself, I take a small sip. And close my eyes as the chocolate/peanut butter combination mixes with a not too hoppy midtaste, followed by a pure chocolate aftertaste. "Ooohhh. Wow. That's…." I lick my lips, savoring the chocolate for a moment more before taking another sip, then a third. There are no words.

"Good?"

"Fucking amazing. I might have a new favorite beer."

Chris laughs, reaching to grab a pen and an invoice sheet, then scribbling some quick notes. "I'll order in a keg or three." When he's done filling out the form, he studies me. "You're looking a lot better," he says, coming out from behind the counter and taking the next stool over, his own bottle of Sam Adams in hand. Chris doesn't care for the sweet stuff, but he sure knows what I like.

"Thanks," I answer him. I've spent the last two days in bed, mostly with Genesis, and though that might sound like fun, once she helped me deal with the immediate needs of my power usage side effects, I slept most of the time.

Then came the issue of a burst baggie full of herbs and spices that we ruptured when I was fully rested and the sex got a little wild. It stained everything cumin yellow, stunk up the whole room, and though *my* bag was still intact and in my sleep shorts pocket, without Genesis's baggie for extra reinforcement, I kept expecting my mother to pop in while I had my head between Gen's legs.

Between that disturbing thought and the spice smell, I waited for Gen to fall asleep and snuck out. And yes, I took my baggie with me. It's somewhere crunched down in the pocket of my jeans. Despite the fact that Chris will call her as soon as he leaves me, it's worth her wrath to see something besides the four bedroom walls. And at least she won't yell at me for going out without her "Mom Repellent."

I return my attention to the conversation at hand. "I owe a lot to you." I've meant to thank Chris before now, but this is the first I've seen him since he saved me on the lawn.

"Forget it." He shoves my shoulder in a brotherly manner. "Though if you'd lose a few pounds, that would make carrying you around a little easier."

I shove him back. "I don't intend to repeat the experience."

"Good." He's dead serious now. The pub's pretty empty, it being a workday afternoon, but he lowers his voice anyway. "Thought we might lose you there. Actually thought we might lose you several times in the last few weeks. You're giving Genesis fits, you know."

Guilt tugs at my insides, but I don't let it smother me. "Until Granfeld's dealt with, I can't afford to play it safe."

"I know that too." He sighs. "Gen always was a sucker for a hero."

I open my mouth to remind him that it will all end soon. We've got a gathering of the Orlando contingent tomorrow to make final plans. Then I'll do one last time walk, find Granfeld, and—

The pub's outdoor patio… shifts.

That's the only way I can describe it, a flickering like a half-changed channel on an old-fashioned television set, a station frequency that won't come in. One second I'm seeing the bar, the outdoor dining tables and chairs, familiar faces of regulars coming and going, Todd, the busboy, wiping down the surfaces.

The next, I'm... somewhere else. Somewhere almost familiar. Somewhere small. Four walls. A toilet, sink, and tub/shower combination. A blurry bathroom I can almost place, all the feelings I associate with it painful and negative. If I could just see it clearly....

My teeth clench. The bottle drops from my suddenly nerveless fingers and shatters on the patio, but I can't concentrate enough to mourn the loss. Pressing my palms flat against the surface of the bar, I will the world to stop moving—and fail. Maybe getting out of bed wasn't such a great idea.

"Flynn? Flynn, what's wrong? Hey!"

I hear Chris as if we stand at opposite ends of a long tunnel, his voice echoing to make the words almost unintelligible. He waves his hand in front of my face, further disorienting me as I flip back and forth between the two scenes at a dizzying rate.

I reach out to swat his hand away... and connect with empty air.

Then I'm falling, not too far, three feet at most, my ass landing on tile, the ice-cold of the flooring seeping through my thin cotton shorts.

Except a second ago I was wearing jeans.

What the fuck?

I blink away the blurriness, focusing in on the bathroom in the alter-image, much clearer now and completely recognizable—because it's mine.

Or it was, anyway. My bathroom. Back at the rent-by-the-week Sunrise Suites where I lived before moving in with Genesis. A dump of a place, complete with the cracked mirror, yellowish stained walls, mold-colored leak marks on the ceiling from the room above mine, and chipped tile.

At first I think I've gone out-of-body and time walked, but I'm not nauseated or dizzy like I usually am after going walkies. My arm hurts, though. More specifically, my left wrist stings like a sonofabitch, and when I look down I'm horrified to see a thin slice starting at the wrist and running lengthwise along that arm, blood welling up in the stinging cut. My right hand clutches a razor blade.

"Yahh!" I shout, flinging the metal away from me to clatter in the filthy tub.

I scramble to my feet and turn on the sink, run water over the cut, clean it with soap, then rinse it again and wrap it in some gauze I find in the tiny medicine cabinet behind the mirror.

It's only when I swing the mirror back to shut the cabinet that I get a good look at myself. And stop and stare.

I hardly know the woman looking out of that glass. Gaunt—it's the best word I can come up with, eyes sunken like the sockets in a skull, shadows around them making them seem even further recessed. My flesh hangs off my bones, all muscle tone gone and my ribs showing through my threadbare T-shirt.

The shirt's familiar at least, a Pink concert tee I bought back before RPL Construction picked up the Festivity job. Back before I was out of work for months and months. Back when I could afford tickets to a show and an overpriced souvenir. But it didn't look like this—stained, torn at the left shoulder, the bottom hem unraveling. My shorts have holes in them too, like I've worn them almost every day for a year.

Year. What fucking year is it? I have to have time walked. It's the only explanation. I'm back in that awful period when I was broke and Kat had just left me.

Except as low as I got, I never tried to kill myself, though I'd thought about it a few times. And the aged state of my clothes….

Nothing makes sense.

I stumble out of the bathroom, amazed by the condition of the rest of my "suite."

Maybe the place was a total hole, but I always kept it clean and orderly. It was something I could control in my out-of-control life. But now—

Liquor bottles—some half-full, most empty—cover every available surface and a good portion of the ratty carpeting. The unmade bed has its sheets and thin blanket hanging off the corners. Springs poke up through the mattress. The pillow's on the couch, as if someone's been sleeping there instead.

My cell phone's on the nightstand.

I practically dive for it, kicking bottles out of the way so they rattle and clang against one another, rolling off to both sides like I'm parting the Red Sea. Seizing the phone, I turn it on and check the date.

Thursday, November 14, 2019. 3:47 p.m.

That's… today.

I mean, it's the same day as when I—left—the Village Pub. About the same time, too, give or take however long it took me in the bathroom just now. I stare at the screen another full minute before I remember that I no longer own this cell phone.

It's a way older model than the phone I recently bought, but I remember it from when I first started dating Genesis.

I scroll through the numbers, searching for hers. She'll know what's going on, what to do.

But I can't find her number. Not the landline at the mansion. Not her cell. And when I dial both from memory, I get nothing but a message telling me they've been disconnected. Same goes for her business line.

My breathing picks up. I have a terrible, horrible thought as I dial the number for the Village Pub, then let it go in a rush of relief as Chris's voice answers on the other end.

"Village Pub, Chris speaking."

"Chris? Oh God, it's good to hear your voice."

"I'm sorry, who is this?"

The terror creeps back in. "It's Flynn, Chris."

"Flynn?" A pause. Then, "Jesus, Flynn. Are you all right? It's been months. I'd just about given up hope of hearing from you again. You haven't come by since the funeral."

My world stops. Because I know with absolute certainty the answer to my next question. And yet I have to ask. "Whose funeral, Chris?"

Another pause, longer this time. "You're not okay, are you, Flynn? Have you been drinking again?"

Have I been? The room decor would certainly suggest so. I staggered when I first got off the bathroom floor, but I figure that came from shock more than anything else. My stomach's sore like I've been vomiting. I'm having a hard time interpreting this body's signals. But though my brain's going in fifty directions, they're all pretty clear.

I think I'm stone-cold sober. I wish I was wasted.

Chris is still speaking on the other end of the phone. "I can come get you, wherever you are. I told you you could call me anytime, honey. No one's mad at you. No one blames you."

God, what can *that* mean? I force my next words through a constricted throat. "Just answer my question. Whose funeral?"

"Aw, hon." His voice breaks, and I can hear him holding back a sob on the other end. In all the time I've known him, I've never heard or seen Chris cry. It terrifies me. "Gen's funeral, Flynn. It was Gen's. Now let me come and get you, and we can talk."

Chapter 58
Timelines

ROBERT PUNCHED the first digit of Nathaniel's phone number into his cell.

The scrap of paper vanished from his fingertips.

Oh dear God, Flynn. What have you done?

He made it to the nearest hotel room bed before the rest of his world tilted. Shifting images, disorientation. Impossible to adjust to except for a being like himself, and even then, it was one of many reasons why succubi and incubi had a disturbing tendency to go insane even without the Registry's "assistance."

Someone, most likely Flynn, had altered a timeline that his own lifestream directly intersected. He had no idea what had actually changed, only that something definitely *had*. And it affected him somehow, and in some way that meant he was never given Nathaniel's phone number at Starbucks a few days ago.

Carefully, he studied the room around him. Nothing different that he could discern. He'd regained his inner balance enough that he could rise from the bed, so he went to the closet and sorted through his suitcase—his closed suitcase, with everything still in it. A moment ago he'd had his meager belongings strewn all over the room, searching for the phone number, but since the scrap of paper no longer existed, he hadn't tossed his suitcase. He also wasn't naked, because he hadn't flung himself from the shower to make that call. The shower was running, though, with steam pouring through the open bathroom door, so he'd planned on taking one, and he'd been at the phone, so he'd been about to call someone. An open room service menu rested next to the phone—a small enough detail he'd overlooked it at first. So that's what he'd been up to in this timeline.

He finished his suitcase inspection. His other possessions seemed complete and intact. So. Same hotel room, same belongings, minor changes. Whatever Flynn had altered, presumably in her hunt for Tempest Granfeld, it had only indirectly impacted him. Which meant she hadn't succeeded in destroying Granfeld yet. If she had….

He doubted he'd be around to be aware of it at all.

And it had to be Flynn. Other than Granfeld herself, no other succubi were jumping around in time, and Granfeld shouldn't even know of his existence… though she could have affected him indirectly as well. Hmm.

Two possible suspects. Still, Flynn seemed more likely. He needed to find her now. If she was mucking around in time, and clearly *someone* was, it had to stop.

He thought about calling Nathaniel anyway, but after six tries and six wrong numbers, he realized he hadn't memorized enough of that phone number to recall it.

He tried Genesis again, but even in this altered world, he couldn't reach her. Only this time, a disturbing difference—the unlisted landline was no longer unlisted, but rather disconnected. The psychic reading business number had been disconnected as well.

Robert had interacted with Genesis's brother, the owner/manager of the Village Pub…. Chris McTalish, if his memory served him correctly. If anyone from Festivity other than Genesis had access to Flynn, he would be it.

Robert tried information again first, but Chris had his home number unlisted. And when he called the pub itself, a pleasant woman's voice informed him that Chris had just left to handle a personal emergency.

Why did Robert have the feeling that emergency involved Flynn?

It hit him then that if Flynn were the primary victim of her time meddling, she'd also retain all her old memories in a whole new world. If enough major circumstances had altered, she'd be going crazy right about now.

He hoped she had enough mental strength to handle the impact.

Robert grabbed his jacket from the back of a chair, turned off the shower, and headed for the door. A fifteen-minute cab ride would have him at the Village Pub. Sooner or later, Chris would return there.

And maybe he'd know where to find Flynn.

Chapter 59
Worldly Wise

A SEARCH for vital clothing pieces such as underwear and a bra goes a lot harder when you're doing it through tears, but I find some relatively clean undergarments, a pair of filthy jeans with just a few holes, and a T-shirt that isn't so worn as to be see-through. Despite the heat, I also grab a jean jacket to cover my makeshift bandaging job. Then I stumble into the setting sun of the early evening and wait for Chris out front of the Sunrise Suites.

It's a little awkward when he arrives, like meeting an old friend after a long time apart, even though in my head I just left him forty-five minutes ago at the Village Pub… "left" being a relative term in my world, apparently. I climb into his sedan without a word, facing forward out the front windshield, but I feel his eyes on me.

"Where do you want to go?" he asks.

"Festivity. I want to see Genesis."

In my peripheral vision, his shoulders stiffen.

I hate doing this to him, but I have to. I have to make sense of all this. I have to *know*. "She is buried there, isn't she?"

"Yeah," Chris says, voice tight. "You were there, Flynn."

"Right."

Dead and buried. So why isn't her spirit here? If there's one ghost I wouldn't mind seeing, it's hers. And I should be able to see it. I'm closer to her than anyone else in my life.

We drive in silence.

My old place is only about fifteen minutes from Festivity. We pull into the parking lot of the nondenominational church in town, a small, neatly kept graveyard beside it, flowers on almost every grave. Gen is… was… Wiccan. Not a lot of Wiccan churches around. Guess this was as close as they could get.

My legs tremble as I get out of the car. Chris politely makes no comment, but he takes my arm to steady me. A minute later, I'm standing over her grave.

Her.

Grave.

It's nothing showy or ostentatious, just a simple marker, but it's so covered in flowers that I have to crouch and shift some of them aside to read it.

Here lies Genesis McTalish
Loving Sister
1996-2019

Fuck.

Damn good thing I'm already close to the ground, because I pretty much fall over right there. Chris seats himself on the grass next to me, draping a cautious arm around my shoulders. Tears stream down both our faces, and for a long time, we say nothing, just lean on each other for support.

Finally I accept the tissue Chris offers me, blow my nose, wipe my eyes, and get my shit together. "When? How?" I ask, knowing the reaction I'll get.

I'm not disappointed. He stares at me like I've grown a second head. "You doing drugs with the alcohol, Flynn?" he asks softly. "I know you were in a bad way last time we talked on the phone. Really wish you'd taken me up on the job offer and the spare bedroom."

He'd offered me a job and a place to crash? Even without Gen to connect us? I remember he'd inherited his apartment from his deceased parents. It had a second bedroom he'd turned into an office.

Putting it back to a bedroom would have been a major undertaking, but he would have done it for me. I couldn't ask for a better brother-in-law.

I stop myself. Not brother-in-law. Not anymore.

"No drugs," I say, clearing my throat. None that I know of, but I hadn't seen any paraphernalia in my hotel room. How do I make myself sound less crazy? "I've had a sort of… mental break."

Okay, that's probably not the best choice, but it's all I've got. "I can't remember some things, and I need to. I need the details."

He gives a humorless laugh. "I've wished I could forget every day since July first, and you want that nightmare back."

July first. Oh holy hell.

That date is emblazoned in my mind. It's the day I dove into Dead Man's Pond to save that waitress, what's-her-name, from drowning in her sinking car. The same day I earlier almost got sucked into the pond myself. The same day Kat managed to leave a remnant of her spirit in me, which Genesis ended up having to exorcise with Leo VanDean's help.

But if Gen died that day…?

I do a quick internal search, using my power to seek out anything foreign so I can *push* it from me, but there's nothing. Either I figured out on my own how to remove Kat during the last four and a half months or that never happened in this timeline.

I press a hand to my forehead, fighting off a mother of a headache. "Details, Chris. I need the details."

"You aren't making this easy on me."

No, I suppose I'm not. "I'm sorry." I take his hand and hold it.

He blows out a breath. "Okay. Well, I'll give you what I know. There's not much. No one's exactly sure what happened that night." He hesitates, staring at the gravestone for a long moment. "You'd gone to your place to pack up your stuff. You were moving in with her for good."

I remember that much. But instead of going straight to her place, I went out to the cursed pond. Really, I'd been drawn there by whatever evil forces were attached to the charm sunk at its center, but I didn't know that then.

"Genesis came down to the pub wondering if anyone had seen you. It was getting kinda late, and she had a tendency to worry about you, especially after the odd… experiences you'd had not long before then."

"Yeah, that was some weird shit," I say to let him know I'm listening, even if I'm not sure exactly what he's referring to. Me seeing Kat's ghost out at the lake? Her coming to visit me in Gen's apartment, trying to take over my body? I shudder. Chris grips my hand more tightly.

"When no one knew anything, she went out back to look for my car that you'd borrowed. Then she just froze, standing there, like she was listening to someone. I watched her from the kitchen entrance, but I didn't interrupt. I figured she was having a spirit contact. It happened that way, sometimes."

Spirit contact. Yeah. And I could just bet exactly which spirit had contacted her.

Granfeld.

"She took off running, practically tore the door off the Charger, and peeled out of that parking lot like demons were chasing her. I knew something was wrong, but I didn't have my car."

No, I had it.

"So it took me some time to borrow one from one of the waitstaff. Then I couldn't find her." His voice breaks. I give him a minute to compose himself. "I must have driven up and down every street in Festivity, searching. She wouldn't answer her cell. It kept going to voicemail. And you weren't answering either."

I'd dunked my phone when the lake drew me in, but it had dried out and worked fine later. It's the same one I used to call him. I look at Chris, his eyes haunted by memory.

"When I finally drove past Dead Man's Pond, I saw the hole in the sign wall and I knew. I just knew. My car was parked there, so I knew you were around, and pieces of the Charger led into the lake...."

Wait. *Genesis* went into Dead Man's Pond? Not the waitress I'd saved?

"I dialed 911 and searched for you, finally spotted you way out in the water, coming up for air before you went back under again. You must have done that three or four more times while I dove in and tried to swim to you. But when I reached the center, you weren't coming up anymore. Neither of you came back up."

He's crying again and not trying to hide it. I rest my head on his shoulder. Shivers pass through me, despite the heat of the evening. He lets go of my hand and wraps both arms around me. I can't stop shaking. I don't have the memories he's describing, but I can imagine....

Diving down, finding her in her sinking car, unable to open the door or work her free of the seat belt she always wore, or whatever it was that prevented me from saving her. Maybe she was awake, pounding on the inside of the glass, begging me to help while the water slowly seeped in. Or maybe she'd lost consciousness and all I could do was watch her die as I dove again and again and my arms and legs and lungs tired....

Chris's voice jolts me from the nightmarish images. "The paramedics and fire rescue showed up. They got to me first. I fought them, but they dragged me from the lake before I could do anything, and went after the two of you. When they pulled the both of you out, you responded to CPR. Gen... didn't."

I lived. She died. She died because Granfeld must have told her I was in trouble, and the lake's curse drew her and her car in.

"I'm sorry," I whisper.

Chris shakes his head. "Not your fault. It was never your fault. You damn near died yourself trying to save her, *were* dead until they revived you. When they hauled out the car, it was full of water, windows down, airbags deployed. The seat belt had jammed, they said. They'd had to cut it off her to get her out. And the crash had knocked her unconscious. X-rays showed head trauma. She never had a chance. No way you could have gotten to her before she drowned."

But I'm betting the me of this timeline never saw it that way. Judging from my current state, I blamed myself and kept right on doing it… until I finally decided to end the pain and guilt with a razor blade.

Either that or I just didn't want to live without her. The impulse to walk in front of an oncoming bus is pretty intense right now.

I roll up my jacket sleeve and stare at the gauze-wrapped slice. All those times I wondered where I'd be without my Genesis, well, now I know.

Chris follows my gaze. "Aw, Flynn, no."

"I stopped myself," I tell him. Because there's still something I can do. Doubt the me from this timeline would have stopped, though, if I hadn't shifted into this body.

"She would never have wanted you to get like this," he says, taking my arm and gently tugging the sleeve back down. "She loved you. Told me she wanted to make a life with you. And I know you loved her. I remember the engagement ring you showed me at the funeral."

My gaze flicks to my own hand, the ring I never take off gone from my finger. "Yeah, I loved her. Still do." And there's no way in hell I'm letting it end this way.

Now that I have specifics, I can go back to July first, stop Granfeld from interfering….

No, I can't. I can't beat Granfeld. Not while she's in spirit form. Not without help I no longer have. Even knowing an exact place and time where I can find her, I don't have Genesis. Even with her, we only managed to run the fight to a stalemate.

I dig my hands into the earth covering Gen's grave. Somewhere six feet beneath me lies her lifeless body. Any guilt I might once have had over eliminating Granfeld before she'd harmed anyone has vanished.

I can follow through on the original plan. Find Granfeld alive, before she became this monster.

And kill her.

Chapter 60
One Last Kiss Before I Go

"WHAT IF I told you there might be a chance to bring her back?" I say, pulling away from Chris and sitting up on my own.

The two-headed Flynn look returns.

"I'd say you need some serious help. Was gonna say that anyway, given your arm. I know you don't have insurance, but please. I'll foot the bill. You can pay me back if it will make you feel better, but let me help. I have a friend who works at Festivity Health. She can get you some counseling and a good rehab program." He gestures across the street from the church, where Festivity's huge state-of-the-art hospital stands. I spent some time there in *my* timeline. I have no intention of going there in this one.

Shaking my head, I get to my feet, but it's hard. This body is so weak. If I'm going to do this, I'll need food and sleep and Chris's help as an anchor.

He stands beside me and we walk to his car, but once we're inside, I lay my hand over his, preventing him from starting the engine.

"Hear me out," I say. "I have a story for you. You're probably not going to believe it, but I can give you proof if I have to."

He studies my face in the fading light of evening, then nods once. "Whatever you need, Flynn."

So he's humoring me. Whatever. So long as I get out what I have to say.

I talk. He listens. A couple of times he starts to interrupt, but a glare from me sets him quiet again. Even if he doesn't believe me, I make it clear that I believe every word I'm saying. When I finish, the sun is long set, the shorter days of fall turning the air crisp and cool. The car sits silent beside the graveyard. Beside Genesis.

When the minutes stretch to fifteen, I tell him, "You're allowed to talk now."

"I don't know what to say." He stares out the front windshield at the passing cars on Festivity Boulevard. Across the street, a medical helicopter lands on the hospital's helipad. Except for us, the church lot remains empty, nothing and everything happening here on a Thursday. "I want it to be true," Chris goes on. He shifts in his seat to face me. "You have no idea how desperately I want it."

"Oh, I have some idea," I say with a sad smile.

He ducks his head. "Sorry. Of course you do. But maybe that's all this is, a desperate wanting on your part? A fantasy you've created with a possible happy ending when no happy endings are really possible?" When he looks up, I meet his gaze but say nothing more. The minutes pass. "Hope is a wonderful and dangerous thing, Flynn," Chris says at last. The pity and doubt have returned.

"I told you I could give you proof. I'd rather not. As bad off as I am, it'll take a lot out of me, and the side effects will probably be worse." Not sure what I'm going to do about that, especially one in particular, with Gen gone, but one problem at a time. "I'm going to need all my strength to take on Granfeld, whether she's as strong alive as she is dead or not. She's still powerful, at any point in her existence. But I'm also going to need your help, someone to call me back. I don't think that'll be a problem if I succeed. But if I fail, you'll have to help… guide me home."

Chris shakes his head. "Sorry, Flynn. I'm not going all in on this, not letting myself hope without proof. It's too much."

I put a hand on his shoulder. "I understand. How about we go back to your place? I should be lying down for this." My stomach growls loudly. "And I could use some energy before I start."

He drives us to the Village Pub and parks in the rear lot. Standing outside the kitchen entrance, I wait for him to duck inside and grab us some dinner. Then we walk up the back steps to the trio of apartments above the restaurant.

Gen and I had the middle one. Chris's place is on the right, and he unlocks the door while I stare at the next one over.

My heart aches. Mansions are nice, but I miss the coziness of the one-bedroom unit, me and Gen cuddling on the couch, watching football and me teaching her the nuances of the game, dinner for two in the tiny kitchen—her famous shepherd's pie, nights in her big comfortable bed beneath the whirring, creaking ceiling fan.

"Anyone live over there?" I ask as Chris gets his door open.

He gives me an odd look I can't quite interpret, then says, "No. There've been a couple of renters since the accident, but they haven't stuck around long."

Huh. Well, rent runs high in Festivity. They may have taken on more than they could financially handle.

We go inside and try to make small talk while we eat, not very successfully. Chris can share what he's been up to lately, but I have no idea what my alter ego has been about, and I don't think I want those details. I had to pay for all that booze somehow. I'm coming up with some pretty scary means of employment for an alcoholic ex-construction worker, 'cause I know I haven't been up on rooftops while intoxicated.

When we're done, I stretch out on the living room couch, a brown leather affair with cup holders built in at both ends. Very bachelor chic. Chris busies himself rinsing off the dishes and storing them in the washer, though he doesn't turn it on. The whole place is neat and orderly, exactly as I figured it would be since he runs his pub the same way. I've actually never been in here, since we always hang out downstairs or at our mansion with more space.

"Okay, what do you want me to do?" he says, drying his hands on a towel, then tossing it back through the archway onto the kitchen table.

"Dim the lights a little, and come over here," I tell him, nervous now. What if I can't do it from this body? I mean, it's me, but not. My brain knows the ropes, but I haven't actually gone walkies from here. And if I can't, he'll be calling his hospital friend and having me put away in a nice padded room.

Chris does as I ask, leaving the kitchen lights on but switching off the lamps on the end tables. I point to the beige carpet near my head, and he kneels beside me.

"I'm going to go out-of-body," I say. "Everyone tells me it's like watching me sleep. My breathing slows down. So does my pulse rate. I can touch stuff while I'm in spirit form, but not people, so I'll move some things around, let you know I'm here. Don't start calling to me unless it looks like I'm in distress. I don't really need a tether when I'm this close to my… home base, but you're a safety net, okay?"

"Uh-huh." In other words, right, sure, let's get this over with so I can call the funny farm.

"Oh, and you might want to have a trash can handy. I have a tendency to throw up after I walk."

That earns me an alarmed look. He reaches beneath the end table, drags out one of those mini wastebaskets people use for junk mail and such, and sets it beside me. "Good enough?"

I eye it dubiously, but I nod, really wishing I hadn't had dinner right before this. Then I close my eyes, take a couple of cleansing breaths, and *push.*

I'm relieved when I slip out-of-body within seconds, my spirit-self rising and standing beside my feet. I'm not so relieved when I glance down and I'm already flickering. This weak and tired, I'm using up my spiritual energy at an alarming rate. Better make this quick.

Chris yelps when I toss a throw pillow at his head, his eyes darting around, trying to figure out where I am. I shift a few knickknacks, flip the TV on and off, recline the La-Z-Boy, and for my grand finale, bring him a beer from his fridge, since it looks like he's going to need it.

He takes what appears to him to be a floating bottle from in front of his face, twists off the cap, and chugs half in one go. But in addition to shock, I'm seeing something else in his expression— hope. Because he just figured out that I might be able to save Genesis.

I let myself sink back into my body, take a deep real breath, cough a couple of times, then roll over and dry-heave over the useless little trash can. Thank goodness nothing comes up. By the time I slump against the cushions, he's ready with a cold cloth, a glass of water, and a couple of Motrin.

Good man.

"You really can do it," he breathes in a whisper, standing over me.

"Yeah."

"You were telling the truth? All of it?"

"Yeah."

"You can bring Genesis back."

I open my eyes to see him crying again and pull him down beside me on the couch. We hold each other a long time.

"I'll try," I tell him. Actually, I'll do it or I'll die trying. I've already made up my mind. "I'll need a good night's sleep before I make an attempt." I cross my legs against the sudden onslaught of arousal. Crap. It's stronger than usual, much more intense than it should be after such a short expenditure of power, but though my walk didn't last long, I did lose a lot of energy. That must be it. I've already learned I can't easily satisfy the need myself. Besides, doing that in Chris's apartment would be really weird. But I can sleep it off if it doesn't get much worse.

I'm about to suggest that I hit the sack for the night when a rapping sound comes through the wall—the wall his apartment shares with Gen's old one.

I glance at it, raising an eyebrow. "I thought you said no one lives there."

He doesn't meet my eyes. "No one does."

That doesn't make— Oh. Shit. Of course. People move in, but they move out fast. Yeah. A haunting would scare away most potential tenants. "Are you telling me that's Genesis?"

"Yeah," he says, shifting the trash can back to its original spot.

"Has she been communicating with you?" I can't quite keep the disappointment out of my voice. Gen's been talking to him but not me? I know Chris has no spirit-seeing ability, but I bet they've worked something out.

"Yes." He studies my face. "She tried to talk to you, too, but I guess after all that's happened, you wouldn't remember."

She tried to talk to me? I don't get it. I can't imagine attempting suicide if I could still see and hear and, considering my skill set, possibly touch Genesis. "What went wrong?"

He sighs and sits next to me again. "You freaked out. Completely. Totally. You called me, scared out of your wits, said she kept appearing, trying to speak with you. It wasn't that long after the Kat thing, and you couldn't handle it."

I chew on that awhile. Yeah, I was a different person four months ago. I'd seen two ghosts, my grandmother's, which put me into child

counseling sessions for half a year to get rid of
the nightmares, and Kat, who possessed me and
scared the quite literal piss out of me. I've come a
long, long way since then.

"The very last time we spoke on the phone
you were completely wasted, said you'd found a
way to block her out. I guess the alcohol interfered
with her ability to reach you. Not long after that,
she told me she'd given up trying."

My heart sinks. I can't imagine how much that
must have hurt her, dead or not, watching me turn
myself into an alcoholic to keep from seeing her.
Shit.

"And you talk to her, how?" I ask, staring at
the separating wall.

He shrugs. "We have a sort of yes-and-no
guessing game going on." Chris shifts toward the
wall as well. "Gen? You here? Did you see what
Flynn just did?"

It's silent for a long moment, then two solid
raps.

Chris looks at me. "That means yes."

"What about writing? Or a computer?"

Chris shakes his head. "No. She was pretty strong psychically in life, so we gave it a try.
She could turn the computer on but couldn't manipulate the keyboard. She could move a pencil
around but didn't have the fine motor skills to
write any words I could make out. It frustrated the
hell out of her. We decided to give up trying. She

was banging against the wall for hours after every failed attempt."

Yeah, I could imagine. Thinking, feeling, and only able to communicate by yes and no? That would drive me nuts.

Out-of-body, Gen and I could both interact with objects in the real world. But I have a feeling we might have more energy in that form than as a completely disembodied spirit.

He raises his voice again. "I don't know how much you heard or saw, but Flynn thinks she has a way to go back and stop your death," he says, speaking to the wall.

One very loud, resounding bang, so violent it shakes the framed seascape hanging above the couch.

I'm up and out the front door before he can say another word.

Chapter 61
Waiting Game

ROBERT DALTON remained in the Village Pub until the 2:00 a.m. closing. He'd had two beers, three sodas, and feigned interest in a baseball game and some late-night talk show. All for nothing. No sign of Chris McTalish. No sign of Flynn.

He paid his check, then wandered around Festivity's central lake for another hour, hoping he might spot their return. But no. When the mosquitoes decided he looked tasty, he knew he should call it quits for now.

Instead of returning to his Doubletree Suites, he took a second room in the Festivity Bohemian Hotel, only a block from the pub. Money posed no problem. He possessed substantial funds, had multiple lucrative investments. And if those ever ran dry, well, he was an eraser. He'd simply erase any record of debts he might incur.

He opened wide the curtains of his new lodgings, having requested a room facing downtown, and therefore, the Village Pub. Festivity lay silent, all nightlife ended, a misty fog blanketing the lake like a thousand gathered ghosts.

He'd return to McTalish's establishment as soon as it opened for business once more. In the meantime, he'd sleep and gather his thoughts. But if he didn't find Flynn on his next attempt, things could get messy. He'd be entering his madness days.

And by the time those passed once more, he would likely be too late to help Flynn.

Or himself.

Chapter 62
Hope Eternal

CHRIS HAD seen some crazy shit in his life.

Okay, he hadn't actually seen it, but he'd heard about it through Genesis: spirit contact, possession, curses. When he realized she could still speak to their parents after their deaths, he'd been jealous at first. So unfair that Gen had that connection, that closeness, while he struggled through being both brother and parent to her without their guidance, running the business, making it successful, trying to keep Gen out of trouble of all sorts, including dark magic addiction.

And that's what turned the tide for him—Gen's addiction, seeing what these "gifts" could do to a person, how they could control, how hard she fought them. She let him sit in on a few client sessions too. He witnessed the pain the spirits of the dead conveyed through her, Gen experiencing every bit of it along with them, and the exhaustion afterward. He often wondered if her invitation to watch her work had been carefully calculated, if she knew he'd felt cheated, though he tried so hard to never let on. Her gift wasn't her fault. She hadn't chosen it, and he wasn't sure she would have if given the option.

Then came Flynn. And he knew, with absolute certainty, that he'd never want to go through what she was currently going through.

Chris had never seen a more lost soul than Flynn's when she'd told her tale. To have had Genesis and then not, in the blink of an eye, to have had her entire world ripped away from her and yet remember what she'd had seconds before.

To have not only her fate but Gen's resting squarely on her shoulders.

When Flynn proved the whole thing true, he couldn't believe her strength.

Four months gone, Chris had begun to accept Gen's loss. He still grieved; every time he went to place fresh flowers on her grave, he lost it. But having a channel of communication with his sister, even one so limited, helped. Then Flynn came along and tore the half-healed wound wide open.

He might get Gen back, might never have to go through the last four painful months, might remember none of these dark, horrible times.

Chris followed Flynn into the hallway to the apartment next door, where she was yanking hard at the knob, trying to get in. Lights flickered on and off in the windows, bright flashes he'd come to interpret as Gen's anxiety. Knocking resounded on the inside of the door, sporadic, staccato bursts of her frustration. The last time he'd seen her so worked up was the night Flynn had finally succeeded in shutting her out.

"Key. I need a key. But... dammit." Flynn pulled harder on the knob, wrenching it back and forth so hard it loosened in its setting. "If I had my tools...." She backed off as far from the door as she could, pressing her spine against the railing of the narrow walkway that ran in front of the three apartments, like she intended to throw herself into the barrier separating her from the woman she loved, break it down.

"Flynn," he said, stopping her midlaunch. "I have the key."

She froze, fixated on the door. "Key? But...."

"Yeah, hon, let me just go get it." Once he reassured himself she wouldn't do damage to her body or the door, he fetched his key ring from inside his own apartment, worked Gen's key off the ring, and pressed it into Flynn's palm.

The lights and banging continued, now at counterpoint with hard rock music blaring from the stereo in Gen's living room—one of the CDs Flynn had brought over and left behind after the drowning. He was surprised the neighbors on the other side hadn't come out to investigate all this racket in the middle of the night. Maybe they were away.

Flynn returned to the door, fumbled the key on her first attempt, cursed, picked it up, and finally managed to get inside. The moment her booted foot touched the foyer tile, everything stopped— no lights, no sound. The pitch-dark interior lay before them like a pathway to the Twilight Zone.

"What… happened?" Flynn whispered, staring into the darkness. "Why the light show?" She glanced at him over her shoulder, her face pale and stricken.

He shrugged. "Not sure. She's upset about something." Pissed would probably be the better term. He had some guesses at the cause, but if he knew Genesis at all, Flynn would find out soon enough. His sister could get furious, but she couldn't stay silent, not for long.

Flynn ran her hand along the wall until she found the switch and turned on the living room lamps. She gasped. Chris stared into the corners, searching for what had her so startled and seeing nothing.

"It hasn't changed," Flynn breathed.

Ah. Right.

"After I figured out she'd come back and the second set of tenants moved out, I, um, rented it myself. I pulled all Gen's stuff out of storage and put it back as best I could. Figured it would make her more comfortable, having familiar surroundings and all. I'm sure I screwed up some of the details, but the big pieces are in place."

"It's perfect," Flynn said, tears falling again.

She crossed the living room, past the Laura Ashley couches Gen had loved so much, popped the CD tray on the stereo, then lifted out and held the disk. "Aerosmith. Thought I'd lost this for good." Flynn returned it to the slot almost reverently and slid it closed. "I wonder if it's still there back in my timeline." She turned toward him and explained, "We bought a new sound system when we moved. But I think the old one's still in a box in the garage somewhere."

"Once you fix this, you'll have to look," Chris said.

Another bang on the wall, louder than that first one had been. A vase leaning against it began to topple, but Flynn dove for it, saving the ceramic from shattering on the floor. She righted it carefully, moving it a few inches away from the wall.

"What the hell, Chris? Doesn't she want to live? Doesn't she… doesn't she want to be with me anymore?" She reached up and swiped the tears from her eyes, then scrubbed at her face with both hands.

I think she wants you *to live, Flynn.* But he didn't say it out loud. This was Genesis's argument. He'd let her have it.

"I can't see her. I should be able to. Why isn't she here? Why did she stop communicating?"

"I think she's waiting for me to leave," Chris said.

Two raps, softer, almost apologetic.

"It's okay," he said to the room at large. "I understand." For a moment, Chris thought Flynn might beg him to stay. Her eyes were wild, skin pale, breathing too fast. Then she shook herself, settled her shoulders, and nodded.

"I'm staying here tonight, if that's okay with you… and her," she said.

"Fine by me," Chris told her. The walls said nothing. "Come over in the morning, when you've made a final decision on all this."

"The decision is made," Flynn said, jaw set, fists clenched, expression fierce.

"Yeah. I kinda figured that."

The apartment remained as silent as a tomb.

Chris turned and left, excluded once again, but he didn't mind. Flynn and Genesis were meant to be together, in whatever way they could.

Chapter 63
Confessions

THE APARTMENT door shuts. It's dead silent. I'm alone.

The lights go out.

Okay, not entirely alone.

"Gen?" I call in almost, but not quite, a whisper. The back of my neck prickles. Goose bumps flare along my arms despite the jacket I'm wearing. It's too much like the first time Kat tried to possess me, right here in this very room.

I wonder if this is some kind of test.

"Not nice, Gen. I know you're pissed at me, but can't you be angry with some lights on?"

Nothing.

Fuck. Four months ago, Gen liked to test me on lots of things, one being how well I could handle all the psychic magical crap. I failed most of them back then. I have to remember, this Genesis never got past that point in our relationship, never saw me grow and change and adapt.

Holding both hands out in front of me, I cross the room, baby steps taking me to the big curtained windows facing Front Street. One pull has the heavy fabric open and streetlight shining in to cast long lit streaks across the cream carpeting. Now that I can see a bit, I reach for the nearest table lamp. It shocks my fingertips. I jerk my hand away.

Fine. We'll do this in the dark.

But after standing beside the coffee table for a full minute, I have no idea what to say. The arousal from my earlier power usage still taunts me, every inch of flesh too sensitive, but I force that away.

"I… I'm guessing you're mad at me. When you're mad, it pretty much always has something to do with me," I begin, speaking into the darkness, ears and eyes straining for the slightest indication of her presence. "Really wish you'd come out and tell me what I've done wrong."

Nothing.

I'll just keep guessing, then.

"Is it… is it because I shut you out? That must have really hurt. And I'm sorry. So sorry. I can't believe she… I… did that. I just wasn't ready for that, I guess. But I'm not the same person. If you heard what I told Chris, well, you know I'm not. I'm ready to hear you now. Really, really ready, because…." My voice breaks. "Because I need you. I need you so much." Sobs shatter my speech, gut-wrenching sobs that sink me to the floor, my arms wrapped around my abdomen because this pain runs so deep it's become physical.

With all the fucking crying I've done the past few days, you'd think that well would have dried up by now. And when it finally does and I'm sniffling and wiping my eyes on the shoulder of my T-shirt, the apartment is still silent.

"Shit, Gen. What else? What do I have to say? What do I have to do?"

A sudden, horrible thought occurs. Maybe it's something I *didn't* do.

"Is it because I didn't save you?" I whisper. "Is that it? I tried. I know I tried. I died trying. It wasn't the same me, but I know I would have given everything I had to keep us together."

My head jerks toward a soft sound coming from the kitchen archway. A sigh? I search the darkness, but my eyesight can't penetrate it.

"It's not my fault the paramedics brought me back. I swear to God, Gen, if I couldn't save you, I would have rather stayed dead."

And there it was, the absolute truth. When I first arrived in this timeline, I couldn't conceive of why I'd be killing myself. But I hadn't known that Gen had left my life. Now I'm surprised I managed to stay alive as long as I did.

"I'll make it right, Gen, I swear. If that's what you want, I'll make it right." I'm practically shouting now, desperate for her to hear me, to acknowledge anything I've said. I sweep a hand around at the apartment. "I never wanted anything but this.

No magic, no mansions. Just this—this apartment, you doing your readings for your clients and me working construction, coming home every night to you… every night… just me and you…." My vision blurs. My throat closes up.

Using the coffee table for leverage, I push up to my feet and stagger toward the bedroom and through it, where the lavender potpourri arouses every fond memory of the two of us together and tears at my soul like I'm being flayed. My hand hits the wall and what I hope is a light switch, but instead I only succeed in turning on the old, creaky ceiling fan. I crash through the door to the master bath, moving by memory since I still can't see a damn thing.

"Fuck it. Fuck all of it. The Registry can fight their own damn battles. Get another hero. I'm done."

I flip on the bathroom light, surprised when it works, and blink in the sudden glare, then jump at my own reflection in the mirror. Just me. Alone. So fucking alone. Well, not for long. I pull off my jacket and throw it on the floor, then unwrap the gauze from my forearm, tearing it away when it won't come loose. It takes opening three different drawers before I find the razor blades—Chris was right about messing up some of the details when he put Gen's things back—but there's an open package in the bottommost drawer. She never did care for the electric razors, said they couldn't get her legs smooth enough.

I rip a blade out and hold it up, the light glinting off the sharp metal. Perfect.

"Mom always complained I never finished what I started." I laugh, a semihysterical sound. It takes a minute before I regain control. I focus on my face in the mirror. "You hear me, Gen? If you won't come to me, then I'm coming to you." I lower the blade to start at my wrist, the edge just piercing the skin.

It hurts. God, it hurts. And it's going to hurt so much more. But it will be nothing compared to the pain I have inside. I'll cut that pain out of me... I'll... I'll....

I dig deeper. Blood flows....

A soft hand covers the one holding the blade, stilling me.

"Stop, Flynn. If you love me, please stop."

Chapter 64
Declarations

"LET GO of the blade," Gen told her, holding Flynn's hand still. Blood welled up from beneath her fingers. Had she already cut too deep?

Flynn didn't move. "I'm not sure I can," she said, voice raw and strained. She had a white-knuckled grip on the metal, all her determination behind her actions.

"Sure you can. I'll help you." One by one, Gen pried Flynn's fingers off the razor blade until it clattered into the sink, spattering the white ceramic in tiny dots of red. Once revealed, the wound didn't seem much worse than it had when Flynn started this in her hotel room. Gen had watched her there, too, almost as helpless to stop her now as she was then.

Almost.

"Come on," she said. "Clean that off and wrap it back up and we'll talk."

Flynn moved as if on autopilot, robotically turning the water on, rinsing the new slice, and re-wrapping it. "You couldn't have shown up a little sooner?" she asked with a low humorless chuckle.

"No," Gen said, "I couldn't have."

That earned her a raised eyebrow in the mirror. Then Flynn blinked. "Why can't I see your reflection?"

"That requires more energy. If you want to see me, turn around."

Flynn froze. Genesis sighed.

"I thought you weren't afraid of me anymore," she said.

"I'm not afraid of you. I'm afraid that if I turn around, you won't be there." She choked a little on those last words, *and I'm not sure I can take that* going unsaid.

Genesis placed her hands on both Flynn's arms and turned her around. The stricken expression on Flynn's face hurt even worse than when she'd seen it in the mirror. For a couple of breaths they stared at each other; then Flynn practically fell into her, wrapping her arms around her like she'd never let go.

Except she'd have to.

The once strong body shook hard, but it felt warm and alive, and Gen reveled in it. So long since she'd held someone, since she'd felt this closeness. For four months she'd wanted this and Flynn had denied her. She gripped Flynn back, and though as a ghost she couldn't really cry, she wanted to.

"I can't stay too long," Gen said at last, pushing Flynn away just a little. "We should say what needs to be said."

"I'm sorry, I'm so fucking sorry," Flynn began. "I didn't mean… I couldn't control…."

Couldn't control what her other self had done. Genesis got it. It wasn't what she was after.

"I know," she said, rubbing Flynn's back, soothing her as best she could. "I know, shhh." It scared her, this Flynn, so powerful she glowed with magic to Gen's spiritual sight, so weakened by loss. Gen sensed the instability in her, how precariously she hung on the edge. Whatever she did or said to Flynn tonight, she had to tread carefully. This wasn't the woman she'd lost. It was someone better and worse in a hundred different ways.

"Please don't go," Flynn whispered, as if that was all she could manage.

"I won't by choice," Gen assured her, taking Flynn's hand and tugging her toward the bedroom. "Come on, let's sit somewhere comfortable. The bathroom is no place for this conversation." She led Flynn to the bed and pressed her down upon it, then sat next to her. She didn't bother with the lamp. The bathroom light lit the room well enough.

"Why are you so mad at me?" Flynn sounded almost childlike, and Gen stroked her hair like she would a little girl.

"That's not why I didn't come. Or why I made you stay in the dark. I wasted a lot of energy in my earlier… um… tantrum, and I had to recharge before I could manifest." If it were possible for a ghost to blush, she'd be doing it. "I'm sorry about shocking you with the lamp. I was drawing from the electricity. That's why I needed most of the lights off. Even so, I kind of rushed things, and I can't stay too long, so let me get out what I need to tell you."

Flynn sniffed and wiped her face on her sleeve. Genesis passed her a tissue from the box by the bed. "Okay."

"I don't want you to do this thing, stopping Granfeld. I don't want you to risk your life again."

Flynn's features hardened. "Not negotiable," she said, facing forward, not looking at her.

She reached out and turned Flynn toward her. "I want you to live. I already watched you die once."

Flynn's brow furrowed in confusion.

Genesis swallowed hard, then took a deep breath she no longer needed and went on. "When you dove down to the Charger, I was already gone, Flynn. But I was watching. The windows were open. The car was full of water and I wasn't breathing. You knew. You had to have known." Everything poured out in a rush. "And yet you wouldn't stop. No matter how hard I tried to tell you, reach you, you wouldn't hear me, and you wouldn't stop. You kept going up for more air, kept going down, though the car was sinking lower and lower and it was getting harder and harder, and all the while I was screaming, *screaming* for you to give up, but you wouldn't." She paused, struggling with the memory, then continued. "When you finally realized you'd never get me free, you wrapped yourself up in my seat belt, opened your mouth, and *sucked* the water *in*. Then you just held on to me and waited for it to end."

She didn't mention the way Flynn had convulsed, the way her eyes had bulged, then gone blank, the way her grip had loosened and she'd floated away toward her rescuers. Her worst nightmare come true again, being so close to someone while they died. She'd felt her parents drown, too, in a simultaneous connection that haunted her for years afterward.

As a ghost, this would likely haunt her for eternity.

Genesis trembled hard, her ghostly form flickering with pain. Flynn pulled her in close and held on, just like she'd done in the car that night.

"So," Gen said, clearing her throat, "I want you to live."

"This isn't living," Flynn said. "Not without you. It hurts like I've swallowed a thousand needles and they're all trying to tear their way out of me."

Oh, Flynn. "You can *have* me. Don't you see? Now that you're willing to hear and accept, you can have me. You can quit drinking to block me out. You can take the job Chris is offering you, move back in here, and get on with your life. And I'll come to you—"

"What?" Flynn said, pushing her away and standing to face her. "Once a day? Once every two days? Three?"

Genesis dropped her gaze to the floor. "More like once a week," she admitted. "That's still more than most ghosts can manage. But it's something, Flynn. And maybe, if you get yourself together, you'll find someone else and—"

"No!" Flynn grabbed Genesis by the shoulders and shook her, hard. "Don't you get it? Don't you feel it? There. Is. No. One. Else. No one, Gen. Not for me. Not ever." She released one hand, slamming her palm against her chest, the thud of the impact making Genesis wince in sympathy, though Flynn hardly seemed to notice it. "You're in here. Since the day we met at that stupid dog festival, you've always been here. That day, I vowed to make you mine. And I am never, ever letting you go."

Chapter 65
Battle Ready

WHEN I finish my pronouncement, Genesis just looks at me. Getting a lot of that lately. I blow out a frustrated breath. "What?"

"You just... I mean.... You've barely been able to tell me you love me, and now...."

"We're married, Gen," I say quietly.

"We really are," she says, incredulous.

"Yeah." For a terrifying moment, I wonder if she never quite felt what I feel for her, but then she pulls me down and kisses me with more passion, more desperation, than I've ever experienced from Genesis, and that's saying a lot.

"You're part of me too," she says, laying me back on the bed and resting her head on my chest. "If you don't succeed in this plan of yours, you'll end up here, with me, right?"

"Sure, Gen. Sure." But we both know that if I don't manage to destroy Tempest Granfeld, it will only be because I've died trying.

We make love, slowly and sensuously at first, but with more urgency as Gen starts to fade. In the end, I'm crying out so loudly with the pleasure she gives me that Chris yells from his apartment, "Hey, Flynn, Gen, you two okay over there?"

Before Genesis can waste energy responding, I reach behind me and rap twice on the wall above the headboard. It's not the wall his apartment shares with this one, but I know he'll hear it. We heard *him,* after all. They're all thin, and I blush, thinking about what else he might have heard over the year that Gen and I lived here. She covers her mouth, not that anyone but me would hear her giggling, but it's still adorable.

Except, I can see her face right through her fingers.

I reach to take Genesis's hand, and mine passes through hers. My throat tightens. "Don't go," I manage to force out.

She offers a sad smile. "I have to." Her image flickers, then goes so transparent only an outline remains. "I love you, Flynn," she says, rushing through the words. "I'll always love you. Please, please be careful."

"I'll try," I promise, though it's the worst of all the empty ones I've ever given her. All the times I've left her to worry, the crazy risks I've taken, I regret putting her through that. And yet I'm going to do it again.

I want to touch her just once more, but my fingers clutch at empty air.

"Live, Flynn. Live." The breeze from the creaking overhead fan carries her voice away.

I AWAKEN to a damp pillow and morning sunrise glowing through the bedroom windows. I didn't sleep long, but I slept hard, the emotional outpouring of the night before exhausting me and crashing me into oblivion mere minutes after Genesis left. The smell of coffee and bacon rouses me further, and I grab a shower, throw my clothes on, and stumble into Gen's kitchen, where Chris has breakfast ready and waiting on her table.

"If I were straight, I'd marry you," I tell him, slurping down the caffeine as fast as its molten temperature will allow.

Chris laughs, as I hoped he would. "I take it things went okay last night." He tugs on the tag at the back my shirt.

I go to tuck it in, then realize the whole thing's inside out. "Um, yeah," I say, heat rushing to my cheeks.

He shakes his head. "Still the same old Flynn."

I wish. The old Flynn might have embarrassed easily (and still does), but she had no powers, no supernatural stressors, and all the love she'd ever need. Cliche or not, you truly don't recognize what you have until it's gone.

We finish eating in companionable silence, both lost in our own thoughts. I sop up the last bite of eggs with a bit of toast, push away from the table, and stand. "Let's get this over with."

"What do you need me to do? Same as last night?" He sets the dishes in the sink.

I nod. "Pretty much, only I *will* need you to call me back, let's say after about forty-five minutes."

Cassie let me run out-of-body for at least an hour at a time, but that body had been stronger than this one.

"Sooner if I seem to be in physical trouble here. We may have to do this a few times, and over a few days before I catch up with her."

He follows me into the living room, where I stretch out on the larger of Gen's flowered Laura Ashley couches. The huge purple flowers with green leaves covering them always made me want to gag, but I never told her.

I never told her a lot of things. And the things I did say, I never said enough.

I shake myself from the onrushing wave of depression, knowing I'll need all my focus for what's next.

"What happens when you do catch up with her?" Chris asks, tossing down a throw pillow and kneeling on it beside the couch.

"I suspect you'll never know any of this happened. *I* will. I remember everything this version of me experiences. At least I think I do. But you? You'll probably be picking me up off the Village Pub patio where I fell when all this shit went down, none the wiser." I stop, rolling on my side to face him. "We're close, you know, in the other timeline."

He takes my hand and squeezes it. "I can see that. And it doesn't surprise me at all. You're exactly the kind of person I'd want for Genesis and for a sister-in-law."

My eyes mist over. I blink the forming tears away.

"What happens if you fail?" he asks, quieter now.

It's hard to shrug while lying down, but I manage it. "I either end up back here… or I don't."

Chris doesn't bother asking what that means. He already knows.

I spent some time researching early-1900s New York while I was convalescing after Leo's attack, so even though Granfeld's actual address had no images on the internet from that time period, I can get to the general vicinity.

Closing my eyes, I take a deep breath, picture the neighborhood in my mind, and *push*.

As my spirit leaves my body for its hundred-plus-year journey, I'm vaguely aware of a pounding in the background, like maybe someone is knocking on Chris's door one apartment over, but it's too late to stop myself, and I'm gone.

THE WORLD reforms around me, and my knees hit dirt road. After the requisite nausea, blurred vision, and dizziness pass, I push to my feet and take stock. I'm back in my kickass Flynn gear, so go me, and in my recreated image, I'm no longer gaunt and pale.

Clapboard houses run down both sides of a tree-lined street filled with horse manure alongside wheel ruts from both wagons and early motorcars. Tempest's address lies on the outskirts of the city, in a time when the city was much, much smaller. I've never been to modern-day New York. Someday I'll have to go, just for the comparison.

Too aware of my time limits, I walk a block from where I landed to the front stoop of the smallest house on the street. Can't be more than three or four rooms, with chipping paint, a porch that sags in the middle, and two of the steps up to it rotted through. The windows facing the street are dark, but that's not surprising, considering it appears to be about midafternoon. I confirm the house numbers against my memory of her address. Yep, this is the place.

As I stare at the abode of my greatest enemy, it occurs to me that I have no plan of action beyond 1. Find Granfeld. 2. Kill Granfeld. Yeah. That's me. Always prepared.

I slip around to the back of the house, down a narrow space between her place and a slightly larger home next door, faint singing and the sound of a crying baby coming from within it. Discarded bottles and newspapers litter the ground.

The backyard resembles more of a junkyard—no more than a patch of mostly dirt with a few bursts of green poking up here and there and discarded household items: an icebox, a radiator, some other random rusted metal parts.

A smaller set of steps leads to the rear entrance, and I climb them to peek through the single windowpane embedded in the door… and catch my breath.

She's home.

And she's not alone.

The room beyond the door appears to be a combination living space/kitchen, though the kitchen consists of a few cabinets, a slightly newer-looking icebox, and a hotplate on a counter. The living area holds a wood table, a few chairs, and a single couch, though she and her guest are making full use of the latter.

Granfeld, wearing only her bloomers and a bra-type thing, lies atop a man wearing nothing at all. I can't discern much more than that. She's blocking my view of his face. But from their movements, it's not hard to guess what they're up to.

I grasp the doorknob and turn, stunned when it actually does. Ah, 1900s living. Everybody trusted everybody, and doors got left unlocked. Or, considering the state of the property, she figured she had nothing worth stealing, so why bother? I push it inward, ducking and cringing when it creaks. I'm not sure if Tempest can see me when I'm out-of-body. I can't see her that way, but as a spirit at least, she's stronger than me. And if she's drawn energy from a seer, then she'd have the ability herself. I'm not taking chances.

"Who is it?" the man calls, his voice muffled.

"No one. The wind. That door's always coming open. Landlord won't fix it."

"So long as it's not my wife."

They both chuckle. Lovely couple.

Once the grunting and groaning pick up volume and speed, I nudge the door farther, then farther still until I can slip inside. They're really going at it now. Granfeld's bloomers lie on the floor, and she's riding him in all her skinny, sweaty, pale glory. Ick. I will never be able to unsee this.

On the upside, it's driven away every ounce of arousal my coming here might have caused.

I'm halfway into the living room when she glances over her shoulder at the open door and I freeze. If she can see me, there's no hiding now. But she stares right through me, shrugs, and carries on.

At this point, I'm torn. Her partner is no angel. He's cheating on his wife. But that doesn't mean he deserves the sort of feedback he might receive if I pull power from Granfeld while he's here. On the flip side, I'm on a tight schedule. I estimate it's been about twenty minutes already. If this doesn't get done soon, I'm going to have to make a return trip, and I so don't want to do that.

I head on over to one of the wooden chairs, settle into it while facing away from them, and wait. It doesn't take all that long. Big surprise.

The man gives one final grunt, the couch squeaks beneath them, and then silence except for heavy breathing.

"Well then," he says when he can speak without gasping, "that was ten dollars, wasn't it?"

Hah. Homemaker my ass. I nearly laugh before I remember that ten bucks was a lot back then. *And*, a little voice in my head whispers, *you don't know what* you *were doing for cash to pay for all that liquor your other self has been drinking. Succubi need sex.* I tell the voice to shut the fuck up.

"Twelve," Granfeld counters. So the only cookies the homemaker's been baking are his.

I shift in my seat to watch the impending battle.

The man raises her off him to look her in the eyes. "Hell, you weren't worth more than seven. Maybe I don't pay you at all," he says, fingering his mustache. "Maybe you just consider yourself lucky I don't turn you over to the cops. And don't you even think about telling my wife. Lieutenant McGuire's a buddy of mine. He'll stick you in a cell and throw away the key if you do."

Instead of firing off a comeback, Tempest smiles like sweet honey. My stomach turns. I have a bad feeling.

"How about I give you something special instead? Something worth the money." She shifts her body, positioning herself over his limp dick, rubbing herself sensuously back and forth over it. I swallow bile.

"Eh?" His lips curl in a predatory grin. "What've you got in mind?"

The next instant, she hits him with everything she has. Hands raised, arms outstretched, her power flares out of her in two fiery orange streams, nailing him midchest and pulling not magic, because as far as I can tell he has none, but life. "We could have done this the fun way, but since you're planning on stiffing me—" She laughs, head thrown back and eyes wild. "—not that you're capable of making anything stiff enough for my taste…."

I couldn't see it when she attacked Chris, but it's visible to me while I'm in this form—sparkling energy like a waterfall of diamonds. No magic comes close to its beauty. The most precious commodity, and she's sucking it out of him.

His face pales, eyes bulging, mouth agape like a fish on a hook.

The guy's an asshole, but no one deserves this. I stand, raising my own hands, preparing to interrupt her little party. My energy gathers in my core, writhing like snakes, ready to draw every ounce of her power into me and….

The open back door slams against the interior wall with a tremendous bang. Everyone jumps, even the poor guy on the couch, as the last person in the world I'd expect to see staggers into the room.

"Dad?" I say, heading for him at a quick pace and catching him as he falls. "What the fuck are you doing here?"

I ease him to the floor and glance back over my shoulder. Granfeld stares at the now wide-open door, oblivious to the two out-of-body spirits in her midst. Her client pants for breath beneath her, barely conscious. After a moment, she shrugs and returns to sucking his life force dry. If I don't intervene soon—

"You can't do it, Flynn," Dad grinds out between a gasp and a groan. His spirit sends an odd crackling energy through mine—not warm and comforting like touching Gen's out-of-body essence, but not unpleasant either. Still, something about it feels wrong. It's inconsistent, like he's not entirely here.

"Do what? And you didn't answer my question. I didn't know you could time walk," I say.

"Neither… did I. Not without piggybacking on your power. Have to go back. You too."

I set my jaw. "Not until I do what I came for. Gen's life depends on it."

"If you destroy Tempest Granfeld here and now, *your* life depends on it, as does mine."

Behind us, the man cries out, a long, painful howl, then silence. Another look confirms my fears. He's not moving, not breathing. And there won't be any psychic healers happening by to revive him. He's gone. I'm too late to save him.

"What are you talking about?" Not my fault. If Dad hadn't distracted me—

"She's pregnant, Flynn."

I blink at him, then study Granfeld, who's just climbing off the couch, her body suffused with an unearthly glow of stolen energy only visible to me and probably my father. Her flat belly shows no sign of pregnancy, but I suppose she could be in the early months.

Okay, no, I don't want to kill a pregnant woman. I've got enough guilt to carry around. It's not the fetus's fault its mother is a raving lunatic sadistic bitch. Guess I'll have no choice but to return at a later date. And I appreciate Dad for coming all this way to keep that off my conscience. But what does any of that have to do with…? Wait.

"No," I breathe. "Oh fuck no. Do not tell me this." Still supporting his ethereal body, I force him to meet my eyes. "You didn't just erase yourself and Mom from the archives. You tried to erase Granfeld too. I thought you'd removed the two of you to protect yourselves and me, that clearing most of Granfeld's entry was an error. But it wasn't, was it?"

He shakes his head. "Someone came down and interrupted my work. I wanted to get it all."

"Because Tempest Granfeld is my…?" Come on, Dad. You hid it. You're going to have to spell it out.

"She's your great-grandmother, my grandmother. And if you kill her before she has that baby that she doesn't even know about yet, you'll wipe out the entire family line."

Chapter 66
Family Ties

FOR A heartbeat, Robert thought Flynn might deck him. Which would have been a neat trick considering he was already down for the count. Coming to warn her had taken almost all he had. Upon arrival, he'd nearly faded out.

And he had no idea where he would have ended up if that had indeed occurred.

The archival records he'd erased didn't state how Tempest Granfeld had died, even prior to him erasing them. But he'd done other research early on to remove as many traces of the family as possible. According to an obscure newspaper clipping from a 1908 *New York Times*, she'd passed away giving birth to her first and only child. In reality, she'd gone out-of-body seconds before that death. Otherwise, she wouldn't have the power she held now. Not a true spirit, but with no body to return to, she'd quickly gone mad. Or at least that was Robert's theory.

And the child? Placed in foster care until he was adopted by the Dalton family at the age of two.

He shared all this with Flynn as she scowled and helped him outside the ramshackle hovel Granfeld called home. Part of him wasn't surprised Tempest had turned to dark magic. A being of her power reduced to this poverty? Ridiculous. "You can't get her while she's giving birth. The timing's too delicate, and the backlash could still manage to kill the newborn."

"So what am I supposed to do now?" Flynn asked, her semisolid figure seated on the back step and sinking a little into it. They couldn't remain out-of-body much longer.

"Destroy her after she's physically dead."

"Been there. Tried that. Didn't work." She rested her face in her palms, though he could see her hopeless expression right through them.

"You didn't have me along the last time," he said.

Her head came up. "No offense, but you aren't exactly a powerhouse, here."

"If you feed me energy, over the course of a day, I'll have enough to assist you in a two-pronged attack. It will have to be carefully done, of course. Just as your mother nearly drained me, I, being of the opposite sex, could accidentally drain you. But my control is excellent, and you are the stronger in this pairing. Besides, it's pretty clear you've tried to destroy her before and failed. I'm guessing you had help then too?"

Flynn's face flushed. "Yeah, a couple of other members of the Registry, including Genesis and President Argyle."

"There are reasons why a team of gifted psychics couldn't defeat her." He had all her attention now. Good. "It isn't common knowledge, and for our own preservation, I wouldn't want it to be, but only another incubus or succubus can kill an incubus or succubus. We are that powerful, Flynn. We can be temporarily weakened, even contained for a short period of time, but we cannot be permanently destroyed by anyone other than our own kind. Our plan to share power between us is a good one. It should work."

"It has to." She gazed across the backyard. "Granfeld attacked Chris right before the wedding. We can catch her then."

Robert shook his head. "That never happened. You're no longer in that timeline, remember?"

"Fuck."

Yes, she apparently did.

"This. This right here is why succubi go crazy," she said.

Robert nodded. "One of many reasons, but for the ones who can regularly time walk, yes, that may be true."

"Only one place, then," she went on. "I didn't want to cut it close, but, well, I know she appeared to Genesis right before Gen's... death." Flynn swallowed hard. "If I destroy her there, then anyone else she took before then will be gone forever."

He rested a hand on her shoulder, and though it sank a few inches into her spirit, he knew she felt his touch. "You can't save them all, Flynn. And in the long run, you'll do far more good alive than dead."

Flynn snapped her head around to stare at him.

"No, I'm not telepathic. But even in the short time I've become reacquainted with you, I know you're something of a hero type. Don't try to tell me it never crossed your mind to go ahead and kill Granfeld here, even if it meant your own death, if it would save Genesis and all the others."

Flynn didn't answer. It was answer enough.

"You can't save them all," Robert repeated. "Save the ones you can."

Chapter 67
Plan B

CHRIS IS heartbroken when I pop back into my body and he doesn't immediately snap into a world where Genesis still lives. I can't comfort him, though. I'm too busy vomiting and getting out of the way of Dad doing the same. We've only got one trash can between us, and we make quite the mess of Gen's cream-colored carpet before we're through. But as Genesis would have said, that's what carpet cleaners are for.

I hate to admit it, but I'm kinda glad Gen's too wiped out to manifest for a few days. I don't think I could handle her disappointment over our failure to bring her back to life. On the downside, I don't get to see her or spend time with her, and the sexual arousal from my power usage is a whole other issue. It's not too bad, since I only made one trip so far, more of an annoyance than a need, but it's a distraction I might not be able to afford if things get dicey in our second run.

Chris rallies from his funk once we tell him our new plan. Over the next hours, he gives us every detail he can remember about what he saw outside the Village Pub's kitchen entrance the day Gen died. When he's gone over it for the fourth time, he takes off to grab some things from his place. In the meantime, I let Dad pull energy from me.

"Normally, this would be done through sexual contact," he says, simply resting a hand on mine. My fingers tingle with pins and needles, and I'm a little lethargic. Otherwise I notice nothing. "But since that would be inappropriate and distasteful in oh so many ways...."

I suppress a shudder. "Thanks so much for that mental image, Dad."

He offers an apologetic smile. "You are a sensual, sexual being, Flynn. While societal taboos forbid sex between fathers and daughters, brothers and sisters, and I am wholly in favor of those restrictions," he hastens to add at my raised eyebrow, "our ancestors practiced no such beliefs. At their origin, there is only one line of succubi and incubi. Somewhere in medieval Europe, your mother and I share some common ancestry. The legends have much in them that is incorrect about our kind."

"Wait. I thought we were only called 'succubi' or 'incubi' because we can pull others' powers and because of the sexual side effects." Am I understanding him correctly? Because if I am....

We pause the conversation as Chris returns with some plastic bags of groceries and heads through the arch into the kitchen.

"No, Flynn. We are the creatures of legend. It's just that the legends are often wrong. And I erased most of the information about us from the archives."

I let that sit for a bit. Cooking smells carry from the stove into the living room, and the fridge opens and closes, Chris humming some tune all the while. Really glad he's not in here right now. "You're saying we're not actually human," I whisper.

"We're human enough," Dad says, patting my hand. "The rest is semantics… and a little sexual power."

"Hey," Chris obliviously interrupts, coming back into the room, "I was wondering, how did you even know Flynn was up here?" He brings us each a grilled cheese sandwich from Gen's kitchen made with the supplies he gathered from his own apartment.

"I bribed one of your patio waitresses to tell me where you lived," Dad says to him without remorse or any indication of the massive change of subject. "Then I saw the flare of Flynn's power through the curtains of the unit next door to yours, and I ran over here as quickly as I was able."

"Speaking of able," I say around a mouthful of gooey cheese and bread, "you're still looking a little pale. Won't you be better after a good night's sleep? You can take this couch." No way am I letting him sleep in Genesis's bed, whether I'm there or not.

He gives me a sheepish smile. "It needs to be tonight, I'm afraid. Unless, of course, you wish to wait an additional three days."

Oh. Right. The whole temporary madness punishment thing. Totally sucks.

"We'll go tonight."

Chapter 68
Turn About

WE DO catch a nap before our second try at Granfeld. Dad does take the couch. I lie in Gen's bed for a while before dozing off, feeling her all around me, knowing she's there even if I can't see or touch her. I catch a whiff of her perfume, and it lulls me into a sound sleep that Chris has to shake me from or I'd sleep all night.

This time around, I take the smaller couch, draping my too long legs over one of the armrests so that Dad can remain on the larger sofa. "Don't forget," I remind Chris. "You need to pull me back after about forty-five minutes. Then I'll have to guide Dad in."

That's what happened on the first go. Chris, being the closest person alive to me in this time-line, was able to bring me home. But Dad had to follow my voice or get stuck in 1907 where he would have eventually become permanently de-tached from his body. He's not a time walker, and he still seems shaky to me. But with my energy, I'm assuming he'll be okay.

Chris nods his understanding, and I lie back, closing my eyes. When I reopen them, I'm downstairs, on the Village Pub patio, arriving seconds before Dad, who staggers into me. I grab a hold of him, propping him against the bar well away from any customers who might pass through him and make things worse. I manage to snag my favorite seat and pull myself up into it while we wait for the initial sickness to pass.

"Is it always like this?" he asks, still a bit green.

"Always, though I'm getting used to it." It's true. The tables and chairs stop undulating a lot faster on this go-round. The more trips I take, the less adjustment I seem to need. Though it's not something I'd do for mere sightseeing. Beyond the discomfort, there are too many opportunities for disaster, fucking with time. "Can you walk?"

"I'll manage," he says, gritting his teeth.

I'm doubtful, but I nod, leading him to one of the low swinging metal gates in the fencing surrounding the patio. He follows, dodging a waitress with a full tray of drinks. Not that he'd knock her over, but he's figured out how bad the vertigo gets when two souls intersect.

No one notices the gate opening "by itself" as we leave. There's a Yankees game on the big-screen TVs. Someone just hit a double, and everyone's facing away.

We tried to time it so that we arrived a bit before our quarry. Chris remembered the game being on, the approximate hour, because Gen had been concerned about me being late, so we dropped in before that, assuming Granfeld would also show up ahead of her.

She must have been popping all over the place in the timeline to figure out the best moment to send Genesis into a risky situation. I wonder just how much of our lives she's watched, and it makes me squirm inside. Nothing too up close and personal. Gen would have seen her if, say, she dropped into our bedroom. But in a crowd? Especially before Gen knew what she looked like from the children's hospital? Yeah, she may have been studying us for quite a while.

Freaky.

My father and I stand in the walkway between the Village Pub and the diner next door, a cute '50s-style place that does most of its business at breakfast hours, so not many patrons occupy their patio. Almost every restaurant in downtown Festivity—and there are fourteen of them, counting bakeries and Starbucks—has outdoor seating as well as indoor. The townsfolk prize their pets, and they take them everywhere. If you want to have a successful eatery in this town, you provide a place for people to sit with their dogs, hence the Pampered Pup Festival where Gen and I met.

I lean against the pub's exterior wall and breathe in the humid July air. So weird to think

I'm also walking into Dead Man's Pond at this very moment, drawn in by the cursed charm at its bottom. Almost weirder to think Genesis is still alive and—

My thoughts cut off as a pop/flash alerts me to Granfeld's arrival. I blink the sparkles from my vision, taking a couple of blind steps in her direction before my sight fully clears. I have to stop her before she speaks with Genesis, before Gen even comes out of the kitchen, because if Gen sees me and my dad out-of-body here, it will screw up the timeline in God knows what other ways.

Granfeld comes into focus, standing at the back corner of the pub, leaning around it to watch for Gen's imminent exit. Odd. She's elected some more modern clothing for herself, maybe to keep Genesis from becoming suspicious? And she seems taller....

Dad's hand comes down on my shoulder, stopping me from raising my arms and beginning the power drain. Don't know what the hell he's thinking. Timing is everything. I shake him off and launch a blast of *pulling* energy at Granfeld's back, grinning when I nail her just below her shoulder blades.

She jerks and twists, wrenching herself around to face her assailants.

And I know why Dad tried to stop me. Why he hasn't joined me in my attack.

Tempest Granfeld didn't cause Genesis's death.

The woman glaring back at us is Mom.

Chapter 69
Judgment

MY CONCENTRATION falters. It's the briefest of lapses. I fully intend to destroy her, mother or not, for what she's done, what she's become. Her eyes spark with madness and self-righteous indignation. God, is this what all succubi deteriorate to if they leave their bodies at death? Is this what I have to look forward to? But for a moment, a few precious, vital seconds, I flash on a memory of the night of the freshman spring dance.

She'd bought me a dress. A beautiful one, all blue satin and white bows. Even if dresses weren't my thing, I'd liked the color. She'd done my hair, my makeup, lent me her jewelry—a white pearl necklace and matching bracelet. Looking back, I think it was her last-ditch effort to turn me into a girl.

I'd gone off to the high school gym, primped and powdered and perfumed, tottering on one-inch heels I'd never worn before. I met up with some friends—one of whom I'd had a crush on for years, a girl. At that age, I didn't have a name for what I felt for Isa, but I knew it went beyond friendship, beyond that pseudo-sisterhood close girls claimed for themselves. And damn, she looked hot that night—she'd left her house in a lacy pink knee-length dress with capped sleeves but changed in the locker room as soon as we arrived at the gym into a skintight strapless red number that barely came low enough to cover her perfect ass.

We hung out together at the dance, holding up a wall since few freshman boys had the bravery it took to approach a girl. Or maybe even then the guys could sense more about me than I knew about myself. Our other friends found partners, but we stood alone. Looking back, I kinda wondered if Isa didn't find anyone because she was standing with me. When the third slow song came on, I nudged her with my arm and said, "If the guys won't ask us to dance, we should just dance with each other," not even quite realizing what was coming out of my mouth.

Isa turned and stared at me, eyes wide. "What are you, a lezzie?" Then she laughed, making the whole thing a joke, assuming I had been, too, or hoping I had. There was just enough nervousness beneath the humor to clue me in—if I hadn't been kidding, what I'd just asked would end our friendship.

I faked some chuckles of my own, and we never mentioned it again.

When I got home, I burst into tears—something I almost never did, even then—crying that no one liked me. I didn't get specific. I knew better from comments Mom had made. She took it as I'd hoped, gathered me into her arms and assured me that someday I'd meet the right boy for me. She'd comforted me for hours, made brownies at two in the morning, and we'd sat at the kitchen table eating the entire pan.

And when, the following year, I came out to my closest friends, Isa stopped speaking to me permanently.

"You'll find the one to sweep you off your feet. I know you will," Mom had told me.

I had, and she'd taken Genesis away from me.

The reminder snaps me out of my reverie, but those vital seconds had passed, and in my moment of distraction, Mom broke free of my draining power.

She hurls a beam of her own, catching me in the abdomen, doubling me over as my strength is *pulled* from me one molecule at a time.

"Do you… really… hate me… this much?" I gasp, fighting the drain as Dad catches me by the shoulders and holds me upright.

"Let her go, Caroline. Let them both go," Dad says.

"I don't hate you, Flynn. I'm trying to help you. Go back to your new life. Start over. Find a few nice men to enjoy. It's who you are, *what* you are." The sucking away of my energy increases.

I gasp as my knees buckle, and Dad and I both hit the walkway. "Better to be… a slut, than a lesbian? Is that… it?"

"Better to be a succubus who accepts her nature in the eyes of the gods *and* God." However, Mom casts one longing glance at Dad, the regret over what happened between them evident and obvious.

She eases up for a moment, gathering more of her power and leaving me panting, tears leaking from the corners of my eyes. Tired. So fucking tired. One hand sinks several inches into the concrete. With Dad's help, I pull it free.

The squeak and bang of the pub's kitchen door catches everyone's attention, and my mother turns toward the rear of the building, knowing her moment is passing her by. When she takes a step in that direction, I rally what little strength I retain, force it into a blast, and throw everything I have into her.

Maybe she only meant to scare me into going back, but I intend to end this, here and now. I'm leaving in victory, or I'm leaving permanently.

Orange energy envelops my mother's body, takes her to the ground, and wraps her up like a fly in a spider's web, strands crisscrossing over her legs and back. But it's enough. Footsteps clang on the stairway up to the apartments on the second floor, a tread I know as well as my own.

A warmth suffuses my essence, filling a void I'd felt, though I hadn't acknowledged it or identified the cause. It's love and comfort and safety and home. It's Gen's life force. The time-lines have shifted again.

Genesis has escaped.

Now it's just me who has to.

My form flickers in the early-evening sun, arms and knees transparent. Dad can't hold me anymore. His hands pass right through.

Mom seizes the opportunity, disentangles herself from the strands of my fading power and gathers it into her own body, then hurls another draining band at me.

I groan and writhe, flopping sideways on the pavement, twisting and jerking as I struggle to, quite literally, hold myself together. "I won't let you live that life," she says. I no longer retain the energy to *push* back to my physical body. I can barely form a coherent thought.

"You're killing her!" Dad shouts at Mom. "Can't you see that?"

I'm so tired, it's hard to tell. Sleep. I want sleep. But instinct tells me if I go to sleep now, I don't wake up. My eyelids grow heavier. I force them open.

"I'm not killing her," Mom huffs, one hand on her hip, the other pointed at and draining me. "I'm removing an aberration of our kind, an im-perfection. You and I so clearly weren't meant to be. Look what happened to us. Look what we produced."

Gen would say that Mom is to be pitied, that somewhere, deep inside, my mother loves me. After that pronouncement, I no longer cling to that illusion. I struggle to take a deep breath and fail. If I die here, do I wink out of existence at the Village Pub in the future? Or am I left there as an empty shell? If that's the case, at least Gen will have something to bury.

Either way, one thing is certain. Mom's crazy as a freaking loon.

"She's more powerful and crazier than ever. You didn't tell me she was dead," Dad says, accusing.

I attempt a shrug and fail. "You didn't ask."

Without further questions, he unleashes his own energy at Mom, and the world around me turns bright with green fire.

Chapter 70
Repayment

ROBERT ROSE to his feet, moving to stand between his ex-wife and his daughter. The green power flowed from his fingertips in a steady beam, the dark energy tingling up both his arms to the elbows.

"You didn't tell me you were still using dark magic," Flynn growled, feebly trying to block him from protecting her and failing.

Robert focused his energy on his ex-wife, though he kept what he'd taken from Flynn earlier in reserve. "You never asked," he returned.

She was weak, so very weak. If she lost much more power, she'd fade altogether. And he was *not* letting that happen.

"I'm not a nice person, Flynn," he went on, gritting his teeth when Caroline switched her attention to him. Their powers met in mid-arcs, clashing with one another in orange and green sparks—a stalemate, though that wouldn't last long. "I may have regretted abandoning you, may have felt enough remorse to try and make things right between us. But that doesn't make me a good man. Never forget, I'm the one who taught Leo VanDean his dirty tricks."

From the expression on her face, Flynn hadn't known that. Well, now she did.

"I used dark magic to protect myself from your mother, regardless of whom the practice might have hurt. You were part of the fallout from that, I suspect. Having you hate me—it was some of the price I paid. I'm an enemy of the Registry, Flynn, not the hero father you always wished you'd had."

She looked up at him, face a mask of pain, eyes pleading, the tendrils of orange fading beneath her semitransparent skin. "I still love you."

It almost made him stop his assault, made the power flicker just enough to bring Caroline's energy a few inches closer to his own form, but he regrouped and held her off. Flynn's essence solidified a bit, then a bit more as she pulled strength from the world around her. Beside the pub's patio, several flowering plants died.

"You will not be the one to destroy her," he told his daughter. "While the myths of the succubi and incubi hold truth, so do the tales of punishment for eradicating one's parentage. I will not let you be forever cursed, regardless of how in the right you would be." He faltered, staggered a step back, braced himself.

"This was your plan all along," she hissed, rising to her knees, then her feet, palms braced on her thighs as she sucked in a harsh breath. "That's why you came with me."

He favored her with a lopsided grin. "Not so much, no. I thought you had mucked up the timelines. I found you to stop you from doing any more damage. This," he said, turning one of his palms upward toward Caroline without breaking off his power blast, "was more of a spur-of-the-moment decision." He paused in his speech, making her meet his gaze, see his intent. "But it's the right one."

"Dad," she began, one last effort to convince him.

"You saved the one you love," he said, offering her the most paternal smile he could muster. "Now let me save you." And with that, he broke one hand from his attack on Caroline and aimed it at Flynn, blasting her with all the energy he'd taken from her back in Genesis's apartment—her own power, not dark magic.

She opened her mouth in a silent protest as her form completely solidified, then vanished. Gone. Returned to her body and the timeline where she belonged to be with the other half of her soul.

Now he had to deal with the other half of his own.

Chapter 71
Back to the Future

"No!"

I'm quite literally thrown by the force of my own power into my body. It's like running headlong into a brick wall, and the impact knocks me off my barstool onto the pub's patio.

Barstool. Patio.

I'm back. And sitting in a puddle of spilled beer and broken bottle glass, surrounded by Chris, two waitresses, and a number of bemused regulars.

"Didn't know you were such a Yankees fan, Flynn. Red Sox are only two runs up. That double won't cost us the game." Sam, the guy who owns one of the kitschy gift shops in Festivity, waves a hand toward the wide-screen TV over the bar where irrelevant guys in irrelevant red-and-white uniforms round some irrelevant bases in an irrelevant stadium in New York City. "Crying shame to waste good beer that way."

"Are you hurt, Flynn?" Mandy, the patio wait-ress, asks.

I glance down at myself. The glass shards didn't pierce my jeans, but I turn my right palm over and yank a piece from it, then toss it aside to land with a soft clink. Blood wells up in the wound. But my wrist isn't cut. I'm not wearing any bandages.

"Ouch. Let me get the first aid kit," she offers.

"No…," I manage, struggling to my feet and weaving where I stand. "No, I'm okay." Lie of the century. I'm far from it. Vertigo and nausea and worry vie for dominance. I swallow bile, brace my knees, and try really hard not to hyperventilate, without much success. "I've gotta go." I make eye contact with Chris, who's giving me a look that says he knows damn well I didn't shout or fall off my seat because of a playoff game. I'm not a base-ball gal, and definitely not into the Yankees, most-ly because Chris is a rabid fan and I like to goad him. "Can you settle my tab? I'll pay you later."

"Suuuure," he says, taking me by the elbow and leading me away from the crowd, out the swinging metal gate I just used four and a half months ago and into the same walkway between the two buildings that I'd just been blown out of by my father.

God, Dad. Had he survived that? Had he won? He must have. I'm here. Things seem back to nor-mal. But without any of my power, without me knowing where his body is in this timeline so I can call him to it, he has no way back....

I think... I think I've lost them both.

Once we're out of earshot of the others, Chris leans in close. "I'll take you where you need to go. No way am I letting you drive looking the way you look."

I wonder exactly how I *do* look. Probably crazed and panicked and pale. When I go to brush my hair out of my eyes, my hand shakes.

"Genesis," I tell him. "I need to get to Genesis."

He doesn't blink in surprise. Doesn't turn ashen or tear up or do anything that indicates I haven't made a reasonable request.

"I'll drive you home," he says simply.

"Oh no, don't bother," comes an all too familiar voice from beside the nearest parked car in the lot behind the pub. "I'll be happy to *drive* Flynn *home*."

We both whirl toward the sound, Chris blinking in surprise when he sees no one there. I can't see her either, but I know the voice. I have one second to mentally curse Tempest Granfeld before her power throws me against the Village Pub's metal dumpster.

Chapter 72
Last Stand

THE RESOUNDING clang the dumpster makes when my spine hits steel is loud enough to carry over the ongoing ball game on the distant patio TVs. I slide to the ground. And it hurts. A lot. I'm not fully recovered from Genesis's dark magic attack. Close, but not 100 percent. And then there was Leo kicking me. And oh, let's not forget the battle from which I was just forcibly removed.

I groan as I roll to all fours, then push up on my trembling knees.

"Flynn, what's happening?" Chris stares from side to side while Tempest laughs. He doesn't react. He can't hear her anymore.

I'm wondering why I can, but my guess is she's choosing to let me do so. Actually, we're family, so I ought to have been able to see her all along, even when I wasn't out-of-body, but maybe it's a matter of emotional bonds rather than blood ones. Doesn't matter now.

"Chris," I say through clenched teeth, "run."

He does, bless him, pulling his cell from a back pocket as he does so and taking cover around the corner of the pub. No idea whom he's calling, but I hope whoever it is brings nukes.

Tempest lets loose with a cackle worthy of gingerbread witch lore, not the least bit concerned with him getting away.

He's not her target.

I am.

And I've been through everything in the past few weeks. Which she knows. I'm sure of it.

"Not so cocky this time, are you, Flynn? Never let it be said that I'm not an opportunist."

The hairs stand up on the back of my neck. "Opportunist" is how Genesis referred to me the first time we met. Must run in the family.

"I merely needed to keep watching until you had burned yourself out." Tempest tosses another blast of green energy in my direction, following it up with a beam of *pulling* power I narrowly avoid with a clumsy dodge.

I cringe inside at her words. When we first met, Gen described me as an opportunist. I wonder if it's a family trait. And God, I hope Gen isn't on the other end of Chris's impromptu phone call. I do *not* want her anywhere near Granfeld and the dark magic. Hell, I just got Genesis back from the dead. I'm not eager to put her at risk ever again.

Tempest aims a few more shots at me, chasing me around the parking lot while I duck behind cars, clusters of apartment mailboxes, and a few more garbage cans, but I get the distinct impression that she's toying with me, wearing my already exhausted self down bit by bit in order to finish me off. I can't pause long enough to regroup or gather my dwindling energy without getting zapped, tossed, or pummeled by power.

"Come now. Why run? You're delaying the inevitable, you know. Besides, do you really want all the mere humans wondering what is happening here?" Tempest gestures with one hand at the space surrounding us while another ball of green fire forms in the other.

I risk a glance from where I crouch behind a BMW. She's right. There are Festivity residents on some of the second-floor walkways lining the rear of the downtown apartments, along with a few stopping by their cars and some employees dumping trash behind the pub. They're staring around at the havoc Tempest has already wrought: a downed lamppost sending sparks across the pavement, a dented Volvo, scattered garbage from the dumpster, but of course they can't figure out how any of the destruction occurred. And then there's me, darting from vehicle to vehicle, probably looking like I'm checking for unlocked doors or cars to vandalize, and all of it while performing some impressive dodges, rolls, and other random acrobatics.

I couldn't care less whether or not the nonmagical population finds out about what exists right under their noses. I'm more concerned about collateral damage, or, you know, personal damage.

Keeping my head down, I crawl under one of those trucks on overly large tires, switching to a row she doesn't expect me to be in, then creep around a bumper, up another few car lengths, and over one more lane until I think I've lost her. Pressing my back against a passenger door, I catch my breath, my chest heaving and sweat dripping into my eyes. My shirt sticks to my skin. It's midafternoon, and even in fall, it's damn hot in central Florida.

I should be focusing on my power, not my breathing, but one kind of has to precede the other. Meanwhile, Tempest is shouting taunts and threats only I can hear.

"You can't defeat me, Flynn. Your daddy was your only chance. The two of you together might have had the strength. But you? You still haven't a clue about *what* you can do, much less *how* to do it."

She's right. But one thing I know now—it has to be me. Dad said as much. Succubus against succubus. And I'm a full-blood specimen. I wonder if Granfeld is. Time to find out which of us is stronger.

Chapter 73
Getting a Clue

I'VE MANAGED to pull some of my power together—what felt like individual snakes tickling about my midsection now resembles something like a writhing ball of energy. Only it's a small ball, and not much energy.

I draw from the few scraggly trees scattered at even intervals between rows of parked cars. I draw from the grass around them—pitiful circles of manicured ambience. Hell, I even pull from every potted plant on every walkway, whispering a quiet, "Sorry," to their owners as they wilt and die.

It's not nearly enough, but I have to do something. I can't run forever. Someone is going to get hurt. Probably me.

"Flynn…." Tempest's voice is singsongy, taunting, teasing… and right… over….

There.

Stepping out from between a pickup truck and a minivan, I launch a tendril of *pulling* power in the sound's direction, jerking back when it *cracks* like a combination of thunder and lightning against an invisible defensive wall.

Nothing. My attack did nothing. Nothing at all.

Oh, wait, yes, it did something. It drained most of the energy I gathered.

I zigzag through the lot once more, seeking refuge, considering and abandoning the idea of entering the pub or one of the other businesses from the rear, and run smack into....

"Nate?"

He's climbing out of a BMW. Of course. I'm so distracted with trying to stay alive that I neither hear the car arrive nor see him exiting the vehicle until I crash into him. We bounce off the open car door. I land butt-first on the asphalt, scraping both palms on the gravelly surface while he falls atop me with his head squarely planted between my breasts.

"Itf Ngtal."

"What?" With one hand in his hair, I yank his face away from my boobs.

He rolls his eyes. "It's Nathaniel. And I might be able to offer some assistance."

"What the fuck are you doing here?"

"I'm with—" He breaks off as the sideview mirror on his rental explodes in a shower of glass fragments. Together we crawl on all fours until we round the sedan and bump into a pair of shapely legs in sensible black pumps. We look up and up until we meet the glaring expression of none other than President Linda Argyle.

Hands on her hips, she gives us a nonplussed frown. "If you're both quite finished with the up-skirt view, maybe we can get on with resolving this situation once and for all."

"Yes, right, of course." Nate rises, albeit carefully keeping his head down and gently pressing Argyle's shoulders lower as well. He brushes bits of dirt from his hands and pants.

I clear my throat. "Correction. What the fuck are *both* of you doing here?"

"Initially, we came to get your training back on schedule," Argyle says, glancing from me to where two other cars pull into spots around the lot. "Then Chris called Cassie, and the Registry archivist called me, within minutes of each other. It sounded like you required assistance, and we have new information to share, so we drove over from our hotel."

I think Cassie is the blond climbing from the Audi in the farthest row from us. I also spot Mimi, the pixie telekinetic from Atlantic City, getting out on the passenger side. A Jeep disgorges the elderly but formidable Niki, a spirit seer who translated for Leo VanDean at my "testing" ritual.

"Nathanial, explain the strategy the archivist discovered," Argyle orders.

He scans the parking lot once, nods, and edges closer so he's crouching right next to me. I'm guessing Tempest is regrouping her own energy and reevaluating her strategies now that reinforcements have arrived.

"More data on psychic succubi has been uncovered," Nate says, his skin flushing pink. "I don't know how we missed it. It was right there in the archives. I'd say someone added it into one of the blank spaces, but that doesn't make sense."

Oh.

Yeah, it does, actually. If my father "died" while stopping my mother, then there's every possibility that things he erased from the records might reappear. I don't know how his powers work, but if they are dependent on his energy somehow, I guess it's as plausible as any other theory.

My heart hurts.

A gentle hand falls on my shoulder. "Flynn, are you all right? I mean, beyond the obvious." Nate's peering into my face, his own etched with concern for me. He really has become a friend.

I extricate myself from his light grip. No way am I exploring my daddy issues right now. "Give me the intel."

He waits a beat longer, making certain I suppose, then dives in. "You can't kill Tempest by pulling her power. A succubus can weaken, but not destroy another succubus that way. It won't be permanent. An incubus could do it, but we don't have one available at the moment…?" His voice trails upward a bit at the end, a question in his tone. He's wondering if my father might be willing to help.

I swallow hard. "No, we don't have one."

Nate nods once. "All right, then. You *can* kill her, just not that way. In fact, *only* a succubus or incubus can kill another succubus or incubus."

That much I got from Dad. I nod and wave my hand in a let's-hurry-this-along motion.

"It's all about the method. There's another option, one we knew nothing about until just before we got here, when the archivist called us. Turns out we've been going about this all wrong. Instead of teaching you how to *pull* the talents Granfeld has stolen and deploy them against her, we should have been offering our magics to you passively."

I shake my head while Argyle keeps watch over the lot, her limited seeing ability enabling her to hopefully spot Tempest before she makes her next move. "No sign of her," Madame President reports.

"I'm not getting the difference," I whisper. "Either way it's me using magic on her, which you said won't work."

"No," he explains, no longer using the condescending tone he used to prefer in our conversations, "it's you using *other people's* magic on her, magic freely given to you so you aren't expending your own energy to get it. And that, according to the records, will work. In the hotel suite, working together, we managed to weaken her a great deal, but ultimately it has to be you casting the final blow, with magic that isn't your own."

Of course it has to be me. Heaven forbid someone else should be allowed to commit the murder. Yes, it's self-defense, but it's me causing a sentient being to reach a final death. No matter how I construct the idea behind a pretty facade, I know it will never sit well with me.

But letting more psychics be erased from existence won't leave my conscience free either.

"Okay," I say to Nate. "How do we start this party?"

He waves a hand over the roof of the car we're hiding behind, I presume gesturing for Cassie, Mimi, and Niki to join us. The other hand he extends toward me. "First, we give you a way to see Tempest," he says, "and then we provide some armor."

Chapter 74
To the Brink

I DRAW power first from Nate and Niki, both of them seers of different sorts. Nate can see the usage of magical energy, and Niki can see ghosts, so whether Tempest is hiding out or not, I'll be able to either find her or at least view where her attacks are coming from.

And it's easy. So very, very easy to *pull* their talents from them without them fighting me. They hold out their hands, I take them in mine, and I concentrate. Next thing I know, I'm watching the electric colors dance over their skin, crossing the connection between us and entering mine. Each psychic I touch feels a little different, and the power has a different hue. Nate's is like warm molasses, slow and steady, a little sticky until I get the flow moving, but not unpleasant. To my sight, it's a rich brown resembling amber sprinkled with glitter. Niki's magic is more brittle, snapping and cracking over my hands and lower arms, painless but startling. It's coal black except for a few spots that sparkle like diamonds.

Cassie comes next, but when she stretches out her hands, I hesitate. This is easy for me, but it's not so easy on them. Nate is using the side of a van to hold himself up, and Niki is seated on the dead grass beneath one of the trees I killed, eyes half-closed and skin ashen. I remember how sick Genesis was when I accidentally drew too much power from her. She was out of commission for days. And she's young and full of vitality. Niki must be in her eighties. Tough as nails and sharp as a tack, but still. And Cassie has little Tracy and Peter to care for.

"I can do this without your skill set," I say to her, keeping my voice low. "Save your magic for family and friends."

She gives me a soft smile and shakes her head. "You're my friend, Flynn. Despite Genesis's unwillingness to let go of the past, you've accepted me." Cassie gives me a sly wink. "And you're about to be family. Chris popped the question last night. He was planning to tell you today, but I guess he never got around to it."

Yeah, Mom rewriting the past, killing Gen, and changing the timeline kind of broke up our chat on the pub patio. And God, I wish and don't wish Genesis was here. I'm burning with need to see her, to confirm that she's really alive and well. (I'm also burning with a different sort of need after all the magic I've been using, but I push that aside.) Instead, I plaster on a happy smile for Cassie, which isn't all that difficult. "Congrats! I'm thrilled for you two. Really. But—"

"No buts. Tracy is stable, in remission, and Peter can handle a few days of discomfort until I rebuild my reserves. Take what I'm offering. Make us all safe." She gestures around the parking lot, where a few more of the Registry have arrived to pitch in. They've removed the lingering bystanders from the danger zone, either by creating some plausible story or via magical means. They've cast some kind of magical shield around the area that supposedly deters nulls from wanting to cross the lot or get in their cars, as well as keeping those with magical ability inside, so Granfeld isn't getting away this time. They've also been reporting in to Madame President that there's no sign of Granfeld, except Nate swore he could sense the power she uses to remain "alive" in at least a mental sense right up until I took his talent for myself. I feel it now, a faint burning sensation that tingles at the back of my skull. She's still here, and sooner or later, she'll show herself again. Cassie is right. No one is protected with Tempest Granfeld around.

I meet Cassie's eyes for a long moment, but there's no doubt or hesitation in them, so I nod, grasp her hands, and *pull*.

The cut on my hand from the broken glass when I fell off the barstool disappears before my eyes. Cassie's magic is by far the sweetest, warming me everywhere it flows until it reaches my core and joins the rest. It's lavender in hue, with dashes of pink and pale blue. Her daughter Tracy would love it, like a pastel rainbow. It would go great in the kid's bedroom. I feel better and stronger even without actively using it. Healing power rocks.

"You need to project it over your entire body, like a shield," Cassie instructs, leaning on the nearest car's roof and breathing heavily. "Damn, that packs a punch."

"Sorry," I mutter. I close my eyes and concentrate, seeking out only her energy, separating it from the others I've absorbed and then nudging it to all my extremities until my entire body tingles with warmth. When I look down at myself, I'm glowing a faint green. "Should I worry that it appears different when I use it? It's green, and green is bad, right?"

She shakes her head, curses softly, and sways where she stands. I grab Cassie's arm to keep her steady. "You're not evil, Flynn. Far from it. That's just how 'stolen' magic looks for you. Don't be concerned. There's nothing evil about you."

I think about what I did to Max Harris and Leo VanDean, both horrible people to be sure, but still, I'm not certain I'm as pure as Cassie thinks. Regardless, I've got one more dirty deed to complete. I rub my hands together, then scrub them over my face. Stolen power or not, I'm fucking tired. Of everything. "So, we need a way to draw Tempest out."

"I have some thoughts on that," Madame President states from behind me, making me jump a little.

Of course she does. She needs to maintain some semblance of control here. There's a large contingent of psychics watching her every move… and mine. I wonder if it's an election year for the Registry or something. I have zero good feelings about her, but she is the expert here. "What have you got in mind?"

Her blink of surprise tells me she didn't expect me to accept her advice. Her shoulders lose a little of their rigid tension. "I'll get to that in a minute, but first, you're forgetting to pull magic from someone."

"Oh?" I know there are other talented individuals here, but I'm not aware of them having skills that I can directly use against Granfeld. "Who?"

"Me," Argyle says, holding out a hand in an offering of power.

And a truce.

Chapter 75
Together We Stand

"FLYNN'S RIGHT, Madame President. This is too dangerous. You'll be completely helpless." Nate is literally wringing his hands in concern. I thought that was something people only did in sappy novels, but nope. Pretty soon he'll be chafing the skin on the backs of his knuckles.

He does have a point, though. I've drawn power from Linda Argyle, at her insistence that her magic-dampening skill would come in handy. She's right. It will. But it's left her pale, shaky, and defenseless. I'm impressed. I never in a million years thought she'd allow herself to be in this position given how threatened she appears to be by me. I could drain her dry right now, and there isn't a damn thing she could do about it.

But I won't.

Granfeld, however, just might. Because the other half of her plan is a surefire way to get Tempest to come out of whatever hidey-hole she's dug herself into. Madame President wants to present the other succubus with a target she can't possibly resist going after—the two of us.

I have to admit, she's finally earned my respect.

And Nate's hand-wringing anxiety meltdown.

"I'll be fine, Nathaniel. I have every confidence that Ms. Dalton can do what needs to be done." Argyle glances at me. My utter shock must show on my face because she adds, "Really."

Really?

With a shared nod, the two of us stand up straight, or as straight as Madame President can manage in her weakened condition, but other than a slight slumping of her shoulders, no one would guess that she's been diminished in any way. I look over my shoulder at the clock mounted high on the downtown Festivity bank's tower. Seventeen minutes. That's how long the entire battle has lasted so far, from the moment Granfeld attacked me and Chris, through the arrival of the other psychics and the drawing of their energy, to now.

Time flies when you're scared shitless, I guess.

We leave the safety of our vehicular barricade, moving to stand in the middle of the center row between parked cars. Nate guessed that Granfeld was hiding somewhere toward the opposite end of the same row. The bait is cast. We wait for her to take it.

While the sun beats down on us and a trickle of sweat runs between my breasts, I watch Argyle in my peripheral vision. "Why the sudden change of heart?" I mutter out of the corner of my mouth.

She hmmphs. "Things weren't what they seemed," she says.

I remain silent, waiting her out.

"My parents…," she begins. And for a few seconds, there is real sadness, a pain and sorrow about her that is the most vulnerable I've encountered from this woman of fire and steel. It's gone as fast as it appears, but it gives me a glimpse into who she might be under different circumstances. "My parents died when I was twelve. Car accident. But I've had glimpses," she says, scanning the parking lot while her words tumble forth. "Flashes of memory. They're older in those memories. Much older. I think—"

"Granfeld erased them," I finish for her. Then, softer, "I'm sorry."

"Me too. They were kind, generous people, and very magically talented. Both had been board members when I was a child, and much beloved by the Registry. I spoke to Nathaniel. He says I was a very different leader prior to about a year ago. I think that's when the timeline was changed. It's all very confusing and hard to follow, but I don't think I'm the person I was meant to be. I'd like to find that person, be that leader."

I nod. And the story makes me wonder, were Genesis's parents taken also? Was the boating accident that killed them really how they were meant to die? "Well, one thing I'm certain of," I tell her.

"You'll have no competition from me. Despite what I said in Atlantic City, I have no desire to be the ringleader of this particular shitshow. So when Granfeld does show herself, you fucking run like hell, you hear me? No heroics. You have almost no power left, and the Registry needs you."

She rests a hand on my shoulder. It's a move so uncharacteristic of her up to this point that I jump a little at the contact, but she solidifies her grip. "No worries. Heroics are your specialty, not mine. But maybe you'll consider running for the board—"

Huh. The old "keep your enemies close" strategy. Because no matter what she's saying now, I still don't count us as friends. I'd tell her where she can shove that idea, but Granfeld chooses that moment to make her reappearance, and it's a dramatic one, all green dark magic lightning and a couple of orange lassos of *pulling* energy thrown in for good measure. I grab Argyle and bodily throw her to the side, taking the brunt of the blast myself. The shield of Cassie's healing energy surrounding my body absorbs most of the impact, but some trickles crack through, beginning the drain on my collected power through a half dozen tiny fissures.

Fuck.

Just like with my parents, it's going to come down to brute magical strength. One of us will drain the other. One will cease to exist. Except this time, I can't tackle her. I can't touch her at all.

I'm not out-of-body and she's a spirit. Only Gene-sis's magic would have allowed me to do that, and thankfully, Gen is at home and safe.

So, which of us has more power? The offspring of both a succubus and an incubus or a gone-mad, hundred-something-year-old undead succubus who's had generations of practice and experience, not to mention knowledge of doing what we do?

The cracks in my shield spread wider.

I think I'm about to find out.

Chapter 76
Stronger United

I CAN'T breathe. I can't think. All I can do is trace the spiderweb of glowing cracks in my protective shield as they spread and grow wider. My own power flows away through them and across the space between me and Tempest Granfeld, sinking into her skin like a tourist soaks up the sunshine. I'm not in spirit form, so I'm not becoming transparent. However, I'm weakening at an alarming rate, knees aching and trembling, hands shaking where I extend them before me in my pitiful attempts to use the energy I've borrowed from the others.

With a scream of defiance, I blast my opponent with a telekinetic bolt. My aim is true, my control perfect. Mimi would be proud, and I wonder with a corner of my mind if she's watching from between the cars. The wave lifts and tosses Tempest end over end to land on the hood of a Corvette. The fiberglass sinks inward with her impact. To anyone without the sight, the entire hood would appear to have spontaneously been sucked in by the engine. She flails all four limbs, a crab flipped on its back but still dangerous with pincers flinging about erratically, as evidenced by the random bursts of energy lancing out in every direction.

I duck and weave, racing toward her as fast as my unsteady legs can carry me. I'm right on top of her, reaching out to connect my *pull* to her power when—

Pop.

Tempest vanishes.

What the actual fuck?

I blink against the flash that accompanies her exit and scrub a hand over my face. I thought the psychics had erected an impenetrable bubble over the parking lot. How could she just—

"Hello, Flynn."

Whirling, I catch her blast full force in the chest. I go down hard, head striking concrete, vision shattering into scattered shards. She's on me before I can draw breath into my expended lungs, both palms on my shoulders, holding me down, dragging away my energy.

Stupid, Flynn. She doesn't have a body. She can will *herself a new one any time she wants.*

And I only have the one to work with in my current state.

I can't breathe. My head hurts. My ears are ringing, and somewhere in the distance I think I hear another car pulling into the lot, which still shouldn't be possible given the Registry members' blockade.

Yet the engine draws closer and closer. The unseen vehicle screeches to a halt. A door opens and slams shut, and a familiar foot tread races toward us.

"Flynn!"

Oh no, fuck no.

"No!" My intended shout is a whisper, but Tempest hears it and laughs manically.

"Oh yes." Her eyes close, an expression of pure orgasmic bliss flowing from forehead to chin, her lips parted in a perfect *O* of satisfaction.

And that's when Genesis body-slams her into the asphalt, straddles her waist, and pummels her with her fists. She's not all that strong, but in Tempest's distracted state, she's doing the job. I push myself up on one elbow, then roll to my knees. The rogue succubus's face is bloody from a split lip, and Genesis continues to pound away. I grab my wife by the elbow and draw her off.

"That's my move," I say, "and it isn't really doing any good. Let me."

Even as I speak, Granfeld's features are reforming into an undamaged representation of her once living self, but it was a distraction she never saw coming. Before she can regain her strength and composure, I press both my palms to her shoulders and *pull*.

Faster. Faster. Instinct tells me I have to draw her power as fast as I can, before she can regroup, recover. Before Genesis loses her barely controlled temper and decides dark magic is the way to end this. But it's not fast enough. Everywhere Tempest begins to fade, she almost immediately solidifies. I can't absorb her energy with sufficient speed.

"Flynn," Genesis says beside me.

All I want is to wrap her in my arms and never let her go. She's alive! God, she's alive. Tears of relief mix with those already pouring down my cheeks. She's alive and I can't stop for one fucking moment to reassure myself.

"Flynn," she says again as Tempest's eyes glow with a faint green.

Oh shit. I'm about to be in some serious hurt.

Well, *more* serious hurt.

"*Pull* from *me*."

Wait. What?

Gen grabs one of my hands, yanking it away from Tempest and planting my palm against her chest. "Me. Take power from me."

Different wording doesn't make her meaning any clearer. What can she be offering that I don't already have?

Dividing my attention, I continue *pulling* Granfeld's energy away, then shedding it by *pushing* it in the opposite direction. I don't like how she tastes and feels. It's slick and oily like hair unwashed for a week. A shudder passes through me. I want it gone as fast as I can expel it.

At the same time, I run through a mental catalog of Gen's skills. Ability to see and communicate with spirits? I got those from Niki. Predicting the future? I'm not sure what good that would do me right now when all I'm likely to see is my own death.

There are other things Gen can do, but they involve dark magic, and I'm not taking that.

"Flynn, she's dead, a spirit!"

She's…?

Oh.

While Tempest's form goes from pliant to solid beneath my right hand, I *pull* power from Genesis with my left. There's no time for grace or finesse, and I know I'm taking too much, but this is it, our last chance. I'm breaking contact with Gen when Tempest throws herself upward with more force than her slight appearance should have allowed. She flips us, reversing our positions. In my peripheral vision, Genesis rolls away, coming to a halt beside a Toyota's front right tire, then lying still, eyes closed, chest heaving.

Granfeld's hands wrap around my throat at the same moment I grip her upper arms. She's stripping energy from me in wide sheets. Meanwhile, I'm fumbling around with a power I've never practiced with, never encountered directly before.

But I've seen Genesis use it.

I close my eyes, searching inside for the purist, sweetest-tasting, lightest energy I can find. And then I *push*.

I know the moment that power engulfs Tempest Granfeld, because even behind my closed eyelids, the brilliance of the light is almost blinding. Her hands loosen their hold. She sucks in a sharp breath, lets it out on the softest of sighs.

And crosses into the afterlife.

Chapter 77
Home

IN THE five-minute drive between the parking lot and home, everything hits me at once: shakes, nausea, fever, arousal, not to mention the mourning-turned-relief at having Gen back from the dead and the real mourning over my only recently reclaimed father. We're in the rear of Gen's Charger with Chris driving. Gen's cuddled against my shoulder, my arm wrapped around her. She's regained consciousness. My *pull* from her only stunned her for a few moments. It looks like she'll recover in a matter of hours, though she's pale and weary.

I think I'm going to take a lot longer.

The landscape rushing by makes the nausea worse, so I focus on my free hand grasping my knee, digging into the torn denim. Wetness runs down my cheeks. I try to get a grip. The shaking intensifies. Fuck it. I let myself shake.

"Flynn, it's over. We did it. This isn't just the power usage. What's going on?" Gen asks, her voice a whisper.

It's too much. I can't answer her.

Chris slows the Charger and turns onto Royal Court Street. "Something… happened… to her at the pub," he says over the seat back. "Before Granfeld showed up, so it's more than the fight. Maybe she shouldn't have gotten out of bed so soon, but I don't think that's it."

Oh. Right. After my battle with Leo, I was supposed to be convalescing. I snuck out. Feels like an eternity ago. Gen tilts her head up to study my face, her expression of concern offset by her frown. She's probably a little pissed at me for going to the pub. Never in my life have I been so happy to have her pissed at me.

The house comes into view, all castle turrets, sloping rooftops, and stone architecture. Then the garage, then the front yard. Chris turns into the driveway. When the car stops, Gen moves to climb out the rear passenger door.

I don't let her. I can't. My grip on her shoulder won't loosen. Now that all the adrenaline has worn off, the very idea of her being separated from me, even for a moment, is unbearable. I lost her. I cannot lose her again. I know it's irrational. It doesn't matter.

She grips me back, holding me together, because I'm falling apart. I don't bother wiping away the falling tears—there's a lot more coming behind these.

"Don't let go," I whisper into her hair, breathing in the scent of her—lavender shampoo, the incense she uses when she's reading the tarot, the orange-and-honey perfume she dabs behind each ear when she gets up every morning. "Whatever you do, just don't let go."

She doesn't. And though I can feel her confusion and concern in every murmur of her comfort, every rub of my back and shoulders, she doesn't press me further.

It's a long time before I can unclench my grip from around her enough to slide out my own door, drawing her with me. I let her lead me inside the house, Chris trailing behind. She tugs me gently into the living room, where Katy prowls nervously back and forth in front of the couch. Gen pushes me down onto the cushions and snuggles under my arm, still holding me, bless her. Katy hops up, though she's forbidden on the sofa, and I bury my free hand in her soft fur.

Rattling of pots and pans and the opening and closing of cabinets tell me Chris is at work in the kitchen, which is confirmed a few minutes later when he appears with a steaming mug of hot cocoa in his outstretched hands.

I give it the old college try, but I can't manage it without sloshing, so Gen holds it for me, bringing it to my lips over and over until I've drunk half. When I can take a solid breath without gasping, choking, or sobbing, she pulls the mug away and sets it aside.

"Now," she says, "talk to me. Please. I think you just scared five years off my life."

Which, of course, has the effect of starting me crying all over again.

When I calm for the second time, I take her hands and try to get the words out, but they won't come. I shake my head. "Not now. I can't go through it again right now." Maybe not ever, but she'll never accept that, so I don't say it. "Let me keep this a bit." She opens her mouth to protest, and I don't blame her, but I cut her off. "I'm not hurt, well, except for some glass in my hand, a bruise from falling off the barstool, and some others from getting tossed around. But nothing's broken." At least I don't think so. If I'm honest, every inch of my body aches like a sonofabitch.

Gen gives me an incredulous look.

Okay, yeah, I'm covered in scrapes, cuts, and assorted other minor injuries, so I rephrase. "There's no immediate danger. Nothing life-threatening. And I'll get through this, so long as you're near me." And when I say near, I mean literally. I can't bear the thought of letting her out of my sight in the foreseeable future, which I'm sure will raise even more questions, but maybe by then I'll be ready to tell her everything. "Just give me some time."

She doesn't like it. I don't have to be psychic to figure that out. But after a long moment, she nods. "Okay. For now. But you are going to tell me, Flynn. You can't scare me like that and not tell me."

"I will. As soon as I'm able. I promise."

IT'S A couple of days before I can manage to share anything. Gen's borne it like a trooper, watching me when she thinks I'm not looking, starting to ask multiple times, then stopping herself and shaking her head in frustration.

And she's stuck to me like glue, with the exception of the first night when she slipped out of our bed to use the bathroom and I woke up, found her gone, and totally freaked out on her. Again.

After that episode, she lets me know whenever she needs to leave my sight, even if she has to wake me to do so.

A few days later, we see the story on the news: "Local man found dead in Disney Springs hotel room. Anyone with any information regarding the situation should contact the authorities." And they flash my dad's driver's license photo on the screen.

Gen's in shock. I've been expecting it.

"Is that why?" Gen asks from her spot on the couch beside me, turning to look up at me with sympathy. She doesn't usually sit here when we're not about to make out. Her favorite armchair is across the room.

Too far. Much too far.

"That's part of it."

"Oh, Flynn, I'm so sorry."

"Yeah, me too." She doesn't like it one bit when I drop it at that, but I'm still not ready.

ONCE THE coroner settles on heart attack, we claim Dad's body, hold the funeral the following week, and then I'm finally ready to share.

But not everything.

Over more hot chocolate in the kitchen, I lay down the basics. My mother. Shifting timelines. Gen's... death.

That's the hardest part, and I don't go into details, but with her sitting next to me, within arm's reach, I'm able to get it out without breaking down again. I refuse to tell her how she died. She doesn't need to know that, and I'll suffer the nightmares for both of us.

I don't share how badly it affected me, either, other than to croak out, "It was the worst day and a half of my life." Considering everything we've been through these past months, that's saying a helluva lot. She doesn't ask for more than that, but I suspect she knows I didn't handle losing her very well.

Gen always knows me.

That leads to my pursuit of Tempest Granfeld, which ended in my dad's apparent destruction of my mom and vice versa, followed by our final showdown with Tempest in the parking lot. I also leave out the whole "I'm a real succubus" part. Am I some mythological monster? Maybe. But I never want to give her reason to fear me.

I fill in as many blanks for her as I can until she draws a deep breath and lets out a long sigh. "Well," she says, "let me tie up one more loose end." She reaches across and into my jeans pocket, dipping her fingers way in.

"What are you—?"

Her hand comes up with the baggie of herbs mixed with my blood that kept my mother away, at least in the present. It wouldn't have been in there in the past or in the alternate timeline, which was how Mom had her opening to attack me and Dad. The baggie was so far down, I hadn't noticed either its disappearance or reappearance, and it had likely been through a wash or two.

"Never good to carry unnecessary magical items around," Gen says a little too flippantly. "Besides, it took me too long to get the cumin from my bag out of the sheets to risk a repeat performance." She slips off her kitchen chair, heading for the door leading to the screened-in pool area behind the mansion. With her hand on the knob, she turns back to me. "I have to dispose of this properly. I'll only be a few minutes, I promise."

I nod. "Sure." But my insides clench when the door closes her off from my view.

We're fine. It's over. Gen's alive and well. We can't spend the rest of our lives glued together at the hip or even anywhere more pleasant, but....

I stand and follow her. She'll roll her eyes, sigh, and shake her head, but she'll get over it. I have been getting better about needing her next to me.

A little.

I step into the pool enclosure just in time to see her throw the baggie into the air above the chlorinated water, where it bursts into one brief flame before hitting the pool's surface.

One *green* flame.

"Shit, Gen!" I shout, startling her so she almost falls in. She teeters on the pool's edge before re-gaining her balance and turning to glare at me. I ignore it. "Did you seriously have to use dark magic to destroy that thing? You couldn't, you know, flush it or something?" My vocal pitch has risen half an octave. I stop and take a deep breath, waiting for an explanation I know I'm not going to like.

She doesn't meet my eyes. "I didn't use dark magic to destroy it," Gen says, focused on her bal-let flats. "I used dark magic to create it."

She used….

How? How could she possibly have used dark magic without me seeing—

The needle. When she pricked my finger, I closed my eyes. And she would have known I'd do that. She must have cast it quickly while my eyes were shut.

"Dammit," I mutter, turning and heading back inside. For the first time in a week, I don't want her near me.

"It was just a tiny bit," she says, running after me. "There was no other way, Flynn. Blood magic requires a related catalyst to work. A psychic who specializes in it could have activated it easily, but

I had to improvise. It was the only way to get rid of her immediately. And nothing else would have stopped her. She would have been hounding you night and day, constantly criticizing and insulting us both, or worse, until the Registry put us in touch with someone. Blood workers are rare. Besides, it would have drawn President Argyle's attention to exactly who your mother *was*."

She lets that hang there. Yeah, having Argyle know the full extent of my family tree would be bad. But that's not a good enough excuse.

"And what about the cost?" I demand, whirling on her.

She backpedals a step. Her brow wrinkles in confusion. "Cost? The cost of blood magic is the blood. The blood paid the price—"

"No, *you* paid it, with a deeper addiction, and *I* paid it. Or haven't you figured that out yet?" I'm shouting. I'm shouting at someone I nearly killed myself over losing. But I am not going to lose her to this.

Tears are forming in her eyes. She really doesn't see it. "I don't know what you're—"

"The timing, Gen! Think. You use just *a little bit* of dark magic, and less than *two days later* you're blasting me in the back with it because you've lost your temper and you're so quick to it that you can't think straight. You really believe that was just coincidence?" At the time, I couldn't figure it out. She'd been doing so much better up until she hurt me, and it had seemingly come out of nowhere. I remember wondering if she'd been sneaking using it behind my back, when really, she'd used it right in front of me. Holy fuck. "You almost killed me, Gen," I say in a small voice. And there it is. I've acknowledged the great big green elephant in the room. Gen said it when she first visited me at Cassie's place, but I never did. It's almost a relief to get that out. Almost.

Well, if Gen didn't understand before, she does now. She's gone pale. "Do you... do you want me to leave?" she whispers.

"No!" I throw my hands up in exasperation. "No. I want you to stop. And if you can't," I add, cutting off whatever she is about to say, "then I want you to let me stop you." I take her shoulders and pull her in to me. She's trembling. "Tell me if you feel it calling. Tell me when you think dark magic might be the best way to deal with a problem and we'll find another solution together. Promise me."

"I promise," she says, muffling her face in my shirt.

"Good."

I can only have faith that it's a promise she can keep.

For weeks and weeks I've been wanting my life back, but I never really lost it until I lost Gen. With Granfeld gone, I can do the thing I love most—focus on my wife, her health and happiness, and my own.

Keep reading for an excerpt from
Threadbare
by Elle E. Ire

Chapter 1
Vick
Not Quite Up to Specs

I am a machine.

"VC1, YOUR objective is on the top floor, rear bedroom, moving toward the kitchen. Rest of the place scans as empty."

"Acknowledged." I study the high-rise across the street, my artificial ocular lenses filtering out the sunlight and zooming in on the penthouse twelve stories up. A short shadow passes behind white curtains. My gaze shifts to the gray, nondescript hovervan parked beside me. In the rear, behind reinforced steel, my teammate Alex is hitting the location with everything from x-rays to infrared and heat sensors.

Our enemies have no backup we're aware of, but it doesn't hurt to be observant.

I switch focus to Lyle, the driver, then Kelly in the passenger seat. Lyle stares straight ahead, attention on the traffic.

Kelly tosses me a smile, all bright sunshine beneath blonde waves. My emotion suppressors keep my own expression unreadable.

Except to her.

Kelly's my handler. My counterbalance. My... companion. My frie—

I can't process any further. But somewhere, deep down where I can't touch it, I want there to be more.

More what, I don't know.

Midday traffic rushes by in both directions—a four-lane downtown road carrying a mixture of traditional wheeled vehicles and the more modern hovercrafts. As a relatively recent colonization, Paradise doesn't have all the latest tech.

But we do.

Shoppers and businessmen bustle past. My olfactory sensors detect too much perfume and cologne, can identify individual brand names if I request the info. I pick up and record snippets of conversation, sort and discard them. The implants will bring anything mission relevant to my immediate attention, but none of the passersby are aware of what's going on across the street.

None of them thinks anything of the woman in the long black trench coat, either. I'm leaning against the wall between the doctors' offices and a real estate agency. No one notices me.

"Vick." Kelly's voice comes through the pickups embedded in my ear canals.

She's the only one who calls me that, even in private. I get grudgingly named in the public arena, but on the comm, to everyone else, I'm VC1.

A model number.

"The twelve-year-old kidnap *victim* is probably getting a snack. He's hungry, Vick. He's alone and scared." She's painting a picture, humanizing him. Sometimes I'm as bad with others as Alex and Lyle are toward me. "You're going to get him out." A pause as we make eye contact through the bulletproof glass.

"Right," I mutter subvocally.

Even without the touch of pleading in her voice, failure is not an option. I carry out the mission until I succeed or until something damages me beyond my capability to continue.

Kelly says there's an abort protocol that she can initiate if necessary. We've never had to try it, and given how the implants and I interact, I doubt it would work.

"Team Two says the Rodwells have arrived at the restaurant," Alex reports in a rich baritone with a touch of Earth-island accent.

The kidnappers, a husband and wife team of pros, are out to lunch at a café off the building's lobby. Probably carrying a remote trigger to kill the kid in their condo if they suspect a rescue attempt or if he tries to escape. They're known for that sort of thing. Offworlders with plenty of toys of their own and a dozen hideouts like this one scattered across the settled worlds. Team Two will observe and report, but not approach. The risk is too great.

Which means I have maybe forty-five minutes to get in and extract the subject.

No. *Rescue* the *child*. Right.

"Heading in." My tone comes out flat, without affectation. I push off from the wall, ignoring the way the rough bricks scrape my palms.

"Try to be subtle this time," Lyle says, shooting me a quick glare out the windshield. "No big booms. We can't afford to tip them off."

Subtlety isn't my strong suit, but I don't appreciate the reminder. Two years of successful mission completions speak for themselves.

I turn my gaze on him. He looks away.

I have that effect on people.

The corner of my lip twitches just a little. Every once in a while an emotion sneaks through, even with the suppressors active.

I'm standing on the median, boots sinking into carefully cultivated sod, when Kelly scolds me. "That wasn't very nice." Without turning around, I know she's smiling. She doesn't like Lyle's attitude any better than I do.

My lips twitch a little further.

Thunder rumbles from the east, and a sudden gust of wind whips my long hair out behind me. Back at base, it would be tied in a neat bun or at least a ponytail, but today I'm passing for civilian as much as someone like me can. I tap into the local weather services while I finish crossing the street.

Instead of meteorological data, my internal display flashes me an image of cats and dogs falling from the sky.

This is what happens when you mix artificial intelligence with the real thing. Okay, not exactly. I don't have an AI in my head, but the sophisticated equipment replacing 63 percent of my brain is advanced enough that it has almost developed a mind of its own.

It definitely has a sense of humor and a flair for metaphor.

Cute.

The house pets vanish with a final bark and meow.

The first drops hit as I push my way through glass doors into the lobby, and I shake the moisture from my coat and hair. Beneath the trench coat, metal clinks softly against metal, satisfying and too soft for anyone around me to pick up.

The opulent space is mostly empty—two old ladies sitting on leather couches, a pair of teenagers talking beside some potted plants. Marble and glass in blacks, whites, and grays. Standard high-end furnishings.

"May I help you?" Reception desk, on my left, portly male security guard behind it, expression unconcerned. "Nasty weather." A flash of lightning punctuates his pleasantries.

Terraforming a world sadly doesn't control the timing of its thunderstorms.

My implants reduce the emotion suppressors, and I attempt a smile. Kelly assures me it looks natural, but it always feels like my face is cracking. "I'm here to see…." My receptors do a quick scan of the listing behind him—the building houses a combination of residences and offices. If we'd had more time, we could have set this up better, but the Rodwells have switched locations twice already, and we only tracked them here yesterday.

"Doctor Angela Swarzhand," I finish faster than the guard can pick up the hesitation. "I'm a new patient."

The guard smiles, and I wonder if they're friends. "That's lovely. Just lovely. Congratulations."

"Um, thanks." I'm sure I've missed something, but I have no idea what.

He consults the computer screen built into the surface of his desk, then points at a bank of elevators across the black-marble-floored lobby. "Seventh floor."

"Great. Where are the stairs?" I already know where they are, but I shouldn't, so I ask.

The guard frowns, forehead wrinkling in concern. "Stairs? Shouldn't someone in your condition be taking the elevator?"

"My condition?"

"Vick." Kelly's warning tone tries to draw my attention, but I need to concentrate.

"Not now," I subvocalize. If this guy has figured out who, or rather *what* I am, things are going to get messy and unsubtle fast. My hand slips beneath my coat, fingers curling around the grip of the semiautomatic in its shoulder holster.

"You're pregnant." The giggle in Kelly's voice registers while I stare stupidly at the guard.

"I'm what?" Sooner or later this guy is bound to notice the miniscule motions of my lips, even speaking subvocally.

Alex replaces Kelly on the comm. "Dr. Swarzhand is an obstetrician. She specializes in high-risk pregnancies. The guard thinks you're pregnant. Be pregnant. And fragile."

Oh for fuck's sake.

I blink a couple of times, feigning additional confusion. "My condition! Right." I block out the sound of my entire team laughing their asses off. "I'm still not used to the idea. Just a few weeks along." I don't want to take the damn elevator. Elevators are death traps. Tiny boxes with one way in and one way out. Thunder rumbles outside. If the power fails, I'll be trapped. My heart rate picks up. The implants initiate a release of serotonin to compensate, and the emotion suppressors clamp down. Or try to.

In my ears, one-third of the laughter stops. "It'll be okay, Vick." Kelly, soft and soothing.

Of course she knows. She always knows.

"Just take it up to the seventh floor and walk the rest of the way. It's only for a few seconds, a minute at most. It won't get stuck. I promise."

"Thanks," I say aloud to the guard and turn on my heel, trying to stroll and not stomp. "You can't promise that," I mutter under my breath.

"It'll be okay," she says again, and I'm in the waiting lift, the doors closing with an ominous *thunk* behind me.

The ride is jerky, a mechanical affair rather than the more modern antigrav models. I grit my teeth, resisting the urge to talk to my team. Alex and Lyle wouldn't see the need to comfort a machine, anyway.

Figures the one memory I retain from my fully human days is the memory of my death, and the one emotion my implants fail to suppress every time is the absolute terror of that death.

When the chime announces my arrival on seven and the doors open, I'm a sweating, hyperventilating mess. I stagger from the moving coffin, colliding with the closest wall and using it to keep myself upright.

There's no one in the hallway, or someone would be calling for an ambulance by now.

"Breathe, Vick, breathe," Kelly whispers.

I suck in a shaky breath, then another. My vision clears. My heart rate slows. "I've got it."

"I know. But count to ten, anyway."

Despite the need to hurry, I do it. If I'm not in complete control, I can make mistakes. If I make mistakes, the mission is at risk. I might fail.

A door on the right opens and a very pregnant woman emerges, belly protruding so far she can't possibly see her feet. She takes one look at me and frowns.

"Morning sickness," I explain, grimacing at the thought on multiple levels. Even if I wanted kids for some insane reason, I wouldn't be allowed to have them. Machines don't get permission to procreate.

The pregnant lady offers a sympathetic smile and disappears into the elevator. At the end of the hall, the floor-to-ceiling windows offer a view of sheeting rain and flashing lightning, and I shudder as the metal doors close behind her. I head for the stairwell—the nice, safe, stable, I'm-totally-in-control-of-what-happens stairwell.

"Walk me through it," I tell Alex. I pass the landing for the eleventh floor, heading for the twelfth.

"The penthouse takes up the entire top level," his voice comes back. "Figures. No one to hear the kid call for help. Stairwell opens into the kitchen. Elevator would have let you off in a short hallway leading to the front door."

Which is probably a booby-trapped kill chute. No thanks.

"Security on the stairwell door?"

A pause. "Yep. Plenty of it too. Jamming and inserting a playback loop in the cameras now. Sensors outside the door at ankle height, both right and left. Not positive what they trigger. Could be a simple alarm. Could be something else."

Could be something destructive goes unsaid. I might have issues with my emotions, but that doesn't make me suicidal. At least not anymore. Besides, with the kid walking around loose in the penthouse apartment, all the doors have to have some kind of aggressive security on them. Otherwise he would have escaped by now.

"Whatever it is, I won't know unless you trip it," Alex adds.

Oh, very helpful. I'm earning my pay today.

My internal display flashes an image of me in ballet shoes, en pointe, pink tutu and all.

Keeping me on my toes. Right. Funny. I didn't ask for your input.

The display winks out.

I take eight more steps, round the turn for the last flight to the top floor, and stop. My hand twitches toward the compact grenade on my belt, but that would be overkill. No big booms. Right. Give me the overt rather than the covert any day. But I don't get to choose.

I verify the sensor locations, right where Alex said they'd be. He's right. No indication of what they're connected to.

And time's running out.

If it's an alarm, it could signal the Rodwells at the restaurant. If they have a hidden bomb and a trigger switch….

"Wiring on the door?" I weigh the odds against the ticking clock. They don't want to kill their victim if there's any chance they can make money off him. If I were fully human, if the implants weren't suppressing my emotions, I wouldn't be able to make a decision. Life-or-death shouldn't be about playing the odds.

"None."

"Composition?" Some beeps in the background answer my request.

A longer pause. "Apartment doors in that building were purchased from Door Depot, lower-end models despite the high rents. Just over one inch thick. Wood. Medium hardness."

"The door at the bottom of the stairwell was metal."

"But the one on the top floor isn't. It's considered a 'back door' to the apartment. It's wood like the front entries." Alex's info shifts the odds—odds placed on a child's survival. I try not to think too hard on what I've become. It shouldn't matter to me, but— The suppressors clamp down on the distraction.

"Give me a five-second jam on those sensors," I tell him and count on him to do it. Damn, I hate these last-minute piecemeal plans, but we didn't have much time to throw this together.

"Vick, what are you—?"

Before Kelly can finish voicing her concerns, I'm charging up the last of the stairs, past the sensors, and slamming shoulder-first into the penthouse door. Wood cracks and splinters, shards flying in all directions, catching in my hair and driving through the material of my jacket.

Medium hardness or not, it hurts. I'm sprawled on the rust-colored kitchen tiles, bits of door and frame scattered around me, blood seeping from a couple of cuts on my hands and cheek. The implants unleash a stream of platelets from my bone marrow and they rush to clot the wounds.

I raise my head and meet the wide eyes of my objective. The kid's mouth hangs open, a half-eaten sandwich on the floor by his feet. I'm vaguely aware of Kelly demanding to know if I'm okay.

Her concern touches me in a way I can't quite identify, but it's… good.

"Ow," I mutter, rising to my knees, then my feet. "Fuck." I might heal fast, but I feel pain.

The kid slides from his chair and backs to the farthest corner of the room, trapped against the gray-and-black-speckled marble counter. "D-don't hurt me," he stammers.

I roll my eyes. "Are you an idiot?"

"Oh, nice going, Vick."

I ignore Kelly and open my trench coat, revealing an array of weapons—blades and guns. "If I wanted to hurt you…."

His eyes fly wider, and he pales.

A sigh over the comm. "For God's sake, Vick, try, will you?"

My shoulder hurts like a sonofabitch. I try rotating my left arm and wince at the reduced range of motion. Probably dislocated. I'm in no mood to make nicey nice.

"You're not the police." Oh good, the kid can use logic.

"The police wouldn't be able to find you with a map and a locator beacon."

My implants toss me a quick flash of the boy buried in a haystack and a bunch of uniformed men digging through it, tossing handfuls left and right.

"I'm with a private problem-solving company, and I'm here to take you home," I continue. "Will you come with me?" I pull a syringe filled with clear liquid from one of the coat's many pockets. "Or am I gonna have to drug and carry you?" That will suck, especially with the shoulder injury, but I can do it.

Another sigh from Kelly.

I'm not kid-friendly. Go figure.

My vision blurs. We're out of chat time. A glance over my shoulder reveals pale blue haze filling the space just inside the back door, pouring through a vent in the ceiling. A cloud of it rolls into the kitchen, so it's been flowing for a while. "Alex, I need a chemical analysis," I call to my tech guru. I remove a tiny metal ball from a belt pouch and roll it into the blue gas. Several ports on it snap open, extending sampler rods and transmitting the findings to my partners in the hovervan.

A pause. "It's hadrazine gas. Your entry must have triggered the release. Move faster, VC1."

Hadrazine's some fast and powerful shit. A couple of deep breaths and we'll be out cold, and not painlessly, either. We'll feel like we're suffocating first. If I get out of this alive, my next goal is to take down the Rodwells.

"Report coming in from Team Two." Alex again. "You must have tripped an alarm somewhere. Rodwells leaving the restaurant, not bothering to pay. They're headed for your location."

A grin curls my lips. Looks like I might get my wish.

I know I'm not supposed to *want* to kill anyone. I know Kelly can pick up that urge and will have words for me later. But sometimes… sometimes people just need killing. But not before I achieve my primary objective.

I'm in motion before I finish the thought, grabbing the kid by the arm and hauling him into the penthouse's living room. Couches and chairs match the ones in the lobby. "Tell Team Two not to engage," I snap, not bothering to lower my voice anymore. The boy stares at me but says nothing. "They may still have a detonator switch for this place." And Team Two is Team Two for a reason. They're our backup. The second string. And more likely to miss a double kill shot.

"You're scaring the boy," Kelly says in my ear.

I'm surprised she can read him at this distance. Usually that skill is limited to her interactions with me.

"Jealousy?" she asks. "What for?"

Or maybe she's just guessing. Where the hell did that come from, anyway? I turn up the emotion suppressors. Things between me and Kelly have been a little wonky lately. I've had some strange responses to things she's said or done. I don't need the distraction now.

"Never mind," I mutter. "Alex, front door. What am I dealing with?"

"No danger I can read. Nothing's active. Doesn't mean there isn't some passive stuff."

"There's a bomb."

I stare down at the boy by my side. "You sure?"

He nods, shaggy blond hair hanging in his face. I release him for a second to brush it out of his eyes and crouch in front of him. He's short for his age. Thin too. Lightweight. Good in case I end up having to carry him. "Any chance they were bluffing?"

The kid shrugs.

"The café manager stopped them in the lobby, demanding payment," Alex cuts in. "Doesn't look like they want to make a scene, so you've got maybe five minutes, VC1. Six if they have to wait for the elevator."

Maybe less if the gas flows too quickly.

Right.

I approach the door, studying the frame for the obvious and finding nothing. Doesn't mean there isn't anything embedded.

There. A pinprick hole drilled into the molding on the right side of the frame. Inside would be a pliable explosive and a miniature detonator triggered by contact or remote. Given the right tools and time, I could disarm such a device. I have the tools in a pouch on my belt. I don't have the time.

"Um, excuse me?" The boy points toward the kitchen. Blue mist curls across the threshold and over the first few feet of beige living room carpet.

I race toward a wall of heavy maroon curtains, shoving a couch aside and throwing the window treatments wide. Lightning flashes outside the floor-to-ceiling windows, illuminating the skyscraper across the street and the twelve-story drop to the pavement below.

Oh, fuck me now.

"Lyle, I need that hovervan as high as you can get it. Bring it up along the east side of the building. Beneath the living room windows."

"Oooh. A challenge." He's not being sarcastic. Lyle's the best damn pilot and driver in the Fighting Storm.

Too bad he's an ass.

The van's engines rev over the comm, and the repulsorlifts engage with a whine.

"Vick, what are you thinking?" Kelly's voice trembles when she's worried, and she rushes over her words. I can barely understand her.

"I'm thinking my paranoia is about to pay off."

I wear a thin inflatable vest beneath my clothes when we do anything near water. I carry a pocket breather when we work in space stations, regardless of the safety measures in place. I'm always prepared for every conceivable obstacle, including some my teammates never see coming.

So I wear a lightweight harness under my clothes when I'm in any building over three stories tall.

Alex teases me about it. Lyle's too spooked by me to laugh in my face, but I know he does it behind my back. Kelly counsels that I can't live my second life in fear.

Sorry. I died once. I'm in no hurry to repeat the experience.

Using my brain implants, I trigger an adrenaline burst. The hormone races through my bloodstream. I'll pay for this later with an energy crash, but for now, I'm supercharged and ready to take on my next challenge.

The hadrazine gas is flowing closer. I shove the kid toward the far corner of the room, away from both the kitchen and the damage I'm about to do.

For safety reasons, high-rise windows, especially really large floor-to-ceiling ones, can rarely be opened. Hefting the closest heavy wood chair, I slam it into the windows with as much force as I can gather. My shoulder screams in pain, and I hear Kelly's answering cry over my comm. With her shields down, she feels what I feel. They're always down during missions. I hate hurting her, but I have no choice. I need her input to function, and I need the window broken.

The first hit splinters the tempered glass, sending a spiderweb of cracks shooting to the corners of the rectangular pane. Not good enough.

I pull my 9mm from a thigh holster and fire four shots. Cracks widen. Chips fall, along with several large shards. There's a breach now. I need to widen it. I grab the chair and swing a second time, and the glass and chair shatter, pieces of both flying outward and disappearing into the raging storm.

Wind and rain whip into the living room. Curtains flap like flags in a hurricane, buffeting me away from the edge and keeping me from tumbling after the furniture. I'm soaked in seconds. When I take a step, the carpet squishes beneath my boots.

"VC1, I think the Rodwells made Team Two in the lobby.... Shit. I'm reading a signal transmission, trying to block it.... Fuck, I've got an active signature on the bomb.... It's got a countdown, two minutes. Get the hell out of there!"

Alex's report sends my pulse rate ratcheting upward. Other than not being here in the first place, no paranoid preparation can counter a blast of the magnitude I'm expecting.

Judging from the positioning of the explosives, anyone in the apartment will be toast.

I take off my coat and toss it into the swirling blue gas, regretting the loss of the equipment in the pockets but knowing I can't make my next move with it on. The wind is drawing the haze right toward the windows, right toward me. I grab gloves from a pocket and yank them on. I unsnap a compartment on my harness and pull out a retractable grappling hook attached to several hundred coiled feet of ultrastrong, ultrathin wire.

Once I've given myself some slack in the cord, I scan the room. The gaudy architecture includes some decorative pillars. A press of a button drives the grappler into the marble, and I wrap the cord several times around the column and tug hard. I'm not worried about the wire. It can bear more than five hundred pounds of weight. I'm not so sure about the apartment construction, given the flimsy back door.

The cord holds. I reel out more line, extending my free hand to the kid. "Come on!"

He stares at me, then the window, then shakes his head. "You're crazy. No way!" He shouts to be heard over the rain and thunder.

My internal display flashes my implants' favorite metaphor—a thick cable made up of five metal cords wrapped tightly around each other. Over the last two years, I've come to understand they represent my sanity, and since Kelly's arrival, they've remained solid. Until now.

One of them is fraying, a few strands floating around the whole in wisps.

Great. Just great.

The image fades.

"Die in flames or jump with me. Take your pick." The clock ticks down in my head. If the boy won't come, I'm not sure I'll have time to cross the room and grab him, but my programming will force me to try.

He comes.

I take one last second to slam myself against the pillar, forcing my dislocated shoulder into the socket. Kelly screams in my ear, but I've clamped my own jaw shut, gritting my teeth for my next move.

One arm slides around the boy's narrow waist. I grip the cord in the protective glove.

"Five seconds," Alex says.

I run toward the gaping hole and open air, clutching the kid to me. He wraps his arms around my torso and buries his face in my side.

"Four."

"Oh my God," Kelly whispers.

"Three."

Lyle and the hovervan better be where I need them. The cord might support our weight, but it won't get me close enough to the ground for a safe free-fall drop.

"Two."

The sole of my boot hits the edge and my muscles coil to launch me as far from the window as I can. There's a second of extreme panic, long enough for regrets but too late to stop momentum, and then we're airborne. Emotion suppressors ramp up to full power, and the terror fades.

My last thought as gravity takes hold is of Kelly. My suppressors have some effect on her empathic sense, but extremely strong feelings and emotions like pain and panic reach her every time.

If she can't get her shields up fast, this will tear her apart.

ELLE E. IRE resides in Celebration, Florida, where she writes science fiction and urban fantasy novels featuring kickass women who fall in love with each other. She has won local and national writing competitions, including the Royal Palm Literary Award, the Pyr and Dragons essay contest judged by the editors at Pyr Publishing, the Do It Write competition judged by a senior editor at Tor publishing, and she is a winner of the Backspace scholarship awarded by multiple literary agents. She and her spouse belong to several writing groups and attend and present at many local, state, and national writing conferences.

When she isn't teaching writing to middle school students, Elle enjoys getting into her characters' minds by taking shooting lessons, participating in interactive theatrical experiences, paying to be kidnapped "just for the fun and feel of it," and attempting numerous escape rooms. She is the author of *Vicious Circle* (original release 2015, rerelease 2020), the Storm Fronts series (2019-2020), the Nearly Departed series (2021-2022), and *Reel to Real Love* (2021). To learn what her tagline "Deadly Women, Dangerous Romance" is really all about, visit her website: http://www. elleire.com. She can also be found on Twitter at @ElleEIre and Facebook at www.facebook.com/ ElleE.IreAuthor.

Elle is represented by Naomi Davis at BookEnds Literary Agency.

DEADLY WOMEN,
DANGEROUS ROMANCE

NEARLY DEPARTED: BOOK ONE

DEAD
WOMAN'S
POND

ELLE E. IRE

Nearly Departed: Book One

No matter how Flynn Dalton tries to avoid it, the supernatural finds her.

At first it's not so bad. Flynn's girlfriend, Genesis, is a nationally known psychic, which makes Flynn uncomfortable for both paranormal and financial reasons, but she can handle it. As long as no one makes her talk about it.

Then, on her way home from her construction job, Flynn almost ends up the latest casualty of Festivity's infamous Dead Man's Pond. And when her ex-lover's ghost appears to warn her away, things get a whole lot weirder.

Flynn might not like it, but the pond has fixated on her to be its next victim. If she wants to survive, she'll have to swallow her pride, accept Gen's help, and get much closer to the psychic realm—and her own latent psychic abilities—than she ever wanted.

www.dsppublications.com